IRON CYCLONE

THE CHOSEN FEW
BOOK ONE

A.M. WENTWORTH

Iron Cyclone © 2026 A.M. Wentworth

Published by Staten House

ISBN 979-8-90329-286-8 (E-book) | ISBN 979-8-90329-289-9 (Paperback) |

ISBN 979-8-90329-287-5 (Hardcover) | ISBN 979-8-90329-284-4 (Audiobook)

Cover by digitaldreams_designs

Editing by Mallory Day Editing

Formatting by InksparkDigital

amwentworthauthor.com

This book is dedicated to my beautiful daughter, Elodie. I hope you achieve all your dreams, sweetie, no matter how big or small.

IRON CYCLONE'S PLAYLIST

Music is a huge influence on the stories I write. Songs, oftentimes, bring about scenes or entire plot points I hadn't thought about previously. With that in mind, I've created a playlist below of the songs that helped mold *Iron Cyclone* into the story you're about to read.

1. Bells In Santa Fe by Halsey
   - Chapters 4, 8, and 10
2. Might Not Like Me by Brynn Elliot
   - Chapters 9 and 13
3. Just Pretend by Bad Omens
   - Chapter 11
4. Risk by Gracie Abrams
   - Chapters 17 and 18
5. Popular Monster by Falling In Reverse
   - Chapter 23
6. Friends Don't by Maddie & Tae
   - Chapters 25, 26, and 38
7. Shameless by Camila Cabello
   - Chapters 29, 52, and 53

TRIGGER WARNINGS

Mention of parental death
Mention of child abuse
Sexual assault (groping)
Torture

PRONUNCIATIONS

Neos Ouranos (NEH-os oo-rah-nohs)
Kalyteros (kah-LEE-teh-ros)
Zoin (zoy-n)
Nero (near-ro)
Fotia (foh-TYAH)
Saros (ser-ross)
Vasilias (vah-see-lee-AS)
Thyia (TEE-uh)
Nerine (ne-REEN)
Tana (tah-nah)
Arete (ah-reet)
Krevos (kre-vos)
Wyver (wee-vr)
Galanis (gah-LAH-nis)
Thyellas (Thy-el-las)
Kipos (KEE-pos)
Ischyros (iss-KUH-ross)
Aeras (air-ras)
Hydor (hy-dhor)
Telos (TEE-lohs)

Kruos (KROO-oss)
Pyrrhus (PYR-ess)
Baros (BAH-ros)
Gi (ghi)
Hieran (hier-en)

The Kingdom of
Kalyteros

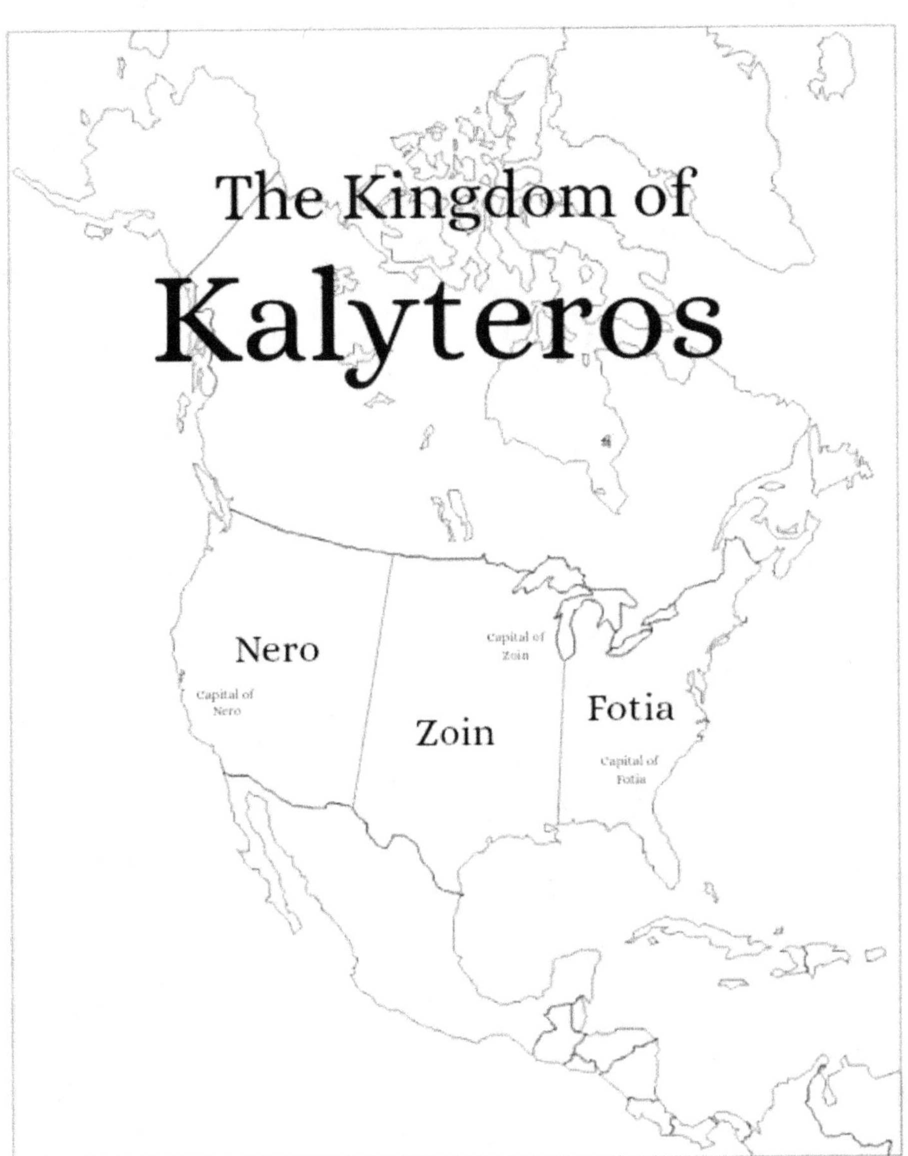

THE STORY OF KALYTEROS
A BEDTIME STORY DESCRIBING THE KINGDOM'S FORMATION IN 1960

No one knows why Vasilias, King of the Gods, would want to invade Earth after thousands of years of separation between the gods and humans, but in 1920, that's exactly what he did.

He and his three daughters—Thyia, Nerine, and Tana—left the heavens to invade the land known as Soviet Russia. It is there Vasilias declared the formation of his new kingdom, Neos Ouranos.

Those who put up little fight during the takeover were granted a small nugget of the god's power as a show of good faith. Vasilias hoped this would make his subjects feel indebted to him.

Unfortunately, the power given was too great for the simple humans and many of them died because of it. It was only the young who seemed to flourish, their resilience making them adaptable to the gift now flowing through their veins.

This revelation excited Vasilias. It meant he now had a people he could mold into whatever he desired. Their lack of experience meant they wouldn't try to tell him how to run things. He might finally have his perfect kingdom.

And for a time, he did.

But, as is human nature, the people of Neos Ouranos grew older and started to question why Vasilias should be king if they all had power. They were too young during the gifting ceremony to appreciate what they'd been given. Instead, they sought more.

That desire only grew stronger as years passed.

Eventually, a group of men decided they would take matters into their own hands. They truly believed they could wrest control from Vasilias and rule in his stead. Their mistake was forgetting that Vasilias was a god.

The result of their uprising was devastating.

Vasilias's daughters watched in horror as their people were either slaughtered or thrown in cages. They begged for their father to let the survivors go, but Vasilias wouldn't listen. He deemed them all traitors and declared they would spend the rest of their lives imprisoned.

Thyia, Nerine, and Tana—now lovingly referred to as The Sisters—decided they needed to stop their father. Being powerful goddesses themselves, they were the only ones who could. They each wielded one aspect of their father's power—storms, water, and fire—and planned to use that to their advantage.

It was on the fortieth anniversary of the formation of Neos Ouranos that The Sisters saved their people—our ancestors.

That night, Thyia met with her father in his garden to talk over cups of tea like they did every night. But this tea wasn't the herbal one they typically shared. Instead, it was laced with Titanium and Vanadium sourced from a nearby coal mine. Ancient lore stated the combination of the two minerals in a god would leave them temporarily powerless.

Thyia distracted her father with conversation in the hopes he wouldn't notice that her cup remained untouched. She was so worried he'd figure out what they were planning. It wasn't until he took his first sip that she finally relaxed.

Vasilias knew what happened as soon as he finished the cup. He could feel the power draining from his body like water washing over him. The stunned King of the Gods couldn't believe his own daughter would betray him in such a way. In a fit of rage, he jumped up, knocking his chair over behind him, and grabbed Thyia by the throat, slamming her against the massive oak tree that was the centerpiece of his garden. He had every intention of killing her.

Thyia struck her father with her lightning until he dropped her, then ran away as fast as she could. She didn't know if she killed him, but she wasn't going to stick around to find out.

When she found her sisters, relief flooded her chest when she saw her people standing before her, no longer caged.

Their plan had worked. Their people were free.

That night, The Sisters fled with our ancestors to the land known as The United States of America. If their father was still alive, they hoped he wouldn't think to look there, since the country wasn't highly spoken of in any Russian texts.

The Sisters then formed the kingdom we now call Kalyteros and split it into three provinces—Zoin, Nero, and Fotia. They hoped the separation would allow each province to adapt and evolve as needed, strengthening them in turn.

It is because of The Sisters' care and dedication to our people that Kalyteros remains a kingdom of love and communion despite their disappearance years ago. We can only hope that we continue to make them proud as our gifts evolve with each new generation. May they always bless us, wherever they may be.

PART ONE
DISCOVERED

CHAPTER ONE

ANASTASIA

From the time I was a little girl, I yearned for more. More experience. More adventure. More *life*. Unfortunately, the sleepy coal-miner town I grew up in was severely lacking in all three.

That isn't to say I didn't love my life. I did. My family brought me so much joy. I loved helping my mom bake her famous chocolate chip cookies on Saturday nights, going hunting with my dad on Sunday mornings, and making up new games with my younger siblings to keep them entertained while Mom cooked dinner. Sometimes I even attended a party thrown by a classmate. It was a good life. A simple life.

Too simple.

I come from a stereotypical ungifted family. The women are expected to be homemakers while the men work as coal miners. There is little else for an ungifted person to do in our part of Zoin.

Even at five years old, I knew I didn't want to be a homemaker. *Couldn't* be a homemaker. It wasn't an option for me. I wanted to be someone with influence. Power. Someone who could make a difference for the province.

Unfortunately, the only way an ungifted person can do that in Kalyteros is by developing a skill and getting top marks throughout their schooling. Then, if they're lucky, they *might* get accepted into an Arete University. There are only three throughout the entire kingdom and they're the only secondary schooling option for the ungifted.

Arete Universities are primarily for gifted students who already have the kingdom at their fingertips. The student body is made up of the children of politicians, high-ranking military personnel, and top province officials who are expected to continue their parents' legacy. Gifted children who come from lesser families must settle for lower tier colleges.

Suffice to say, it's pretty much impossible for the ungifted to get accepted.

My dad knew of my desire to go to Arken—the Arete University in Zoin—from a young age and did whatever he could to help me achieve it. He decided early on that I would become an expert in weaponry, fighting, and stealth. He thought my being an ungifted girl meant no one would expect it of me so the school would be more impressed. Me and my dad then spent many late nights and early mornings practicing wielding and throwing weapons, sparring, and learning whatever else my dad deemed important.

Honestly, I think he just wanted to know I could protect myself. I always got the feeling he hated the idea of me going to Arken but didn't want to deny me my only chance to do something with my life.

During the first half of my senior year, my dad would take me to every open house and college visit that Arken held. Despite his exhaustion from work and the hour drive to the school, he always made sure we were there. A few times, my mom and siblings even joined. It was so exciting to see where I might spend my next four years. Nerve-wracking too. It made my dream tangible, and I was scared it would slip through my fingers.

When Arken began accepting applications, my dad helped me fill mine out and videotaped me demonstrating my skills. He was my biggest supporter and there wasn't a day that went by that I didn't appreciate everything he did for me. I knew if I was accepted, I would owe it all to him.

He never got the chance to see my dream come true. There was an explosion last December in the coal mines where he worked that killed him and seventeen other men. They say it was one of the worst explosions the kingdom had ever seen. They say there were no signs one was imminent. They say he's in a better place now. They say he loved us all dearly.

They say. They say. They say.

I might punch the next person who tries to console me with another empty platitude.

My family was completely heartbroken when we learned of my dad's death. We were numb. I think, even months later, we still are. A piece of our family was gone in an instant. The heart of our family was gone.

My mom couldn't leave her bed for weeks. I couldn't imagine what she was going through. I'd never seen her laugh with anyone else as hard as she did with my dad. He loved to push her buttons, then kiss her right when she was about to snap at him. He would come up to her while she was making dinner, spin her around, and slow dance with her while singing their song. They were my definition of love, but now I'm not sure what it means anymore.

I never want to know what it's like to lose a love like that.

My siblings struggled as well. They'd never experienced a loss of this magnitude. They didn't know how to cope. My sister Daphne would bawl at the slightest inconvenience, my brother DJ's pre-teen angst was now amplified, and he lashed out constantly, and my youngest brother Christos started sleeping with me at night because he was afraid to be alone.

As for me, I just went through the motions. I couldn't confront what I was feeling out of fear it would break me so badly I could never be fixed. Instead, I did what my mom couldn't. I got us all up, packed our lunches, and drove us to school. I made dinner when we got home, got everyone ready for bed, and made sure bills were paid. After the explosion, the government gave us a lump sum of money for Dad's death. It's the only reason we were able to stay afloat.

By April, I think we were finally getting out of the haze of our grief. That was, until my acceptance letter from Arken arrived. I went to grab the mail one morning and saw a large envelope from the school. My heart leapt at what that meant, but it sank just as quickly when I realized I couldn't tell the one person I wanted to: Dad.

Everything I ever dreamed of was held within the contents of that envelope. I should've been excited. I should've been jumping for joy and thanking my dad for everything he did to make it happen. Instead, I felt hollow.

How could I go to Arken now? My family's still functioning on autopilot. They need me. How could I walk those halls again when all I can remember of them was my dad's booming laugh echoing off its walls?

Would my dad still be proud of me if I didn't go?

I went to my mom with my concerns, and she immediately shut them down. She reminded me of all the hard work I put in. That my dad put in. She told me that it'd take some time, but our family would learn how to function again. She also told me that I shouldn't waste an opportunity like the one I'd been given.

"We'll be okay, Annie," she said as she pulled me in for a hug. "You need to do this. For all of us."

I wept in her arms after that. She was right, but it didn't make the choice any easier. I'd still be going to a place haunted with my dad's memory.

That was a couple months ago and my feelings regarding the matter haven't changed. If anything, I think I've only grown more worried.

Will Mom be overwhelmed without my assistance? She just started getting better. After everything, will Daphne fall in with the wrong crowd? Sophomore year is hard enough for a teenager. What if she makes a bad choice? And I can't even begin to wrap my head around all the worries I should have for DJ and Christos. *Have I made a mistake in deciding to go to Arken after all?*

"We'll be fine, Sis. Stop worrying." Daphne's voice cuts through my anxious spiral. "You're going to give yourself frown lines if you keep scowling like that." She sits down next to me on my bed and crosses her legs underneath her.

"Who says I'm worrying about you guys?" I ask, trying to appear calm and collected. "I could be worrying about what I'm going to wear tomorrow. Or what sort of boys will be there. You know, normal stuff."

"Unless you and I switched bodies without my knowing, I highly doubt that," my sister replies with a snort. "You're too responsible to worry about stuff like that. Knowing you, you're probably worrying about who'll take Christos to his third-grade art fair on Thursday or DJ to his karate class on Saturday mornings."

"Well, now that you mention it..."

Daphne nudges me with her elbow. "We'll be *fine*. You just try to live a little now that you're going to Arken. Flirt with cute boys. Meet some friends and go to a party. Do something other than study. I can't be the only one having fun in this family."

She glances around our tiny room. Our matching twin beds are shoved against opposite walls and a small dresser occupies the space between them. An even smaller closet makes up the opposite wall. "I *am* looking forward to having my own room now," she says. "I might be able to hang up all my clothes finally."

"Take good care of it," I respond with a smile. "But remember, I'll be back for winter and summer break so don't change it too much. I do have to use it again at some point."

"Yeah. Yeah. How could I forget?" She waves me off. "Anyway...Mom says dinner's almost ready. She wants you to pry yourself from packing and join us. Get some human interaction."

Had I been packing that long already? "Okay. Tell her I'll be right there. I want to do one last check to make sure I have everything."

"Yeah. I know the drill. I'll tell her you'll be joining us in fifteen minutes."

I roll my eyes and stick my tongue out at her, but say, "Tell her twenty."

CHAPTER TWO

ANASTASIA

My mom seems back to her usual self this morning. Or she's putting on a very convincing show for my sake.

She woke us all up, fed us breakfast, and got us out the door in time for move in. My move in time is 8:30 and we live almost an hour away from the school, so what she accomplished is no small feat. I'm hoping this morning is just the beginning of my mom's comeback. I'll feel much better about leaving if it is.

I glance out my window and watch as fields of green pass by our car. We're now only fifteen minutes away from Arken and my nerves are shot. Today is going to be a whirlwind of changes for me. I'm both excited and afraid of what it holds.

I look down at the outfit I threw on of jeans and an old, faded blue mathletes T-shirt and wonder if it's too simple. I hadn't put much thought into my attire, caring more for practicality than looking cute. My hair quickly thrown into a loose bun emphasizes how little effort I made. I sure hope the other students don't show up well dressed and put together. I'm not ready to stand out just yet.

My mom glances at me from the driver's seat, her strawberry blonde curls bouncing with the movement. "Are you getting excited,

Annie? I know how much you can get in your head. I want to make sure you're taking the time to revel in what's happening today."

I smile. "I am, Mom. I promise. I'm just wondering who I'll be living with. I never got any information about them. I'm hoping they won't be blasting music at all hours of the day or constantly having friends over."

"I'm hoping it's someone who'll drag your butt out to parties for once," Daphne chimes in from her spot behind Mom.

Mom smiles. "You'll meet her soon enough, sweetie. No sense in worrying about it. I know you and you'll find a way to make even the worst of roommates work to your benefit." She reaches behind her seat and squeezes Daphne's knee. "And I don't want you getting any ideas about joining in on these parties, Daph. Your sister knows I strictly forbid it."

Daphne crosses her arms and huffs from the backseat while I grin at her. My wild child sister. I don't know how two people so different could come from the same parents.

But I guess that could be said for my whole family. Other than the strawberry blonde hair that adorns our heads, there's very little we have in common. Despite our differences, my family is extremely close. I think my dad played a huge part in that. He made sure love was the cornerstone of our home.

My thoughts stall. Thinking about my dad brings back that familiar pang in my chest. I tell myself to fight the tears that now threaten to make an appearance. The last thing I want is to show up for my first day at Arken with red-rimmed eyes and a blotchy face.

All too quickly, the iron gates of Arken University come into view and my breath catches in my throat. *This is really happening.* My mom's rusty sedan enters through them and creeps slowly by evergreen trees that line the drive up to the main building of the school.

Thankfully, she finds an open parking spot between a sports car and an oversized SUV and pulls into it. We all pile out of the car and seem to gawk in unison at the buildings that surround us. Their beauty rivals that of Old America universities such as Harvard and Princeton. Universities that now serve as museums for America pre-Kalyteros takeover.

I take a deep breath and make my way toward the check in table in front of us.

Here goes nothing.

I quickly check in, get my room key, and gesture for my family to follow me as I head in the direction of my dorm. It doesn't take me long to find it. It's one of only two dorms on campus that's strictly for first-year students. The Kopela Building is the female dormitory, and the Agori Building is the male. Both are three stories tall and clearly inspired by Old America gothic architecture because of their arched roofs and stained-glass windows. The two buildings frame a large white fountain that's the focal point of the campus.

My family follows me into my dorm while I look for my room. We end up finding it on the second floor. It's at the end of the hall and overlooks the fountain. Its location should be perfect. I'll only have to contend with noise coming from one shared wall which is no small blessing.

As I unlock my door and enter my room, I quickly take in the space and the enormity of the moment. This is where I'm going to be living for the next nine months. Who knows what'll happen in here or the memories I'll make. Butterflies flutter around in my stomach in response.

My room is roughly the same size as the one I have back home. There are two twin beds, two large wardrobes, two small dressers, and two desks with chairs that are to be split between me and my roommate.

I unpack while my mom takes my brothers out to the quad to expend some energy. Daphne leaves a few minutes later to find 'the good coffee.' I much prefer to settle in alone and my family knows that. The act of organizing a new space with only my thoughts to occupy me is so satisfying.

I set my things down on the left side of the room and start the process of moving in by making my bed first. I'd chosen a gray comforter with yellow detailing that looks like daisies with matching yellow sheets. I love the simplicity of it. After that's done, I move on to unpacking my clothes, then to organizing my books on my desk. Before long, my room feels like a living space. The lights I hang above my bed give it a cozy feeling I adore.

As I'm admiring my work and wondering if I should add some of Christos's art to the wall, the door creaks open behind me. I turn to find a tan-skinned girl walking into the room. She has long, dark brown hair and she wears a red sundress that drags across the floor. She's gorgeous.

The girl notices me and exclaims, "Ah! You must be my roommate!" She rushes in for a hug. "Hi! I'm Emilia!"

I smile as I hug her back. At least she seems friendly. "Hi, my name's Anastasia, but you can call me Ana."

When my roommate pulls away from me, her smile is genuine and her eyes gleam with excitement. "It's nice to finally meet you, Ana. It was torture not knowing who I'd be living with."

A knock sounds on our door, interrupting our introduction, and a male voice says, "Mills! A little assistance, please."

"Oh shoot! I forgot I was supposed to be holding the door for him." She rushes to the door and flings it open. A tank of a man shuffles into the room after that, his arms filled with boxes and pieces of luggage.

He gently places the items on Emilia's bed before he turns to her. There's no sign of exhaustion on his face despite how heavy the boxes look. "I didn't realize being your boyfriend meant I was also your pack mule."

My roommate gives him a teasing smile as she looks up at the man who towers over her. "You didn't? Well, shoot. I guess I better cancel all the furniture I ordered. I wouldn't want to put you out any further."

"I know you're joking about the furniture," Emilia's boyfriend says after he plants a quick kiss on her lips, "but I'm always happy to help. You know that."

"I do," Emilia responds with a smile before gesturing toward me. "Nik, this is my roommate Ana." Her boyfriend extends his hand to me and his large muscles flex with the motion. "And Ana, this is my boyfriend, Nikolai."

Nikolai runs his honey-colored fingers through his short, dark hair as he smiles. When I shake his hand, raw strength emanates from him, catching me off guard. He must notice my shocked expression because he says, "I'm super strong. It's my gift. Hence why my girlfriend loves to use me as her one-man moving company." He looks at my roommate and smiles, his stubbled jaw and sharp eyes noticeably softening. The love I see in that look makes me instantly like him.

"I should probably get going, though," he sighs. "I want to make sure I get to the room before Harvey does. He's insistent that we should have bunk beds, and I worry I'll be forced into the arrangement if I don't beat him there."

"Yes. *Go*," Emilia states with a wave of her hand. "The last thing I want is to be banging my head on your ceiling all semester."

They kiss goodbye and Nikolai smiles at me again. "It was nice to meet you, Ana."

"You, too," I say as he hurries out the door.

After he leaves, Emilia gives me an apologetic look. "Sorry about that. I probably should've warned you about the whole boyfriend thing. We'll likely spend most of our time in his room so hopefully we won't bother you too much."

I wave off her concern. "Don't worry about it. He's welcome whenever. I'll probably spend most of my time in the library anyway."

My roommate grins and I find myself thinking we could be friends.

When she turns toward the boxes piled on top of her bed and sighs, I decide to give her space so she can unpack and get settled in without me in the way.

"I'll leave you be," I say as I make my way toward the door. "I need to find my family and say goodbye to them."

"Do you want to meet back here around 1:00 so we can grab lunch before orientation?"

My heart leaps in excitement.

"That sounds great, actually. I'll see you then, Emilia."

"Please, call me Millie."

I smile in response. "See you then, Millie."

CHAPTER THREE
ANASTASIA

I find my family occupying four Adirondack chairs by the fountain, so I grab a fifth and settle in beside them. We spend the next hour reminiscing and watching the other first-year students move in.

It's nice, but it passes by far too quickly.

Before I know it, my mom is standing up and announcing that it's time to go. She hollers for my brothers, who are tossing a ball back and forth on the other side of the quad. They come running over as Daphne hugs me goodbye.

As my sister pulls away, she grabs my shoulders and looks at me, her bright green eyes rimmed with tears. "I know I've joked about it a lot, but please promise me you'll have some fun while you're here. All you've done for the past eight months is take care of us. I hate to think that you won't relax and let loose. You're one of the smartest people I know, but you can be fun too. You deserve to have fun."

Tears prick the corners of my own eyes. "Oh Daph, I'm going to miss you so much. You know you guys were always more important than any stupid dance or party my classmates threw. Taking care of you guys was all that mattered." She gives me a look that says, "That's not the point," and I laugh. "Okay. Yes. I promise to have fun."

She smiles that beautiful smile of hers and says, "Good," while I hug her again.

Gosh, when did my scrawny, obnoxious little sister become such an eloquent young woman? I hope high school is kind to her this year. I'm going to hate not being there for her every step of the way. My tears threaten to fall, so I pull away from her.

My brothers rush to my side next, nearly knocking me over as they do. "Man, am I going to miss you guys," I laugh as I catch myself and give them both a squeeze. "Now, you have to promise me that you'll be good for Mom, alright? And try to help out around the house some."

"Okay," they say in unison but in a noncommittal way.

I kiss them both on the head, then turn toward my mom, whose arms are already open and waiting for me. I hurry to her and collapse into her warmth. "Oh sweetie, I'm so proud of you," she whispers into my ear. "I hope this experience is everything you wanted."

My throat feels raw, and I urge myself to keep it together. I really don't want to cry in the middle of the quad. My mom pulls out of our hug and places a hand on my cheek. "Your father would be so proud of you."

Whatever control I had slips after that and tears trail down my cheeks. My mom brushes them away but keeps her composure somehow as she pulls me in for one final hug. She then gathers everyone's things and turns toward the car. "We'll see you at family weekend next month, Annie. Remember to call us and update us on how things are going, okay?"

"I will. I love you guys!" I hear a chorus of "love you" in return.

I wipe at my eyes as I watch them until they disappear. When I can no longer see them, I blow out a long breath and head back to my dorm. It should almost be time to meet Millie for lunch.

By the time I return to our room, Millie has finished unpacking and is arranging a few flowerpots containing what look like succulents on the windowsill.

"Your side looks great, Millie. I love all the greenery." Vines hang from multiple spots on the ceiling, complementing her white comforter with vine-like detailing. I'm surprised by how real they look.

"Thank you! You're sure it's not too much?" she asks over her shoulder.

"No. I think it's perfect. I already can't wait to settle in and watch movies at some point."

"Awesome! That's the vibe I was going for." She finishes adjusting the pot that was giving her trouble and turns around, putting her fists on her hips while examining her work. With a grin that splits her face, it's obvious she's satisfied with what she sees.

"Are you ready for lunch?" I ask.

"Yeah!" She grabs her wallet and ushers me toward the door. "Let's go. I'm starving!"

As we're walking down the stairs, heading toward the student center, a few girls pass us. Their white-blonde hair and dark blue eyes tell me they're water benders. Likely children from the Aeras or Hydor families—the only prominent water bending families in Zoin.

Most water bending families, especially the strong ones, remain in Nero. That's where Sister Nerine ruled the first twenty-five years after Kalyteros was formed. Those families stay there because they're hoping for a chance at being elected Grand Leader.

Each province has their own Grand Leader who implements and enforces laws created by parliament. They also choose key members of the governing body. It's a very important position— probably the *most* important position.

The strongest water bending families remain in Nero because of our kingdom's constitution. It states that an individual can only be elected to the role of Grand Leader if they have the gift of the province's founding sister. Both Nero and Fotia still have several water-bending and fire-bending families. That means the Grand Leader is constantly changing for both provinces, allowing for new ideas and different points of view. And they are all the better for it.

Unfortunately, the same cannot be said for Zoin. There's only one family that remains that are storm benders—the Thyellas family. They've been in power for longer than I've been alive, which has allowed them to go unchecked and make decisions that have risked our province unnecessarily. They've also created a lot of tension with the other provinces, specifically Fotia. I don't know of any ungifted in my hometown of Wellington who like the Theyllas family because of it.

Most of the coal mines, where the men of Wellington work, are in or near Fotia.

My dad told me one morning, while we were hunting, that working in the mines used to be a lot better. That the people of Fotia would allow them to eat in their restaurants for lunch or go to their bars after their shift ended for a drink. That all changed after some of the decisions Grand Leader Thyellas made. The Fotians no longer trusted our people and banished them from frequenting any of their establishments. Dad said that people who were once kind now spit at his feet. I knew then how desperately things needed to change for Zoin.

It's my understanding, though, that things have only gotten worse between the two provinces since Grand Leader Thyellas was assassinated in his office last December. His Vice Grand Leader came out and said the assassination was committed by a Fotian. With the rising tension, I imagine it won't be long before fighting breaks out between them, if not a full-blown war.

Only the gods can save us if that happens.

"So, how did your family like Arken?" Millie asks as we exit our building and head toward the student center. It's located only a few feet from the first-year dorms.

"They liked it, but it wasn't their first time here," I explain as we descend the stairs that lead to the cafeteria. "We came a handful of times before for college visits."

"Wow. That's awesome. I wish I could get my parents to care

that much about my interests. Most of the time they just throw money at me to get me out of their hair."

My eyes widen. I can't imagine a parent not caring about their kid's interests. My parents always wanted to know what my siblings and I were into.

"I'm sorry to hear that. That has to be frustrating."

"Yep" is Millie's clipped response. "But that's why I spend most of my time out of the house with my friends. No sense in staying somewhere I'm clearly a bother."

Our conversation dies out as we enter the cafeteria. I glance around the space and am once again awestruck by its beauty. It was designed to look like the inside of a medieval castle. School awards hang from the balusters in a similar manner to how a castle would hang its sigils. It's beautiful and old-timey. I find myself speechless every time I come in here.

I quickly grab my food and find a table in the middle of the seating area. The food selection is slimmer than it was during my college visits. They must've been showing off or something. I didn't know what to choose so I grabbed what looked the most appetizing: two slices of cheese pizza. As I settle in at the table, Millie arrives with an overflowing salad.

"*So*, I have to know. Do you have a boyfriend?" she asks as soon as she sits down. She pauses, then quickly adds, "Or girlfriend? Or whatever you're into?"

"No. I don't have a boyfriend," I specify. "I dated a few guys in high school but none of them stuck. They couldn't understand why I didn't want to stay home popping out babies for them after I graduated high school."

"Yikes. Well, that's their loss, then."

"I'll cheers to that!" I say with a smile, raising my glass. "What about you? How did you and Nikolai meet?"

"We met a few months ago, actually. The capital has a send-off party every summer for its local high school graduates. The whole point is to connect students who are pursuing the same specialties and give them a chance to get to know each other. Well, Nik and I might not be in the same specialty, but we definitely got to know each other." She waggles her eyebrows, the meaning loud and clear. "We've been inseparable since."

"You guys seem cute together. I look forward to getting to know him."

"Be careful what you wish for, roomie," she responds with a devious smile. She then leans forward and gives me a sheepish look, "I'm obviously a nosy busybody. You'll hopefully learn to love that about me. But I'm curious, what's your gift? Anything cool?"

I wince but thankfully she doesn't notice. I knew the question was bound to come up and dreaded it. Ungifted prejudice is so prevalent, especially in upper society. My lack of a gift could quickly break whatever relationship I'm building with my roommate. "I'm ungifted, actually," I answer awkwardly. "I was accepted into Arken for my skills in weaponry and stealth."

"Oh. That's interesting," she responds.

I hold my breath, anticipating a snide remark about how great it is that the ungifted are given a chance at something. It certainly wouldn't be anything I haven't heard before. But she doesn't.

Instead, she says, "I've never met an ungifted person before. How cool is it that I now get to live with one?"

I let out the breath I was holding. *Oh, thank gods.* My roommate's cool. She's really, really cool. I then ask the question I know she's waiting for. "What's your gift?"

She smiles and I watch in amazement as a yellow daisy sprouts in her hand. She hands it to me and I take the flower while trying to suppress the shocked look I'm sure I'm wearing.

"I'm phytokinetic, which, in simple terms, means I can grow and manipulate plant life. As you already saw, it won't take long for my side of our room to be drowning in greenery." She laughs. "I mainly specialize in poisonous plants, though, so I don't recommend touching any of them without checking with me first."

My eyebrows jump to my hairline. "Good to know," I say in response to her warning, already worried I'll somehow end up poisoning myself. "But that's a cool gift, Millie. I've never heard of a phytokinetic before."

She smiles wide. "Look at us! Already introducing each other to new things."

My smile mirrors hers, but then my eyes are drawn to the front of the cafeteria where a tall guy now enters. He's muscular but not overly so and his black hair grazes the tops of his eyebrows. He's frowning, which emphasizes his sharp jawline. He approaches a table where another male whoops and hollers for him. He gives his friend a tight smile as he sits down.

"Who's that?" I ask Millie, nodding my head in the guy's direction. She looks where I direct and gasps.

"Oh, my gods!" she whispers while turning back to me. "That's Xander Thyellas! I didn't think he was actually going to come."

"Wait. *What?* Thyellas? As in *Grand Leader* Thyellas?" My mouth falls open as I look at the guy with fresh eyes. There's nothing about him that indicates province royalty. Not in his demeanor or his attire. He's wearing faded jeans and a long-sleeved black shirt that's pushed to his elbows. I can see dark tattoos covering his arms that contrast with his ivory skin, but I can't make out what they are. He seems normal. Average even.

"The very one. You're looking at our future Grand Leader over there. Nik told me something about his uncle requiring him to graduate from college before he could take on the role. I thought it was just a rumor. Nik assumed it was so his uncle could have more time as acting Grand Leader."

"Is that even safe?" I ask. "His father was assassinated. Wouldn't he be a target as well?"

"You'd think," she responds with a shrug. "Who knows. But hey, I won't complain. Not if it means we get that eye candy roaming our halls." She sneaks another peek behind her. "Gods, he's gorgeous."

I laugh. "Don't you have a boyfriend?"

"Well, yeah. I may be off the market, but it doesn't mean I can't enjoy some window shopping," she says with a wink.

I laugh again as my eyes drift back to Xander. Future Grand Leader, huh? Well, if he's anything like his father was, then I better steer clear of him.

I tear my gaze away from Xander as Millie stands. I quickly stand with her, not wanting to be left here alone.

"Nik should be settled into his room by now so I'm going to check on him before orientation. Save us seats?"

"Yeah, sure," I manage to say despite my mind still being occupied by the future Grand Leader and how odd it is that he's here. I look toward him once more before leaving the cafeteria. He's intently listening to one of his tablemates talk now, looking like any other student. The only indication that he's more important than he appears is the way other students keep staring at him and whispering.

A guy like that is probably used to the attention. Maybe even enjoys it.

Either way, I need to steer clear of him. I'm sure he's a jerk just like his father was and I don't need to be around someone like that.

CHAPTER FOUR
XANDER

I don't know if Arken University would've been my top choice for college. I would've much preferred Krevos in Nero or Wyver in Fotia. At least those schools would have the excitement of living in a new province.

But my opinion on what to do with my own life doesn't matter. I accepted that fact a long time ago.

From a young age, I knew the only path laid out for me was to become Grand Leader of Zoin. I can't say it was something I ever wanted, but there was little I could do about it. With me and my father being the last remaining storm benders, there was no one else who could take on the role. Not without changing the constitution or the entire structure of Kalyteros's government.

My father never understood why that made me feel trapped in my own life. He thought having a position of such power was all someone could ever want.

To say that we were different people would be a massive under-statement.

I eventually understood that he put so much emphasis on power because he didn't have much of it himself. He was an only child whose gift didn't manifest until he was almost a teenager. And when it finally did, it was quite weak. He could barely generate a strong enough gust of wind to move a door. From what I've gathered over the years, my grandfather was very cruel to him because of it. Therefore, when my father took over the role as Grand Leader, he made it his goal to be one of the most powerful Grand Leaders that ever existed. No matter the cost.

Even if that meant exploiting his own child.

The Story of Kalyteros is a bedtime story told to children that's meant to explain how our kingdom came to be. But that retelling conveniently doesn't mention the fact that it was only storm benders who turned against Vasilias during the insurrection. And that the entire storm bending population of Neos Ouranos was wiped out afterwards.

This meant Sister Thyia had to implant her gift into a new group of people when Zoin was formed, or her gift would die out. She decided then that she wasn't going to repeat her previous mistake by gifting them her full power. Instead, she would only gift them the ability to control one aspect of a storm, whether it be lightning, wind, or rain. And that limitation was passed down from generation to generation.

That is, until I was born.

The full extent of my gift made itself known at a very young age. A crying fit would result in a flooded kitchen. A scraped knee would cause streaks of lightning that'd short circuit the power to our house. A temper tantrum would send furniture flying across our living room. My mom did her best to hide the scope of my power from my father, but it was an impossible task.

When my father did finally find out, my life changed overnight. Days that were once spent playing with my mom were now spent learning how to control my gift, refining my social skills, and helping my father demonstrate the full strength of *his* gift to the kingdom.

My father decided early on to play off my gift as his own. He wanted everyone to think that he was the strongest storm bender since the formation of Kalyteros. To that end, I was expected to attend every meeting, diplomatic conversation, and conference he was involved in. He'd have me hide in the wings or in an adjoining room and wait for his signal. He gave me a watch in the early days of our charade that was identical to one he always wore. He installed lights on it that would notify me if he needed a demonstration and which element he expected. There was no leniency for mistakes. A demonstration of the wrong element or at the wrong time would be seen as weakness by members of the other provinces.

The punishment for my mistakes varied based on my father's mood. Sometimes it was only verbal harassment via insults and threats. Other times, it escalated to physical abuse. Nothing visible, of course. At least, that was the case until he outsourced my punishment.

After a few years, he decided he was too busy to punish me, so he hired someone to do it instead. The sadistic prick he found, Dr. Diavolos, loved hurting me and wanted his work to be seen. My father had to hire a healer after that to try to hide my injuries, but they could only do so much.

Unfortunately, those punishments continued until I gained full control of my gift when I was sixteen years old and eliminated all mistakes.

I now realize how messed up it all was. I was involved with these demonstrations as early as five years old. Most of the gifted don't even have their powers at that age. And they're definitely not expected to uphold the level of expertise I was.

I can fully admit that it screwed me up. My need for perfection is to an unhealthy degree and I still struggle to connect with new people. My mom, my baby sister Lydia, and my friends Tony and Steven are the only people I trust in this world. And they're the only ones I know aren't using me for their own gain.

Suffice to say, I wasn't heartbroken when my father was assassinated last December. If anything, I felt a sense of relief. Maybe my life could finally be my own.

Though, I did fear what it meant for my mom and Lydia. Were they in danger too?

My Uncle Sebastian is the Vice Grand Leader for Zoin. That means he was the one in charge of the investigation into my father's assassination. It was his office I snuck into when the investigation was complete. I needed to know the truth and I was sure I'd find it hidden amongst the documents piled on his desk.

What I found changed everything.

I assumed after my father's assassination the process would begin for me to take over as Grand Leader. Apparently, my uncle had other plans.

He called me two months ago to let me know I'd be starting at Arken University this fall. I thought he was joking. My father was gone. His death meant I had to take over the role I'd been groomed for my entire life.

My uncle then informed me that I was expected to graduate from college before I could assume the role. That in the meantime, he would be acting Grand Leader.

How convenient.

So, here I am. Settling into a first-year dorm room in a building that I share with fifty-eight other guys.

Thankfully, my room's in a good location—on the third floor and the last room at the end of the hall. It hopefully means minimal disturbance from others. The room itself is small and lifeless, but I can't be bothered to decorate it. What's the point?

Lucky for me, my uncle took my safety *very* seriously and made sure I got a single room instead of a double like all the other first-years. That way, if someone wants to murder me in my sleep, they'll have to fight through a door first before they can get to me. *What a joke.*

I might've been worried if I didn't know what I did about my father's assassination.

Uncle Sebastian informed the kingdom via an emergency tele-conference that my father was murdered by an assassin from Fotia. In actuality, the crime was committed by his own bodyguard—a metal bender named Nicholas Metallo.

I was surprised when I found that tidbit in my uncle's notes. I'd interacted with Metallo a few times while I worked closely with my father, and he seemed normal. Certainly not the killing-his-boss type.

As I investigated him further, I learned that he was my father's bodyguard for twenty years and that he also worked as an assassin when needed. It's not unusual for a metal bender to have a job as either a bodyguard, assassin, or soldier, but Metallo must've been quite skilled if my father thought him capable of handling two of those roles.

I had a lot of questions about the information I gathered. The biggest one being, why would Metallo suddenly kill a man he'd been working with for twenty years? It didn't make sense.

Unfortunately, I don't think I'll ever know why. My uncle killed Metallo once he determined he got all the information he could from him.

But Metallo's death didn't remove the threat to my family. My uncle noted that Metallo has a daughter and circled the phrase 'we need to keep an eye on her' in his notes. Gifted families always train their children to follow in their footsteps. If Metallo wanted my family dead, then it's likely his daughter does too.

Sadly, I couldn't find any information on her. All I had was a photo. It looked like one that would be taken at a high school, but it gave no indication of which one. She was pretty. *Very* pretty. She had long, reddish hair and gray eyes that had an innocence to them. Her smile was easy. There was nothing about her that seemed threatening but that didn't mean anything. The deadliest person I know looks like he couldn't hurt a fly.

I spent months looking for Metallo's daughter without any progress. Imagine my surprise when I walked into the cafeteria and found her there eating. I played it cool, but I could feel her watching me the whole time. Was she spying on me already?

I'm not sure what I'm going to do about her yet. All I know is I have to do *something*.

I'm settled into my room for the evening, wondering what I should do, when I hear a knock on the door. I'm unable to suppress the groan that falls from my mouth. Who could that be?

When I open the door, I see the slender, olive-skinned teleporter I met during my time at the Capitol Building.

Many years ago, a school was set up in a wing of the building and that's where the children of high-ranking officials typically go. It allows them to attend class but also shadow their parents during important meetings and events. I'd met Tony in a finishing class my freshman year and he was always around after that. Eventually, I accepted his presence, and we became friends.

I sigh. Him standing outside of my door this late can't mean anything good for me. "What's up, Tony?" I ask, not bothering to hide my annoyance.

He leans against my door frame and crosses his arms with a smile. The gleam in his eyes tells me he knows he's bothering me and doesn't care. "Steven and I are heading to an upperclassmen party on Wyndell Way and thought you might want to join."

My mouth opens to tell him no, but something stops the word from coming out. A thought then pops into my head.

What better way to draw out a spy than to give them bait?

"You know what? Sure. When are you guys heading out?"

CHAPTER FIVE
ANASTASIA

After sitting through an excruciating orientation, Nikolai informed me and Millie that there's an upperclassmen party on Wyndell Way tonight. He wanted to know if we were interested in going. Apparently, he knows the guys throwing it from high school. Millie was ecstatic, of course, and accepted the invitation for both of us. I didn't share her excitement. Instead, I fought back a groan and had to tell myself it couldn't be worse than sitting through the Director of Student Affairs going over the Code of Conduct again.

That's how I ended up in my room, getting ready for my first college party.

I can't remember the last time I went to a party. I want to say it was during my junior year of high school. The introvert in me always preferred to stay home. The thought of going somewhere I didn't really know anybody, with drinking as the only source of entertainment, didn't appeal to me. But I promised Daphne I'd get out more so here I am giving it the ol' college try. Literally.

I'm busy doing my makeup while Millie straightens my hair. Upbeat music keeps a steady rhythm in the background while our conversation easily drifts from favorite movies, to the guys we've dated, and our expectations for tonight.

When I'm done with my makeup and Millie finishes my hair by pinning half of it up, I change into my outfit for the night: a pair of ripped skinny jeans with a frilly black tank top I found while out shopping with Daphne last weekend. I round out the outfit with my favorite black booties, simple earrings my mother gave me years ago, and a small diamond pendant from my first homecoming.

In contrast, Millie throws on a black mini dress with a jean jacket and white tennis shoes. She chooses to leave her hair down, stating, "It won't stay up with all the dancing I'll be doing so why bother?"

Millie's phone rings and she quickly answers it, turning her back to me. "Hey baby! Are you almost here?"

While Millie's occupied, I slip my favorite knife into my boot. I like to always have one with me. You can never be too careful at these sorts of things.

"Okay. See you soon," Millie says before she hangs up the phone and faces me. "Nik said he's going to meet us at the party. I guess him and a few of his friends are heading over together. He also wanted me to tell you that there's a blonde kid coming that he wants you to meet. Apparently, he's ungifted too."

"Really?" I'm unable to keep the excitement out of my voice. "That's cool. Yeah, I definitely want to meet him then."

"Great! You ready?"

I nod. "Yeah. Let's go."

It's a ten-minute walk to the party. Thankfully, it's a beautiful night so I don't mind. The path we take is lined with Sycamore trees that are cast in a silver glow from the full moon.

Most upperclassmen live on Wyndell Way or the few streets that surround it. There are various apartments and homes available for rent that allows the students some autonomy while minimizing risk for the university. It's a win-win.

"Have you seen any guys you're interested in yet? I can be your wing woman tonight," Millie says as she loops her arm through mine.

My thoughts immediately go to the strange guy in the cafeteria. *Xander.* I mentally shake my head, while my body follows suit. *Nope.* Definitely not. He's *not* an option.

"I can't say I have," I respond. "But I'll let you know if that changes at the party."

"Good." She beams, then pauses, seeming to ponder her next question. Is that nervousness I detect? "So, what do you think about Nik?"

"I like him," I answer with a smile. "He seems nice. He also seems *crazy* about you." I playfully bump her, hoping to ease her worries.

"Oh, good," she says with a sigh of relief. "You know, I've dated a few guys before, but I never felt about them the way I feel about Nik. He knows just what to say to make me laugh and he always treats me like a queen."

The happiness I feel for my friend is genuine as I smile at her and give her arm a squeeze. Her responding grin quickly falls and she forces us to stop suddenly. I glance around to see what the problem is and realize we've made it to Wyndell Way.

Two story homes line the street on both sides and loud music can be heard pouring from several of them as their front doors open. I didn't realize there would be so many parties tonight.

"Uh, did Nikolai tell you which house he's at?"

"Let me check." Millie pulls out her phone and opens it. "He says they're at 306." She looks up and takes in the chaos lining the street. "I guess we better go find him."

We start the trek down Wyndell Way, checking mailboxes as we pass them. One of the houses has a group of guys outside, who are clearly drunk. They're trying to toss around a football, but they're all too drunk to throw it, much less catch it. I cover my mouth to stop myself from outwardly giggling at the sight.

"Oh, here it is!" Millie shouts as we pass a house on our right. "306."

I look up at the small colonial style house in front of me. Its classic red brick facade is in stark contrast to the strobe lights flashing through its front window. I can just barely make out a group of students dancing inside when a streak of red illuminates the space.

When Millie walks toward the front porch, I suck in a breath and blow it out slowly. *Here goes nothing.*

We enter the house, and my eyes take a moment to adjust to the craziness. The room to my left is the source of the music and those annoying strobe lights. It looks like that's where most of the students are dancing. To my right, there are a couple tables set up for beer pong. A guy whoops as the ball he throws lands in one of the remaining cups in front of his opponent. There are stairs in front of me that are roped off with a sign stating, "No one's allowed upstairs. We mean it!"

Millie grabs my hand and pulls me through the hallway next to the stairs.

We end up in the kitchen, where the music dulls enough to hear the person next to you. Nikolai stands near the fridge, talking animatedly with a group of guys. He looks across the room as we enter and grins when he sees it's me and Millie.

"Finally!" He smiles at his friends. "Looks like we can call off the search party, boys."

Millie laughs as we approach them, then stands on her tiptoes to kiss her boyfriend. When she leans her back against him afterwards, he wraps his arms around her. They look cute together. And happy.

A tall, dark-skinned male with a charming smile puts his hand out for me to shake. "Hey! The name's Harvey." He juts his thumb in Millie and Nikolai's direction afterwards. "Please tell me these two disgust you as much as they disgust me."

I shake his hand and smile. "Ana." I then look at my loved-up friends as if I'm assessing them before I turn back to Harvey. "Nah. I think they're cute."

"Hell yeah!" Nikolai shouts as he high-fives me.

Harvey throws his hands up in mock defeat and says with a chuckle, "You all make me sick."

"Yeah…so that obnoxious fella is Harvey," Nikolai says as

Harvey winks at me. "He's the heir of Nero's General and a grade A pain in the ass."

Harvey bows, happily accepting the title.

"And the brooding guy in the corner is Kasper. He's the heir of Fotia's General."

I smile in Kasper's direction while noting with fascination the red and gold hues in his short hair that give it the appearance of a roaring fire. *He's a fire bender for sure.* He's nearly as pale as I am, but that's probably where our similarities end. He looks like he spends most of his time frowning.

Kasper nods, his only acknowledgement of the introduction. I then note the flame tattoos that cover both of his forearms. *Yep. He's definitely a fire bender.*

Millie gently pats the side of Nikolai's face. "Nik here's the heir of Zoin's General so you'll find we're surrounded by a lot of testosterone. We can only hope they keep their talks about war strategy amongst themselves. Somewhere far, far away from us."

I laugh while my attention drifts to the fair-skinned blonde standing next to Kasper. He must be the ungifted guy Nikolai mentioned to Millie.

"The blonde next to Kas is Graham. He might not look like much, but he's quite the tech genius," Nikolai explains. "He was accepted into Arken for his hacking skills."

Graham's cheeks flush. "It's nothing. *Really.*"

A dimple appears as Graham smiles at the group and it has me swooning. *He's cute.* His square glasses give him the appearance of sophistication and intelligence, but his round face and soft eyes give off kindness.

I definitely want to get to know him.

"It's nice to meet all of you," I say with a smile, and they all smile back at me. Well, everyone except for Kasper.

Harvey rubs his hands together once introductions are over. "How about a round of shots to start the night?"

We all whoop in agreement.

Shots were a mistake.

Whatever Harvey poured for us tasted like straight gasoline and felt like fire going down my throat. It didn't take long for its effects to kick in. I feel lightheaded already and a little fuzzy…but also free. My usual anxiety is nowhere to be found.

Millie pulled all of us onto the dance floor once the shots were drained. I'm not sure how much time has passed since we started dancing but it's been a while. I'm sure the six of us make for an unusual sight as we move and twist around, but it doesn't matter because we're having fun.

Millie is swaying with her hands in the air while her hair tosses back and forth in time with the music. Nikolai's matching her step for step, but his arms remain by his side at a ninety-degree angle. They'll randomly catch each other's eyes and smile. It's like they're the only two people in the room.

Harvey, on the other hand, is well aware of all the other girls in the room. I think he's currently dancing with his third girl of the night. I'm not sure, though. I don't like to look in his direction for longer than a few seconds. If he isn't making out with a girl, then he's dancing with her in a manner that's better left between them.

Kasper had an extra shot in the kitchen, and it seems to have loosened him up. He, Graham, and I are currently attempting to outdo each other's corny dance moves, and I can't say when the last time I laughed this hard was.

"I'm going to grab another drink," Kasper shouts when the song finishes. "Do you guys need anything?"

"I'm good," I shout back, not wanting to risk the nice buzz I have turning into something less appealing.

"Me too," Graham says.

"Okay. Be back in a minute."

Once Kasper leaves, Graham leans toward me and shouts so that I can hear him, "Do you want to go outside? I'm getting hot."

I smile. "Sure."

He grabs my hand as we weave through the gyrating bodies on the dance floor and his touch sends shivers down my spine. When he lets go once we're out of the living room, a pang of disappointment shoots through me.

We leave the overcrowded house and settle onto the top step of the porch.

"Did you go to many parties in high school?" Graham asks, his eyes locking on mine. The light from the moon reflects off his glasses, giving him an ethereal appearance.

I look down at my hands, suddenly feeling self-conscious. "No. Not really. I went to a few, but I mostly spent my time studying in high school. I was always trying to get here," I say, gesturing around us.

"To this porch?" he asks with a joking smile.

I playfully shove him and laugh. "No. To Arken, you goof."

"Ah. Yeah. That makes more sense," he replies teasingly. "I was the same way, though. I always knew I wanted to go to Arken so a lot of my time was spent making sure I got here. Even if it meant I missed out on what everybody else was doing."

My body relax in a way it hasn't in years. "Someone finally gets it! My sister, Daphne, thought I was crazy for feeling that way. You'd think I told her that I kick puppies for fun with the way she reacted."

Graham throws his head back and laughs. When he looks back at me, he smiles a cocky grin. "At least it paid off for us." He gestures to himself. "Well, it did for me at least. I got into Arken and now I'm getting to enjoy this beautiful night with an even more beautiful girl. Life can't get much better."

Damn. That was smooth.

"Is that so?" I ask as a shy smile spreads on my lips.

His gaze drops to my mouth, and I realize we're a lot closer than I thought. It has my breath catching in my throat.

"The lovebirds want to go to another house." Kasper's deep voice interrupts us from behind. "I'm going to try to chisel Harvey off his current exploit, then we'll be heading out. You guys coming?"

Graham and I look at each other and smile. We then say in unison, "Yeah!"

CHAPTER SIX
ANASTASIA

The next few hours pass by in a blur as we hop from house party to house party. Thankfully, we find different ways to entertain ourselves at each.

Our time at the second house is spent playing drinking games like Kings and Flip Cup. This is where I learn that Kas is unnaturally skilled at games involving any type of hand eye coordination. His ability to flip a cup and have it land on his first try gives even my skills a run for their money.

At the third house, we play classic party games like Truth or Dare and Never Have I Ever. Harvey reveals during the latter that he once froze his 'little soldier' while trying to hook up with a girl. An unfortunate tidbit shared after Millie stated she's never done something embarrassing with her gift.

After all that, we're spending time at the last house winding down.

As I sit here and think about what's transpired tonight, I decide I'm glad I came out. Maybe I *can* be someone that enjoys partying.

It's weird how being in a house full of strangers can feel so intimate. To think I met this ragtag group only hours ago is insane. I feel like I've known them forever. It's as if we were meant to be friends.

I glance around the party, admiring each of them. Millie and Nik are cozied up in an armchair talking while Kas flirts with a pretty blonde on the couch next to them. Harvey, having exhausted all his opportunities with the ladies, is now playing beer pong with a few guys who needed a fourth.

Graham and I are spending the time talking closely in a corner of the room, our mutual attraction palpable. We spent most of the evening getting to know each other and subtly expressing our interest, so at this point the kindling for whatever this is has been placed. It's just waiting for one of us to strike the match.

Millie stands from her place on Nik's lap and makes a beeline for me. She then leans in close and whispers, "I'm going to stay with Nik tonight. Is that okay?"

"Of course," I answer sincerely. "Don't worry about it."

"We're leaving now. Do you want to head back with us?"

I glance at Graham in front of me, Kas on the couch (now making out with the blonde), and Harvey in the middle of his game and decide I'll be okay. I feel comfortable heading back with any one of them.

"I'll be fine. One of these knuckleheads can take me back. Are we still on for brunch in the morning?"

"Definitely," she replies with a smile. "But let's plan for 11:00 so I can get some sleep." With a wink, she says, "I don't think I'll be getting much of it tonight."

I laugh. "That works for me. Have fun."

She hugs me goodbye, then signals to Nik that it's time to go. He stands and shouts to me while pointing at Harvey, "Take care of my roommate."

I give him a thumbs up to show my acceptance of his task.

After they leave, I look around the house and take stock of the party. It seems to be on its last leg. The music was shut off twenty minutes ago and party goers have been slowly trickling out since.

When I glance toward the back of the house, my heart stutters when I see Xander standing there. He's leaning against the back wall, casually sipping from a beer.

What's he doing here? It can't be safe for him to be out like this.

There's a group of guys surrounding him that he seems to be entertaining, though the muscle working in his jaw tells me he wishes he wasn't.

The party allows me to study him without being noticed.

He's a good few inches taller than the guys around him and has an air to him that is both intriguing and bemusing. The way he carries himself shows years of refinement and training, but there's also a sense of confidence and power mingling there that's interspersed with something I can't quite put my finger on.

I can see why people are drawn to him.

My eyes skirt the room and find several girls staring at him, their eyes focused on the muscles peeking out from his black T-shirt and the tattoos that encircle them. I don't blame them. There's no denying he's attractive.

I would think Xander's loving all the attention if it weren't for that muscle in his jaw working overtime.

An intriguing individual for sure.

My gaze returns to Graham, and I see that he's zoned out. There are now bags under his eyes that highlight his exhaustion.

I touch his arm to bring him back to reality and say, "I'm going to go to the restroom. Do you want to head out once I get back?"

He nods slowly.

I graze his shoulder as I leave the room, then head toward the back of the house. I'm grateful when I find a clean restroom there. I use it quickly and wash my hands with haste. My own exhaustion is settling in now and I long for my bed.

When I leave the bathroom, I run face first into the one person I said I should stay away from. As I stumble back, he catches me by the arm and a jolt of energy passes between us. I straighten, making sure I don't fall, and catch sight of the tattoos on Xander's arms that I couldn't make out in the cafeteria: storm clouds and lightning bolts. They cover the length of both his arms.

I tear my eyes away from them and look up at the future leader of our province. "I'm sorry," I blurt out as a blush creeps up my neck. "I didn't realize anyone was waiting."

He tilts his head, seeming confused about something, then lets go of my arm and says, "You're fine."

When it doesn't seem like he's going to say anything else, I hurry past him and return to Graham. He notices the blush on my cheeks immediately. "Is everything alright?"

"Yeah. I'm fine. I'm just ready to go."

"Okay," he says, accepting my dismissal of the subject. "Then let's go."

I look toward Harvey and find him already watching us. "Are you guys leaving?"

"Yeah."

"Then I'm coming with you," he responds while putting down the tiny white ball in his hand.

"That's not necessary," I say, trying to brush him off. "We'll be fine."

"Nonsense. I'm not letting my two ungifted friends wander around in the middle of the night unprotected. Not on my watch." He looks at the guys he was playing beer pong with and salutes them. "'Til next time, comrades."

I glance at Graham for support, but he shrugs his shoulders.

I guess Harvey's coming with us…

A few seconds later, the three of us are heading toward the front door when Harvey shouts, "Kas, you good to head back on your own?"

Kas gives us a thumbs up while still making out with the girl on the couch. I highly doubt he'll be heading back alone.

Once we leave the house and get a breath of fresh air, Harvey runs his hands over his short locs and exclaims, "*Wow*. Now that's how you start your first year of college."

Graham and I voice our agreement in a more subdued manner.

Harvey wraps his left arm around Graham's shoulders. "Well, Graham, buddy, it looks like you and I are homeless tonight. Our roommates seem to have commandeered our rooms for their own exploits."

"And to think the night started out so promising for you," Graham jokes.

A giggle escapes from me that I try to cover up with a cough. It doesn't work and Harvey playfully shoves me before responding to Graham. "I know, right? I burned out too soon. At least now I know better for next time."

We fall into a comfortable silence after that, and I use the time to take in the open fields that surround us. Their stillness at this hour is both beautiful and eerie. The full moon is now hidden behind clouds, so the area is cast in shadow.

Graham's voice cuts through the quiet. "You really think Kas is bringing that girl back tonight?"

"Oh, definitely," Harvey responds. "What I saw was a done deal."

"Where are we going to sleep, Harv?" Graham groans. "I'm not sure of the protocol in these types of scenarios."

"Well, you have two options," Harvey explains while putting up two fingers. "One, you go back to your room and pretend to be asleep when Kas comes back, then hope to gods he's quiet. Or two, you come sleep with me in the common room. The couches shouldn't be too bad. We could treat it like our own little slumber party."

"Option two. Definitely option two," Graham responds. "I like Kas, but I don't need to know him that well."

Harvey pumps his fist in the air. "Hell yeah! Sleepover!"

I smile at Harvey's antics before my eyes drift toward the first-year dorms as we arrive back on campus. Most of the lights in the rooms are shut off, their inhabitants already sleeping. My exhaustion has me nearly collapsing right there once my body realizes how close my bed is.

We arrive at the boys' dorm first, so I hug Harvey goodbye and tell him that I hope he gets a good night's sleep.

"Me too, Ana. Me too. I'll see you at brunch either way," he says, hugging me back.

I go to hug Graham next, but he stops me. "Let me walk you to your dorm."

"Okay," I reply with a smile.

As we begin the short walk to the girls' dorm, Graham grabs my hand. The butterflies in my stomach respond to the touch with a flurry of excitement.

"I had a lot of fun with you tonight," Graham begins, his voice wavering slightly. My heart swells at his nervousness. "Maybe we can do it again sometime?" He pauses. "Without our entourage."

I face him as we reach my dorm. "I'd like that."

"Good," he responds while his nervousness is replaced with something that looks a lot like desire. He then places his hands on my waist and pulls me in close. Seconds later, his lips meet mine and the butterflies in my stomach still as they're replaced by a heat that surges in my abdomen.

His tongue brushes against my lips until I part them for him. His right hand then tangles in my hair as our kiss deepens.

Gods, it's been a long time since I was last with someone. I imagine a night with Graham would be nice. Maybe even great.

Right when I think about inviting him up to my room, he pulls away and smiles. "I'll see you at brunch, Ana. Sweet dreams."

"Goodnight, Graham," I say as he turns away and walks back to his dorm.

I quickly climb the steps to my building and work on tamping down the remnants of my desire while I make my way to my room.

Tonight was great. I hope it's only the beginning of an amazing four years here.

CHAPTER SEVEN
ANASTASIA

Millie stumbled into our room *way* too early this morning and woke me up with all the noise she made.

Apparently, Harvey and Graham were kicked out of the common room when their RA found them sleeping in there, so Harvey had no choice but to return to his and Nik's room. Millie left after that, not wanting to impose any further.

Unfortunately, I was unable to fall back to sleep after that, so I decided I'd get ready for our brunch with the boys. As I did, I told Millie about what happened between me and Graham.

"Oh my gods! That's *awesome.* You guys looked so cute together last night." She beamed. "I was going to kick you if nothing happened between you two."

I smiled at my roommate, my own excitement mirroring hers. I was eager to see Graham again so we could solidify plans for our date.

The excitement I felt this morning still roils in my gut when we meet the boys outside of the student center.

"Well, who might these two beautiful ladies be?" Harvey asks as we approach. He pulls us in for a hug and kisses both of us on the side of the head. "I'm glad to see you guys made an effort this morning. The same cannot be said for your companions."

Harvey side-eyes the rest of the guys and I chuckle to myself when I see how haggard they look. Kas, appearing the most out of sorts, has his shirt on inside out and his hair is sticking straight up. He seems too tired to care, though.

"Are you guys ready to grab some food?" Millie asks and the boys grunt in response.

As we descend the steps to the cafeteria, I sidle up next to Graham. He smiles while I tell him good morning with a grin plastered across my face.

"Good morning, Ana. You look beautiful today."

My cheeks flush at the compliment. I then note the bags under Graham's eyes and ask, "Did you sleep okay last night?"

"Harvey definitely romanticized the idea of sleeping on the common room couches. I was able to get some sleep, but I don't know if my neck will ever recover from it."

"Yikes. I'm sorry to hear that."

He waves off my concern. "It's okay. It's what you do for friends. I'm sure Kas would do the same for me."

I voice my agreement before we swipe into the cafeteria and head in different directions for food.

I look around at all the options available to me and decide on a lighter fare. Today's going to involve a lot of preparation for classes tomorrow. I already know I'll be a jumble of nerves so smaller meals will probably be best.

With that in mind, I grab some scrambled eggs and bacon—my favorite.

When I enter the seating area, I find Kas face down at a table in the far corner. As I make my way toward him, I see that his hair is still sticking straight up, blending in with the tattoos that cover his forearms.

"You okay, Kas?" I ask once I sit down across from him.

He grunts in response.

"Not much of a morning person, huh?"

He grunts again.

"Would you like me to grab some food for you?"

He peers up at me that time, his golden eyes highlighting his exhaustion. "Did they have any waffles?"

"Yeah. Do you want me to grab you one?"

He nods and lays his head back down, so I let him know I'll be right back.

Unfortunately, when I reach for the tongs to grab Kas's waffle, someone else does at the same time. Our hands graze each other, and a jolt of electricity passes between them. I jump back in surprise and turn to find Xander standing there. My mouth drops open without thinking and I blurt out, "We really gotta stop meeting like this."

He stares at me with narrowed blue eyes for several seconds before saying, "I agree." His voice is a deep baritone that tugs at something deep within me. He then takes a step back and gestures for me to use the tongs first.

I quickly throw two waffles on a plate and give Xander a polite smile before I hightail it away from him. I make a pit stop at the toppings station after that and deck Kas's waffles out with butter, syrup, and lots of whipped cream. All the excess sugar should give him some energy and that's what he desperately needs right now.

When I place my creation in front of Kas, his pupils dilate, and he wastes no time digging into it. He thanks me between bites and the look he gives me makes me think he might consider me a friend now. The thought has a smile forming on my lips.

"No problem," I say as I sit down next to Millie and across from Graham. "I know how rough sleepless nights can be."

"Speaking of which…" Harvey cuts in, giving Kas a devilish grin. "Did you and that blonde have fun last night?" Kas glares at Harvey, conveying how he feels about discussing the topic, so Harvey puts his hands up in a placating manner. "Okay. I get it. You don't kiss and tell. My bad."

Millie looks between Harvey and Kas, making sure their conversation is over before she asks, "So, what classes is everyone taking this semester? Do we have any classes together?"

Millie's question began a conversation that lasted most of the meal. It turns out, I have classes with Kas, Harvey, Nik, and Graham.

Kas, Harvey, and I will be taking a specialized weapons course together; Nik and I are in hand-to-hand combat; and Graham and I are taking a history class that discusses how the nature of Kalyteros's government has influenced governments throughout the world.

As I look around the table, I can't help but smile. It'll be nice to have friends in most of my classes. There are only two classes that I won't—Intelligence Gathering and Coded Messaging—which are specific to my specialty.

Once our schedules are figured out, the six of us depart brunch with the promise to meet again for dinner that evening. It sounds like everyone plans on heading back to their rooms to get a few more hours of sleep. I, on the other hand, will be finding my classes and scoping out the best study spots so that I'm ready for the first day tomorrow.

Graham stops me before I get too far in the direction of my first class. "Hey. I just wanted to catch up after last night," he says with a nervous smile. "I had a lot of fun and would love to finalize details for that date if you're still interested."

"*Yes*. I'm definitely still interested. My class load is pretty light on Tuesdays and Thursdays. Wanna try to grab dinner Thursday night?"

"I'm down for that. Let me look up some options and we can discuss which one sounds best, okay?"

"Sounds good to me."

I swear I must be beaming right now. I'm so happy.

"Good." Graham plants a gentle kiss on my lips before he leaves to go to his and Kas's room.

A smile remains plastered on my face as I continue to the location of my first class. I don't know how things could get any better.

CHAPTER EIGHT

XANDER

I arrive at the Stratos Building just in time for my first class. I hurry inside while resisting the temptation to stop and gawk at the ugly building. It's one of the newest ones at Arken, which is emphasized by its modern design. Its sharp angles, large windows, and monochromatic color scheme leaves it without character. What's left is a cold, lifeless space that doesn't fit with the rest of the buildings on campus.

The facility encompasses the back ten acres of the university, appearing like a small compound when you first approach it. It contains six training areas, four shooting ranges, and a handful of lecture halls.

It's mentioned in all of Arken's marketing material that several high-ranking military personnel donated money for the building. They wanted to ensure the school was developing viable recruits.

I personally think it's absurd they did that. Their money could've gone toward much better things—the ungifted families living in squalor outside of the capital, to name one.

I shake my head at the thought and force myself to focus on finding my class.

Thankfully, I find the correct lecture hall just as the professor starts speaking. He stops as I enter, his dark eyes following me until I plop into a seat at the back of the class.

The eyes of every student in the room are also on me, but I ignore them. Attention is nothing I'm not used to.

The professor smooths his short, gray hair and clears his throat before he continues. "As I was saying, my name is Professor Hawke, and this is Weapons Training I. The purpose of this course is to teach all of you how to properly handle and use various types of weapons. Each class will be evenly split between lecture and application. You *will* be expected to demonstrate what you're being taught. This is a hands-on class, after all."

The next fifteen minutes are spent listening to Professor Hawke describe why he's qualified to teach this class. Apparently, he's a retired Fotian General that worked alongside Sister Tana right before she disappeared forty years ago. That's not something I'd personally brag about, but maybe that's just me.

As Professor Hawke begins his lecture on the origins of throwing knives, I scan the room to see if I recognize anyone. My heart rate spikes when my eyes land on the spy: Ms. Metallo.

What's she doing in this class?

I learned while out with Tony and Steven on Saturday that she's posing as an ungifted student. That all but confirmed my suspicions that she's a threat.

I haven't decided what I'm going to do with that information yet. Part of me wants to confront her and end this now, but the other part of me wants to wait to see what she'll do. I honestly don't know which choice is better. Either option puts my mom and Lydia at risk.

My eyes narrow when the redheaded guy next to her leans in close to whisper something in her ear. She covers her mouth to stifle a laugh and the lanky guy on her other side questions her. This leads to more laughter from Ms. Metallo and her fire-bending friend. They shut up almost instantly when Professor Hawke glares in their direction.

The spy was with those two guys at the party on Saturday. It was the three of them, a blonde guy with glasses, a beautiful brunette, and another guy who was as muscular as one could naturally be. The muscular one seemed familiar, but I never got a good look at his face.

How does she know these guys? And how well do they actually know her?

For thirty minutes, Professor Hawke discusses the different types of throwing knives that exist and the various throwing techniques one may use. I zone out for most of it. It's nothing I haven't learned before. My father forced me to take classes like this throughout my entire childhood.

Once the lecture is finished, the class moves to the adjoining training facility. As we file into the space, most of the students look around in awe at the sheer size of it. It's large enough to allow our class of eighteen to spread out comfortably while also leaving room for another dozen students or so.

Professor Hawke clears his throat to bring our attention back to him. The ticking of the muscle in his jaw shows his frustration, though his full, gray beard masks it well.

"For class today, I want to establish a baseline for all of you. That way, I can track how you improve throughout the course." Professor Hawke turns to the spy and gives her a wicked grin. "And who better to start with than the ungifted student that was accepted into Arken for her skills in weaponry?"

Lies, lies, and more lies.

How was she able to convince the school to believe all her lies?

"Ms. Galanis, why don't you step up and show us what you're capable of?"

Galanis? Is the spy using a fake name? I make a mental note to search for the name 'Galanis' when I get back to my room.

The spy steps up to the marked spot on the floor, about ten paces in front of the rest of us. I note her tense shoulders and the way she keeps flicking her wrists, an obvious nervous tick.

Professor Hawke hands her four throwing knives and gestures to the targets he expects her to hit, roughly forty feet away. She takes a deep breath to steady herself, then lines up with them.

I watch in amazement as she throws each knife, and they hit

their mark with a quiet *thud*. I struggle to hide my surprise. I didn't see any hints of her using her gift, which means she hit those targets based on skill alone.

What she did is extremely impressive. And *very* concerning.

The only person I know who might be better than her is Tony, but that's because he's practically an expert when it comes to throwing knives and daggers.

"Nice display, Ms. Galanis," Professor Hawke says with a scowl that highlights his annoyance. "Maybe the school wasn't wrong for accepting you. We'll see, though. I'm sure any one of these gifted students will be able to do what you just did."

Nice display? *Really?* Who's he kidding? There probably isn't a single person in this room that could do what she just did.

Surprise flashes across the spy's face, but it's quickly replaced by a quiet resolve. I gotta hand it to her. She does a good job of pretending to be offended by the ungifted prejudice thrown her way.

But whether *she* has a right to be offended or not, I'm annoyed on behalf of those who actually are. Ungifted prejudice is not okay. Especially from a professor.

"*Dick*," I quietly hiss.

His head whips in my direction. "Do you have something you'd like to say, Mr. Thyellas?"

"Nope," I respond as I fold my arms across my chest and glare at him.

"Well, since you so desperately want to be the center of attention in my class, why don't you go next?"

"Gladly," I say as I grab the knives he holds out to me and position myself on the marked spot. I place two of the knives in my left hand and two in my right. I then take a deep breath and throw them all at once.

A flash of lightning streaks across the ceiling, following the path of the knives. It then strikes each knife as they land with a *thud* in the center of their target. I hear the gasps of the other students behind me when my lightning cracks before it disappears.

I turn to Professor Hawke and quirk an eyebrow at him. He

looks at me with undiluted fury. His anger, now noticeable, causes my classmates to shuffle in discomfort.

"The use of gifts is not allowed in my class, Mr. Thyellas," Professor Hawke snarls. "You may be the future Grand Leader, but that means nothing here. Use your gift again and you'll have to leave. Understood?"

"Understood."

I breeze past him nonchalantly and settle in next to my classmates. I smirk to myself, knowing that my lack of care toward his posturing likely upset him more. One look at his face confirms my assumption.

I watch as he forces himself to calm down before he turns back to the rest of the class. "Do I have any volunteers who'd like to go next?" When no one raises their hand, he says, "If no one volunteers, then I'll begin choosing at random."

The remainder of class is spent observing each student's ability to hit the targets that me and Metallo's daughter—I mean, Ms. *Galanis*—had four perfect bullseyes on. It appears that Professor Hawke's proclamation that any gifted student could accomplish what the spy did was incorrect. Most of the students were at least able to hit the targets, but very few got anywhere near their center.

My interest is piqued by the spy's friends, though. They're the only other students who land all four throwing knives on the targets and they each have a bullseye of their own.

I study them closer and notice a familiarity that I try to place. Suddenly, the faces of the Generals for Nero and Fotia flash in my mind and I realize I'm staring at their sons. That would certainly explain why they're so skilled. The children of Generals are expected to follow in their footsteps, so a certain level of training is required.

Interesting. I wonder why they chose to come to Arken instead of going to the Arete Universities in their own provinces.

My chest tightens as a thought pops into my head. Could the spy be working with these two to bring down my family? Is that why the three of them seem so close already? Is this all for some grander plan that Nero and Fotia put together?

I suddenly feel like I can't breathe as I realize my family is in a lot more danger than I thought. How the hell am I supposed to protect them now? I'm just one man against two provinces.

When lightning sparks at the tips of my fingers, I force myself to take controlled breaths. I can't let the spy and her friends figure out that I'm onto them. Not until I know how bad the situation really is.

The last student finishes her demonstration as I regain some semblance of control over myself. Professor Hawke then, unconvincingly, tells us that we did a good job today and dismisses us with a "see you all on Wednesday."

As we file out of the training facility, I decide that I need to find out more about Ms. Galanis and the friends she keeps.

I can't risk anything happening to my family.

CHAPTER NINE

ANASTASIA

"Geez, what's wrong with that guy?" Harvey asks as soon as we leave the training facility. "I can't believe he would treat you like that. If he keeps it up, I'll have to have a word with him." He cracks his knuckles to indicate the kind of talk they'd have.

My thoughts flash to the moment in question and the shock I felt. I knew I was going to experience prejudice at a gifted school, but I didn't think it'd come from a professor. I thought there were rules against that sort of thing.

I look at Harvey and Kas to see if they're as upset as I am. From the ice forming on Harvey's fingertips and the fire in Kas's eyes, I'm guessing the answer is yes. They look pissed. I move to rejoin them, hoping to squash any retaliation, when I hear Xander Thyellas mumble something behind me. It sounded like he called the professor a dick, but I must've misheard him. Why would he care if Professor Hawke was rude to me?

My thoughts return to the present and my friend standing next to me. I grab Harvey's hand and give it a squeeze to try to calm him.

"Don't worry about it, Harv. It's nothing I haven't dealt with before. I can handle it. Trust me."

"The dude's a quack, anyway," Kas cuts in. "General Hawke worked as an advisor for several years before he retired, and my father said Hawke never knew what anyone was talking about. Even if they were discussing basic war strategy and common modes of attack. My father doesn't think Hawke did much while he was General."

Harvey shakes his head in exasperation. "Class will definitely be interesting if that's the kind of guy he is." He playfully nudges me with his elbow. "Speaking of interesting…What did you think about Xander Thyellas stepping in to defend you? It looks like you caught the Grand Leader's eye."

I shove Harvey's shoulder when he waggles his eyebrows. "I did *not.* Xander was just trying to rile up Professor Hawke. That's all. It had nothing to do with me."

"And even if it did, you should steer clear of that guy, Ana," Kas states, his deep voice taking on a protective tone. "My father worked closely with Xander's and constantly talked about how awful of a person he was. I don't know Xander personally, but I can't imagine that apple falls far from the tree. His father was doing anything he could to cause trouble with Fotia. Who knows what Xander's plans are once he takes office."

Before I can tell Kas not to worry, I hear someone shout my name from behind me. I turn to see Nik walking my way with a goofy grin plastered across his face. "You ready to go kick some butt?"

I smile wide, my excitement making me bounce on the balls of my feet. "Hell yeah!" I turn back to Kas and squeeze his arm to show my appreciation for his concern. "I'll be fine. You guys don't need to worry about me, okay?" I look between my two friends, and they nod their understanding.

Nik waves goodbye to Harvey and Kas as we head in the direction of our hand-to-hand combat class. Once we're out of earshot of our friends, he asks, "What was that about?"

"Kas was doing his best protective older brother impression," I say with a shake of my head and Nik chuckles.

"Yeah. He'll do that. He can't help it. You looking a lot like his younger sister, Tally, probably doesn't help either." Nik blows out a breath and stretches in preparation for class. "How was your first class with them? Did you smoke 'em?"

"I did, but I expected that," I answer as a sense of nostalgia creeps up on me. "It wasn't anything I hadn't done a million times with my dad."

"Your dad was the one who trained you?"

I nod. "Yeah. He knew of my desire to go to Arken from the time I was a little girl. He trained me in whatever way he thought necessary to get me here."

I fight to numb the familiar pangs of loss as Nik says, "My dad trained me too. Those are some of my favorite memories from when I was a kid."

"Yeah. Same," I whisper as tears well in my eyes.

Our conversation's cut off by the arrival of our professor, so I quickly wipe my eyes and hope Nik doesn't see that I was crying. I then take in the intimidating man now standing before me. He's of average build and appears to be of Asian descent. He's barefoot and wearing a gi. There's nothing out of the ordinary about him, but I still feel a chill run down my spine when his eyes scan me and my classmates.

He introduces himself as Professor Fonias, then states he's ungifted, but that his expertise in eight different fighting styles is what led to his admission into Arken many years ago and his eventual rise to bodyguard for Grand Leader Vepo in Nero.

I can't help the smile that spreads across my face when Professor Fonias mentions he's ungifted. It gives me hope for my own future.

"I think it goes without saying, but I'll say it anyway. In my class, the use of gifts is strictly forbidden." Professor Fonias looks at each of us to ensure we're listening before he continues. "The purpose of my class is to learn how to use your body to defend yourself. Nothing else. Understood?"

Affirmative mumbles carry throughout the room.

"Good. Now, my class is only an hour long, so I'll typically spend the first few minutes demonstrating a move or fighting style to you. After that, you'll break off into pairs and practice what I taught you. The last half hour of class will then involve students challenging each other to sparring matches. There'll be two going at the same time and they'll both last five minutes. Is that clear?"

We all nod our understanding.

"*Good.* Now, since this is our first class and a portion of it has already been spent on introductions and expectations, I thought it'd be fun to spar for the remainder of our time together. That way I can get a baseline for everyone, and you can learn the intensity that will be expected by me. Do I have any volunteers for the first match?"

Nik nudges my arm, and I look up at him with furrowed brows. "I think we should volunteer," he whispers.

"*What?* Why?"

"Most students probably know you're ungifted by now and the gifted love making a spectacle of those they believe are beneath them. I imagine any one of our classmates is itching to challenge you for a quick ego boost. If we spar and they see how talented you are, maybe they'll leave you alone."

My stomach drops. *Nik's right.* Of course my classmates think I'm beneath them. I don't know why I expected anything different. Especially after how Professor Hawke treated me.

"It's worth a shot," I grumble as my anger boils to the surface. I'll show all of them just how wrong they are.

Nik raises his closed fist to me, and I bump it with my own.

"I volunteer," Nik announces Nik to the entire class before pointing at me with his thumb. "And I would like to challenge Anastasia Galanis."

I note surprise on the faces of my classmates. A few even look disappointed.

"Alright," Professor Fonias says. "You may both approach the center of the sparring ring. The match will begin as soon as you finish bowing to each other."

Nik and I move to our starting points and face one another. I grin while I bow and teasingly say, "Good luck."

"You too," he says with a smirk, matching my movements.

I ended up beating Nik during our match, but it wasn't for a lack of trying on his part. We banged each other up pretty good.

Thankfully, Nik was right. No one dared to challenge me after I beat him. I guess most of them know Nik isn't someone you want to mess with and if I won, then that must mean I'm not either.

The rest of the day flies by and before I know it, it's dinner time.

I groan as I sit down at the table my friends are already gathered around, my muscles aching from the movement. Unfortunately, my injuries are nothing compared to the dark bruise on Nik's chin from where I kicked him earlier and nearly knocked him out. I feel awful for hurting him like that, but Nik brushes off my concern, stating it's an inherent part of his specialty.

Dinner is spent catching up with everyone and hearing about their day. It sounds like they all had similar days to mine, which I guess is expected at a school like Arken. We all agree that it was a great start to the semester.

After dinner, I go back to my room and settle into bed while I ice several of the bruises that give me trouble. With it being the first day of class, I don't have any homework or studying to do so I spend the rest of my evening watching trashy reality TV with Millie.

I call my family before I go to bed to check in and tell them how my first day went. What was supposed to be a short phone call ends up being over an hour long. They wanted to know every detail about my day, then Daphne needed assistance with a wardrobe crisis for her first day on Wednesday.

When our conversation finally dies out, my mom makes sure to tell me how happy she is that I had a great first day. She then makes me promise to call her in a couple days before she hangs up. I tear up when the line dies, suddenly realizing how much I miss my family. Being away from them like this is so hard.

62

CHAPTER TEN
XANDER

I wake up for the second day of class with my head spinning. None of the information I found on the spy last night made any sense and I have no idea where to go from here.

Why was she raised in an ungifted town? And why did she go to an ungifted high school? I feel like I'm losing my mind at this point, and I hate it.

Why won't she just try to kill me already and put an end to all this? I don't like waiting to see if she'll do something.

My thoughts are preoccupied with Ms. Galanis during my first two classes and before I know it, it's time to meet Tony and Steven for lunch.

Steven's another friend from high school that forced himself on me—I guess that's the only way I make friends. He's an earth bender who's incapable of reading a room. The dude has no filter, and it's caused a lot of problems for me over the years.

As I approach the student center, I see Tony and Steven waiting by the stairs. When Steven notices me, he starts bouncing up and down. "*Dude*, Xander, I think I met the love of my life today."

When I register what my friend's telling me, I respond in the only way I can. "That poor girl."

In typical Steven fashion, he starts describing the girl, oblivious to what I just said. "She's drop dead gorgeous, man. Like she could be a model, she's that gorgeous. And she's smart too."

Tony and I exchange a look while Steven continues talking about the current girl that has his attention. How many times have we heard him talk like this?

"She says she can grow plants, but I can tell you one thing she's *definitely* growing." Tony groans when Steven waggles his eyebrows at us.

"I stand corrected," I respond. "Your love story is one for the ages."

He smiles while pushing his floppy hair out of his face. "Mark my words, boys. She'll be mine by the time we graduate."

Tony chuckles and wraps his right arm around Steven's shoulders. "Whatever you say, Romeo. Let's go get some lunch."

I follow behind my friends as they descend the stairs. I then quickly grab my food in the hopes of going unnoticed. If anyone sees me, they'll stop me and talk at me for gods knows how long. My classmates aren't exactly subtle about their desires for a spot in my cabinet when I become Grand Leader and it's extremely annoying.

Thankfully, no one sees me and I'm able to grab an open table in the back of the seating area, out of sight. Tony sits down across from me a minute later with a plate full of some type of pasta. I don't think I've ever met someone that eats as much as he does, yet doesn't gain a single pound. He attributes that fact to his gift.

"Guess who I saw today," he says while digging into his food.

My brows furrow. "Who?"

"Just your favorite person in the whole world, Nikolai Ischyros. Looks like he's going to school here after all."

I groan and put my head in my hands, already dreading what that could mean for me and my friends.

If a high schooler could have an arch nemesis, then Nikolai would've been mine. He and his friends were always picking on Tony, Steven, and I, but they were especially cruel to Steven. I never tolerated any of it so Nikolai and I would have heated exchanges often.

Surprisingly, our fights only turned physical once, but I imagined kicking his ass at least a hundred times over the years. I hoped a new school would mean I was finally free of him. I guess I should've known better. Of course he wouldn't leave his father's side.

Tony laughs at my response. "I'm sure everything will be fine as long as you don't hook up with any more of his girlfriends."

I groan again. "Ugh. Don't remind me. My body *still* hasn't recovered from that fight."

"You won, though," he reminds me while taking another bite of food. "You made sure that prick finally got what he deserved. It was a long time coming after what he did to Steven on the roof."

Anger surges through my veins at the mention of what happened to Steven during our sophomore year of high school. The memory of it flashes in my mind and has my hands clenching into fists. For some stupid reason, Nikolai got it into his head that it would be funny to hang Steven over the side of the Capitol Building and act like he was going to drop him. We could hear Steven's screams all the way from the cafeteria. That was the first time Nikolai and I almost came to blows. The only thing that stopped it was the sudden appearance of our math teacher, Ms. Clary.

My thoughts are brought back to the present when Steven slams his tray on the table as he sits down next to me. He then opens his mouth, but whatever he was about to say dies in his throat when he notices our expressions. "Why the long faces?"

"I was just telling Xander that I saw Nikolai Ischyros today."

There's a flash of fear in Steven's eyes that quickly disappears when he grins. "I wonder if that big lug has missed me."

"I prefer we not find out," I grumble as phantom pain spreads through my right arm. Nikolai broke it when we fought and the feeling of him snapping it in two still haunts me.

"Don't worry, man." He pats my shoulder reassuringly. "I can steal his girl this time. That's a sacrifice I'm willing to make because I love you."

Tony laughs and nearly chokes on his food in the process. While he pounds on his chest, I roll my eyes at both of them and say drily, "You guys are hilarious."

Steven claps me on the back and leans in close. "Oh, you know you love us."

"Yep. About as much as one loves a lobotomy."

Tony and Steven exchange a look before they smile wide. "I didn't hear him say he *doesn't* love us, did you, Steven?"

"Nope. Sure didn't." Steven pinches my right cheek and drawls, "You love us."

I push Steven away from me, but I can't help the smile that tugs at my lips. I'm unable to deny how good it feels to get back into a routine with these guys. We've been through so much together over the years and I like knowing I can count on them. Even if they do drive me crazy most of the time.

The rest of lunch is spent discussing our classes. It seems we're all in agreement that they're too easy after everything we learned at the Capitol Building.

Before I know it, it's time for my next class so I say goodbye to my best friends and make my way toward the Admin Building.

When I find the classroom I need to be in, I see that it's already packed full of students, so I put my head down and go to the only open desk near the window.

As I take my seat, I'm surprised to find the spy sitting next to me. It's obvious by her stiff posture and the way her eyes keep glancing in my direction that she's also noticed me, but is trying to act like she didn't.

You know what? *Fuck it.* Let's see what she does if I introduce myself.

I lean over my desk and extend my hand toward her. She notices and her eyes widen while I say, "Xander Thyellas."

The spy slowly places her hand in mine and a jolt of energy passes between us from the contact. Concern flashes in her eyes, but it quickly fades when I smirk at her, letting her believe the spark was intentional. Her gaze narrows after that. "Anastasia Galanis."

Anastasia. Huh. That's not what I expected her name to be at all, but I kinda like it.

"It's nice to finally meet you, Anastasia," I state as I let go of her hand. "I thought I should introduce myself to the person who's been running into me wherever I go."

I watch her closely to see how she responds to the subtle accusation in my words, but she doesn't react the way one would if they thought they'd been caught. Instead, a blush creeps onto her cheeks. I don't have time to question her reaction because our professor enters the room and a chill travels down my spine when I recognize his voice.

"I'm so sorry I'm late, class," says the voice from my past and I look to the front of the room and see Dr. Farrogow standing there. A pit forms in my stomach at the sight of the man I once considered a friend. "I got caught up helping a student that fell down the stairs."

His eyes scan the room, noting the students he'll be teaching this semester. When they land on me, he pauses his sweep and a small smile spreads across his lips.

That has me wondering if it's too late to switch classes. I glance at the spy out of the corner of my eye and sigh. I can't. Not when this is the only time she's alone. I have to find out what she's up to and this class might be the only way I can. That means I'm stuck with Dr. Farrogow. *Great.*

While he introduces himself, I lean back in my desk and cross my arms, waiting to hear whatever nonsense he's about to spew.

"Welcome everyone! My name's Dr. Farrogow and I'll be your professor for the next few months." He looks around the room and smiles at everyone before he continues. "The purpose of my class, Intelligence Gathering, is to teach all of you how to gather information discreetly without being discovered. I'll also show you how to analyze that information efficiently, so you'll actually get something valuable from it.

"Now, I'm sure many of you are wondering why a healer of all people is teaching this sort of class. Well, it's because they couldn't find anyone better." He pauses for a moment before laughing—a contagious one that carries throughout the space. "I'm kidding, of course. I was chosen because I worked as a healer for Grand Leader Thyellas's family for several years."

Once he mentions our history, the spy glances at me with a confused look on her face. I ignore her as Dr. Farrogow drones on.

"In that role, I was also expected to assess threats to the family. I'd do this by intercepting and analyzing communication between the staff. If I saw anything of concern, I was to report it to security. It was a different role for me, but one I absolutely loved."

His attention drifts to me and there's a sadness in his eyes that does nothing but make me angry. "Eventually, my work for the Grand Leader became too much. I decided then that I wanted a more lowkey job. That's when I switched to teaching and I've been doing it since."

I nearly laugh out loud at his explanation for why he left. It became too much for him? More like he ran away because he was a selfish jerk who only thought of himself.

After that, I can't listen to another thing he says. I pull out my notebook and scribble in it while I do my best to tune him out.

Unfortunately, I get so lost in thought that I lose track of time. It's not until I see my classmates stand and gather their things that I realize class is over. I quickly shove my stuff into my bag and hurry toward the door, hoping Dr. Farrogow doesn't try to talk to me.

I just make it to the exit when I hear him call out behind me, "Xander!" He pauses. "I mean, uh, Mr. Thyellas! Can I have a moment?"

I swallow the groan on my lips and turn to face the man who healed and comforted me for years. That is, until he decided he no longer cared and left me alone with those monsters.

My displeasure with being forced to talk to him is clearly written on my face as I slowly approach his desk. He waits until everyone's gone before he says, "How've you been, Xander? I've thought about you a lot over the past two years. I really wanted to reach out, but figured it was best if I didn't. When I saw your file in Arken's records, I hoped you might end up in my class someday."

"I'm fine," is my clipped response.

"Good. That's good. I'm glad to hear it." Dr. Farrogow fiddles with and adjusts the items on his desk.

"Do you need something?" I ask, annoyance lacing my words. "I have homework to get to."

"No. You're right. I'm sorry for keeping you." He tries reaching for my arm, but I quickly pull it away. After that, he blows out a breath and runs his hands over his face. "I want you to know, Xander, that I'm here if you ever need anything. I'm still your friend."

"You were *never* my friend," I snarl while I try to push down the hurt that's clawing its way into my chest.

I don't wait for him to respond before I storm out of the room.

I'm good and angry by the time I leave the Admin Building. It's a concerted effort to keep my gift in check despite my spiraling emotions.

Dr. Farrogow has some nerve acting like we can just pick up right where we left off. *He's* the one who abandoned me when I needed him the most. That means *he's* the one that has to suffer the consequences.

As I aimlessly wander the campus, trying to work through my anger, my thoughts drift to the spy. When Dr. Farrogow mentioned seeing my file in Arken's records, I immediately thought about Anastasia and wondered if she had one too.

My anger shifts into something more useful. Something that feels a lot like hope. If the spy does have a file, then maybe it could provide some insight into who she is and maybe it can even help me figure out what she's up to.

Welp, it's settled. Looks like I'm breaking into the Admin Building tonight.

CHAPTER ELEVEN
XANDER

It's nearly midnight when I approach the Admin Building. Its dark facade looms in front of me, engulfed by shadow, giving the usually inviting space an ominous feel. I don't shy from it, though. Instead, I welcome the shadows as I disappear within them.

The Admin Building is the heart of the university, both in location and function. It's used not only for administrative purposes on the first floor, but overflow classes are held on the second, and the third is where old records are stored.

My destination tonight is the first floor. Specifically, the Administrator's office. I'm hoping that's where they keep the records for current students.

The Admin Building has three separate entrances, and the west entrance is the one I make my way toward since it's the one most concealed by shadow. Once I reach the set of double doors that make up the entrance, I lean against them and send my lightning to search for any alarms and cameras within. I short-circuit each one as I find them, then use my wind to unlock the door nearest me and slip inside.

I wait for my eyes to adjust to the darkness before I continue.

The last thing I want is to run into something and make unnecessary noise.

Once I can vaguely see the hallway looming before me, I creep along it and make my way to the center of the building. I trail wisps of my wind behind me as I go. They act as motion detectors, sending a chill down my spine if someone walks through them. They'll notify me if anyone's coming and give me a chance to hide.

I easily find Administrator Spana's office in a cluster of similar looking rooms. The door is unlocked so I sneak inside. I'm instantly surprised by how small it is. There's a large desk in the center of the space that's covered with family photos and memorabilia for a second-tier college I don't recognize. Bookshelves line the right wall, and they're filled with various copies of the student handbook. It's the filing cabinets on the left wall that draw my attention. I quickly approach the one in the middle labeled with the letter 'G' and begin rifling through it, searching for Ms. Galanis's file.

I struggle to read the names on the files in the dark, so I pull out my phone and turn on its flashlight. My stomach leaps when I immediately see the spy's. I'm surprised by how thick it already is when I take it out.

While I rifle through it, I discover the first handful of pages are her application to Arken, followed immediately by the review of her showcase. It looks like whoever reviewed her was very impressed by her skill, stating, 'Ms. Galanis is an exceptional candidate who demonstrates an expertise in skills that haven't been seen in this school for decades. We could use someone like her. I recommend her immediate acceptance.'

There's a separate note from the Dean of Admissions that has my head spinning. 'Ms. Galanis is denied admission to Arken University. Yes, she shows great skill, but her skill set falls under a specialty that's already saturated with talent. There are other ungifted applicants that are better suited for our university at this time.'

Wait. So, the spy wasn't accepted into Arken? Why is she here then?

I quickly flip to the next page, hoping it provides answers, and find a letter from President Forester. In it she declares, 'Anastasia Galanis is to be accepted as a full-time student at Arken University immediately. This decision was made following a recommendation from Acting Grand Leader Aeras.'

What? My uncle's the reason the spy is at Arken? Why the hell would he push for her to be accepted? He knows just as much about her as I do. What's he playing at?

I need to find out what he said to President Forester that convinced her to accept the spy. Unfortunately, that means I'll have to break into her office, which will not be an easy task. The offices of the President, Vice President, and the various Deans of the university are housed in a separate building at the front of campus. One with a top-notch security system.

I groan before I skim through the rest of the spy's file, not finding anything else of note. I return it to the filing cabinet, fully ready to give up for the night.

A note taped above the filing cabinets makes me pause.

'The files for graduated students <u>must</u> be returned to the records room on the third floor. This ensures efficient organization. If you have any questions about the filing system, please talk to the secretary.'

Huh. I wonder if Metallo has a file up there. I'll have to check.

Great. That makes two places now that I need to search.

But it'll have to be another time. My alarm will be going off in less than five hours and I really need to get some sleep before then.

I quickly scan the room, making sure everything looks like it did when I came in. Once I'm satisfied, I prepare to leave. I stop when my phone starts vibrating in my hand. A pit forms in my stomach when I see that my mom's calling. Why's she calling so late?

I answer the phone and immediately ask, "Mom, what's wrong?"

"Hi, honey," she answers, her sweet voice calming me in a way I didn't know I needed. "I'm sorry. I didn't realize how late it is. I hope I didn't wake you."

"You're fine, Mom. You didn't wake me. Why're you calling so late? Is something wrong?"

"No. Nothing's wrong. I'm just sitting here with Lyddy, watching one of her favorite cartoons. It made me think of the silly shows you and I used to watch when you were her age. She has a fever right now so she's fighting sleep."

Lydia's sick? My chest tightens with worry. "Do you need me to come home? I could be there within the hour."

"Oh, no, honey. There's no need. Lyddy has a stomach bug. It's just something her body has to work through on its own. I've already given her medicine to help. Honestly, the biggest thing she needs right now is sleep." I hear my sister laugh in the background as my mom tickles her. "Of course, that's the one thing she's fighting. But we're okay. I'll get her to crack eventually." I hear my mom sigh. "I selfishly wanted to hear your voice. I've missed you. You leaving for college feels too much like…" The weight of what's left unsaid settle between us as her voice trails off.

I don't know if my heart will ever stop breaking for my mom. She's been through so much because of my father.

"'This isn't like last time, Mom," I say, trying to ease her worries. "I can come home whenever I like. Whenever *you'd* like. I have some free time on Saturday. Do you want me to stop by?"

"I couldn't ask you to do that, Xander. I'm sure you'd rather hang out with your friends." Her voice takes on a determined tone while she says, "I'm fine. *Really*. You living on campus is just some-thing I need to get used to."

"I'll come over on Saturday, Mom. I need a break from this place, anyway."

"Is it that bad already?" I can hear my mom's smirk through the phone.

"*Yes*, actually. My classes are terribly boring, and my classmates have decided that the men's restroom is the perfect place to tell me why I should hire them someday."

My mom's light laugh in response eases the ache in my chest. "That does sound awful," she says, laughter coating her words. "You should definitely come home then."

"Oh, I will. Though it'll probably be early. I can text you that morning so you know when to expect me."

"Okay, sweetie. That sounds good to me." I hear her blow out a breath. "Well, I should probably stop bothering you and let you get some sleep. It sounds like you need it. You need to be alert if you're having to fight people off in the bathroom."

I chuckle before I say, "Okay. Goodnight, Mom."

"Goodnight, honey. I love you."

"I love you, too."

Once I hang up the phone, I run my hands over my face and sigh. I then feel along my wisps of air, making sure the coast is still clear before I leave Administrator Spana's office.

As I exit the Admin Building and head back to my dorm, my thoughts drift to my mom and how drastically her life was changed the day my father learned of my gift. It happened during my third birthday party. I was upset that one of my cousins was playing with my favorite toy and my anger caused a rumble of thunder. My father confronted my mom about it after the party and she couldn't come up with a convincing enough lie to explain away what happened. My father knew then that my mom had been hiding my gift from him, and he was very angry.

That night, he dragged me to the condo he bought that over-looked the Capitol Building. He initially got it so that he had a place to stay on nights he worked late. But after that awful night, it became our sole residence.

A month later, my father met with my mom alone, where he proceeded to tell her that she wasn't to call me or try to see me. If she did, then she'd lose the few visits he would allow her to have with me each year. My mom told me that she wanted to fight it, but that there was nothing she could do. My father was too power-ful. Had too many connections.

I never considered what my mom was going through while I was with my father. I was too busy trying to keep him happy, so I'd make it through another day. It wasn't until he died, and I moved back in with her, that I realized how hard those years were for her. I prob-ably should've known they weren't good since she begged to have another baby with a man she hated. At least they had Lydia via a surrogate, so they didn't have to spend any time together to make it happen.

My mom tries her best to hide how those years affected her, but when you look close enough, you can see just how badly they broke her. I find it's the most noticeable when she's laughing and playing with Lydia. Her eyes always have a sadness to them during it. As if she remembers playing with me like that and knows how much time she lost.

I've gotten used to the heartbreak I feel whenever I look at her. I just wish I didn't see it mirrored back at me.

Unfortunately, we both still have a lot of healing to do from the damage my father caused. I thought we were making some progress with it, but then I had to move to Arken and it set us back. I think I'll have to make Saturday visits a regular occurrence, for all our sakes.

When I finally return to my room, my shoulders sag as the weight of everything I must carry settles on them. Between my family, my friends, classes, and looking into Metallo and the spy, I'm spread thin. I hope something gives soon, otherwise, I'm going to burn out.

CHAPTER TWELVE
ANASTASIA

It's finally Thursday night and I'm buzzing with excitement. Graham should be showing up for our date any minute now and I can't stop fussing with my outfit while I wait for him. I have no idea what he's planned, but Kas told me I'd love it.

I check my reflection in the mirror for the hundredth time and adjust the sleeves of my favorite mini dress. It hugs me in all the right places and should drive Graham wild. Especially when paired with the strappy black heels I'm wearing and my hair hanging loosely down my back.

I can't believe how nervous I feel, but I guess it makes sense. It's been a couple years since the last time I went on a date, and I was still being driven around by my parents then. This is my first *real* date.

My heart skips a beat when I hear a knock at the door. I do a final once-over in the mirror and smile, happy with what I see. I open the door and suck in a breath when I catch sight of Graham. He looks so handsome tonight in the dark slacks and olive-green button-up he's wearing. He rolled the sleeves up to his elbows, giving him a relaxed appearance that makes me want to throw him on the bed and forget about whatever he's planned.

Desire flares in Graham's eyes as they roam over my body, taking in every exposed inch. It has me feeling all sorts of cocky.

"You look beautiful," Graham says, voice hoarse. He clears his throat and asks, "Are you ready to go?"

I nod and quickly grab my purse off my desk, shutting the door behind me as I join him in the hall. He pulls me in for a quick kiss before he reaches for my hand and guides me toward the exit. I relish in how familiar it already feels.

"So, where are you taking me?" I ask as we exit the building.

I note the twinkle in his eyes as he says, "I found this Italian restaurant called D'Angelo's that's only a ten-minute walk from campus. They have live music and discounted drinks on Thursday nights. I thought it'd be perfect for us."

"That *is* perfect," I respond with a wide smile. "I can't wait to see it."

Our walk to the restaurant is spent discussing the assignment our history professor gave us yesterday. It's a safe topic—one that keeps our nerves in check until our date officially starts.

The path to the restaurant takes us through an older neighborhood with tree-lined streets. The houses contained within are a mixture of Colonial and Tudor style—my favorites. I find myself imagining what it must be like to live in one of them.

With Graham's hand in mine, I also find myself wondering about my future and what it might look like. Will I end up in a home like the ones we're walking past? Will I be married? If so, will we have kids? Do I even want all that? My thoughts wander to how devastated Mom was after she lost Dad. Do I really want to risk the same thing happening to me? I don't know. *I don't think so.* I don't see how it could be worth it.

I look at Graham through the corner of my eye and sigh. Will all my relationships now be tainted by the memory of my mom sobbing in bed for months? No amount of love is worth it if that's the outcome.

I'm brought back to reality when we reach D'Angelo's, and I take in its beautiful exterior. It's located at the end of a row of businesses, but its brick facade and the greenery that lines its windows makes it stand out. I note the covered patio to the right of the restaurant that has a fire pit in its center and string lights hanging above. I can already see myself coming back here just to enjoy that patio.

I see Graham assessing my reaction out of the corner of my eye, so I squeeze his hand and turn to him with a smile. "I love this! It's so cute."

He smiles wide, happy that he made the right choice. He then pulls me along into the restaurant and gives the hostess his name. She leads us to a table in the back corner that's situated next to a dimly lit fireplace. We're at one of only a handful of tables in the area so it feels intimate.

Graham orders a bottle of red for us before the hostess leaves and I smile at his choice. I love being eighteen now and getting to order drinks at restaurants. It makes me feel so grown up.

I pick up the menu before me and browse my options, trying to ignore the way my stomach flips when I take in the prices. I don't think I've ever been at a restaurant this fancy, let alone one this expensive. The rare times my family went out to eat were usually spent at a local diner. If Graham and I decide to go on any more dates, I'll have to tell him that I don't need to be taken to places like this all the time.

We order a few minutes later, then spend the time before food arrives talking easily. I learn that Graham's an only child of a single mother who nannies for a local High Family. The way he talks about her suggests they're close and that he loves her very much.

We also talk about why he got into hacking. Apparently, there were several teachers in his school district that had no problem failing students solely because they were ungifted. Graham taught himself how to hack into the school's grading system so he could change his and the other ungifted students' grades. The teachers were upset about the change, but they couldn't provide a valid reason why the students should fail so they were forced to keep them as they were. I could see how proud Graham was that all the ungifted students in his year graduated. That wasn't usually the case.

That brought on a rather long conversation about ungifted prejudice and whether we believe things could change in Kalyteros. I remain hopeful, but Graham's unconvinced.

I like how easy it is to talk to with him. I also like how forthright he is. He's open and honest and not afraid to say how he feels. He seems like a really great guy.

We end the night with another stroll through the old neighborhood with the nice houses. I find myself imagining more nights like this with him and I'm excited for them.

When we finally make it back to campus and we stop outside of my dorm, he grabs my hands and says, "I had a lot of fun tonight, Ana. I would love to do this again, if you're up for it."

"I had a lot of fun, too," I respond with a smile. "I'd absolutely love to do this again. But, honestly, I'm not ready for tonight to end yet. Do you want to come upstairs and watch a movie or something? Millie's gone for the night."

He nods and follows me upstairs. We then spend the rest of the evening familiarizing ourselves in a different way.

CHAPTER THIRTEEN
ANASTASIA

Classes have been in session for a few weeks now and I think I've finally settled into a good routine. When I'm not in class, studying, or working on homework, I'm either with my friends or spending time with Graham alone.

After another great date, Graham asked me to be his girlfriend, and I said yes without hesitation. We've been inseparable since and find any opportunity to sneak away together.

I'm grateful for the distraction he and my friends provide because without them, I don't think I'd like being here that much. Which is a disappointing realization.

I always knew there was tension between the gifted and the ungifted—I faced discrimination plenty growing up—but I had no idea how bad it really was. Not until I was forced to face it daily.

Many of my classmates have made it clear that they don't like me solely because I'm ungifted. Some even go out of their way to try to prove I'm beneath them. One classmate in particular, Sean Levinio, constantly challenges me in our hand-to-hand combat class, hoping to do just that. Nik's usually able to change his mind with a pointed glare, but Sean refused to back down yesterday and I was finally forced to fight him. When he lost, he got in my face and accused me of cheating. I thought he was going to hurt me when I saw the hatred in his eyes and heard the vitriol spilling from his mouth. Thankfully, Nik stepped in and separated us before Sean could do anything.

My thoughts have been preoccupied with that moment since, and I can't shake the feeling that Sean's going to confront me again. But this time, he'll make sure to finish what he started. I just know it. Guys like him don't accept losing to someone like me.

I'm grateful it's family weekend at Arken because it means my family will distract me from my worries. I'm currently following them as they visit each booth that's been set up and partake in the various festivities scattered across campus. They seem to be having a good time, which helps ease my nerves.

My mom and Daphne were happy to hear about the friends I've made and that I have a boyfriend now. But they were disappointed when I told them they won't be able to meet them today. My friends are all too busy entertaining their own families—or making themselves scarce—and don't have time for an introduction. That's probably for the best, though. Knowing my sister, she'd probably embarrass me around them or would become obsessed with Kas or Harvey and neither outcome is something I want to deal with.

Once my brothers play every game available and my sister triple checks that Graham can't join us, we pile into my mom's car and head to the capital for dinner. Millie told me about a new barbecue place in the city and my family is eager to check it out.

There's no wait when we arrive at the rustic looking restaurant, so we're seated immediately. Within a few minutes, our orders are taken, then we're left to talk amongst ourselves. We get so caught up with updating each other on our lives that hours pass without us noticing. It isn't until our waitress approaches and tells us that the restaurant is about to close that we realize the time. We quickly leave after that, not wanting to put our waitress out any further.

By the time my mom drops me off at Arken, the campus is quiet. Most of the students are either out partying or have retired to their rooms for the evening. That means I'm the only one walking the dark path back to my dorm.

My entire body goes rigid when I hear the scuff of shoes behind me, followed by a familiar voice saying, "Well, well, well. What do we have here, boys?"

I turn and find Sean lingering in the shadows of a tree with two guys I don't recognize standing on either side of him. I back up slowly, trying to put some distance between us. Sean pushes away from the tree and smirks in response. "What? Not feeling so tough now without your bodyguard around?"

The other two guys follow Sean's lead and approach me with wicked grins on their faces. The taller of the two looks between me and Sean with a confused expression. "*This* is the girl who's been giving you trouble?" When Sean nods, the tall guy gets an evil glint in his eyes. "But she looks so *breakable*." The way he says the last word has a chill running down my spine.

I reach for the knife tucked into my boot, but my fingers only graze it before Sean's friends grab my arms and force them behind my back. Sean then comes to stand in front of me with a satisfied smile. With a crack of his neck, he says, "You think you're tough, huh? Let's see how tough you are against the three of us."

"I don't know," I respond, somehow finding a way to contort my fear into a controlled cockiness. *Don't let them see that they've rattled you.* "If your friends are anything like you, then I think I'll do just fine."

Sean punches me in the stomach, and I double over, gasping as the air rushes out of my lungs. A sharp pain radiates through my ribs that I try to breathe through. His fingers then dig into my face as he forces me to meet his eyes. They have a crazed look to them that has my fear skyrocketing.

"You bitch! You're nothing! *Nothing!* Arken only accepts your kind because they feel sorry for you. It's not because you deserve to be here. You're worthless." With a nod of his head, his friends' hold on me tightens and I brace for what's to come. "It's about time you ungifted losers learn your place."

My head snaps to the side when Sean's fist connects with my

chin, and I have to bite my tongue to keep from crying out. I spit out the blood that pools in my mouth and taunt, "Is that all you got? My littler sister punches harder than that."

Sean's eyes flare in anger and I steel myself for the kick he aims at my side.

CHAPTER FOURTEEN

XANDER

Unlike the rest of my classmates, I decided to go home for family weekend rather than have my mom and Lydia come to me.

I knew if they came to Arken, it would just be a mess. Our little family can't do anything publicly without being asked prying questions—usually about my father's death—and I didn't want my mom to have to deal with that. Especially not for an event I couldn't care less about.

Instead, I left as soon as classes were over yesterday and grabbed food from our favorite Indian place. We then spent the entire evening watching movies while Lyddy played on the floor in front of us.

I could've spent the entire weekend doing just that, but unfortunately, I had to get back to campus. I still hadn't found Metallo's file in the records room and I hoped I might tonight. I was convinced it had to be in there somewhere. There's no way he started working for my dad at such a young age without going to Arken or one of the other Arete universities.

That's why I'm currently heading toward the Admin Building while the rest of my classmates are either out partying or relaxing in their rooms. I'm desperate for answers and won't rest until I find them.

I turn onto the path that'll lead me to my intended destination and instantly come to a stop.

There are four figures concealed by shadow several feet in front of me. From the little bit I can make out, it looks like two of the figures are holding a third person between them while the fourth taunts and hits that person. I debate turning around and taking a different way to the Admin Building until I hear a familiar voice come from the one being restrained.

"What's your plan here, Sean?" asks the spy as she spits what I can only assume is blood at her feet. "You gonna kill me?"

I hurry toward them without understanding why when the guy says, "So, what if I do? It's not like anyone will care. Ungifted trash like you don't matter."

I sidle up behind the man and the only sound is the crackle of my lightning as I snarl, "Are you guys really that scared of Ms. Galanis that you can only take her on when it's three against one? That seems a little unfair, don't you think?" The spy tenses when she realizes who's speaking. It has a smile forming on my lips while electricity crawls up my arms. "How about we even the odds?"

My threat has barely left my mouth when the three guys drop Ms. Galanis and take off running to the guys' dorm. My eyes track them until they disappear into the building. I then stoop down and help the spy up.

"Are you okay?"

"Yeah. I'm okay. Thanks to you," Anastasia says as she brushes herself off. Even in the dark, I can see the nasty cuts and bruises that cover her face. Whoever those guys were, they really wanted to hurt her.

"Why were those guys attacking you?" Do they know something about the spy that I don't?

She crosses her arms in front of her chest while her jaw sets. "The guy that was hurting me—his name is Sean Levinio—was upset that I beat him in our sparring match yesterday. He wanted to show me that I was nothing more than 'ungifted trash.' As if beating me up while his friends held my arms behind my back somehow proved that he's tougher than me."

The spy rolls her eyes in response to the absurdity of the situation, and I find myself respecting how strong she is. She literally just got her ass kicked, but she isn't letting it break her spirit.

"Do you want me to take you to the nurse so you can get looked at?"

"No. I'll be okay." She brushes off my concern with a wave of her hand. "It's nothing I haven't been through before. I'll ice my injuries when I get back to my room."

"At least let me walk you to your dorm, then," I insist.

Her eyes meet mine and I feel her analyzing me, trying to figure out why I'm helping her.

Why *am* I helping her? I'm supposed to be figuring out how big of a threat she is to me and my family, not swooping in and rescuing her like some knight in shining armor.

If she ends up killing me in my sleep after this, then I'll only have myself to blame.

Idiot.

My inclination to help those in need is going to be the death of me. Literally.

When Anastasia doesn't find the answers that she seeks, she nods her head reluctantly and I gesture for her to follow me. We spend the entire walk to the girls' dorm in silence.

As we make our way there, I notice that she's favoring her right side and realize she's more hurt than she's letting on. It has anger coiling in my gut, and I find myself itching to make those jerks pay for what they've done.

I don't understand why she didn't use her gift to defend herself, though. She could've easily stopped them. Especially with the knife I saw tucked into her boot. It doesn't make sense. Why would she risk her life to keep up the charade?

I swear, each new thing I learn about her only leaves me more confused.

When we finally reach her dorm, I tell her to be careful and she thanks me again for saving her. Once she's safely inside, I turn and head back to my own dorm—any plans I had to sneak into the records room forgotten.

CHAPTER FIFTEEN
ANASTASIA

Today's the first day I'll see Xander since he saved me from Sean, and I have no idea what I'm going to say to him. I've been able to cover up the bruises Sean gave me so my friends don't know what happened, but there's no hiding them from Xander. He was there. He saw firsthand how badly I was hurt even though I tried to downplay it.

I was able to avoid him yesterday in Weapons Training, but I won't be that lucky today. He sits right next to me in Intelligence Gathering. There's no way I'll be able to act like he isn't there without coming across as ungrateful or rude.

I still don't understand why he cared enough to save me. Other than my friends, none of the gifted at Arken like me. And they definitely wouldn't go out of their way to help me if I was in trouble. So, why did Xander?

I don't get it.

It feels like my heart stops when Xander waltzes into the classroom and slides into his seat next to me. My cheeks immediately heat as a fresh wave of embarrassment crashes over me. I'm supposed to be this great fighter—that's why Arken accepted me—

but he knows I got my ass kicked three days ago. Does he think less of me because of it?

Xander glances at me through the corner of his eye, obviously analyzing me, but he doesn't say anything. I could leave it at that. I *should* probably leave it at that, but he saved my life. I can't ignore that fact just because I'm embarrassed.

"Xander?" His eyes meet mine and he tilts his head in a questioning manner. My gaze instantly drops to my lap where my fingers are fidgeting with a loose thread from my shirt. "Thanks again for saving me. You didn't have to"

Now it's his turn to avert his eyes. "Those guys won't be a problem for you anymore. I let them know this morning what will happen if they mess with you again."

My mouth drops open as my eyebrows shoot to my hairline. I blink rapidly as I try to wrap my head around what he just told me. "But…but why? I didn't think the gifted cared about what happened to the ungifted."

There's an intensity to his gaze that pins me in place as he says, "No one should ever feel hopeless and be left wondering if anyone cares enough to save them. It doesn't matter if they're gifted or not."

My mouth drops open again and it's an effort to close it.

Is this really the same guy that Kas warned me to stay away from? Someone who truly believes what Xander just said can't be all that bad, right?

I can't shake the feeling that there's more to Xander Thyellas than everyone thinks. Especially after his recent statement. Something about the way he said it makes me believe that he once felt hopeless and wanted someone to save *him*. But why?

I'm still mulling over what Xander said when Dr. Farrogow announces our big project for the semester.

"The entire purpose of my class is to teach you how to uncover information that others might be trying to hide. What better way to put those skills to the test than for a project that'll make up forty percent of your grade?" Dr. Farrogow smiles at the groans now filling the room. "Oh, come *on*. It'll be fun. You'll see.

"For the project, you'll be broken up into pairs. Each pair will then research an event in Kalyteros history. The goal will be for you to find information about the event that someone else tried to hide—whether it be the government or those involved directly. I think many of you will be surprised by how often that actually happens." Dr. Farrogow gestures around the room. "I've already chosen your partners, so you don't have to worry about finding one. The only thing you'll need to do in the immediate future is tell me what event you'll be researching."

Dr. Farrogow names the pairs he came up with and my stomach drops when I hear that I'm paired with Xander. *Dang it.* I guess any lingering questions I have about him will be answered during the hours of researching we'll be doing together.

I sneak a peek at Xander to see how he feels about us being paired together, but his expression gives nothing away. I guess that's better than him being openly upset about it.

It's Thursday night and instead of hanging out with Graham like I normally do, I find myself standing awkwardly outside of Xander's room. I'm currently trying to work up the nerve to knock and get our first research meeting over with.

When Xander suggested that we meet in his room, I was hesitant to agree with him. Not when Arken has a large library with plenty of meeting rooms in it. But Xander insisted. He didn't want us to be interrupted by other students trying to talk to him the whole time. I couldn't argue with that logic so that's how I ended up here, standing in front of his door like an idiot.

I finally get the courage to knock and the sound of it carries through the hall while I take a deep breath.

Here goes nothing.

Seconds later, Xander opens his door and gestures for me to come inside. I'm surprised to find a mostly empty space. I would think no one lived here if it weren't for the comforter on his bed. There are no photos, memorabilia, or *anything* that might provide insight into who Xander is. The room is void of any kind of personality or character. I guess it's fitting for the stoic man I know absolutely nothing about.

I immediately sit down at Xander's desk and pull out a notebook, getting right to it. I don't want to be here longer than necessary. "Have you thought about an event you'd like to research?" I ask as I finally look at the storm bender standing in front of me.

He leans against his bed while his lips form a thin line as he nods.

"Okay. Which one?"

"There was a storm bending family—the Kataigida family—that was found dead in their home years ago. All six members were suddenly gone, and I've never believed it was because of a faulty furnace like my grandfather claimed. I think they were murdered, and I'd like to find out if my theory is correct."

I quickly jot down what he's saying into my notebook. "When did they die? I've only ever heard about your family. I didn't know there were other storm-bending families around."

"There's not. The Kataigida family died about thirty years ago and they were the only other storm-bending family besides mine at the time."

My brows furrow at that. "So, what makes you think they were murdered?"

"Robert Kataigida was running against my grandfather in the election that year and he was projected to win. That would've meant my grandfather was only Grand Leader for one term—something he would've viewed as an embarrassment. I think my grandfather killed them to ensure his victory and wipe out any future competition."

My mouth drops open as I struggle to find an appropriate response. Eventually, I say, "Why doesn't anyone know about this?"

Xander shrugs. "I don't think my grandfather wanted people talking about it. He just wanted to brush it under the rug, so no one looked too closely. My father told me about it in passing years ago and the way he bragged about their deaths made me question what really happened."

"Huh." I chew on the edge of my pen while I review everything I wrote down. I heard rumors that storm-bending families would kill each other to stay in power, but I never thought they were true. It's wild to realize they might've been. "Well, based on what you've said, I think that's the perfect event to research for our project."

Before I'm able to ask him where we should start our search, a different question falls from my mouth. Followed immediately by a second. "How does being a storm bender work? Can you truly only control one aspect of a storm?"

Xander's entire body tenses, but he doesn't brush off my questions. Instead, he says, "Yes. Storm benders can only control one aspect of a storm. Some have controlled rain, others wind, and a few lightning."

"Is that how it's always been?" I ask, confusion lacing my words. "I thought I saw your father controlling multiple elements during one of his telecommunications."

His eyes focus on his feet while he mumbles, "My father was different."

"So, he *could* control multiple elements. Wow. Did you take after him in that regard?" Xander's eyes jump to mine and they bore into me with an intensity that has me fidgeting uncomfortably. "Sorry. I didn't mean to pry. I just don't know much about any of this. They don't exactly talk about the gifted at an ungifted school. I guess they didn't want to make us feel more inadequate than we already did."

His shoulders relax a bit as he sighs. "No. *I'm* sorry. I forget that you weren't raised around all this. Where did you come from again?"

I spend the next hour telling him about where I grew up and what it was like going to an ungifted school. I also tell him about my family and what made me want to go to Arken.

As I share more details about my life, Xander starts to look confused, but he doesn't say anything about it. He just listens to me talk and asks questions when my stories require them.

When I finally leave his room after our conversation dies down, my cheeks heat when I realize I shared so much about myself but didn't ask him a single question. Next time, I'll make sure to ask him

some. I'm desperate to find out who he is so I can understand why
I'm drawn to him in the way that I am.

CHAPTER SIXTEEN
ANASTASIA

At breakfast this morning, Millie suggested that our little friend group should go explore the capital today. She complained that there wasn't much to do on campus this weekend and made it clear she desperately needed a change of scenery.

I personally loved the suggestion. Other than going to that barbecue place with my family, I'd never been to the capital, and I was eager to see the museums everyone spoke so highly about. Graham, Nik, and Harvey were on board with the idea too. The only one who seemed against it was Kas, but thankfully it didn't take much convincing before he begrudgingly agreed to join us on our adventure.

After that, it wasn't long before we were all piled into Millie's SUV and driving the few minutes it takes to get to the capital from Arken.

We start our day at the massive farmers market that's set up in an old warehouse on the outskirts of the capital. I'm overwhelmed the minute we step into the place. There must be close to two hundred different vendors stationed throughout it and they're all selling various types of wares or baked goods.

Immediately, Kas and I are drawn to the antiques shop situated to the right of the entrance. The vendor is selling all sorts of items, but it's their vases that interest me. They have the most intricate detailing I've ever seen. Kas, on the other hand, is intrigued by the collection of rare coins that are on display.

He has just picked one of them up and is turning it over in his hand when the vendor notices him and snarls, "We don't serve your kind here!"

When the vendor rips the coin from Kas's hand, I look between him and Kas with a puzzled expression. What the hell is this guy talking about? Why is he singling out Kas?

It's the set of Kas's jaw and the quiet anger that radiates from him that has realization dawning on me. Kas is from Fotia. The man is refusing to sell anything to him because he's a Fotian.

Apparently, Graham and I aren't the only ones in our friend group that faces discrimination on a regular basis. It looks like our fire-bending friend does, too.

The explosive anger I'd grown to expect from Kas is nowhere to be found in this moment. Instead, he stuffs his hands into his pockets and walks away without saying a single word to the vendor.

Something about Kas's lack of response fuels my own anger. I turn on the man and shout, "What the hell is your problem?! He's a paying customer."

The man practically spits as he says, "I don't serve Fotians." His eyes bore into Kas's retreating back and the hatred I see in them shocks me. My dad told me about the growing tension between Zoin and Fotia, but this is the first time I've actually seen it. I guess Grand Leader Thyellas's efforts to incite hatred against Fotians worked.

"Who says he's a Fotian?" I ask, wanting to make the man feel stupid. "Fire benders don't just come from Fotia, you know."

The man chuckles. "*Please.* I'd know the golden eyes of the Pyrrhus family anywhere."

My brows furrow. I hadn't realized Kas's golden eyes were unique to his family. That means there's no way for him to hide who he is or where he comes from.

Before I'm able to respond, the vendor wrenches the trinket I'm holding from my hands. "I also don't serve the friends of Fotians so move along before I call security."

I glare at the jerk one last time before I chase after my fire-bending friend. When I catch up to him, I try to grab onto his arm, but he wrenches it out of my grasp. "I'm *fine*, Ana," he says dismissively. "It happens all the time. I don't need to talk about it. Just go find Graham, okay?"

I want to tell him that I understand what he's going through, but Millie grabs me before I can and excitedly pulls me toward a shop that's selling hand-stitched dresses. "Check these out, Ana! Aren't they gorgeous? Feel free to pick one out. I'm buying!"

The interaction with the antiques vendor sours how I feel about the place so I'm happy we don't stay long.

Our next stop for the day is The Sisters' Memorial and the Old America Museum.

The Sisters' Memorial is a beautiful fountain located outside of the Old America Museum. There are statues of each Sister on top of it that smile at you as you walk past. It honestly seems more creepy than anything.

As the six of us stare at it, Nik tells me that it was built a few years after The Sisters disappeared to honor all they'd done for Kalyteros.

To this day, no one knows why The Sisters just up and vanished nearly forty years ago. Some believe they went into hiding, while others think they died. I'm not quite sure what I believe.

None of it makes sense, honestly.

We admire The Sisters' Memorial for a few minutes, then make our way into the museum. There, we get to see snapshots of what life was like for Americans before The Sisters took over their lands and formed Kalyteros. The people of America looked happy, but they also seemed to struggle with the same things we do—poverty, discrimination, classism.

The photos of Old America aren't what shock me, though. What shocks me are the ones of Kalyteros right after its formation. There are dozens of them that show Americans getting pushed out of their homes so that the gifted could live in them instead. There are also several photos of people living on the street afterwards. The sight of it makes me feel sick. Americans lived here first, yet they were treated as if they didn't belong as soon as The Sisters moved here. I can't imagine what those poor people went through.

There are more pictures that depict the American flag being burned and statues of former American presidents being destroyed. Monuments that held any importance were demolished. The Sisters were literally trying to erase American history from existence. How in the hell did anyone want to worship them after that?

By the time we reach the end of the museum, I no longer believe Kalyteros was the 'Better World' The Sisters claimed it was. How could it be when people were being thrown out on the street like garbage?

Our kingdom was literally built on chauvinism.

The last photo in the museum is probably the one that makes me the angriest. It's of The Sisters smiling with their hands clasped together over their heads as Old America's White House burns behind them. They look so happy, and the photo's caption reads, "The Sisters were happy to establish a better world for their people." It's a fight to keep my eyes from rolling. A better world for whom? Certainly not the ungifted. Or any of the Americans that were forced to either assimilate or find somewhere else to live.

Graham sidles up next to me and jerks his head toward the photo. "That's crazy, right? The Sisters did whatever they could to erase what happened here, but insisted we should be happy about it. As if letting us keep a few holidays and traditions from before could soften the blow."

He gives an exasperated chuckle, and I smile in response. I'm happy I'm not the only one who sees how insane it was.

"I'm glad you feel the same way. When no one else seemed bothered by it, I started thinking I was being dramatic."

Graham tucks an errant strand of hair behind my ear and gives me a look that's full of adoration. "If it's something you care enough about to get upset, Ana, then I wouldn't call it being dramatic. I'd call it being passionate and it's good to feel that way."

My smile widens and I give him a quick kiss on the lips. My chest tightens as gratitude for my boyfriend has me feeling all warm and fuzzy. It's nice having someone who understands what I deal with.

After we leave the museum, Harvey suggests we stop at a burger place around the corner. It's there that I forget about whatever anger I was feeling and enjoy the time with my friends again.

We go to a club afterwards and spend hours dancing.

I'm exhausted by the time we return to campus, but I have an exam in Weapons Training on Monday that I desperately need to study for. I let Millie and Nik have some alone time in the room while I settle against my favorite tree, hidden behind the guys' dorm.

I should probably feel some degree of worry that I might be attacked again, but my dagger is now strapped to my wrist for easier access. That and Xander's promise that Sean and his friends will leave me alone helps ease my anxiety.

I only study for about thirty minutes before my eyes are drawn to a cluster of trees to my left. I'm surprised to find Xander walking past them, dressed entirely in black. He looks around as if he's worried about being caught and it has me wondering what he's up to.

Before I can question if it's a good idea or not, I stuff my notebooks into my bag and stalk after him. My friends' warnings about Xander echo through my head as I do.

Even if Xander is as bad as Kas believes, there must be some good in him since he saved me from Sean and his friends. That has me feeling like I should stop him before he does something he'll regret.

I follow him for a couple minutes, but the woods are so dark that I eventually lose sight of him. I'm just contemplating turning back when a deep voice behind me has me freezing in place.

"Why are you following me?"

CHAPTER SEVENTEEN
XANDER

"I'll only ask one more time. *Why* are you following me?" I growl as the spy turns and looks up at me with a panicked expression.

Electricity dances along my fingertips as my anger grows. I can't believe I started to fall for her crap.

I listened to her talk for over an hour on Thursday about her childhood, her family, and what it was like to grow up ungifted. I spent the entire time trying to find inconsistencies with what she was telling me, but there weren't any. She was so convincing that night I actually wondered if my uncle was wrong about her.

Turns out I'm a fricking idiot because the minute I let my guard down, I find her following me in the woods.

Well, I won't be making that mistake again. Whatever game she's playing ends tonight.

Despite her initial nervousness, her voice doesn't waver when she says, "I saw you sneaking around and wanted to make sure you weren't doing anything you shouldn't."

"So, you're spying on me?"

Anastasia's mouth opens, then immediately shuts. She doesn't know how to respond to my accusation.

It has me getting in her face and snarling, "I know who you are, Spy."

Her brows furrow. "What are you talking about, Xander? *Spy?* What do you mean?"

"It means this innocent, nice girl act you're playing at doesn't fool me."

"I have no idea what you're talking about," she responds, a hint of fear returning to her voice. "Look, you saved me from Sean, so I wanted to return the favor. I thought I'd stop you from making a mistake you'd regret, but clearly there's something else going on here, so I'll leave you be."

She turns to leave, but I grab her arm while I laugh drily. She's really quite convincing if you don't know the truth. "Okay. *Fine.* If that's how you want to play this, then I'm game. Since you're so keen on following me, you might as well see it through." I tug her arm as I start walking again. "Come on, Spy. It's time you confront who you truly are."

Anastasia hesitates at first, like she's wondering if she should try to resist me. She must realize there's no point because she sighs and lets me pull her along toward my intended destination.

"Where are we going?" she asks after a few minutes. There's a steely resolve in her tone now.

"To the Archives Building. It's about a mile off campus. It's where they store the records for students who attended Arken over twenty years ago. I'm hoping to find your father's record there."

Unfortunately, I didn't learn about the Archives Building until after I thoroughly searched the records room and came up empty.

"My dad's record? But my dad didn't go to Arken. He was ungifted. Why would his information be in the Archives Building?"

I don't answer her. There's no point responding to her lies.

After that, the spy doesn't ask any further questions, so we spend the remainder of the walk in silence. The only sound is her boots crunching on the few leaves that have fallen—a sign of autumn's slow arrival.

Thankfully, the Archives Building is exactly where the map said it'd be, so we find it without any excess wandering. I force Anastasia to stand next to me while I break into it. I note the concern in her eyes when she sees how easily I'm able to unlock the door and shut off the security system. *Good.* Let her be scared.

I gesture for her to enter first, then follow after her. The flashlight I brought illuminates the dark space, and I find rows of filing cabinets covered with a thick layer of dust. It doesn't look like anyone has been here for a long time.

The spy hovers by the door while I walk amongst the filing cabinets, looking for the one labeled 'M' for the years 1995 to 2000. Based on how long Metallo worked for my father, I think it's safe to assume he attended college sometime during those years.

It takes a few minutes, but eventually I find the right one. After a few more, a grin spreads across my face when the name *Metallo, Nicholas* appears before me. *I knew it.* I knew he went to Arken.

I pull out the file and shove it into Anastasia's hands when I return to the front of the building.

She looks at it with a puzzled expression. "What's this?"

"Your father's file."

"*No.* I don't know who Nicholas Metallo is, but he's not my dad. My dad's name was Damian Galanis." She tries giving me back the file while saying, "I don't know what kind of game you're playing, Xander, but it's not funny."

I tap the folder, telling her to read through it, then lean against the nearest set of cabinets. I'm eager to see the realization that she's been caught dawn on her face.

The spy sighs but does as I request. While she skims through the file, I watch her features slowly change from annoyance to confusion. Not anger like I expected.

When she holds up a picture and asks why there's a photo of her dad in the file, I find myself feeling confused too. That's the only question she has? Not how did I know about her father? Or how did I find out about her?

My bewilderment only grows when tears prick the corners of her eyes. There's no way she's that good of an actress. Did she really not know her father was gifted? Could my uncle have been wrong about her?

It's at that moment I decide to tell her the truth about her dad and his involvement with my father's murder. That way I can gauge her reaction and see just how much she knows.

Tears are streaming down her face by the time I'm done. "That's not possible. My dad was just a coal miner. He wasn't gifted. He couldn't have worked for your father. And he definitely didn't kill him. You clearly have the wrong person, Xander."

Huh. So maybe she didn't know.

I'm hesitant to believe that this was all just a misunderstanding, though. What about her closeness to the Kruos and Pyrrhus heirs? That can't be a coincidence. It all has to be connected somehow.

I cross my arms and shrug my shoulders. "I've heard of metal benders hiding their true identities from their families to protect them. It's pretty common for assassins, actually."

"Assassin?" Her question comes out in a breathy whisper. She quickly recovers and states, "Now I know you have the wrong person."

I shrug again, maintaining my mask of indifference. "The photos I have in my room seems to suggest otherwise."

"Photos?"

I nod.

"What photos?"

I don't answer her question. Instead, I give her a blank stare. I'm not going to tell her about the pictures I found. Not here.

She releases a defeated sigh when she realizes I'm not going to answer, then wraps her arms around her middle. She doesn't ask any more questions after that, but it's clear by the look on her face that the information I just threw at her is overwhelming.

With that, I decide to take her back to Arken. She's clearly spiraling and needs to work through it. The last thing I need is for her to break down here and get us caught.

She's quiet the whole way back, but once I drop her off in front of her dorm, she asks, "Can I see the photos you have tomorrow?"

I sigh. "Yeah. You know where to find me."

Gods, this night didn't go at all like I thought it would.

When the spy finally enters her building, I let out a groan. What did I just get myself into? If tonight wasn't just an act, then I'm now stuck guiding this girl through some tough personal stuff. Stuff she'll only be able to talk to me about.

Dammit. I really am an idiot.

CHAPTER EIGHTEEN

ANASTASIA

I wake up before the sun rises, still in shock from everything Xander told me last night. There's no way it's true. It *can't* be. This whole thing must be a cruel prank Xander's playing on me because I'm ungifted.

I can't believe I ever thought he was better than the rest of them. I'm such a fool. I should've listened to Kas's warnings.

After that thought, I force myself out of bed and dress quickly. If Xander's going to be a jerk, then I just want to get it over with.

A few minutes later, I'm knocking on his door, and he answers, bleary-eyed and confused. When he sees that it's me, he runs a hand over his face and asks, "Did you get any sleep?"

"Not really."

He sighs and opens his door wider. "Come in."

I do as he says but stop once I reach the middle of his room and cross my arms. He walks past me and leans against his bed, waiting for me to say something.

My eyes find my feet and focus on them as I ask, "Is this all some prank you're playing on me because I'm ungifted?" No more dancing around whatever this is. I want him to tell me the truth.

I hear him suck in a breath, but I refuse to look at him. I don't want him to see the hurt on my face. The hatred I deal with on a regular basis weighs on me, but not like this. I thought I found someone outside of my friends who saw me for me rather than how I was born. It hurts to realize I was wrong.

"I'm not playing a prank on you, Spy."

There's that name again. Why does he keep calling me that?

I watch him through my eyelashes as he crosses the room to his desk and rifles through its drawers. He grabs something out of the bottom one and closes the space between us.

"These are the photos I told you about," he states, handing me an envelope.

I take it from him and am surprised to find photos of me and my siblings inside of it. "How did you get these?" I ask, my eyes jumping to his.

There's no amusement on Xander's face when I look at him. Just silent assessment.

"I found them in my uncle's desk. I assume he took them from your father after he interrogated him."

"So, you were telling the truth last night?" My stomach drops as the question falls from my mouth. *My dad was a killer?* I struggle to wrap my head around that fact. My dad was one of the nicest people I knew. How could he have hurt people for a living?

Xander rubs his temples as a look of exhaustion crosses his face. "I'm too busy to be making up elaborate schemes just to mess with you, Anastasia. Trust me."

My cheeks warm. Of course he's too busy to do something like that. He's the future Grand Leader for gods' sakes. I'm sure between that and school, he's spread thin enough already. What was I think-ing? I'm so stupid.

"And just so we're clear, I wouldn't care if you were ungifted."

Well, that's good to know. Though, it doesn't explain why he was so hostile toward me last night.

"Why would your uncle keep photos of me and my siblings?"

"Because he thought one of you might be a threat."

"*What?*" I ask. "But we're all ungifted. What sort of threat could we pose?"

He rubs his chin as if deciding how to answer my question. After several excruciating seconds, he states, "My uncle believes you're a metal bender like your father was."

I laugh out loud. That's the only response I can possibly give to that ridiculous statement. "Is that why you've been calling me a spy?" I can't help the amusement in my voice as I ask the question. "You thought I worked with my dad to kill yours? What did you think I was doing here, then? Trying to kill you?"

When he shrugs, I laugh again. He *did*. Oh my gods.

Xander rolls his eyes and says in a frustrated tone, "You don't know how far people are willing to go for power. I know of a son giving his own father suppressants so he could easily kill him and take over as Grand Leader. A father having his child help him kill a few people is mild in comparison to that."

Xander's statement makes me pause. Who could he possibly be referring to? If the person killed his own father to become Grand Leader, then it must've been someone in his family. That's the only way the role would've been passed on like that.

There's no way he could be talking about his own father, right?

I know it's a dangerous question, so I don't entertain it. Instead, I ask, "Suppressants? What are suppressants?"

Xander angles his head. "You don't know what suppressants are?" When I shake my head, he says, "They're exactly as they sound. They're a supplement you can take that will suppress your gift. They're usually given to children with powerful gifts until they learn how to control them." Xander's eyes widen suddenly. "Did your father ever give you something that he said you had to take every day?"

I nod. "Yeah, but it's not a suppressant. It's medication to help with my migraines. I used to get them really bad as a kid." They'd leave me bedridden for hours at a time. My dad hated to see me hurting like that, so he went to a local apothecary and found something to help. I haven't had one since.

"Are you still taking it?"

I nod again.

"Then I suggest you stop for a while."

"What? *Why?*"

"Because my uncle was convinced you're a metal bender. It's entirely possible that the 'medicine' your father gave you is actually a suppressants" He gives me a sympathetic look. "I recommend you stop taking it for a week and see what happens. That's the only way we'll be able to know for sure if my uncle's right."

"And what will I do if he is?"

"We'll figure that part out later. All you need to worry about right now is stopping your medication."

I note the dismissal in his tone, so I don't linger. I tell him that I'll think about it and head for his door.

"You know where I am if you have any questions."

I thank him, then leave his room and building as quickly as possible. My movements feel stiff, almost robotic, as I do. My head spins and I don't know what's real anymore.

Am I really gifted? Was my entire life a lie? The thought has me feeling like I'm going to puke. By the time I reach my room, it seems extremely likely that I will. I throw myself onto my bed and force my eyes closed while I will the nausea to pass.

For a second, I contemplate waking Millie so I can tell her everything that's happened, but my fear stops me. What if she thinks I'm a killer like Xander did? Would I be able to convince her otherwise as easily as I did him? If not, would she report my family? It's Nik's dad that'd arrest us so I can't rule out the possibility.

The risk isn't worth it. Not until I figure out who my dad really was and why he killed Grand Leader Thyellas—if he even killed him. Until then, I can't tell my friends anything.

In the meantime, I'll stop taking my medication like Xander suggested and see if there's any legitimacy to his claims. I can't throw away everything I thought I knew about my dad just because Xander says otherwise. Even if he is pretty convincing.

I'm going to figure out the truth. No matter what.

CHAPTER NINETEEN
XANDER

It turns out Anastasia really didn't know she's gifted. It was never an act.

That realization threw me for a loop. Why did my uncle want to keep an eye on her then? Why did he push for her to be accepted into Arken? Unfortunately, I don't have time to search for answers to those questions because I'm now stuck helping her.

I don't know why I offered to help her. The last thing I wanted was to add more to my plate, but the sadness in her eyes had me blurting that we'd figure it out together. As if that was a totally normal thing for me to offer.

Ugh.

My bleeding heart is going to be the death of me because Anastasia pulled me aside this morning after Weapons Training with fear lining her face. The minute I saw the shadows under her eyes, I knew what was happening. She stopped taking her medication and now her gift was making itself known.

"I think something's wrong," Anastasia says with worry-filled eyes. "I've been feeling weird since Wednesday and it's only getting worse. It's like there's some-

thing inside of me that's fighting to get out. What's going on, Xander? Is it my gift? Am I really gifted?"

When her voice cracks, I grab her by the arm and pull her to a quiet part of the atrium. The last thing we need is for her to be overheard.

"Yes. It's your gift," I say in a calming voice, hoping it'll ease her growing worries. "After being suppressed for so long, it's begging to be released. You're going to have to use it soon, or it'll get worse."

"But how do I do that? What if I hurt somebody when I try?" Tears well in her eyes as she wraps her arms around herself. "I have no idea what I'm doing here, Xander."

Dammit.

"I'll show you how to control it," I grumble as I cross my arms and fight back a string of curse words. I only have myself to blame for this. I was the one that just had to search my uncle's office after my father's murder. And I was the one hell bent on proving the spy was out to get me.

Next time something major happens in the province, I'm staying out of it.

Relief floods Anastasia's face. "You will?" It's quickly replaced with guilt. "I can't possibly ask that of you. You have enough on your plate already."

I wave off her concern. "It's fine. It's not something that can be easily explained anyways. I have to show you how to do it. Besides, I'd prefer not to be stabbed by an errant knife during Weapons Training. It's just better for everyone if I train you."

"Okay," she responds while blowing out a breath. "Then I'm willing to meet whenever you can. I'll make whatever time work."

"I have some time on Saturday afternoons. We'll meet then until you figure out how to control it."

She nods and thanks me. "I appreciate your help, Xander. I'm glad I can talk to you about this. You're the only one I really can."

Yeah. I know.

CHAPTER TWENTY
ANASTASIA

I've had two training sessions with Xander so far and they were both more productive than I thought they'd be.

We met at a secluded clearing about a mile from campus and that's where he taught me the basics of wielding my gift. I was grateful for the space because it let me do what I needed to without worrying about being seen or hurting anyone. And I definitely would've hurt someone if they'd been around. I nearly took Xander out a couple times as it was.

Xander's a surprisingly good teacher. He's nothing but patient with me and does a great job explaining how I should channel my gift so I get my intended result. I think that's why I'm making as much progress as I am. I don't think I could handle my own in a fight yet, but I could stop a knife if it were thrown at me which is a crazy thing to realize.

Even though I've manipulated metal at least a dozen times now, I'm still struggling to wrap my head around the fact that I'm actually gifted. It feels like it's all a fever dream that I'm going to wake up from any minute now.

My gift refuses to let me forget about it, though. Xander warned me it might grow stronger as the suppressants leave my system, and he wasn't wrong. It's roiling within me, begging to be released and it reacts differently every time I try to use it. What would've caused a dagger to float a couple inches above my hand initially had it shooting toward Xander during our last training session. Luckily, he dropped to the floor before it hit him. When he stood back up, he joked, "Are you sure you're not trying to kill me?"

I was grateful for his humor. Just when I'd think I was getting the hang of my gift, something like that would happen and I would immediately feel discouraged. Xander has a way of lightening the situation that keeps me going.

The more time I spend with Xander Thyellas, the more I think my friends were wrong about him. He doesn't seem anything like the asshole his dad was. He's actually kind and understanding, even if I have to force it out of him sometimes.

Toward the end of our second training session, I asked Xander if I could go with him the next time he looked into my dad. Now that I'm figuring out who I truly am, I want to know who my dad was too. I need to know that the man who raised me wasn't entirely a lie.

"Absolutely not," he responds sternly.

"Why not? You're doing these investigations to find out why your father was killed, right?" When he nods, I say, "Well, you say my dad was the one who killed him. I have a right to know why, too."

He sighs. "I don't think it's a good idea, Spy. There are too many risks involved. If we're caught, then you'll be kicked out of Arken."

"I don't care. I need to know the truth about my dad." I smirk at him. "Besides, I think you underestimate me. My dad trained me for this sort of thing for years. I'm not going to get caught."

He runs his hands over his face, but with a shake of his head, he states, "Fine. But if we're caught, don't say I didn't warn you."

After our training session that day, Xander told me he'd let me know the next time he was going to do some research on my dad.

Unfortunately, with everything going on, I've become distracted. I'm not really present during class or when I'm with my friends. I can tell Graham and Millie have noticed, but they haven't pried yet.

I look up from my plate when I hear Graham say my name and he has a concerned look on his face. We're on a date at a local Mexican restaurant and I must've zoned out.

"Is everything okay, Ana? I keep having to repeat myself and even when you answer it feels like you're a million miles away."

Oh crap. I didn't realize I was being that bad.

"I'm sorry, Graham. I'm just distracted by the Intelligence Gathering project Xander Thyellas and I are working on." The lie comes easy, though guilt gnaws at me as the words leave my mouth. "We're looking into the deaths of the Kataigida family and it's heavy stuff."

"*Wait.* You're hanging out with Xander Thyellas?"

I furrow my brows. *That's* the question he has?

"Yeah. For class."

"Do the two of you hang out a lot?"

I note the tension in his voice and it has me hesitating. After that, I choose my response carefully. "Just once or twice a week."

"Hmm."

He doesn't ask any further questions, but I see the way the muscle in his jaw is ticking. He's frustrated and I don't understand why.

CHAPTER TWENTY-ONE

XANDER

For some reason, I seem incapable of telling this woman no. I try to, but she continues to find ways to make me give in to her requests.

That's how I ended up in the library with her on a Tuesday night looking up information on her father. I thought the library would be a good place for her to start since it's less likely that she'd be expelled for breaking into it, especially if I'm with her.

Unfortunately, there's not a lot of sensitive information about Nicholas Metallo stored in the library so there's nothing for me here. But Anastasia seems happy with what we've found. Her gray eyes light up every time she finds another article about her father.

She's currently reading through a feature piece about his time as captain of the archery team. Apparently, the team was sectional champions all four years her father went to Arken

"That seems a little unfair, don't you think?" I ask as she places the article on top of the stack of documents she's already read through. "I mean he was a metal bender. Wouldn't that mean he always got a perfect score?"

"I'm sure they had rules against him using his gift." She gives me a look as if her response was the obvious answer to my question.

"One can hope," I say as I pick up a document that lists those who were in Metallo's graduating class. I skim over it, then hand it to her, tapping her father's name as I do. "It looks like you and your father had more in common than you realized."

She takes the document from me, and I know the moment she finds her father's name and the note indicating he was valedictorian because tears well in her eyes. She then whispers, "I never knew he was good at school, too."

Without thinking, I reach for her hand to comfort her. I don't know why seeing her upset always affects me in such a way, but she seems like a happy person despite everything she's been through, and I want her to stay that way.

Once our hands touch, a jolt of energy passes between them that has us both gasping and wrenching away from each other. It's the same energy that's passed between us any time we've come in contact. I still have no idea why it happens and it's driving me crazy.

Her brows furrow as she gives me a shocked look. "Does that happen every time you touch someone?"

I shake my head. "No. Only you."

She looks between our hands. "Well, that's weird."

"Yeah," I say exasperatedly. "You're telling me."

She examines our hands once more before she decides to change the subject. With another whisper, she asks, "Do you hate my dad for killing yours?" Her eyes are full of concern when they meet mine and something inside my chest tightens.

"No. My father and I didn't exactly get along." I blow out a breath as I run my fingers through my hair. "I just wish I knew why your father did it."

Her gaze drifts over the articles we've read. "Yeah. Me too."

"When did you learn of his passing? Your father, I mean."

She chews on her bottom lip, contemplating how best to answer. "It was on Christmas. He was supposed to be home in time for dinner, but he was late. My mom thought he picked up a couple extra hours to help pay for the gifts they got us. He'd do that some-times, so we didn't think anything of it." Her eyes get a haunted look to them as she says, "I'll never forget the way my mom screamed and fell to the floor crying when the cops told her about the explosion. I was in such shock that I just stood there and watched her sob. My siblings did, too."

Damn. Her poor family. I can't imagine how hard that must've been for them.

"What about you?" she asks as she swipes the tears from her face. It's an effort for me not to brush away the one she missed by her lips.

"My friend Tony was the one who told me, actually. For some reason, my father requested an urgent meeting with Tony's dad that day. Manuel Telos is a war strategist so I can only assume my father wanted to discuss the tension between Zoin and Fotia with him. Since it was Christmas, Manuel brought Tony along with him. The minute Tony figured out what happened, he teleported to me and told me everything. I then had to tell my mom."

"Oh geez. I'm sorry. That must've sucked."

I shrug my shoulders. I can't exactly tell her the truth. To do that, I'd have to explain why I was seeing my mom for the first time in almost a year. I'd also have to tell her that my mom knew my father was dead the minute I showed up on our front stoop without him.

No. I definitely can't explain any of that to her. Not without delving into all the crap my mom and I went through. *Not gonna happen.*

After our conversation comes to an awkward end, I decide to return the articles we found to their original locations. It's probably after midnight by now and we should get to bed. Anastasia notices and jumps in to help, speeding up the process.

Once we're done, we sneak out of the library, and I walk her back to her dorm.

She doesn't immediately go inside, though. Instead, she scrapes the toe of her sneaker on the sidewalk and says, "Thank you for letting me investigate with you tonight, Xander. I know you weren't keen on the idea, but I appreciate you doing it anyway." Her eyes meet mine briefly before they quickly drop to her feet. "And I'm here if you ever want to talk about what happened with your father. I know there's probably not many people you can talk to about it."

I blink a few times, taken aback by her offer. Before I can figure out a response, she gives my hand a squeeze and hurries inside. I'm then left standing there, speechless, as I wonder about the strange girl who's been thrust into my life.

At what point did all this stop feeling like a burden to me? And why am I already looking forward to the next time I get to see her?

I shake my head before promptly returning to my own room.

None of it means anything. It can't.

CHAPTER TWENTY-TWO

ANASTASIA

My hands are on my knees and I'm forcing myself to take deep breaths after I stopped the slew of daggers Xander threw at me. He wasn't kidding when he said he was going to push me today. I could collapse any minute now from exhaustion.

Xander approaches me with a smile on his face. If I wasn't already struggling to breathe, that rare smile would've made me breathless.

"That was good, Spy. It seems like you're really getting the hang of your gift."

I give him a thumbs up in thanks, unable to put it into words, and his smile widens with amusement. "Are you going to be able to walk yourself back to campus now?"

I shrug my shoulders. That's a good question.

When he leans against the nearest tree instead of leaving, my brows crinkle in confusion. "What're you doing?"

"Waiting for you."

"*Why?*"

He sighs as if my question is the stupidest thing he's ever heard. "Well, I'd prefer that you not die out here and given your current state, that's a real possibility."

I straighten and roll my eyes. "I'm not going to *die*."

With a finger, he gestures around the clearing. "Do you know what roams these woods at night?" When I shake my head, he says, "Neither do I and I'd rather not find out by stumbling upon your corpse tomorrow. Hence why I'm waiting for you."

I fight back the smile that threatens to spread across my face. Xander still tries to act like he's only training me because he feels obligated to, but it's obvious that he's starting to care for me. At least, to whatever degree means he doesn't want to find me dead in the woods.

I close the space between us and grab him by his arm. "Lucky for you, I'm good now." He makes a surprised noise when I loop my arm through his and tug him in the direction of Arken. "Wanna grab dinner when we get back? I'm starving."

"Uh…"

"Do you already have plans?" I ask with a tilt of my head, finally releasing his arm. When he tells me he doesn't, I say, "Then I guess you're eating with me."

He sighs but there's a ghost of a smile on his lips.

Twenty minutes later, we're just entering the cafeteria when I hear someone shout Xander's name. He immediately drops his head and groans. He then puts his hand on my back and steers me toward the person.

"I was hoping you'd never have to go through this, Spy."

The tone of his voice has me looking at him with worry creasing my brow. "Go through what?"

"Meeting my friends."

My gaze snaps to the table we approach while my eyes widen. Xander's introducing me to his friends? *Oh my gods*. That's huge. It feels like I'm being welcomed into his inner sanctum or something.

I'm a jumble of nerves by the time I'm standing in front of one of the tables in the back, looking between the two guys Xander has only mentioned in passing.

The one with floppy black hair and porcelain skin stands and Xander tenses next to me. His friend, who clearly comes from an

Asian background, extends his hand to me and asks, "Well, who might you be, beautiful?"

"This is Anastasia Galanis," Xander says in a casual manner, but I can hear the threat lingering underneath. "We're working on a project together for one of our classes." When his Asian friend opens his mouth to say something, Xander warns, "Don't even try to flirt with her, Steven. She'll cut your tongue out before you can finish whatever crude comment you're planning."

Steven quickly sits back down, but he beams at me while running his fingers through his hair. "*Feisty.* I like it."

"So, that's Steven. He's obnoxious ninety percent of the time, but I'm sure you'll tolerate his antics better than I do." Xander then gestures toward the other guy at the table and I'm met with hazel eyes. "And that's Tony. You'll probably like him the best. He tends to be the voice of reason out of the three of us."

I smile and shake Tony's hand. When he smiles back, I find myself breathless for a second. His olive skin, sharp jawline, and dark features all come together to create one beautiful package and I'm not sure how to respond to it.

Xander guides me into the seat next to Tony while Steven chuckles and says, "Yeah… Tony tends to have that effect on people. Unfortunately for you, our boy swings in the other direction."

Xander sits down across from me and must notice the blush creeping up my cheeks because he says, "Ana has a boyfriend, so she's not interested in either one of you knuckleheads."

Wait. How does Xander know that I'm dating Graham? I never told him.

"So, what's your story, Ana?" Tony asks, thankfully changing the subject. "What awful thing did you do that has the universe forcing you to spend time with our grumpy friend?"

Xander and I lock eyes, and for the first time, I like the secret that binds us. In this moment, it doesn't feel like some awful lie. Instead, it feels like a special connection that only the two of us share.

I laugh at Tony's joke, then proceed to tell him and Steven about myself, already liking how easy it is to talk to them.

CHAPTER TWENTY-THREE
KASPER

Halloween has to be one of the stupidest holidays ever created. Whose bright idea was it, anyway, to dress up little kids and have them go door to door asking strangers for candy? It's like parents are just begging for their kids to be kidnapped or poisoned.

But that's not even the worst part. Somehow, college students have taken that stupidity and amplified it. Girls dress as skimpy as possible, and guys try to look like bad asses—all in the hopes of getting the other sex's attention. It's pathetic, honestly.

I hadn't planned on coming out tonight for that very reason. I didn't want to deal with it. I was already having a bad day and knew seeing everyone's tacky costumes and attempts at flirting would annoy me. My friends forced me to come out, though, without bothering to ask why I didn't want to. They never do.

But it's not like I'd tell them that another jerk was rude to me today because I'm a Fotian. There's no point. They couldn't have stopped the slur that fell from the dick's mouth as he shoved me. And they definitely can't stop me from feeling like I deserved it.

My father tells me the hatred I'm dealing with is what I get for choosing to go to Arken instead of staying in Fotia for schooling. As if being reminded of what happened there would be any better.

No. Even with all the disdain thrown my way, Arken's still the better choice for me. I just wish my father would understand and stop trying to make me feel guilty for leaving.

I note the tension in Graham's shoulders as he sidles up next to me and hands me another drink. His eyes then drift across the room to where Ana's playing beer pong with Xander Thyellas. I guess she's been spending time with him for some class project and it has Graham all freaked out. He had a couple girlfriends in high school and every single one of them ditched him the minute a gifted guy gave them attention. I keep trying to tell him that Ana's not like that, but this particular insecurity runs deep for my friend. And I can't exactly blame him in this situation. If there was any guy you'd need to worry about stealing your girl, it'd definitely be Xander. He not only has the status and looks, but the power as well. That's a very enticing combination for anybody.

I'm honestly surprised Ana's hanging out with the storm bender, though. I thought she'd at least heed my warning about him, given my experience with his father. I guess she decided she'd form her own opinion about the future Grand Leader. I have to respect that, even if it annoys me.

"What's wrong, Pyrrhus? No one to talk down to?"

Speaking of annoying…

I turn to my left and find Tony Telos standing there, smirking. I roll my eyes at him and try to ignore how good he looks in his fighter pilot costume. His handsome face doesn't matter when all he does is annoy me. He loves to nitpick everything I say in our Strategies of War class, and I can't stand it. Or him.

"What do you want, Telos?"

"I just came over to compliment your costume." His hazel eyes look me up and down, taking in my plain T-shirt and jeans. "What are you exactly? A grumpy college student?" He ponders for a few seconds before he snaps his fingers and says, "*Wait.* I know what you are. You're dressed as a mediocre General. I guess you didn't need to put much effort into that one, huh?"

I bare my teeth at the teleporter as I snarl, "Mediocre General?

Really? Says the strategist who couldn't come up with a well thought out plan."

Tony and I were forced to work together in class this week for a mock war and we were the first team to lose. It was embarrassing and entirely Tony's fault, yet here he is trying to blame *me* for *his* screw up.

"It's not my fault you couldn't execute it properly, Pyrrhus. Even Professor Bracker said my plan should've worked."

"Professor Bracker is nothing but a washed-up has-been. He has no idea what he's talking about," I bite back as flames dance along my fingers.

I'm not in the mood for Tony's crap tonight. One more word out of his stupid mouth and I'll fight him. I don't care where we are and who might see. Let them believe I'm nothing but a Fotian jerk. That's all they think of me anyway.

Rather than backing down or trying to diffuse the situation like all the others I've threatened at Arken, he angles his head and smiles when he sees how angry I'm getting. There isn't an ounce of fear on his face. The prick is enjoying needling me and it has my anger boiling over.

I get in his face, but before I can tell him off, he pats me on the cheek and walks away with a smirk. I turn with my jaw clenched and see him rejoin Xander and their annoying earth-bending friend. It takes every bit of control I have not to follow after him. The tele-porter loves getting under my skin and it's getting to the point where I'm going to have to fight him or risk another explosive outburst.

I don't know why I ever considered hooking up with the jerk, but it was obviously a momentary lapse in judgement. One I'm glad I didn't act on. It's clear he's obsessed with Xander, and I'm not inter-ested in sharing who I sleep with.

At some point, Graham left to talk to Ana while I was arguing with Tony. He returns now looking like he wants to break some-thing. Clearly, their conversation didn't go well.

"You wanna get out of here?" he asks once he's standing next to me.

"Yes, please," I say as I cast one final glance in Tony's direction.

He's laughing at something Xander said and it has me fisting my hands at my sides.

I let Graham lead the way out of the house but keep an eye out for anyone who might want to cause trouble. There are several guys at Arken that love to mess with him because he's ungifted and I like to know when they're around. I've already threatened them a couple times, but it hasn't stopped them yet. I find myself wishing that one of them will try something tonight. It'd be nice to release some of this pent-up frustration.

Fortunately for Graham, we make it outside without disturbance.

Once we're on the path that leads back to campus, I ask, "Are you and Ana okay?"

He shrugs. "I'm sure we will be. She didn't understand why I was upset that she left me to hang out with Xander and his friends. I'm not sure how to explain it to her without coming off like a possessive asshole."

"Does she know about your past?" When he shakes his head, I sigh. "You should tell her, dude. It'd help her understand why you react the way you do and would probably stop you two from fighting about it."

"But I don't want her to see me as this insecure guy, you know? What if that pushes her away?"

"I think Ana's more understanding than you think. I'd give her a chance if I were you."

"Yeah. Okay," Graham responds, sounding unconvinced. "I'll think about it."

CHAPTER TWENTY-FOUR
ANASTASIA

Xander's letting me search President Forester's office with him tonight and I'm shocked. I thought he'd at least make me break into the library a few more times or maybe even the records room to prove myself. Nope. I guess he thought I was ready for the big leagues because I'm currently rifling through the drawers of the most important person on campus.

During the handful of minutes it took for Xander to shut off the security system to the building, he filled me in on what he found in Administrator Spana's office. A feeling of dread settled in my gut when he told me that Sebastian Aeras is the reason I was accepted into Arken. It confirmed something I've been thinking since Xander and I started working together—there's more to our fathers' deaths than we realized.

"What am I looking for exactly?" I ask as I open the bottom drawer of President Forester's desk.

"There should be some sort of log that outlines what's discussed during important phone calls," Xander responds from where he's rifling through the filing cabinets on the other side of the room. "Since my uncle is acting Grand Leader, any phone calls from him would immediately be flagged as important."

After I flip through a few documents, I ask, "Why does President Forester keep so many paper copies when everything's handled electronically nowadays?"

He shrugs. "I don't know. Some people prefer it that way, I guess. I know my uncle is big on keeping physical copies of important communications. My father used to make fun of him for it, saying spies would know all our secrets because of him."

"Your father had a good point there," I muse as I move on to right side of the desk and open the top drawer. "Speaking of your uncle, do you think he gave President Forester a reason for why I should be accepted?"

"Knowing him, no. But it doesn't hurt to look anyway."

I'm about to close the drawer when I notice a white binder tucked into the back. I shine my light on it and feel excitement instantly hit me.

"Xander, I found it!" I whisper-shout.

Xander's standing next to me within seconds, looking over my shoulder.

It takes a couple minutes of skimming through the binder, but eventually I find the notes detailing President Forester's phone call with Xander's uncle. Apparently, he told her that I'm a student of note that should be accepted immediately. He didn't give her a reason, but it seems he didn't need to. His recommendation was enough.

"Why would he ask President Forester to report everything you do to him?" Xander asks after he takes the binder from me to get a closer look.

I shrug my shoulders. "You did say he made a note that I was gifted after he interrogated my dad. Maybe my dad told him that I was and your uncle wanted to keep an eye on me to make sure I wasn't going to retaliate."

"No. I don't think that's why," Xander states confidently. "Your dad clearly didn't want anyone to know you're gifted if he went to the trouble of getting you those suppressants. I doubt he would've just given up that information."

"Even if your uncle tortured him?"

"No. Your dad was a tough dude. I don't see him cracking, even under torture. Not when it would put you and the rest of your family at risk."

I have to agree with Xander on that one. My dad was always super protective of me and my siblings. My mom, too. He wouldn't willingly put us in danger—not even to save his own life. So how did Sebastian Aeras know I was gifted? And why did he want to know what I was doing?

Suddenly, Xander's head snaps up and his attention shoots toward the door. His eyes narrow for only a second before they widen. He then grabs my arm and pulls me into the closet next to us.

When I start to protest, he covers my mouth and puts a finger to his lips, telling me to be quiet. It's at that moment, I realize just how small the closet is. He's pressed up against me and I find my body responding to his proximity in a way it shouldn't. *You have a boyfriend, dummy*, I remind myself as I try to ignore the charged energy between us. Can he feel it, too? Gods, I hope not.

Once he's sure I'll stay quiet, he removes his hand from my mouth and turns around so that his back is to me. *He's trying to hide me. Someone must be coming.*

He shoots a bolt of lightning at the door that quickly spreads throughout it, charging it. If anyone tries to open the door now, they'll likely be zapped. He then flicks his wrist in a circular motion and a gust of wind starts blowing around the small space.

Wait. He's able to control wind, too?

A creaking noise outside of the closet diverts my attention from him. The sound of two voices quickly follows and Xander pushes back into me, shielding me. I can hear one of the desk drawers slide open while whoever's on the other side of the door continues to talk. It's slammed shut seconds later and the voices drift off as they leave the room.

Xander waits a few minutes to make sure they're not coming back before he gestures for me to follow him, and we leave the closet.

As soon as we're out, I turn to him and demand, "What the

heck was that Xander? You can control wind? I thought you said storm benders can only control one aspect of a storm?"

"I didn't lie about that," he says while rubbing the back of his neck. "Storm benders *should* only be able to control one aspect of a storm. That's just never been the case for me."

"*Wait.* What does that mean? Are you saying you can control all the elements of a storm?"

He nods.

"How? Did you get it from your father?"

"*No.*" The conviction with which he denies my question has a puzzled expression crossing my face. He sees it and sighs. "My father lied about the true strength of his gift. He could only control wind. He used me to make himself seem stronger."

My mouth drops open. "The demonstrations he'd do during his telecommunications were all you?"

He nods again and it feels like my head is spinning. If Xander can control every aspect of a storm, then that means he's the strongest storm bender that's existed since Kalyteros's formation. It might even mean he's the strongest out of any of the gifted.

"Does anyone else know about this?"

"I think Tony and Steven do, but I've never outright told them, and they've never asked. My mom's the only one who knows for sure." He pauses. "And now you."

CHAPTER TWENTY-FIVE

ANASTASIA

After the night in President Forester's office, Xander and I have only grown closer. I think him telling me the truth about his gift broke down any walls that remained between us. I can now confidently say he's my friend.

Unfortunately, while my relationship with Xander has gotten stronger, the same cannot be said for the one between me and Graham. Graham's clearly uncomfortable with me hanging out with Xander and I don't understand why when I've explained numerous times that it's just for class. It's a lie, but he doesn't know that.

The growing tension between us finally came to a head when I told him I was going to a tournament with Xander, Tony, and Steven today. He wasn't happy about it and made sure I was well aware of that fact. We ended up getting into an argument and I left before we could work through it.

I'm trying not to let our fight take away from the event, but it's hard not to when he keeps texting me. I look at his newest one and sigh. *You don't even know these guys. Why are you choosing them over me?*

A shout from Steven has my attention returning to the arena floor where the reigning champion, Zeus, has knocked down his opponent. It looks like he might win this one pretty quickly, which makes Steven very happy since he bet a lot of money on him.

I didn't know anything about tournaments before Steven invited me. It's not something people in Wellington talked about or even followed. Apparently, they happen every month and it's a chance for the gifted to show off their skills in a controlled setting.

It's primarily for the gifted that come from lower ranked families. They hope that if they win, then they'll get recruited for a better job opportunity. Maybe even one in the capital.

It's brutal, though. The contestants that have faced each other so far have not held back at all. I'm not sure it's something I'd ever want to participate in, even knowing the benefits that come from it.

When Steven stands up and twirls a towel above his head while he chants Zeus's name, Xander and I exchange a look. The energy from the crowd is making him more obnoxious than usual and it's pretty entertaining. Tony must feel the same way because he keeps making stupid comments that encourage his antics.

Luckily for Steven, Zeus wins and the entire stadium erupts. This is Zeus's fifth win in a row, officially setting a record. He'll now get to decide if he wants to remain the reigning champion with an opportunity to return next month or accept one of the job offers I'm sure are coming his way.

Once the tournament is over, Steven drags us to a nearby bar. Based on the crowd already inside, it looks like many tournament goers had the same idea. Xander and I sit down at one of the tables toward the back while Tony and Steven stop to talk to a group of people lingering by the entrance.

"Is this how all nights out with them go?" I ask while I watch two guys exchange a look to decide which one of them gets to pursue Tony.

Xander nods. "It's not as bad as it seems. It's actually quite fun to watch all the ways Steven can ruin his chances with a woman."

I grimace. "He's that bad?"

"I think he'd stand a better chance if he learned to keep his mouth shut. As with every other part of his life, Steven comes on a little too strong and it scares off most girls that'd give him a chance."

He nudges my arm. "I'll be right back. I'm gonna go grab us some beers." Ah, I love being eighteen.

I thank him, then scan the bar once he walks away. It seems like your typical sports bar. Large TVs hang on every wall and there are pool tables, dart boards, and a couple arcade games in the back left corner. What surprises me is the throwing range that takes up the entire right half of the space. It seems like a fun idea, but I'm not sure it's safe when most of its potential clients are drinking heavily.

My eyes find Xander leaning against the bar while he waits to order, and I see two separate girls approach him. He barely acknowledges them as they try to flirt with him. He just says something that has both girls walking away with disappointed looks on their faces. I really don't understand him. He could have any girl he wants, anywhere, but he couldn't care less. That's so strange to me.

While I wait for him to come back, I check my phone and see that I have three missed calls and five unread texts. All from Graham. I roll my eyes and shove my phone back into my pocket. I'm not in the mood for him right now.

The annoyance I feel has me slamming the beer Xander got me as soon as it's placed in front of me. His eyes widen, but he doesn't say anything. Instead, he hands me his as well.

I'm four beers deep by the time I suggest that Xander and I should play a game of darts. He gives me a cocky grin as he agrees. He clearly thinks he's going to beat me. It's hilarious.

I grab the first dart as soon as we're in front of the board and say, "Prepare to lose, Your Highness." I add as much sass and sarcasm as I can into the nickname.

He chuckles. "In your dreams, Spy."

"How about we make it interesting?"

He eyes me suspiciously. "What do you have in mind?"

"If I win, then you have to tell Professor Hawke that you love him."

"Oh *gods*. I can't lose now," he responds with a groan. With a playful shake of his head, he asks, "And if I win?"

"Then the next time Steven's flirting with a girl, I'll confront him and act like a jilted lover." Xander laughs out loud at that and I think it might be my new favorite sound. "Do we have a deal?"

He nods while shaking my hand. "We have a deal."

Thirty minutes later, I'm grinning at Xander while he groans again. It was close, but I won in the end. That means he now has to tell the professor he shares a mutual hatred with that he loves him.

"When do I have to do it?"

"By the end of our next class and I won't take any excuses."

He sighs. "You're a cruel woman. I hope you know that."

"I know," I say with a grin. I then catch sight of Steven flirting with a girl by the bar and decide I'll mess with him anyway. "I'll be right back, Xan." He smirks when he sees where I'm headed.

I school my features into my best angry expression as I approach Steven and his latest victim. I then shout, "Steven Gi! I haven't even been gone for five minutes and you're already flirting with someone else?"

He gives me a confused look. "Uh, Ana, what are you doing?"

"What am *I* doing? What are *you* doing?" I snarl as I pretend to wipe away tears. "I can't believe I trusted you when you said you'd remain faithful this time. I'm clearly an idiot."

He looks at the girl next to him and raises his hands to try to show his innocence. "I have no idea what she's talking about. She's just a friend. She came with my buddy Xander tonight."

"Just friends, huh? That's not what you told me when we were in bed together last weekend!"

He releases a frustrated sigh as he finally realizes what I'm doing. Xander laughs from somewhere behind me when the girl throws her drink in Steven's face.

After she storms away, he gives me an exasperated look while the remnants of her martini drip from his hair and the tip of his nose. "Xander's a horrible influence on you."

Xander sidles up next to me with a huge grin. "That was all Ana, dude."

"You two are too much alike, then," he responds with a groan.

Xander and I look at each other and our grins widen.

CHAPTER TWENTY-SIX

XANDER

Within a few minutes, Steven recovered and was flirting with another girl. However, he didn't fare much better with her.

Ana and I talk while we wait for Tony and Steven to give up for the night. I do enjoy spending time with her like this. Whatever trepidations I had about becoming her friend have long since disappeared.

When Tony randomly joins us, Ana challenges him to a throwing competition. After a couple short rounds, though, she returns to the table with a frustrated look on her face. "How's he so good at that? I started training years before he did, yet he kicked my butt every time."

I find my teleporting friend standing by the throwing area, flirting with the guy who runs it, and smile. I then pat Ana on her hand and say, "You'll get him eventually."

I know it's a lie, but the last thing I want is to trigger her competitive side. Tony's been training tirelessly for years. There are few out there who can match his skill with a dagger.

Unfortunately, Tony's reasons for training so hard are much sadder than Ana's. He didn't do it to help him get into Arken or for bragging rights. He did it so he knew he could always defend himself. I didn't learn why until the summer before my junior year of high school.

Dr. Diavolos had beaten me pretty badly one night that summer and my father never came to release me. I guess I embarrassed him horribly enough that he thought I should hang there all night and think about what I did. He didn't realize I was bleeding so severely I wouldn't make it that long.

Somehow, I was able to break myself out of my chains and crawl out of the storage closet. I must've passed out at some point because when I woke up, I was lying on the table in Dr. Farrogow's office.

Dr. Farrogow must've seen the confusion on my face because he said, "Your teleporting friend found you passed out in the hallway and brought you to me."

I planned to confront Tony when I saw him at school the next day, but I didn't need to. He was waiting outside of Dr. Farrogow's office for me.

I stayed at his house that night and we spent most of the time talking. He didn't go into too much detail, but he told me that he was abused as a kid, so he knew what an abused person looked like. Apparently, that's why he befriended me freshman year. He didn't want me to go through it alone like he had.

I hadn't realized until then how badly I wanted someone to be my friend for who I was and not because of what my last name could offer them. It turns out Tony was always that for me.

Eventually, Steven learned of our pasts too and that's when the three of us really got close. Sure, we'd defended each other and had lunch together before that, but for me it was more out of convenience than anything. It was weird to feel it shift into something more.

Their friendship is what finally helped me gain control of my gift.

My thoughts return to the present when Ana downs another beer and says something I don't understand because she's slurring so badly. If Tony and Steven don't come back soon, I'm going to have to cut her off. The last thing I want is her hurting herself.

I breathe a sigh of relief when my friends return a couple minutes later.

"You guys ready to go?" I ask as I look between the two of them.

Steven nods, but Tony side-eyes Ana. "How drunk is she right now?"

I glance at Ana while she's furiously texting someone and note the flush to her cheeks and the way her eyes are glazed over. "I'm guessing pretty drunk."

Steven grins. "I have a way we can know for sure." He leans into her and gives her a flirty smile. "How you doing, beautiful?"

Ana looks up from her phone with a playful smirk. "Not too bad, handsome. How 'bout you?"

He winks at her before he turns to Tony and says, "Oh yeah, she's plastered."

Tony's gaze shifts to me. "What do you want to do, man? I can't teleport her home like this. It'll just make her feel worse and she'll probably puke all over us."

"You guys go ahead," I say with a wave of my hand. "I'll find a taxi to take Ana and I back."

"Are you sure?" he asks with concern in his eyes.

"Yeah. We'll be fine. We'll head out as soon as you guys leave."

"Okay," Tony responds reluctantly. "Just be careful. And call me if anything happens. I'll come right back."

I brush off his concern but promise I'll reach out if I need him. Tony seems happy with that, so he and Steven disappear seconds later.

Ana looks up from her phone after that and scans the space around our table. "Where did Tony and Steven go?"

"Home. I think it's time we do, too."

She nods and jumps off her barstool. She only takes a few steps before she stumbles. I quickly grab her arm to steady her while she laughs about how clumsy she is.

When she stumbles again with her next step, I sigh and wrap my arm around her to keep her upright. She's going to end up hurting herself if I don't. I guide her out of the bar and into the nearest taxi while she mumbles something about loving my laugh.

Once we're settled into the backseat, she links her arm through mine and leans her head on my shoulder. I stiffen at the intimacy in the gesture but find myself leaning into her as the taxi pulls away from the bar.

As we drive through the capital, she sighs and looks up at me through her eyelashes. "You know, Xan, you're a better person than people think you are. I wish my friends could see that."

Her friends don't think I'm a good person? What the hell? They don't even know me. Why would they think that?

Her gaze focuses on the tattoos that cover my left arm. "I don't think I'll ever understand why you ignore all the girls that hit on you. There were so many checking you out tonight. Any one of them would've gone home with you." She pauses, seeming to realize what she's saying. "I'm happy you didn't, though. It meant I got to spend more time with you."

Yep. She's definitely drunk. Ana would never be so forthcoming with her feelings about us hanging out. We've both been restrained when it comes to admitting how we feel about our growing friend-ship. I'll certainly never tell her that somehow over the past month she's slowly become one of the most important people to me.

She's silent for a few minutes after that. I start to believe she's fallen asleep until she whispers, "Sometimes I think about breaking up with Graham so I could hang out with you without him getting mad and ruining it. I have more fun with you anyways."

I don't respond to her ramblings. It's not my place to. But the thought of her breaking up with her boyfriend has a strange energy coiling in my gut. Is that excitement? Or trepidation?

It's not important, I tell myself as I brush the feeling away.

When we finally get back to Arken, I realize that Ana did fall asleep this time. It has me quickly paying our driver, then scooping her up into my arms and making the trek to her room.

CHAPTER TWENTY-SEVEN
XANDER

In the weeks following the tournament, I've found myself wanting to spend every moment I can with Ana. At this point, I'm chalking up my need to constantly be around her to the fact that she's my first female friend. I'm sure the excitement will wear off eventually.

Ana's lucky I've been wanting to spend so much time with her. It's the only reason she was able to drag me to Dr. Farrogow's house for dinner tonight.

I'm still shocked she was able to convince me. I've rebuffed every attempt the healer's made to reconnect—I have no interest. Yet the minute a pretty girl bats her eyes at me, I'm spending hours in his house eating and making small talk as if it's completely normal. I should probably get my head checked.

Though, I hate to admit it, but the guy makes a mean pot roast. It's full of flavor and super moist. I focus on eating while Ana asks Dr. Farrogow all sorts of questions about being a healer.

It's strange watching the man at ease in his own home. Before Arken, I'd only ever seen him in his office at the Capitol Building and he was always worried then. Especially in the weeks before he quit.

I wouldn't have taken him for a crocheted quilts and knickknacks sort of guy, but they're scattered throughout the space, making it appear more like an old lady's home than a middle-aged professor's.

You think you know someone…

He lives in one of the cottages on the outskirts of campus that are specifically for the faculty and staff of Arken. It's a small place, but it works for a single guy like him. It has a small living room in the front with a guest room off the back. A hallway next to it then leads to the enclosed kitchen, the bathroom, and Dr. Farrogow's room. It's very outdated, but it clearly fits his quaint style.

When dinner's over, I'm forced to discuss our research project with him. Thankfully, Ana does most of the talking.

We were able to gather enough circumstantial evidence that we're confident my grandfather did in fact kill the Kataigida family. It wouldn't hold up in court, but it should be enough to get us a good grade at least.

"Was it difficult to find this information?" Dr. Farrogow asks once Ana's done talking, his eyes drifting to me.

I shake my head. "Not if you looked in the right places."

Ana puts her hand on my shoulder and states, "Ignore him. It took hours of *me* searching before we found anything. Princess over here was just along for the ride."

"Hey! I helped," I respond with a laugh. "I made sure we had plenty of coffee and snacks."

"No. You're totally right. Those were essential for our research," she responds in a placating tone. I roll my eyes at her, and she grins in response. It's infectious and before long my face mirrors hers.

My phone ringing interrupts the moment. I see that it's my uncle, so I take it outside.

"I need to meet with you right away, Xander. I received a letter from Grand Leader Pyrrhus, and she says she'll only communicate with the true Grand Leader of Zoin. I need you to come here and help me draft a response that she'll actually pay attention to." He mumbles something I don't understand, then says, "This woman drives me insane. I understand why your father hated Fotia so much if he had to deal with her all the time."

I sigh. Of course my uncle would insist that I drop everything and come help him deal with a matter that's probably not even that pressing. He always wants things done on his schedule.

When I hang up the phone, I go back inside and tell Ana and Dr. Farrogow that I have to leave. "My uncle needs my assistance with something." I turn to my professor. "I guess let me know if you need anything else from me for the project."

He nods while I give Ana a hug. After that, I force myself to leave so I can talk my uncle off whatever ledge he's found himself on.

CHAPTER TWENTY-EIGHT
ANASTASIA

After Xander leaves, Dr. Farrogow stares after him, seemingly lost in thought. Several seconds pass before a pained expression crosses his face. "I haven't heard him laugh like that in a long time."

"Were you and Xander close?" I ask, my curiosity getting the better of me. I know Dr. Farrogow worked for Xander's family, but he hasn't said much about what sort of relationship they had. Xander hasn't either.

He gives me an assessing look. He must be satisfied with what he sees because he says, "Xander and I have a complicated relationship." He blows out a shaky breath before continuing. It's obvious something happened between the two of them that weighs on him. "As you know, I was the healer for the Thyellas family for nearly a decade. During that time, I healed Xander quite a bit and we developed a sort of camaraderie because of it. I wouldn't say we were friends, but we were as close as an adult and teenager could be. The kid was going through a lot at the time, so I wanted to be there for him. All that went out the window when I quit suddenly. I know he feels like I abandoned him, and I don't blame him."

My brows furrow in confusion. I'm not sure what to say. Very little of what he just said made sense.

He notices my confusion and states, "Let me start from the beginning and I promise it'll all be clear by the time I'm done."

I nod and gesture for him to go on.

"So, I grew up in a wealthy fisherman town in Nero called Saros. It was the same town that Xander's mother grew up in." His features turn wistful. "Kate was smart, popular, and loved by everybody. Imagine my surprise when she showed an interest in me."

"What happened between you two?" I'm not sure how this connects to Xander, but my interest is piqued.

He smiles. "We fell in love."

My eyes widen and he blows out a breath before saying, "Kate's family never believed I was good enough for her. When they realized she wasn't going to break up with me no matter how much they demanded it, they arranged for her to marry Alexander Thyellas."

"*Wait.* Alexander Thyellas? As in Grand Leader Thyellas? Xander's father?"

"Yep," is his clipped response. "We were both devastated by the arrangement, obviously. It all just happened so fast. Before we knew it, she was married and shipped off to live at the Thyellas Estate."

There's sadness in his eyes and my throat tightens in sympathy. I can't imagine how badly that must've hurt.

"She'd only just graduated from high school," he whispers. "All our plans to run away together were suddenly up in smoke. We tried to stay in contact, but it was too hard. Whatever communication we had was inconsistent.

"She reached out to me randomly a few years later. She was worried about Xander and didn't know who else to turn to. His gift developed a lot younger than normal, and it was very strong. She was worried her husband would use Xander for his gift and was looking for a way to hide it. As a healer, she thought I might know how." He runs his fingers through his hair and shakes his head. "That weekend, I met her at a park in a small town not far from where she lives. It was the first time I'd seen her since she got married and it was a lot harder than I thought it'd be. That's also when I met Xander. He was a sweet little boy teeming with power. I gave Kate a few recipes I knew for poultices that should suppress his gift. Sadly, they weren't enough. Alexander still found out the truth about Xander."

"How did he find out?"

"I don't know," he responds with a shrug. "But Alexander took Xander away after that and Kate was only allowed to see him a few times a year. She was devastated. I tried my best to be there for her, but there's really nothing you can do to ease a pain like that. She ended up falling into a deep depression."

"Oh my gods," I gasp while covering my mouth with my hand. "That's horrible."

Dr. Farrogow's expression is grim as he agrees with me. For some reason, though, I get the sense we haven't reached the worst part of the story yet. That realization has dread pooling in my gut.

"A couple years later, I was offered a job to be the Grand Leader's personal healer. I assumed Kate had something to do with it, so I called her right away. Apparently, she'd noticed some bruises on Xander during Christmas and was worried. She hoped I'd be able to figure out what was going on." His voice is strained when he says, "I consider that job my greatest failure."

What?

"When I first started working for the Thyellas family, Xander would come to me every few days needing healing for various cuts and bruises. His father would try to explain them away, but I knew the signs of abuse. I should've left with Xander then, but I was young and stupid and only thought about myself. I was worried what would happen to me or my family if I tried to take Xander."

"At some point, Alexander hired a low life to 'discipline' his son for him. That's when Xander's injuries got a lot worse. He was coming to me every day after that, needing healing for black eyes, broken fingers, and even a fractured..." He trails off, then takes a deep breath and blinks away the tears forming in his eyes. "Like I said, that job is my greatest failure."

I don't know what to say. What Dr. Farrogow has shared is so much worse than I imagined. And Xander was just a kid.

"I felt so much shame for what I was allowing to happen that I stopped talking to Kate. I couldn't face her knowing I was letting her son be abused and wasn't doing anything to stop it."

"When did it finally stop?" I ask. "When his father was murdered?"

He shakes his head. "It stopped suddenly the summer before his junior year. I never knew why. I was just happy he wasn't being hurt anymore."

I blow out a sigh of relief. Thank gods.

"When school started back up, Xander began dating a blonde girl named Suzie. I saw him laugh a few times then. It gave me hope that we were finally past all the pain."

But... I have to stop myself from saying the word out loud, though I know it's coming.

"Unfortunately, they broke up a couple months later and I watched Xander turn into a shell of the person he'd become. Some of the staff heard rumors that the girl was only using Xander for his last name. Apparently, she grew bored once she realized dating him wasn't elevating her status like she thought it would. My heart broke for the kid. After that, I couldn't work there anymore. Not when it seemed like Xander's entire life was going to be a rollercoaster of pain. Mentally, I could no longer handle it." He lifts his glasses and swipes at the tears in his eyes. "I was weak and selfish and made Xander's pain all about me."

He gives me a sad smile. "He seemed happy tonight. I think you're largely the reason. Your friendship is good for him."

My heart swells as I realize the truth in Dr. Farrogow's words. When I first met Xander, he rarely talked, let alone smiled. Now there isn't a single conversation we have where he doesn't.

"I know I just threw a lot at you, but I can see you're a good person, Anastasia. And I know that you care for Xander. He's been let down by so many people in his life. He just needs someone he can count on. I'm hoping that'll be you."

Tears well in my eyes while I say, "Of course, Dr. Farrogow. I'll do whatever I can to help him."

He gives me a pained smile. "Good." He wipes his eyes again while glancing at the clock above his mantle. *Oh my gods. Is it really* after 8:00? I'm so sorry, Anastasia. I didn't mean to keep you here for so long. Here I am blabbing your ear off when I'm sure you have plans with your friends."

I brush off his concern with a wave of my hand. "Don't worry about it, Dr. Farrogow. I enjoyed talking with you."

"Yeah." That pained expression returns to his face. "Thanks for letting an old man get his regrets off his chest."

He stands from the couch, so I follow his lead. He then ushers me toward the front door and says, "Feel free to stop by anytime you need. My door is always open."

"I will," I respond with a smile. "Thank you again, Dr. Farrogow. For everything."

He nods. "See you in class, Ms. Galanis."

"See you later, Dr. Farrogow."

When the front door shuts behind me, I lean my back against it and run my hands over my face. I kept my cool in front of my professor, but I'm reeling from everything he told me. *Poor Xander.* I had no idea things were so bad for him growing up.

Eventually, I'm able to convince my body to move and I make my way back to campus. While I do, my thoughts spiral. I wish I would've known everything Xander was dealing with. I wish he felt safe enough to share it with me. But now that I do know, I'm going to help him in whatever way I can. He won't be alone anymore. I'll make sure of it.

When I return to campus, I head to Nik and Harvey's room. I'm going out for drinks with them and Millie at a local taco place and I'm looking forward to the distraction they'll provide.

Once our history class is over, Graham joins me in my room.

I'm looking forward to catching up with him. I haven't talked to him since I told him I couldn't go to the concert he sprung on me at the last minute. Xander and I already had dinner plans with Dr. Farrogow that day and I couldn't cancel. Graham ended up taking Kas to the concert instead.

I wanted him to have fun even though I couldn't go. Unfortunately, I have no idea how it went because he hasn't responded to any of my texts since Friday.

"How was the concert?" I ask sweetly as he settles onto my bed. I sit at my desk to give him some space since I know a fight is brewing.

"It was fine. Kas liked the band. But honestly, I think he was just happy to be back in Fotia."

"Good. I'm happy to hear that," I say with a genuine smile. "I'm sorry I had to miss it."

His eyes narrow. "How was your dinner with *Xander?*" There's a bite to his tone.

"Our dinner with *Dr. Farrogow* was nice," I answer, ignoring the fact that he's trying to bait me into a fight. "I learned so much about him and what it's like to be a healer. I definitely have a newfound respect for him."

"Hmm."

My patience frays. "Graham, you're obviously upset. Do you want to talk about it? Or do you want to continue doing whatever this is?"

The muscle in his jaw works as he contemplates how to answer. Finally, he says, "I guess I just find it interesting that you blew off plans with your *boyfriend* to hang out with Xander."

"That's not fair and you know it!" I exclaim, unable to contain my frustration. "I didn't know you bought the tickets. We scheduled the dinner with Dr. Farrogow weeks ago. I couldn't just cancel it last minute. Not when my grade depended on it. If the concert had been any other night, you know I would've gone with you."

"Yeah. Sure. Whatever you say."

"What's that supposed to mean?"

"It means you can believe whatever you want, but it doesn't make it true. I've tried making dinner plans with you for weeks now, but you've blown me off every time for *him*." He practically spits out the last word in his anger.

"It was for class and you know that!"

"Do I? Because whenever I ask about what you're researching, you either brush off my question or tell me it's too complicated to explain." I watch his eyes darken. "If you're sleeping with him, just tell me so I can be done with all this."

I gape at him, not knowing how to respond to such an absurd claim. That's when a knock sounds on my door. I shoot a glare in Graham's direction before I go to answer it. My stomach drops as soon as I do.

Xander's oblivious to the worry lining my face as he walks past me and asks, "What're you up to, Spy? Wanna grab some lunch?" He stops once he sees Graham sitting on my bed.

"How convenient," Graham snarls.

I watch as Xander looks between me and Graham. When he notices the tension in the room, he subtly positions himself between us.

"You know what? Screw this!" Graham shouts as he jumps off my bed and storms out of my room. I try to grab his arm as he passes but he pulls away from me.

"Graham, come *on!*" I shout after him, then turn to Xander. "This isn't a good time, Xan. I'll catch up with you later, okay?"

He hesitates for a moment while his eyes drift to where Graham just left, but then he sighs and says, "I'll be in my room if you need me."

I nod as he leaves and closes the door behind him.

Once I'm alone, I fall to my knees and put my hands over my face as tears spill from my eyes.

Did Graham and I just break up? Is that what just happened?

How did everything get so messed up?

CHAPTER TWENTY-NINE

XANDER

Ana found me this morning before class and asked if we could do another search tonight. I couldn't say no to her. Not when there was a hint of desperation in her request. That's why we met at our training spot shortly after midnight to start the three-mile trek to the capital. After our last search on campus, we both agreed that we exhausted our options at Arken.

Due to my familiarity with the Capitol Building, we determined that was our next location to investigate. Unfortunately, that means ·we're walking through pitch black woods in the middle of the night to get there. Our only source of light is the dull flashlight I brought with me.

Thankfully, it's a clear night but the temperature has definitely dropped now that winter's approaching. I gave a pair of gloves and a hat to Ana before we left, knowing she wouldn't be prepared for the cold. When I look at her now and see that she's wearing them, a smile tugs at my lips.

I tear my eyes from her to slowly examine the path ahead of us. I don't know what types of animals roam these woods at night and I have no desire to find out.

Once I'm sure we're safe from any unwelcome followers, my

eyes find Ana again. She has a sadness to her tonight that I'm certain is due to the guy she's dating, *Graham*. I interrupted a fight between them a few days ago and she hasn't seemed like herself since.

When I can no longer stand the thought of her sad, I decide to break the silence between us. "Hey, Ana, are you okay?"

She takes a moment to answer, seeming to ponder how best to reply. Finally, she blows out a breath and says, "Graham and I have been fighting a lot lately. He hates how much time I've been spending with you." She gives me an apologetic look. "He thinks I'm cheating on him."

She stops walking so I stop too and turn to face her. The glow from the flashlight lights up her face, highlighting the tears that well in her eyes. It's like a punch to my gut. I could kill that idiotic boyfriend of hers for hurting her like this. She doesn't deserve it.

"I just don't know what to do," she says, her voice wavering with emotion. "I hate hurting him, but I can't exactly explain this." She gestures around us to emphasize her meaning. "What we're doing is so important to me. I have to figure out the truth about my dad." She pauses, blowing out another breath. "I just hate how it's hurting my relationships with the people I care about."

A tear trails down her cheek, so I wipe it away with my thumb. I then lift her chin so she's looking me in the eyes. I want her to know I mean what I'm about to say.

"I hate how badly this is hurting you, Ana. And I'm so sorry for whatever my father did to drag your family into all this. Once we find the truth, I promise you can go back to the life you were building. I'll make sure no one from my world ever bothers you again. You deserve that much. You deserve to be happy."

"Does that mean you'll be out of my life, too?" Her expression is now pained but I don't understand why.

I look away, not wanting her to see how hard this is for me. "Yes. It's probably for the best. The last thing I want is to hurt you further."

She grabs the hand I just dropped from her chin. "But that isn't what I want, Xander. That's the last thing I want."

She presses into me while tightening her grip on my hand. Her proximity affects me in a way I try not to acknowledge. Though, one look at her face, and I realize she's affected too. I stumble back at the desire building in her eyes.

She wants me?

I watch her struggle to keep her gaze from falling to my lips. The sight has me clenching my hands at my sides to keep from grabbing her. *Get it together, Thyellas. She has a boyfriend*, I try to remind myself. When her eyes return to mine and I see her growing need there, whatever chains were holding me back loosen.

Gods, I want her too.

I grab her and pull her against me while literal sparks fly between us. We're plunged into darkness as the flashlight I was holding falls to the ground and breaks. The only source of light now comes from the streaks of moonlight shining through the trees.

I whisper her name as I search her face. Her name is my plea. Does she truly want this? I need to know before I can move forward.

Her nod is the final key I need to unleash myself.

My right-hand tangles in her strawberry blonde hair and yanks her head back so she's looking up at me. I smile and lean down to kiss her. We're both startled by the surge of energy that passes between our lips when they meet, but we quickly get used to it.

I kiss her hungrily, my lips moving urgently against hers. I didn't realize I was starving until I finally had a taste of her. Now, I can't imagine wanting to kiss anyone else.

There is no one else but *her*.

She grips the front of my shirt while my hands move to cup her face, my tongue brushing the top of her lips, begging to be let in. My knees nearly give out when she opens her mouth for me and my tongue begins dancing with hers.

I didn't realize a kiss could be this good. It's unlike anything I've ever experienced. My body feels electrified, and it wants to be closer to her. It begs to be closer. I *need* to be closer.

I stop kissing her and pick her up, so her legs wrap around my waist. My left hand then holds her in place while my right tangles back in her hair. The pressure now being applied to my dick has me moaning against her mouth.

I break our kiss long enough to search her face. I have to know with complete certainty that she wants this. If I have sex with her and it ruins our friendship, I'll never be able to forgive myself. Ana seems to understand why I'm hesitating because she places a hand on my cheek and says, "I want this, Xander. I want *you*."

My shoulders sag in relief. *Thank gods.*

There's a flush to her cheeks now that highlights the effect I have on her. The sight makes me realize how badly I've wanted this —how badly I've wanted *her*—since the moment I confronted her in the woods two months ago. I kiss her slowly this time, savoring it.

We continue to kiss as I walk us to the nearest tree and lean her against it while making sure to avoid any jagged parts that could hurt her. I then pull her hoodie over her head and throw it on the ground. She tosses the hat and gloves I gave her next to it.

Before long, our clothes are removed and the only sound in these dark woods are our grunts and groans. That is until a loud beeping noise sounds to my left.

I jolt awake, breathing heavy. I then sit up and look around a dark room, trying to figure out where I am. As my eyes adjust to the darkness, I realize I'm in my room.

It was all just a dream.

I fall back on my pillow and rake my hands over my face. A sense of disappointment washes over me that I quickly brush away.

What the hell was that? Why am I having a sex dream about Ana?

I put my hands over my face in exasperation. *What have I gotten myself into?*

CHAPTER THIRTY
XANDER

Sex dreams are the *worst.*

You'd think I actually had sex based on how sluggish I feel this morning, yet the ache in my balls is an unwelcome reminder that I hadn't.

I went through my morning routine without issue, but I worry a strong gust of wind will cause a situation downstairs I don't want to deal with. I keep reminding myself that it was only a dream in the hopes my body will calm down. So far, it hasn't worked.

I know there are ways I could take care of this situation myself, but I worry I'll just end up thinking about Ana while I do. I definitely don't want that to happen, so I'll figure something else out. I have to.

As soon as I walk into Weapons Training, I collapse into my seat and groan. It's going to be a long day. I look up when I hear Ana laugh as she enters the classroom and my traitorous dick twitches at the sight of her. *Oh no.*

She glances up at me and must notice my distress because her eyes crinkle with concern. I know any second she'll be coming to check on me. I silently plead for her to just sit down and leave me be. The last thing I need is to be near her right now. Unfortunately, my efforts are useless because Ana motions to her friends that she'll be right back. *Dammit.*

As she climbs the steps toward me, I keep repeating to myself, 'it was just a dream, it was just a dream, it was just a dream,' hoping it'll help me gain some semblance of control over my body.

When she finally reaches me, she asks, "Hey Xan, is everything okay? It looked like something was wrong when I walked in."

"Yeah. I'm okay," I say, trying to brush off her concern. "I didn't sleep well last night so I'm struggling a bit this morning."

I will Professor Hawke to come barreling into the room so I can end this conversation with Ana before my body betrays me.

"Okay. Well, try not to fall asleep during our demonstrations. I'd hate for you to miss me beating you," she says with a smirk before squeezing my shoulder and walking away.

I roll my eyes at her, but I'm unable to stop a smile from forming on my lips. I love how competitive she is.

That's when Professor Hawke finally decides to show up. "Morning, class. I'm sorry I'm late. I was finalizing our lesson and lost track of time." He puts his briefcase on his desk and folds his hands behind his back. "Over the next week, we'll be learning about battle axes and the various ways to wield them. Today, we will focus specifically on the techniques involved with throwing them."

When he starts droning on about the history of using axes in battle, it doesn't take long for me to zone out. I spend the entire lecture portion of class trying to figure out how to fix my current predicament. I can't keep getting hard anytime Ana's close to me or smiles at me. She's my friend. Honestly, she's probably my best friend. I don't want to risk that just because my body doesn't know how to separate dreams from reality. But what do I do?

By the end of lecture, I decide the best way to rid myself of my problem is to find release via some other avenue. Steven told me there's a party at 306 tonight. A pretty second-year named Kaylee has made her desire to bed me very clear. Maybe giving in to her advances this time wouldn't be such a bad idea. It'd certainly be better than letting this continue.

As class moves over to the training arena, I resign myself to doing just that.

The demonstration portion of class begins like it always does. Professor Hawke first shows us how the ax should be thrown, then he gives it to us to practice with. There are always a few students who try to show off, but they always end up falling short of Ana. I would say the only students who've impressed me, other than Ana, are her friends Harvey and Kasper.

They step up once all the showoffs are done.

I first watch Kasper throw the ax with a deadly calm and hit the bullseye with a *thud*.

Harvey steps forward right after, determined to show up his friend. He looks back at Kasper as he throws the ax with a cocky smile. It ends up landing just right of the bullseye. The fire bender tries to cover his smirk with his hand, but Harvey sees it and shoves him.

Ana shakes her head at both of them and laughs. She then steps up to give her own demonstration. I can't help the smile that spreads across my face as she does. I love seeing her skill in action.

I note a nervousness in her today that's unusual. I watch her line up on the marked spot with shaky fingers and try to steady herself. When she throws the ax, I realize why she's nervous. This is the first time she's thrown a weapon in class since she stopped taking the suppressants. She's probably worried her gift will show itself.

I turn and watch the ax glide through the air. When it starts to sway unnaturally, I decide to intervene. We can't risk her gift being exposed. Not when it could be the very reason both our fathers were killed.

I shoot out a gust of wind toward the ax as I cover up the gesture with a coughing fit. I also throw a breeze around the room for good measure. I want the class to believe my coughs are what caused the draft.

As I finish my performance, I hear the ax clatter on the floor several feet from us.

"Mr. Thyellas! Control yourself! I'll not have you disturbing my class," Professor Hawke shouts. I hear him grumble while shaking his head, "Fricking storm benders and their control issues."

"I'm sorry, Professor," I say between coughs. "I think I have a cold coming on. I'll do my best to control it."

He grimaces. "Good. You better. If it happens again, I'll have no other choice but to remove you from class today. Understood?" His eyes narrow in my direction, assessing me.

"Understood," I answer while pounding on my chest with my fist to sell it.

"And keep your germs away from us, too."

I notice the questioning look on Kasper's face out of the corner of my eye. I assume he sees through my charade, but doesn't understand why I'm putting one on.

When Ana gives me a grateful smile, it makes it all worth it.

She retrieves the ax on the other side of the room and prepares to throw it again. This time, it hits the bullseye with a *thud*. *There you go, Ana.*

After that, I make a mental note to teach her control techniques during our training session tomorrow. They'd help her in situations like this.

I'm the last one to throw the ax and it lands just left of the bullseye. Ana smirks at me, having won our little competition for today.

Professor Hawk sighs once I'm done and dismisses us with nothing but, "See you all on Monday."

I hurry to catch up with Ana outside of class afterwards. She waves off her friends as she stops to talk to me.

"Are you coming to admit your defeat?" she asks with an eyebrow waggle.

I laugh. "*Never.* I went easy on you today. Don't get used to it."

"*Sure.* Whatever you say."

I clear my throat, suddenly nervous to discuss my idea for training tomorrow. I push on anyway. "So, I was thinking that tomorrow we could work on some control exercises."

Ana blushes. "I can't believe that happened," she says in an exasperated tone. "Someone could've seen it."

I put my hands on her shoulders as she looks me in the eyes. I take a deep breath and beg for my body to keep control of itself. Thankfully, it listens as I say, "Hey, don't be too hard on yourself, Spy. It takes the gifted years before they gain any semblance of control. You're doing very well, considering. We'll work on strengthening it during our training sessions and before long, you won't have anything to worry about."

I nod my head in the direction of her next class, indicating that I'll walk her to it. She smiles and falls in step with me.

"Thank you for everything, Xan. Truly. I don't know how I could do any of this without you."

My chest tightens at her sincerity. I playfully bump her arm to lighten the mood. "Don't worry about it. We're in this together."

Our conversation then drifts to Professor Hawke and how "nice" he's been to me since I told him I love him. We're busy laughing about his reaction to my coughing fit when we arrive at Ana's class.

Nikolai scowls when he sees that I'm dropping her off. I ignore him and tell Ana that I'll see her later. She gives me another heart-stopping smile, then makes her way to her friend.

Nikolai and I exchange one final glare before I leave for my own class.

CHAPTER THIRTY-ONE
ANASTASIA

I pull Graham aside once our history class is over. "Can we talk?"

"Fine" is his clipped response.

"Do you want to talk in my room? Millie has class right now so we wouldn't be disturbed."

His mouth is a thin line as he nods.

We spend the few minutes it takes to get to my dorm in awkward silence. I rub my arms as we make our way there, hating how distant we feel, despite the mere inches between us.

When we finally make it to my room, I sit down on my bed and gesture for Graham to join me. While he gets settled, I say, "I'm sorry our argument was interrupted on Monday. I hate that we couldn't resolve things then."

He rolls his eyes. "It was interrupted by the very person that's causing all our problems, Ana." He practically spits while he says, "*Xander.*"

I rub my temples before I respond, but it's an effort to keep my voice even. "I don't understand why you're so bothered by him. He's just a friend. I only spend time with him because of our Intelligence Gathering class. You know we're paired together for the final project."

It shouldn't be this easy to lie to my boyfriend. And I should feel guilty about it, right? I'm not sure why I don't.

"I just don't understand why you have to get together so often. Especially in his room. *Alone*," he explains. "I don't like it."

"*You* are my boyfriend, Graham. *You* are the one I care for and who I share my bed with." I can no longer contain my frustration. It finds its way into every word I say. "No one else means as much to me as you do. What about that don't you get?"

He lowers his head in shame. "Xander's the future Grand Leader of Zoin. Girls are constantly throwing themselves at him." His voice drops to a whisper. "I guess I don't understand how you could want me when you have someone like him interested in you."

My chest constricts at his words. I hate that he feels that way. He's a great guy when he doesn't let his insecurities get the better of him. I place my hand on his thigh while my voice takes on a cajoling tone. "Graham, none of that matters to me. You should know that. Do you truly think so little of me?"

His response is a whispered, "No."

"Then can we please move past this? I'm with you. You're the one I want to be with. Nothing will ever happen between me and Xander."

Graham finally looks at me and I see guilt lining his face. "I'm sorry, Ana. I messed up. I know that. I need to do better. I *will* do better. For *you*. I understand if you're not ready yet, but will you please forgive me?" There's a tenderness in his gaze as his thumb grazes my cheek. "I hate fighting with you."

My shoulders sag before I smile and tell him I forgive him. I'm eager to move past this needless fight, too. He grins and kisses me.

The kiss quickly turns passionate as I lay back on my pillow and pull him down with me. We then spend the next twenty minutes doing the one thing we *are* good at.

Once we're done, I rest my head on his chest while he drapes my comforter over us. He strokes my hair as we lie there in silent contentment.

"I love you, Ana. I hope you know that," he confesses in a whisper.

My heart drops at his admission. I hoped we were still a long way from 'I love you.'

My mouth drops open as I struggle with what to say. I told myself I'd never fall in love. Not after it nearly broke Mom when she lost Dad. But how do I tell Graham that after what he just said? I *can't*. He wouldn't understand. In this instance, a white lie is probably better than hurting him right now.

"I love you too, Graham," I say and pray that he can't see through my lie.

When he smiles and pulls me closer, I breathe a sigh of relief. *Thank gods*. The last thing I want right now is to have another fight.

After we lay there for a few minutes, he says, "Harvey told me there's a party at 306 tonight. It might be fun to go."

I sit up, already excited. "Yes! We absolutely should."

Going out was the right choice.

There's been so much unspoken tension between me and my guy friends because of my friendship with Xander and how it upsets Graham. I think we all needed a night out to let loose and remember why we're friends in the first place.

With the end of the semester fast approaching, it looks like most of our classmates had the same idea. 306 is so packed that the party has spilled into the front yard. Shouts from upperclassmen about the party moving to their houses can be faintly heard over the music blaring in the living room.

My friends and I choose to stay at 306 since it's our go to spot.

Kas and Harvey are busy flirting with a group of girls in the other room while Graham and I dance beside Millie and Nik. The two of them make out as they sway back and forth in time to the music. Normally, the level of affection they're displaying would make me uncomfortable, but Graham and I don't exactly have room to talk right now. We're dancing just as close to each other and we're not being subtle about how turned on we are.

As the shots we took ten minutes ago set in, a boldness creeps over me that's unusual. I'm about to tell Graham to meet me in the bathroom when something across the room has me freezing in place.

My heart stutters at the sight of Xander making out with a pretty brunette. He's pressed against the girl and his hands are tangled in her hair. I can no longer hear whatever song's playing over the speakers. It fades as a feeling of dread settles over me, mixed with confusion. Xander's never paid attention to any of the girls that have showed interest in him. Including the one he's currently kissing. What changed?

I feel like I can't breathe when I watch him pull away from her and whisper something into her ear. When she nods in response, he grabs her hand and leads her to the front door. *Oh my gods, he's leaving with her.*

I turn to Graham and tell him I have to use the restroom while struggling to hide how flustered I feel. I quickly make my way to the back of the house, finding the bathroom with ease. Its interior is grosser than I'd like but I brush away my disgust since I have no intention of using it. I just need some air. And a quiet place to get my thoughts in order.

I lean over the sink and study myself in the mirror. Why did seeing Xander with that girl make me feel like my world was suddenly out of orbit? He's single and attractive, of course he should take advantage of the attention that brings him. What he chooses to do in his spare time is no concern to me. Right?

I splash some water on my face and take several deep breaths to try to ease my growing anxiety. Once I've calmed down, I leave the bathroom and make my way back to Graham. Thankfully, he's right where I left him.

"Are you okay?" he asks, brows crinkling with concern.

"Yeah," I lie. "I don't think those shots are settling well."

"Do you want to leave, then?" I shake my head.

I'm just about to ask if we can sit down somewhere when I hear Steven behind me. "*Dude,* Ana! I don't know what you've done to Xander, but your friendship with him has changed him for the better." He claps me on the back as I turn to face him. "He took home a girl tonight and he never does that. *Never.*" He wipes a fake tear from his eye as he says, "I'm so proud."

"I'm glad you're happy, Steven," I say with a forced laugh.

"Happy? I could kiss you." Graham tenses behind me at Steven's declaration. "You helped change my boy from a perpetual grump to someone who actually has fun and lets loose." He mockingly bows before me. "I'm indebted to you."

I genuinely laugh this time. "You're insane, Gi."

He waggles his eyebrows before he running off to find Tony. At least, that's what I assume he's doing.

I blow out a breath once he's gone and turn back to Graham. His furrowed brows has me pausing.

"Who was that?"

"A friend of Xander's. His name's Steven. I guess he's happy that Xander's hooking up with a girl tonight," I respond dismissively.

"And he believes you're the reason." I see the flash of annoyance in his eyes. It's become his standard reaction whenever Xander's mentioned. I need to diffuse this situation before it turns into another fight. I can't handle that right now.

"Yeah, that's just Steven," I say with a wave of my hand. "He's loud and over dramatic. Don't pay him any mind." I look at the clock on the mantle to our right and feign surprise. "Whoa! It's already almost 1:00? We should probably get going."

It looks like he wants to say more but decides to drop it. "Yeah, okay. Let's say goodbye to everyone, then we'll head out."

CHAPTER THIRTY-TWO

ANASTASIA

I arrive at the training site a few minutes before our usual time and quickly realize I beat Xander here—which is a first. I lean against the nearest tree to wait, knowing he'll be here any minute. Unfortunately, a cold wind picks up that chills me to the bone and makes me wish I brought a coat.

The sound of leaves crunching underfoot several minutes later signals Xander's arrival. Though, I'm now so cold I'm unable to greet him. All I can do is keep my arms wrapped around myself to try to contain my body heat.

"Hey, Spy," Xander says as he drops his backpack at his feet. "I'm sorry I'm late."

"You know, I think we should find a better location to train," I struggle to say as my teeth chatter uncontrollably. "Preferably one that's indoors."

"Why do you say that?" he asks, finally looking at me. His eyes widen when he sees how badly I'm shivering. "Hold on." He flicks his right hand in a circular motion and a warm gust of wind blows around us in response. It warms me instantly and eases my aching limbs. "Is that better?"

"Yes," I say while my whole body relaxes.

"Okay. Good." Once he confirms I'm no longer freezing, he claps his hands to mark the beginning of our training session. "*So*, I thought we could start with our usual warm up, then I'll go through some of the control techniques I know."

"Sounds good to me," I say while trying not to show how embarrassed I feel about yesterday.

Xander smiles in response, clearly seeing through my mask. "Okay. Let's get started then."

He takes off the green hoodie he's wearing and throws it onto the ground, leaving him in only a black T-shirt. After that, he gestures for me to follow him into the center of the clearing so we can start our warmup.

As we cycle through the exercises, I find myself analyzing him closely to see if he seems any different after last night. I'm thinking if he does, then it'll give me some idea of when he has girls over. I don't know why I need to know that but I do.

I don't see anything of note, though. If anything, he seems back to his usual self, the nervous energy he had yesterday nowhere to be found.

I continue assessing him until he lifts his arms above his head to stretch his shoulders. When the motion gives me a clear view of the perfect V that makes up his lower abdomen, I quickly avert my eyes while my cheeks warm. I've always known Xander's attractive but damn. It's starting to feel like he's a god or something with how perfect he is.

My conscience lectures me about how I shouldn't objectify my friend, but my eyes ignore it. Instead, they sneak another peek. I am only human after all.

My attention snaps back to the task at hand—my face growing even redder—when Xander clears his throat and states, "Okay. That should be enough of a warmup for us."

He crouches and digs through the bag he brought with him. I give him a puzzled look when he pulls out a red Arken University sweatshirt and hands it to me. He notes my confusion and explains. "I have to drop my wind, so it doesn't interfere with our lesson. I

170

figured you wouldn't be prepared for the cold, so I brought this, a hat, and some gloves for you."

My heart swells as I accept the items. He really brought all this just for me?

I quickly pull the sweatshirt over my head and get a whiff of Xander's scent—warm summer rain with a hint of pine. The sweatshirt's huge on me, falling just above my knees, but it adds an extra layer of warmth I'm grateful for. I pull on the hat and gloves and relish in the fact that they also smell like Xander.

Once he sees that I'm covered, he drops his wind and the cold quickly seeps back into the clearing with a vengeance. Thankfully, the extra layer makes it manageable, and I watch as Xander puts his own hoodie back on.

When his wind has completely disappeared, he grabs several knives from his bag and brings them to me, dropping all but one at my feet. He places that one in his hand.

"Do you feel that restless energy reverberating throughout your body?" He looks to me for a response, so I nod. "I want you to gather all that energy and direct it toward the knife in my hand."

I do as he says and watch the knife lift a foot above its original location. It sways uncontrollably back and forth while it hovers there.

"Okay. You see how unsteady it is? That's because of the worry you're feeling. My goal is to teach you how to prevent your emotions from affecting your gift in such a way. To start, I'd like you to take several deep breaths."

I breathe in and out slowly, following Xander's lead. When I feel myself calm down, the knife steadies itself, its swaying stopping completely. I look at Xander with an excited smile once it does and he smiles back, clearly pleased.

"If you ever feel like you're losing control of your gift, the first thing I recommend is taking a few deep breaths," he explains. "I find that's usually all I need."

We spend the next hour working on a couple other control techniques Xander knows. By the end of it, the knife never wavers—even when thrown—no matter how angry or upset I get. Annoyingly, Xander really enjoyed that part of our training. He'd trip me, shove me, and heckle me to try to get me to lose control, but I never did. Not once.

When the hour's finally up, he hugs me and says, "You did great, Spy. I think you have a good handle on your gift now. If you follow those techniques, then you shouldn't have any further control issues. Even when I annoy you."

He winks when I pull away from him and I laugh sarcastically. "Oh, thank gods for that." My expression turns serious. "But really, thank you, Xan. I don't know what I'd do without you."

He brushes off my gratitude with a wave of his hand. "It was nothing, Spy."

I smile at his inability to accept a compliment, then loop my arm through his.

We make our way back to campus as the sun begins its evening descent. We spend the time admiring the gold and pink hues surrounding us in silence, content with the results of today's training session.

CHAPTER THIRTY-THREE
ANASTASIA

We didn't learn anything new during the last two weeks of class. Instead, the time was spent reviewing material that might be on the final. That's when it truly sank in for me that the semester's almost over.

I've been bouncing between worry and excitement because of it. Worry for the finals I still have to take, but excitement for what next semester might hold. If it's anything like this one was, then it'll be one hell of a ride.

All in all, the end of my first semester at Arken is bittersweet.

Thankfully, it looks like I'll still have friends in most of my classes next semester. Kas, Harvey, and Xander will be in Weapons Training with me again and Nik will be in my Mixed Martial Arts class. I even have a class with Millie: Poisonous Plants and Their Effects on Nature. She pushed me to take it with her since I was looking for another class to fill my schedule. Unfortunately, the only one I don't have a class with is Graham. Surprisingly, he wasn't bothered by that. He just said we'll have to be more intentional with setting aside time for one another.

Next semester is still a month away, though. In the meantime, I get to go home and spend a few weeks with my family. I'd be lying if I said I wasn't looking forward to it. My mom goes all out for the holidays and I'm excited I get to be there for it. Christmas is my favorite.

When Kalyteros was first formed, The Sisters had a tough decision to make regarding holidays. Apparently, they considered banning all except the ones they created. In the end, I guess they changed their minds because they only banned the holidays that were specific to Old America—holidays like Fourth of July and Thanksgiving.

I'm grateful they didn't go through with their original plan. I love holidays and couldn't imagine not celebrating them. They help break up the monotony of the day-to-day and give you something to look forward to.

With the holiday spirit in mind, Millie, Graham, and I went to a thrift store this morning and bought some ugly Christmas sweaters. 306 is having a Christmas-themed party tonight and we fully intend on going all out for it.

Unfortunately, Nik, Kas, and Harvey are away for the weekend, shadowing their fathers, so they're unable to partake in the festivities. Millie said we'll have to celebrate on their behalf. I worry what she means by that.

The party is packed by the time we arrive. It looks like my classmates wanted one last hurrah before they're consumed by finals. To that, I wholeheartedly agree.

I hear someone shout Graham's name as we enter the crowded living room. Graham smiles and waves when he sees that it's a few of his friends from his Cybersecurity class. He then leans in close and tells me he's going to hang out with them for a bit. "I'll find you later, okay?"

I nod and shoo him away with a shout of, "Have fun!"

With a smile, I turn to my roommate and link my arm with hers. She laughs as I proceed to drag her to the dance floor. Within seconds, we get lost in the crowd of people as our bodies sway to the music.

I'm eager to spend some quality time with Millie tonight. She's made several comments recently that she never gets to see me anymore and I hate how true they are. I need to do a better job of making time for her.

While Millie and I dance, I can't help but feel at peace. I don't think I'll ever get tired of dancing. I love how free it makes me feel. Every bit of stress and worry that usually hangs over me disappears the minute I let the music take over.

I'm busy twirling around with my hands in the air when my gaze is drawn to the front door. That's when Xander enters the house with Tony and Steven close behind. We instantly lock eyes and give each other a small smile before he makes his way to the back of the house.

"So, what's the story between you two?" Millie asks as she gestures toward Xander's retreating back. "You seem pretty friendly."

I'm taken aback by her question.

"There's no story," I say, making myself appear as nonchalant as possible. "We just worked together on a project for Dr. Farrogow's class all semester. He's a nice guy."

"Uh-huh," she responds, unconvinced. "I guess him carrying your unconscious butt back to our room was just part of your project then?"

My cheeks warm. I hadn't realized Millie was in our room that night when Xander dropped me off. There's no simple way to explain that away.

"Have you two hooked up?" she asks without waiting for a response to her previous question.

My eyes widen in shock. "*No*. Of course not. Why would you ask that?"

She shrugs. "Xander's an attractive guy. He's also the future leader of our province. A guy like that would be hard to resist. I'd understand if you had." She places her hand on my shoulder and gives me a reassuring smile. "And I say that despite your boyfriend being my best guy friend."

My face grows warmer, so I quickly brush off her implication by saying, "No. I'm with Graham. It's not like that with Xander."

"Okay," Millie says, emphasizing the final syllable. It's clear she doesn't believe me.

I grab her hands to get her dancing again, wanting desperately to end this uncomfortable conversation.

We're still dancing about twenty minutes later and I haven't seen Graham in just as long. I think he went downstairs with his friends to play pool.

When the song ends, Millie shouts that she's grabbing another drink. I wave her off and continue dancing. My favorite song just started and I don't plan on going anywhere until it's over.

Graham sidles up behind me and wraps his arms around my waist seconds after she's gone. I'm surprised he's already back, but happy, nonetheless. I smile and lean into him when his thumbs find the waistband of my skirt and trail torturous circles beneath it.

My blood runs cold when a voice that isn't Graham's purrs into my ear, "Why don't we move this party elsewhere?"

I quickly pull away and whip around to find some random guy smiling at me.

The guy must notice my surprise because his smile is instantly replaced by narrowed eyes. "What? You think you're too good for me or something?"

I shake my head and put my hands up in a placating manner, trying to diffuse the situation. "*No.* I just thought you were somebody else."

"So, you do think you're too good for me," the guy snarls. He roughly grabs me by my arms. "I know who you are. I know you're nothing but ungifted trash. I don't know what makes you believe you're better than me, but I can promise you're not. You're lucky I even wanted to dance with someone like you."

"Let go of me!" I shout but it's drowned out by the music. I try to pull out of his grip, but he only tightens the hold he has on me. I look around to see if anyone has noticed and can help, but those dancing closest to us are too wrapped up in what they're doing to care.

The man smiles a wicked grin when he also realizes no one's coming to help me. Nausea settles in my gut when he pulls me closer and grazes the inside of my arms with his thumbs.

"A pretty ungifted thing like yourself should be grateful I'm interested in you."

My entire body stills at the unwanted contact and a pit forms in my stomach when he licks his lips. Oh gods, he's going to try to kiss me.

My thoughts spiral as I look for a way out of my current situation. There's a large metal clock sitting on the mantle behind the guy and my knife's tucked into my boot. Either could help me, but they'd require me to use my gift. Xander was adamant that no one can know I'm gifted until we figure out what happened to our fathers so they're not viable options.

True fear weighs on my chest when I realize I can't get myself out of this.

The creep's right hand grabs the back of my neck while his left slips under my shirt. I try to fight him off now that my arms are free, but it's like hitting a brick wall. I dig my nails into his skin but his hold on me doesn't loosen.

When the man's mouth is about to meet mine, I do the only thing I can think of. "Xander!" I shout as loud as I can, my fear and desperation intertwining with his name. I know if anyone can save me from this prick, it's him.

The guy freezes and I think I see a flicker of fear cross his face when he asks, "Who did you just call for?"

Seconds later, a scary calm voice sounds from behind me. "I suggest you let her go. *Now.*"

The creep's eyes widen when he realizes who threatened him. He shoves me toward Xander and puts his hands in the air, feigning innocence.

Xander steadies me and gives me a quick once over. "You okay, Ana?"

I nod, though tears gather in my eyes. My hands are shaking as the adrenaline coursing through me starts to crash. That guy forced himself on me for no other reason than to show he could.

Xander takes in my expression, and I watch his nostrils flare. He then guides me toward Tony and Steven—who stand behind him—before he turns back to my assailant. Tony wraps his arms around me while Steven blocks me from the creep's view.

Millie returns at that moment and rushes toward me with a concerned look. "Oh my gods, Ana! What happened?"

CHAPTER THIRTY-FOUR

XANDER

I was settled into my usual spot at 306, watching Tony and Steven play beer pong, when Ana's scream had me rushing to her. I could hear the fear in her voice and knew immediately that something was wrong.

Finding her trying to fight off one of my old classmates while he forced himself upon her had a lethal calm settling over me. It took every bit of my self-control not to kill the prick the moment I saw his hand up her shirt. But the fear in Ana's eyes confirmed he was going to suffer. I'd make sure of it.

Ethan Caravo has no idea how badly he messed up. He hurt the one person I care about the most and I won't let him get away with that.

The idiot digs himself a bigger grave by trying to blame Ana for what happened. "I just wanted to dance with her, man. *She's* the one that acted like she wanted more than that." His voice takes on a pleading tone as he says, "You have to believe me, Xander."

"I suggest you leave now before I make you," I snarl as electricity gathers at the tips of my fingers. If he so much as breathes wrong, I'll strike him down right here. The fact he's still standing at this point is more than he deserves.

I hear a commotion behind me, but I'm not worried about it. I know Ana's safe with Tony and Steven. Instead, my gaze is locked on Ethan, daring him to spew more lies. He scoffs, though it appears he isn't entirely stupid because he doesn't argue with me. He just mumbles an apology and quickly leaves the party.

My eyes follow him until he disappears, then I turn back to Ana with concern tightening my chest. The sight of her boyfriend arguing with Tony, insisting that Tony let her go now that he's here, instantly angers me. Where the hell was he when she was getting attacked?

Tony ignores Graham's threats, keeping his arms tightly wrapped around Ana while her head is buried in his chest. Even she's ignoring her boyfriend, knowing he can't protect her. Steven watches them closely, waiting for Graham to do something that'd require him to intervene. I quickly approach the four of them, wanting to break up the confrontation before it escalates. That's the last thing Ana needs right now.

Tony lets go of Ana as soon as I'm next to them and Graham bares his teeth at my best friend. I ignore his posturing and focus on Ana instead. Her expression is hollow, and I watch her wrap her arms around herself.

"Are you sure you're okay, Spy?"

She nods and thanks me for saving her, but her eyes tell a different story. I so badly want to hug her right now. I don't, though. Not when it'd cause a fight between her and her boyfriend.

That means I do the only thing I can. "His name is Ethan Caravo," I explain. "We went to high school together. He's an entitled jerk. I'll talk to him and let him know what'll happen if he goes near you again."

"It's not your job to protect her," snarls the useless bag of bones Ana calls her boyfriend.

I finally look at him and quirk an eyebrow. Is he serious? Where was he then when she needed protection? If she was left to rely on him, who knows what would've happened tonight.

"Graham, Xander just saved me from that guy. A guy that was

assaulting me," Ana snaps. "This is not the time to fight over whose job it is to defend me."

Graham works his jaw, but he doesn't say anything else. I have to fight back a smirk. I'm glad Ana told him off. Personally, I think she should ditch him, but her yelling at him is good enough for now.

"So, what now?" Steven asks, trying to ease the tension.

Thankfully, Ana says she just wants to go back to her dorm. That's the best place for her right now. Tony offers to take her and Millie, and they're gone seconds later. That leaves me, Steven, and Graham standing there awkwardly.

Several seconds pass before Graham says under his breath, "Thanks for saving her." He looks between me and Steven with a mixture of annoyance and shame on his face, then leaves to go to another room.

"Wow! I've never seen such a display of gratitude," Steven jokes once Graham's out of earshot. "That dude is definitely happy you saved his girl."

"Well, he should be. It's not like he was there to help her."

Tony reappears at that moment. "What now, boys?"

"You guys do what you want," I say with a wave of my hand. "I have something I need to take care of."

He gives me a knowing smile. "Want some help?"

"No. I got it. I'll see you guys tomorrow."

When I arrive at my intended location, I lean against the wall before I knock on the door. The last thing I want is for Ethan to see me through the peephole and hide. Breaking down his door is a hassle I don't want to deal with tonight.

"Hello?" I smile at the worry I hear in his tone when he opens his door.

"Ding dong motherfucker," I say before I punch him in the face. He falls to the floor and I slowly stalk after him.

Ethan's roommate jumps from his bed once he sees me, but before he can reach Ethan's side, I growl, "Try to help him and you'll be next." The roommate quickly sits back down, his fear palpable.

I return my focus to Ethan and stoop over him while he tries to scramble away from me. I grab him by his shirt and lift him up so that we're face to face. "So, you think you can force yourself on whoever you want, huh?"

He puts his hands up defensively. "It wasn't like that, Xander. She asked for it."

I punch him again and his head snaps back. Blood trickles from his now split brow.

"She did! I swear!"

This time when I punch him, I snarl, "Go ahead and keep lying to me, prick. I can do this all night."

"*Fine.* You're right," he says desperately. "I just wanted to show her how worthless she is. I wanted her to know she's not better than me."

"That's what I thought." I throw him back on the ground, then crouch next to him. The lights in his room flicker as lightning gathers in my eyes. "You so much as *look* at Ms. Galanis again and I'll come back here. Except next time, the only way you'll be leaving is in a body bag. Do you understand?"

He nods quickly, eyes full of terror. He's trembling by the time I leave his room.

I use my rain to clean my bloody knuckles while I make my way toward Ana's room. I need to know she's okay. I won't be able to sleep otherwise.

CHAPTER THIRTY-FIVE

ANASTASIA

Tony teleports Millie and I just outside our dorm, then pulls me in for a hug.

"I'm sorry about what happened to you, Ana," he whispers. "If you ever want to talk about it, I'm here."

I squeeze him while fighting back tears. Xander might've saved me from the prick who assaulted me, but it was Tony who comforted me afterwards. I'll never forget that.

"Thank you, Tony. I appreciate it."

He lets go of me and waits until Millie and I enter our dorm safely before teleporting away. My shoulders immediately tense in his absence. Millie must notice because she links her arm through mine and steers us toward our room.

"So, how are you really feeling?" she asks while glancing at me out of the corner of her eye.

"Violated," I admit. "That creep didn't care about how I felt. He was going to force me to do whatever he wanted." I blow out a shaky breath as tears gather in my eyes. "I've never felt so helpless in my life. I've been training since I was a little girl, yet it didn't mean anything when it actually mattered."

She wraps her arm around my shoulders and leans her head

against mine. "I'm so sorry, Ana. He never should've done that to you. You didn't deserve it."

I nod. It's the only thing I can do right now.

I still can't believe I couldn't stop *Ethan* from forcing himself on me. Why didn't I fight him? Why didn't I use any of the fighting styles I know to get him off me? It's like I forgot them the minute I needed them. What about my gift? What's the point of having it if I can't use it when I need it?

"I'm going to take a shower," I announce once we're in our room.

I slowly strip off my clothes, then stare at them, contemplating throwing them out. I don't think I'll be able to wear them again without reliving what happened.

Tears stream down my face as I toss my favorite skirt and the ugly sweater I bought with Millie and Graham this morning into the trash. Why did this have to happen to me? I was trying to be polite when I told him I wasn't interested. Why did he take that as a reason to hurt me? To force himself upon me?

I feel so powerless.

Is that sort of treatment something I should expect now? The thought makes me sick.

I pull on my robe and grab my shower caddy, then make my way to the communal bathroom. I move slowly as I do, the trauma weighing on me.

After a long shower, I return to my room, ready for bed. Millie suggests we watch a movie instead. "It'll help keep the nightmares away."

That's how we ended up snuggling in my bed, watching a cheesy rom-com.

I jump when a knock sounds on our door a few minutes into the movie. "Who could that be?" I ask as I climb out of bed.

"Tell Xander I say hi," Millie responds with a smirk.

I roll my eyes at her, even though I think it's Xander too. I look through our peephole and smile when I confirm that it is in fact my best friend.

I quickly unlock the door and open it. "Hey, Xan. What are you doing here?" The sight of him calms me in a way I desperately need.

His eyes search my face while he says, "I wanted to check on you and see how you're doing."

I glance at Millie and see her shooing me, urging me to go spend time with him. I find myself wanting to do just that.

"Do you want to go for a walk?" I ask and he nods. I gesture for him to come inside for a moment so I can get ready.

"Hey, Millie," he says when he notices her on my bed.

I grab my shoes and pull them on while Millie smiles at him. "Hey, Xander. Thanks again for saving my best friend tonight."

He brushes off her gratitude with a wave of his hand. "It was nothing."

Thankfully, I'm ready to go so I pull Xander out of the room before Millie can ask him about his intentions with me or something ridiculous like that.

CHAPTER THIRTY-SIX
XANDER

We spend the few minutes it takes to leave Ana's building in silence.

I have no idea what to say to her. What do you say to someone who was violated in such a horrible way? I never seem to know. The last thing I want to do is make it worse.

The only thing I can think to do is be here for her. In whatever capacity she needs. Because she does need someone, even if she continues to say she's okay. The haunted look in her eyes tells me so and it kills me. What if I hadn't been there? What would've happened to her?

When Ana and I reach the walkway that leads to the Admin Building, I decide to finally break the silence. "How're you doing, Ana?" I'm hoping she'll be honest now that it's just the two of us.

Before she answers, I send out a warm wind and let it spiral around us as we continue walking. Ana relaxes in response, then says, "I'm okay."

Liar.

"Do you want to talk about what happened?" I ask, subtly nudging her to open up.

She blows out a breath while her eyes lock onto her fingernails. There's blood beneath them from when she scratched Ethan.

"My memories of the attack seem blurry now, but they also haunt me in vivid detail. I know that doesn't make a lot of sense, but it's the only way I can explain it."

She recounts how the assault unfolded, and I have to clench my hands to rein in my need to punch something. Hearing her talk about how scared she was while he threatened her makes me wish I hurt Ethan worse than I did.

"The whole thing made me feel so helpless. I thought about using my gift, but I remembered you saying I shouldn't expose myself. That's why I called for you. I knew you'd be able to help me."

My stomach sinks at her words. I only meant she shouldn't use it openly in class or on campus. I never thought she'd take that to mean when she was in danger, too. This is all my fault. I should've been clearer. Instead, I made my friend believe that exposing her gift was worse than her getting hurt.

I grab Ana's hand and force her to stop. When she looks up at me with furrowed brows, I say, "Ana, your safety is more important than whatever might happen if your gift's exposed. We can deal with the fallout from it. What *I* can't deal with is you getting hurt. You're too important to me." I force her to meet my eyes, and I see tears gathering in hers. "I'll always be here to help you, Spy, but you don't need me. You're so incredibly strong and smart. There isn't anything you can't do if you put your mind to it, including stopping a loser like Ethan. I'm sorry I made you feel like you couldn't use your gift to save yourself. I want you to use it. I want the entire world to know that Anastasia Galanis is not someone to mess with. She's somebody to fear."

CHAPTER THIRTY-SEVEN
ANASTASIA

Tears well in my eyes for what seems like the hundredth time tonight.

Xander's words should make me feel better, but they don't. The woman he's talking about no longer exists. Honestly, I wonder if she ever did. I've been attacked twice now at Arken and both times Xander was the one who saved me. Not me. I don't think I'm capable of saving anybody.

Xander must see everything I'm feeling on my face because he pulls me in for a hug and says, "You're still a strong person, Ana. What happened to you doesn't change that."

"Then why do I feel like it does?" I sob into his chest. "My dad taught me how to defend myself, so why can't I? He'd be so disappointed if he knew what I let happen."

"From what you've told me about your dad, he'd never be disappointed in you, Spy," Please don't think like that."

I pull away from him and nod, but his words don't change how I feel. I let my dad down tonight and it's a shame I'll carry with me for a long time.

I don't want to talk about what happened anymore, so I shift our conversation to a lighter topic. "That was one hell of a way to end our last party for the semester."

Xander chuckles, following my lead. "You're not wrong. I'm not sure how we'll top it in the spring. Other than an outright brawl, I just don't see anything garnering the same attention."

I playfully bump his arm. "I'm sure you'll figure something out. You do love being the center of attention after all."

He rolls his eyes, but the smile that spreads across his face quiets my racing thoughts. Xander always has a way of making me feel better. I have no idea how I'm going to go back to my room and deal with all this without him. I don't want to.

I didn't realize I grabbed his arm until he asks, "What's wrong, Ana?"

I immediately let go of him and apologize. "I'm sorry, Xan. I didn't mean to grab you. I was just thinking about how I don't want to go back to my room. At least, not yet. Not when it means I have to leave you."

Concern returns to his face, and I quickly look away in embarrassment. It's not his job to make me feel better and I shouldn't be putting that kind of pressure on him. He has enough to deal with as it is.

He grabs my hand and forces me to look at him. He then clears his throat and asks, "Do you want to stay with me tonight?" When my eyes widen, he rushes to clarify. "In a completely platonic way, of course. You can sleep in my bed, and I'll sleep on the air mattress I have."

The only thing I can think to ask is, "Why do you have an air mattress?"

He sighs. "Steven gave it to me so he and Tony would have somewhere else to stay if the other brought someone back."

"Have they ever used it?" When he shakes his head, a laugh falls from my mouth that eases the worry lining his face.

I loop my arm through his and contemplate his offer as my dorm grows closer. I know I should say no. Nothing will happen between us, but Graham would still be upset if he ever found out. It wouldn't be fair to him if I stayed with Xander. But I can't picture myself going back to my room tonight either. Not when my greatest source of comfort is saying I don't have to leave him.

Screw it.

I smile up at Xander and say, "Let's have a sleepover."

CHAPTER THIRTY-EIGHT
ANASTASIA

I've been in Xander's room several times before, but none of those times felt like this. Knowing I'm staying here with him tonight has it feeling intimate. Special. I try to remind myself that it's just Xander, but it only heightens the weird energy flowing through me.

I've always been attracted to him, but I never thought much about it. So, why am I feeling this way? It's just a room. It's not like we'll be sharing the same bed or anything.

Xander hands me his laptop and tells me to find a movie to watch while he sets up the air mattress a few feet from his bed. Seeing how close he'll be to me all night has any lingering worries instantly disappearing.

Once his temporary sleeping arrangement is set up, he hops onto the bed next to me and starts the movie I chose. He groans the minute he sees its title. It's a stupid comedy I've loved since I was a little girl.

"What? You don't like my choice?"

He chuckles while shaking his head. "I swear, you and Tony are too much alike. Not only are you both unnaturally skilled with a dagger, but now I learn you have the same crappy taste in movies."

I feign offense. "I'm gonna tell Tony you said that."

"I've already told him. Many times."

"Well, it sounds like I should be spending my time with him instead. Tony clearly has good taste."

When I make like I'm going to leave, Xander grabs me. "Oh no you don't."

I laugh as his arms make their way around my waist and pull me on top of him. He releases me as soon as he realizes what he's done, but I tackle him in turn.

He puts his hands up in mock surrender as I pin him to the bed. "Okay. Okay. You win. No need to hurt me."

I throw a satisfied smirk his way before I sit back down.

When he straightens, he grabs his arm and acts like I hurt him. "Remind me to never insult your movie choices again, Spy."

I pat his leg before I lean my head against his shoulder. "Yeah… That's probably for the best. I'd hate for you to have to type all your important Grand Leader documents while missing a few fingers."

He rolls his eyes, then starts the movie. I end up falling asleep within a few minutes of it being on. Between Xander's comforting presence and the smell of rain enveloping me, I'm lulled into a deep slumber.

Thankfully, I dream of deep blue eyes instead of demanding hands.

The morning after I stayed at Xander's, I woke up to a thermos full of coffee and a plate piled high with eggs and bacon.

"How did you know these are my favorite?" I asked excitedly.

"They're literally the only two things you eat for breakfast. It wasn't hard to figure out," he responded, and it had a smile spreading across my face. It's nice to have a friend that pays attention.

We watched another movie together while I ate, then I begrudgingly returned to my room once it was over. I knew I could only escape reality for so long. Finals were coming, and I needed to prepare for them.

Looking back, though, I was probably more worried than I needed to be since I passed every single one with flying colors.

Now that they're over, I'm packing for the month I'll spend at home.

I'm hoping some time away will help with the nightmares I've been having. I ended up staying with Xander for most of the week because of them and it's not fair for me to keep putting him out like that. Especially since he insists that he sleep on the tiny air mattress every time even though he's way too big for it.

As I squeeze one more outfit into my suitcase, I hear a knock at my door. I turn and find Xander leaning against it and smile instantly.

"You need help with that?" he asks with humor dancing in his eyes. I zip it closed in answer and he smiles. His expression then turns serious. "Are you leaving soon?"

"Yeah. My mom should be here any minute. What about you?"

"I got one more bag to throw in my car, then I'll be outta here." He drifts toward me as if pulled by an invisible string. "Try not to get into any trouble while you're home, Spy."

"*Me?* You're the one I'm worried about," I say, playfully shoving his arm. "You better behave yourself. Don't make me have to rescue you."

He smirks before he pulls me in for a hug. "I make no promises."

PART TWO
UNCOVERED

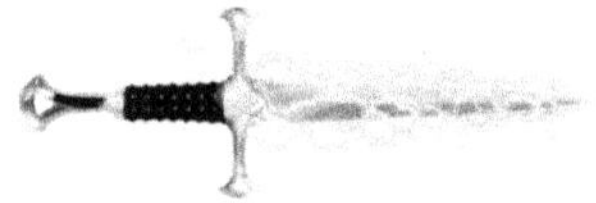

CHAPTER THIRTY-NINE

ANASTASIA

My family and I had a wonderful Christmas. We spent most of the day reminiscing about Dad. Surprisingly, talking about him on the anniversary of his death didn't hurt like I thought it would. It felt good to focus on how great of a dad he was rather than why he's no longer with us.

Graham stopped by that evening and met my family for the first time. We exchanged gifts and watched a Christmas movie together. It was nice to spend time with him without the stress of school hanging over us, even if the awkwardness between us still lingered. I didn't let it affect my holiday cheer, though. It felt great to be home celebrating with my family.

Once the holidays were over, I was eager to get back to Arken. I missed the hustle and bustle of school and getting to see my friends every day. I'd gotten so used to the life I built there that it felt weird being home, doing nothing.

But honestly, I just wanted to get away from my family before I slipped up and told them the truth about Dad. Whenever he was brought up in conversation, it took every bit of strength I had not to tell them who he really was.

I always thought I had the best dad, but after everything I've learned about his job and what was expected of him, I've realized I didn't know the half of it. My dad never showed us how tired he was, he never raised his voice at us, and he never made us feel like we were bothering him. He literally left the stresses of his job at the door.

My dad was an amazing person, and I hate that I can't share how great he was with my family. But I hope I'll be able to once Xander and I figure out what happened to him.

Xander's been calling me every few days during break to check in and see how I'm doing. I think he still worries about me after the assault. I decided to share my struggles regarding Dad with him last night.

"How about I come over tomorrow to take your mind off it?" he suggested. "You could show me around all your old haunts and give me the true Wellington experience."

"I don't think you realize how boring Wellington actually is."

"It can't be any more boring than spending another day staring at these same four walls in my room," he stated. "I might lose my mind if I have to."

"Oh, you poor thing," I said sarcastically, "trapped in your luxurious mansion with only a sprawling estate to keep you entertained."

"I appreciate your sympathy," he said seriously, so I sighed dramatically in response.

"If you're going to twist my arm, then fine, you can come over. I'd hate to be the one to blame for you dying of boredom."

We hung up not long after that and my stomach has been twisted in knots since. Xander's supposed to show up any minute now and I'm worried about how my family will react to him. I didn't give them any specifics on who was visiting. I only told them a friend from school was coming over.

I take a deep breath and blow it out slowly when I hear a knock at the front door. I rush to it before any of my siblings can beat me there, and I'm greeted by Xander's easy smile. He's bundled up against the cold in a long black coat and a black beanie as thick snowflakes fall behind him. I smile back at him and gesture for him to come inside.

As I guide him into the house, I find my family gathered outside of the living room, waiting to be introduced. Daphne's mouth drops open as soon as she sees him. She quickly shuts it, then looks at me with raised eyebrows. I roll my eyes at her and fight the smile tugging at my lips. That's exactly how I expected her to react to him.

Xander immediately walks over to my mom and extends his hand to her. "Thanks so much for letting me come over today, Mrs. Galanis. Your daughter was gracious enough to invite me when she heard I was going out of my mind with boredom."

"It's nice to meet you, Mr...." My mom pauses, waiting for Xander to tell her who he is.

"Thyellas. But you can just call me Xander."

I watch my mom's and sister's eyes widen when they recognize his name.

"Wait! You're Xander Thyellas?" Daphne asks excitedly. "Aren't you the Grand Leader of Zoin? At least, my history teacher said you should be now that your father's gone."

My mom jabs Daphne in the side with her elbow to shut her up, but Xander's unaffected by the mention of his father's murder. "I'm not the Grand Leader yet," he clarifies with a smile. "My uncle wants me to graduate from Arken before I take on the role."

"Oh wow," Daphne says. "And you're seriously friends with *my* sister?"

Xander laughs at that. "I know. Surprising, right? Thankfully, your sister was kind enough to allow me into her social circle. It took a lot of begging, though."

I roll my eyes at him, and he grins in response.

"I'm sorry, Mr. Thyellas," Mom cuts in, wringing her hands. "If I'd known you were coming, I would've prepared a proper meal for you."

Xander shakes his head and says, "That's kind of you, Mrs. Galanis, but not at all necessary. Ana's talked so highly of your cooking that I'm just happy I finally get to try it. I don't need anything special. I'm actually looking forward to the meatloaf she said you were making tonight."

I watch a blush spread across my mom's cheeks as she smiles. It looks like he's charmed even her.

Xander shifts his attention to my brothers, who stand awkwardly to the side. He then kneels so he's at their eye level as he introduces himself.

"What does Grand Leader mean?" Christos asks once introductions are finished.

"It means I get to tell people what to do."

"Really?" DJ asks, clearly surprised.

"Yep." Xander leans in with a conspirator's smile. "If I tell everyone they have to eat ice cream for dinner, then that's what they have to do."

DJ and Christos look at each other with faces full of excitement.

"So, when do you become Grand Leader exactly?" DJ asks and Xander laughs.

"Not fast enough, dude," he says while ruffling my younger brother's hair.

Xander straightens and extends a hand to my sister next. She accepts it with a blush. "I'm Daphne."

"It's nice to finally meet you, Daphne. I've heard a lot about you from Ana." My sister smiles wide at that.

When Xander extracts his hand from my sister's grip and turns to me, I see Daphne's mouth drop open again out of the corner of my eye. It looks like she's already enthralled by my friend.

"Are you ready for the true Wellington experience?" I ask, eager to get him away from her before she makes him uncomfortable.

"I was born ready."

I guess Xander decided a true Wellington experience involved us walking everywhere. It wasn't an absurd idea since Wellington *is* such a small town, but it was a strange request in the middle of winter. Thankfully, we had his wind to keep us warm.

I spent the first few hours of the tour showing him my old high school, the wooded area where my classmates would often throw parties, and the hilltop where teens would go to hook up. We stopped at my favorite cafe, The Lucky Dog, for lunch afterwards. While we ate, Xander asked follow-up questions regarding what I'd shown him so far.

Our last stop of the tour was one requested by Xander: where my dad used to train me. He knew I'd been avoiding it since Dad's death.

Cresting the hill and taking in the field where I spent many nights and weekends with my dad was a lot harder than I thought it'd be. It was the backdrop of all my favorite childhood memories, but it was hard to look at it now without the person that had a starring role in each one beside me.

Somehow, I remained strong as we walked through the clearing, and I told Xander about the different exercises my dad would make me do. That strength instantly disappeared when I saw my dad's favorite knife sticking out of the tree we used for target practice. He forgot it last time and said he'd come back for it another day.

He never got the chance…

The sight of it had my heart feeling like it was shattering into a million pieces. The tears started flowing then and wouldn't stop.

Xander hesitated for only a second before he pulled me to his chest and wrapped his arms around me. He didn't say a word, just held me close and let me cry. His warmth reminded me I wasn't alone, and it helped more than I thought possible.

We stood like that for a long time atop the hill that was once my favorite place in the entire world. I think it was the first time I truly grieved Dad. I didn't have anyone else to worry about so I could finally focus on how *I* was feeling, and I was devastated.

Losing my dad meant I lost not only my biggest supporter, but my best friend too. Going through life without him may be getting easier as time passes, but it still hurts. And I think it always will. I lost a piece of me the day he died. A piece that'll never come back.

The silence that had fallen over us while I cried finally broke when my stomach growled, reminding us it was almost time for dinner. We both laughed despite the situation.

"Looks like I better get you home, Spy. Your mom's meatloaf is calling. Are you ready to go?"

I nodded as I pulled out of his embrace and brushed away the remaining traces of my tears. "Yeah. Let's go."

Sadness still clings to me when we return to my house and see my mom pulling the meatloaf out of the oven. I take our coats so I can hang them up while Xander heads to the kitchen to help my mom with the heavy dish. I'm grateful when we're all gathered around the table, digging into the meal my mom prepared, several minutes later. I don't feel like spending time alone with my thoughts right now.

"Mrs. Galanis, I think this might be the best meatloaf I've ever had," Xander gushes while taking another bite. "Ana definitely didn't exaggerate when she talked about how good your cooking is."

"Oh, Xander, you flatter me," my mom says with flushed cheeks. "It was nothing. *Really*. I just threw some meat into the oven."

Xander smiles at my mom and my heart swells. I love how well he's getting on with my family.

"So…What was it like growing up in a mansion?" Daphne asks. "Did you have parties all the time?"

"Oh, *all* the time," Xander says and I can tell by his tone that he's joking. "If my mom bought a new pair of shoes, then we *had* to have a party. A new pair of earrings? Three parties, minimum. I was drowning in parties by the time I was ten."

Daphne sighs wistfully, oblivious to his exaggerated tone. "I can't imagine what that must've been like." She gives Xander a playful grin after that. "Was it hard to learn how to do your own laundry on campus or do your servants still come and do it for you?"

Xander throws his head back and laughs. He then looks at me and shakes his head. "You Galanis girls are all the same, aren't you?"

"Just wait until I get started," my mom jokes and we all laugh. I can't remember the last time I've felt this happy here. Probably sometime before Dad died.

The rest of dinner is spent in good conversation. My mom and

Xander end up discussing ungifted prejudice. My mom's eyes are gleaming when Xander explains that his biggest goal as Grand Leader is to eliminate the divide between the two classes in Zoin. She even looks at me and nods her approval as he explains how he'll make it a reality.

All too quickly, dinner ends and Xander announces he should head home before it gets too late. My family busies themselves with clearing the table as I walk him to the door.

"Thanks for coming over today, Xan. I had a lot of fun. It was nice getting out of the house. Even if it was just to walk around town."

"Of course, Spy. I had a lot of fun, too." A devilish grin spreads across his face. "I especially loved hearing those embarrassing stories at the hookup spot. I might have to use a few of them to motivate you during a training session."

"You do, and I'll castrate you," I try to threaten as I point a finger at him, but I say it while fighting back a laugh so the effect is ruined.

We're both stunned into silence when I open the front door and we're met with two feet of snow. It completely blocks the exit and piles around Xander's car.

I turn to him and grimace.

He shrugs. "Don't worry about it. I should be able to get myself out no problem."

My mom's stern voice comes from the kitchen. "Absolutely not. It won't be safe to drive in these conditions and I won't have the future Grand Leader of Zoin risking his life. You'll stay here tonight." There's no room for argument in her tone.

Xander gives me a surprised look and I smile at him, excitement already bubbling inside of me. "Welp, looks like you're staying, Your Highness."

"Yeah. I guess so." His smile mirrors my own.

CHAPTER FORTY

ANASTASIA

Xander and I help my family clean up the kitchen. While I'm wiping down the table, I ask them what we should do tonight since we're snowed in and have a guest to entertain now.

"You guys don't have to do anything special on my behalf," Xander insists. "I'm up for whatever you guys want to do."

Daphne and DJ exchange a look as smiles spread across their faces.

That can't mean anything good.

I groan when they both shout, "Game night!"

Xander gives me a confused look, so I say, "You thought I was competitive? Wait until you play board games with my family."

My siblings search the house and pull out all the board games they can find while Xander and I prepare the living room for the war that's about to ensue.

My mom brings us all mugs of cocoa while we settle into our seats. I make sure to sit next to Xander on the couch, positioning myself so I can protect him from any game pieces that may be thrown his way.

"Our guest gets to choose the first game," my mom announces as she joins Xander and I on the couch.

Xander ends up picking Clue and I don't have the heart to tell him he's made a grave mistake. When it comes to the games we have, Clue is the one that tends to cause the most arguments.

I spend the next thirty minutes making educated guesses and deflecting insults as if my life depends on it. Xander gives me a shocked look after he's declared an idiot for guessing the murder occurred in the dining room. He stifles a laugh when I remind him that I warned him my family's vicious.

"The dining room card is right there, Xander," Daphne reminds while pointing to the center of the board. "Pay attention."

Xander and I have a hard time containing our laughs after that. Thankfully, Christos wins during his next guess. Hopefully, that means we can now move on to a less competitive game.

My hopes are quickly dashed when Christos chooses Monopoly —our second worst game for arguments. I blow out a slow breath. *It's going to be a long night.*

Luckily, my mom announces that it's bedtime an hour later, so Monopoly is cut short before any game pieces are thrown at me or Xander. It was definitely getting close to that point.

When my mom and brothers leave to get ready for bed, I hurry to my room and quickly change into pajamas. I don't want to leave Daphne alone with Xander for too long. She'll try to tell him all my most embarrassing stories if I do—the ones I haven't already told him.

I also find a few things for Xander to wear in a box of my dad's old clothes. He gives me a grateful smile when I hand them to him.

Daphne stands after Xander leaves to get changed in the bathroom, stating she's going to bed too, but I can see through her lie. She just wants to leave Xander and I alone, hoping something will happen.

My sister's been giving me looks ever since I sat next to him on the couch. It's clear she thinks we're interested in each other. The way she waggles her eyebrows when she turns off the lights in the living room confirms it.

"Have fun," she drawls as she leaves, and I roll my eyes in response. She's ridiculous.

The fire burning in the hearth casts a warm glow over the living room. I'd consider it romantic if I were sitting here with Graham. As I settle onto the couch and pull a blanket over me, I realize that's the first time I've thought about him all day. *Huh.*

I try not to think about the romantic ambiance as my best friend returns and settles in on the other end of the couch. His long legs stretch all the way to my side, so I position myself between them while he tugs on my blanket, forcing me to share it.

"You weren't kidding about your family being competitive," Xander says with a chuckle once he's comfortable. "I thought DJ was going to bite my head off when I bought the Reading Railroad before he could."

"He probably would've if the game went on much longer. Why do you think I sat next to you? I was trying to shield you from any game pieces they might throw at you."

Xander gives me a playful grin. "And here I thought you wanted to be close to me because you missed me during break."

My heart does a somersault in my chest, and I suddenly find myself breathless. I quickly change the subject to make the fluttering in my stomach cease. "Were you able to get ahold of your mom?"

"Yeah, but I told her I'm staying at Tony's tonight," he explains. "I didn't want to deal with any prying questions she might have about me sleeping over at a girl's house."

"Is she that bad?"

He sighs and shakes his head. "No. She just worries about me and seems to think a girl will solve all my problems. I don't want to get her hopes up or give her the wrong idea about us."

"It's sweet that she cares."

"Yeah…" He trails off before his eyes crinkle with concern. "What about you? How're you feeling after today?"

"Okay…I think." I run my hands over my face. "I know it's good that I finally took the time to grieve my dad, but it also feels a lot like letting him go."

Xander leans forward and puts his hands on my knees. "Your dad will always be with you, Spy. That's never going to change. Everything you do is because of him. I mean, just look at the way you fight or the way you hold your weapons. That's all him and his assassin training. The gift flowing through your veins is also because of him."

Tears prick the corners of my eyes. Xander's right. Everything I am is because of my dad. I grab his hands from their spots on my knees and graze my thumbs over his knuckles.

"I can never thank you enough for helping me learn the truth about my dad, Xan. I feel like I appreciate him so much more now." I bite my lip in response to the feeling gnawing in my gut. It's the same one that pops up whenever I try to connect everything we've learned so far. "I just can't help but feel like we're missing something, though. Nothing we've found explains why my dad killed yours."

"I was thinking the same thing on my way here, but I don't know what it could possibly be." He rubs his chin until his eyes widen suddenly. "Wait. Isn't the apothecary your dad used near here?"

"Yeah. It's about twenty minutes away. Why?"

"I think we should go there tomorrow and talk to the shop owner. Maybe they know something. Your dad had to have visited them regularly for your suppressants. I bet they'd be able to tell us if he was acting weird around the time he killed my father."

"Do you think that's a good idea?" I ask nervously. I want to find answers but not at the expense of Xander's safety. "The apothecary's located in Fotia and Fotians hate your family. Like they *really* hate your family. Who knows what someone might do if they see you."

He waves off my concern. "If I cover my face, they won't know it's me. It's the middle of winter. I can just throw on a scarf and no one will question it."

I smile as excitement builds inside of me. "That might actually work."

He smiles too. "Then it's a plan. We'll go check out the apothecary tomorrow."

After that, we fall into a comfortable silence that's only interrupted by the sound of the fire crackling before us. A feeling of peace falls over me. I don't know if it's from the warmth of the fire or the feeling of Xander's hand in mine as we settle into our respective ends of the couch, but I don't want the moment to end.

"I hope it's not weird, but I got you a Christmas present," Xander says, cutting through my thoughts. He pulls out a long rectangular box he'd hidden beside him and hands it to me. "I saw it while I was out shopping with my mom in the capital and knew I had to get it for you."

I open the box slowly, surprised that he got me something, then gasp at its contents. Xander bought me a Hieran knife for Christmas. My mouth drops open as I look at him with a shocked expression.

"Oh my gods, Xan. You shouldn't have!" My voice is all squeaky with excitement.

Hieran knives are extremely rare. Their steel is sourced from Etna, the dormant volcano that makes up the northernmost part of Fotia. The steel is then forged into a knife by Hieran fire benders and it's their gift that creates the unique carvings on the hilt of each knife. I've always dreamed of having one, but they're impossible to find and incredibly expensive. Most are stored in Fotian armories to be used in times of war.

I take the knife out of its box and turn it over in my hand. Its hilt is pure black but there are etchings in the wood that look like flames. I'm mesmerized by the way the glow from the fire reflects off them. It's a gorgeous knife.

I dive across the couch and hug Xander so tight that the air rushes out of him. As I thank him profusely, he smiles against my cheek and says, "I'm glad you like it, Spy."

I let him go and admire my knife for a few more seconds before I place it back in its box to keep it safe. I give Xander a sheepish smile afterwards. "I got something for you, too." I jump up and run to my room as I shout over my shoulder, "I'll be right back."

Daphne glances up from her phone with a confused look while I pull out the gifts I got for Xander from underneath my bed. I hurry back to my best friend and present the smallest one to him first.

His eyes narrow in bewilderment. "You got me a wristband?"

"Don't laugh," I say nervously. Why do I feel nervous right now? It's just Xander. "It might seem silly, but I know how stressed you can get, and I read somewhere that snapping a wristband can help manage it"

Xander smiles wide and the way his eyes crinkle around the edges sends my heart aflutter. "Thank you, Spy. That's very thoughtful. I'm sure it'll help immensely." He chuckles softly. "Or at least the pain from snapping my wrist constantly will distract me from the stress."

"That's not all…" A shit eating grin spreads across my face as I pull out his second gift.

Xander doesn't bother looking confused this time. "You got me…a second-place trophy?"

"Yeah." My smile widens. "I thought it'd be a good reminder for you. You know, since you're always going to come second to me in class."

He throws his head back and laughs, the sound of it echoing around the room. When his gaze returns to me, he smiles with a shake of his head. "Oh, so that's where we're going with this, huh?"

I nod and mirror his smile.

Before I can say the quip that came to mind, Xander's face is cast in shadow after one of the logs on the fire falls, dimming the room further. I can only see his mouth as he smirks. It's the same smirk he's thrown at me hundreds of times but something about this one is different. A sudden urge to kiss him hits me, nearly knocking me over with its intensity. *Oh no.* I try to brush the feeling away, but it only grows stronger as I watch him stretch his arms above his head. His biceps flex with the movement and it has desire pooling in my gut. There's no denying Xander's attractive, but the dim lighting makes him downright irresistible.

I'm in trouble.

I need to get away from him before I do something stupid. I stand as casually as possible and tell him that I should probably get to bed if we're going to the apothecary early in the morning. We say goodnight to each other, then I hurry to my room.

Once I settle into my bed, I silently curse at myself for even thinking about kissing Xander. He's my best friend. I shouldn't be thinking about him like that. Especially when I'm with Graham.

I'm sure it's just because of the emotional day I had. Everything will go back to normal after a good night's sleep. *It has to.*

CHAPTER FORTY-ONE

XANDER

I woke up to the smell of bacon cooking this morning and was immediately greeted by Ana's mom in the kitchen. She seemed a tad overwhelmed by everything she was trying to make so I offered to help her.

While I was busy preparing the eggs, Ana joined us, and I struggled to smother a laugh. Her hair stuck up in several places and she looked like she didn't get much sleep.

"Good morning, Sleeping Beauty," I said with a smirk. Her entire body tensed when she first looked at me, but she quickly relaxed and flicked me off.

"Good morning to you too, dick," she grumbled. She then noticed I was cooking. "My mom's already put you to work, huh?"

"He offered," her mom interjected from where she was throwing the last bit of bacon into the oven.

"That I did."

"Well, try not to ruin the eggs," Ana said with a look that conveyed how little she trusted my cooking.

"As you wish, Your Highness," I replied with an exaggerated bow.

She ignored me and turned to her mom. "Is there anything I can help with, Mama?"

"Xander and I have the cooking handled. If you could set the table, then go wake up your brothers and sister, I'd appreciate it."

Half an hour later, we were all gathered around the table eating breakfast. As we talked, I learned more about Ana's family, and I pocketed a few more embarrassing tales about Ana that I fully intend to hold over her. Like dinner last night, they all laughed and joked freely with each other. It was nice to see what a loving family looks like without trauma marring every interaction.

Once breakfast was over, Ana practically pushed me out the door so we could go to the apothecary her dad used. Thankfully, the warmer temperature this morning helped melt some of the snow around my car. I used my wind to gather the rest in a pile near the tree line.

Ana knew the shop was located near her dad's work, so she was able to direct me to it easily. We ended up parking at an abandoned store in the little downtown area and walked the few blocks to our destination.

When the shop finally comes into view, I see Ana's shoulders tense out of the corner of my eye. She's nervous and I understand why. The shop owner could have the very answers we've been looking for. Or they'll at least point us in the direction of what we seek—hopefully.

I grab her hand and squeeze it. "No matter what happens in there, I'll be right beside you, Spy. We'll get through it together."

Her eyes meet mine and she gives me a nervous smile before she pushes into the shop. A bell tinkles as we enter.

I peer around the quaint space and find that Ana and I are the only two people in it. It's rather small, but it might feel that way because of the many tables cluttered throughout it, making it hard to maneuver. They're topped with different recipe books, essential oils, and all sorts of herbs and spices.

I scrape my thigh on the sharp edge of one as I examine the natural remedies on the shelving lining the left wall of the shop. The shelves on the right appear to hold more herbs and spices.

The checkout counter takes up one half of the back wall and a drawn purple curtain makes up the other. That's where the owner of the shop appears and greets us.

"How can I help you?" the middle-aged woman asks as she approaches. With her dark hair and almond shaped eyes, she reminds me of someone I've seen before, but I can't put my finger on who.

Ana shakes the woman's hand. "We're hoping you can answer a few questions for us." The shop owner's eyes narrow so Ana clarifies. "My father frequented your shop for many years. He died a year ago and I still don't know why. We're hoping you'll be able to tell us about what he was like in the months or weeks before his death."

"Who was your father?"

"Damian Galanis."

The woman's eyes widen before she rushes to the front of the store and locks the door. When she returns after flipping the sign to say the shop is closed, she gestures for us to follow her.

I make sure Ana stays behind me as we walk through the curtain she disappeared through. We now find ourselves in a small room with a round table in its center. The shop owner has already positioned herself at the opposite end of it and indicates with a wave of her hand that we should sit in front of her.

I nudge Ana toward the chair tucked off to the side while I take the seat directly across from the woman. As I settle into it, I throw out a wisp of wind behind me so it can alert me if someone tries to sneak up on us.

"I apologize for the dramatics. I didn't want us to be interrupted," the shop owner says, her eyes falling on Ana. "You must be Anastasia. Your father talked about you a lot. My name's Esmeralda. Your father came to my store for many years. He was a good man. I'm sorry to hear about his passing."

Ana gives Esmeralda a sad smile. "Thanks. I miss him every day."

"How did he die?"

"An explosion in the mine he worked at. Is there anything you can tell us about the last time he came to your store? Was he acting differently or did he seem nervous at all?"

"No. I can't say he was. He was his usual kind self." A sad look falls upon the shop owner's face. "His kindness is why I still helped despite the tension between our provinces. I would give him what he needed in the alley behind my shop so any troublemakers wouldn't see him."

Ana's voice is full of disappointment as she asks, "So there wasn't *anything* weird about the last time you saw my dad?"

Esmeralda shakes her head. "No. Nothing weird with your dad. The only strange thing that happened around that time was that the Vice Grand Leader of Zoin started snooping around my shop. He wore an awful wig to try to hide his identity, but I knew it was him."

That piques my interest. "And you're sure it was the Vice Grand Leader?"

The woman's eyes fall on me and a strange feeling curls inside my chest. I definitely know her from somewhere. I also feel strangely drawn to her and I don't like it one bit. It's as if my power calls to her.

"Ah, he speaks. And who might you be, boy?"

I extend my hand to her and give her a cocky smile. "The name's Steven Gi." I even give her a wink to sell the charade.

The look the woman gives me while she shakes my hand tells me she doesn't believe me one bit. Instead of asking who I really am, though, she answers my question. "Yes. I'm sure it was the Vice Grand Leader. I'd know his piercing blue eyes anywhere. He kept asking about what rare materials I had in stock. Based on how squirrely he was acting, I thought it best not to give him any specifics."

Ana gives me a confused look. "What reason would Sebastian Aeras have for snooping around a random apothecary in Fotia?"

I shrug. I have a theory, but it's one I'll share with her once we're alone.

"Is there anything else you can tell us about that time? Anything at all?"

When Esmeralda shakes her head, Ana's shoulders sag in disappointment. "Okay. Well, we won't waste anymore of your time. Thank you for answering our questions."

Ana stands and I go to follow her lead, but the shop owner grabs my arm, forcing me to look at her. When my eyes meet hers, it's like she's looking through me instead of at me. Her voice has an eerie quality to it while she says, "You're starting down a path you can't come back from, boy. The winds of change are upon us. You must be prepared to sacrifice yourself for the greater good of the kingdom, otherwise, it'll be lost entirely. Sister Thyia has smiled upon you. Don't let it be for naught."

My eyes widen as I rip my arm from her grasp. I quickly stand and usher Ana through the shop in my eagerness to get away from the woman.

Once we're outside and making our way back to my car, Ana asks, "What the hell did that woman mean when she said you need to prepare to sacrifice yourself?" There's genuine fear on her face. "She's not saying you have to die, is she?"

I brush off her concern with a wave of my hand. I'm not worried about what Esmeralda said. It's likely a money-making scheme of hers. One that'd require me to come back and pay for her to answer my questions. *Not gonna happen.*

"I don't know, but I think the ramblings of that woman are the least of our concerns." She gives me a questioning look, so I say, "I think my uncle had something to do with our fathers' murders."

"*What?* What makes you think that?"

"I don't know. It's just a feeling I have. I mean, why else was he snooping around the apothecary a few weeks before your dad's death? I think we need to look into him and see if there's a connection."

We spend the entirety of the car ride back to Ana's trying to figure out how we'll investigate my uncle. Though, as we draw nearer to her house, we fall quiet. Our time together is coming to an end and I'm already dreading it. I've had such a nice time with her and her family.

I blow out a breath once I pull into her drive and put my car in park. I look at my beautiful best friend once I do and give her a small smile. "Well, it doesn't look like the weather is going to force me to stay this time."

"Yeah. it certainly doesn't." There's a tinge of disappointment in her voice that has a flurry of excitement rolling through my gut.

"I had a lot of fun, Spy. It was great to finally meet your family. They're all wonderful people."

"I don't think Daphne's going to shut up about you visiting anytime soon," Ana says with a shake of her head. "You won't be able to visit again without a flock of her friends waiting to meet you."

I chuckle at the thought. "I'm sure I can handle them." I pull her in for a hug and relish in her scent: vanilla and lavender.

"I think you underestimate the power of a group of teenage girls," she responds while hugging me back.

"You're probably right."

We sit like that for several minutes, neither one of us wanting to let the other go.

Eventually, she sighs. "I should probably get inside and make sure my siblings haven't killed each other."

I nod and force myself to pull away from her.

Classes start back up in about a week. It won't be long before I get to see her every day. I can handle being away from her for a little bit longer.

"I guess I'll be seeing you soon, Spy."

"See you soon, Xan."

As I make my way down her driveway, Ana watches me leave and it takes every bit of strength I have not to stop and ask to stay longer. She has this way of calming the chaos in my mind and it makes me want to be with her all the time.

That must be why it's so hard to leave her. Right?

CHAPTER FORTY-TWO
ANASTASIA

I force myself to go inside once Xander's car disappears down my long driveway. I head straight for my room and lay down on my bed, hoping to distract myself from what I'm feeling. My chest aches for him in his absence and I don't understand why. He literally just left. How can I miss him already?

Daphne walks into our room and finds me staring at our ceiling. She smirks and says, "You're totally smitten with him, aren't you?"

I bolt upright and give my sister an offended look. "What are you talking about? I'm not smitten over Xander. He's just my friend. I'm dating Graham, remember?"

She rolls her eyes as if she doesn't believe a thing I just said, and it has my anger boiling to the surface.

"You could've fooled me. You and Graham were so awkward when he was here on Christmas. It was like you two didn't know how to act around each other." She leans against her bed and smirks again. "You and Xander, though? You two seem crazy about each other. I mean you should see the way he looks at you…"

"He doesn't look at me any sort of way," I snap, unable to restrain my anger any longer.

"Oh, he definitely does. And you look at him the same way, Sis. There's clearly something between you two."

"Oh my gods. Shut *up*, Daphne," I shout. "There's nothing between me and Xander. I'm with Graham and that's that."

"Don't tell me to shut up just because you're too scared to admit how you feel about Xander."

Before I can throw a nasty retort her way, our door opens, and Mom enters our room with a confused look. "Girls, what is with all the yelling?"

Daphne points at me while a pleased look on her face. "Annie's mad because I said her and Xander are into each other." It's clear she thinks our mom will side with her.

Mom turns to me and asks, "Is that true, Annie?"

I huff and shake my head in exasperation. "Daphne's insinuating that I'm into Xander even though I'm dating Graham. She even implied that Graham and I aren't good together. Of course that's going to upset me."

"Do you want my honest opinion, honey?"

My mom's question has my entire body going rigid. She's never given her opinion when Daphne and I've argued. She usually just reminds us that we're sisters who love each other and suggests we revisit the conversation later. If she feels like she has to say something, then she must think it's important.

"I guess," I respond nervously.

"Daphne's right, Annie." My mom puts her hand up to stop the rebuttal forming on my lips. "You didn't seem happy with Graham when he was here during Christmas. If anything, you seemed uncomfortable. Now we don't know if the two of you are always like that, but as your mother, I hope that the man you love makes you feel as happy as Xander seems to make you."

"I don't *love* Graham, Mama. I just enjoy spending time with him. He's great but you guys didn't get a chance to see that because of the craziness with the holidays."

My mom's taken aback by my statement. "You don't love Graham?"

"Of course not. We've only been dating a few months. That's not enough time to fall in love with someone."

"I knew I loved your father within a few days of knowing him."

My voice takes on a bitter tone as I say, "Well, we all know how that worked out for you after dad died."

Instead of getting mad at my bratty response, my mom gives me a knowing, sad look. "Annie, are you afraid of loving someone because of how I acted after your dad died?"

I scoff. "Do you blame me? I saw how losing Dad broke you. I'm not interested in giving someone that much power over me."

"Oh, Anastasia, I'm so sorry. I should've been stronger for you kids. I know that. It was just hard to navigate my grief after your father died. I loved him so much. But the pain I felt after losing him doesn't make me regret falling in love with him." My eyebrows raise at that. How could it not? "I'd find him and go through it all again if I could."

"But it'd still end with him dying. You'd really go through *that* again?"

My mom gives me a pained smile. "Of course I would. I'd relive it over and over again as long as he was the one by my side. He was my soulmate, honey. I'll never have a bond with anyone else like the one I had with him."

"Soulmates aren't real, Mom," I argue, needing to force logic into this conversation so it doesn't upset me.

"They *are*, Annie, and your dad was mine. And I hope you have one out there somewhere and you're not afraid to let them in when you find them. They will only make you better. I mean, they're the other half of your soul, how could they not?" My mom closes the space between us and places her hand on my cheek. "I know love can be scary, honey, but when it's with the right person, it's worth it. The risk of losing them is worth it."

I shake my head, refusing to believe her. First, she spews nonsense about soulmates being real. Now, she follows it up by saying heartbreak is worth the risk of loving someone. Well, I think she's wrong. I saw how devastated she was for *months*. No amount of love I could feel for someone would make that sort of pain worth it.

I stand from my bed and say, "Thanks for the advice, Mom, but I think we're going to have to agree to disagree on this one." She gives me another sad smile that I ignore. "I promised I'd call Graham today. Can I talk to him in your room?"

She nods so I head to her room while trying to forget the conversation we just had. I don't care what my mom says. I'll never fall in love if I can help it. And the way my thoughts kept drifting to Xander while she talked about love makes me think I need to distance myself from him. At least until these confounding feelings I have subside.

I can't give anyone the power to break me in such a way. Not even the person who's helped heal me the most.

CHAPTER FORTY-THREE
XANDER

It's the night before students return to Arken for the spring semester, so I'm trying to spend as much time with Mom and Lydia as I can.

"That princess crown really suits you, Xander," my mom says once she returns to the living room after checking on dinner.

Lydia insisted we have a princess tea party for my last night at home and I couldn't say no. That's how I ended up with a feathered boa around my neck, a crown on my head, and a tutu around my waist.

"Thanks. I'm trying to figure out how I can incorporate it into my Grand Leader uniform."

My mom smiles briefly at my joke before her expression turns serious. "Are you excited to go back to school?"

I shrug my shoulders, trying to give the appearance of nonchalance, even though I'm excited to see Ana tomorrow. "I guess. I'm not looking forward to homework and tests again, but it'll be nice to see my friends."

"Do you have any classes with them this semester?"

"Yeah. A couple. Though, I'm not sure having a class with Steven is a good thing."

I was happy to discover I have some classes with Tony and

Steven this semester. It means I'll get to see them more. Plus, I have Weapons Training with Ana again. The classes might suck, but having my friends with me might make them bearable.

My mom smiles. "I'm sure you and Tony will find a way to reel him in."

"I sure hope so."

The doorbell rings, signaling my uncle's arrival. He likes to stop by occasionally for 'family dinner' and he insisted that we have one tonight. I'm not sure why, but after what Ana and I learned at the apothecary, I can't help but feel suspicious.

I stand and head for the door. When I open it and greet my uncle, his eyes widen as he takes in all the pink I'm wearing. "Well, that's certainly a look, Nephew."

"I call it Tea Party Chic," I say as I gesture for him to come inside. "Mom's in the living room with Lyddy. Dinner should be ready soon."

I follow my uncle as he makes his way toward the living room and watch him kiss my mom on the side of the head. "Evening, Sis."

"Evening, Seb. You look nice tonight."

Uncle Sebastian straightens his three-piece suit as a bashful look spreads across his face. "Thanks. I had a meeting with several High Families tonight, so I thought I should look presentable."

My eyes narrow at that. What possible reason could he have for meeting with the High Families? The only reason he'd need to meet with them would be to persuade them to vote for a motion he's putting forward. And my uncle hasn't made me aware of any plans he has to do such a thing.

What is he up to?

Unfortunately, I get my answer to that question when my uncle pulls me aside after dinner.

"I want to talk to you about my plan to ensure the future of Zoin."

My brows furrow. "Why would you need to 'ensure' the future of Zoin?"

"Well, with you being the last remaining storm bender, the

longevity of the province depends on your survival. I worry that the growing tension with Fotia puts your life at risk. I mean, a Fotian assassin already killed your father. What's stopping them from killing you, too?"

I bite my lip to keep from calling him a liar. He can't figure out how much I know. Not until I find out if he was involved with my father's murder.

"What's your plan?" I ask, contorting my face into one of worry. Let him believe I'm buying the story he's spinning.

"We need to go to war against Fotia."

My mouth drops open. That's definitely *not* what I thought he'd say.

What the hell is he thinking?

He notices my shocked expression, so he explains, "The war has been brewing between us and Fotia for quite some time now. If we don't act first and get the upper hand, we'll be on the defensive when they finally decide to strike and that's not a position I want to be in." He puts his hand on my shoulder as if he's explaining a tough subject to a child. "Honestly, we should've hit them the minute we found out they killed your father and it's my fault we didn't. I didn't want to act too rashly while we were all grieving."

I'm shaking my head before he finishes his statement. "We should be trying to resolve the tension between us and Fotia, not imploding the remaining shreds of our relationship with them. A war is not the answer here, Uncle Sebastian. It should never be the answer."

He rolls his eyes as if I'm too young to understand. "Sometimes war is necessary for change, Alexander."

My left eye twitches at his use of my full name—he knows how much I hate it.

I'm pissed now.

"No amount of 'change' is worth putting our people's lives at risk."

I throw off the hand he uses to pat my shoulder while he says, "This is obviously a lot for you to deal with on top of the stress with school. Why don't you give up your claim to the position of Grand

Leader? I can take it over. I know you never wanted it in the first place."

"*No.* I'll be the Grand Leader of Zoin as soon as I graduate from Arken. It's what I've been groomed my entire life to do and I'm going to do it."

My uncle blows out a long, frustrated breath. "Very well."

He leaves immediately after that and I'm more convinced than ever that he's up to something. Why else would he be trying to start a war?

CHAPTER FORTY-FOUR
ANASTASIA

Classes have been back in session for a few weeks now and I've spent most of that time with Graham.

After the conversation I had with Mom and Daphne, I'm more determined than ever not to fall in love. That's why I've distanced myself from the one person I could see myself falling for.

Graham doesn't understand why I'm suddenly eager to spend my evenings with him. I certainly can't tell him it's to distract myself from how much I miss Xander, so I've made him believe it's to make up for the time we lost over break.

I've been lying to Xander since we came back to Arken, saying my new classes are stressing me out and I need to just focus on them for a while. He knows how important school is to me, so he hasn't pushed me to hang out or talk beyond a few texts here and there. I know eventually I'll have to explain why I'm avoiding him, but I'm hoping that won't be for another week or two. I'm not ready for the fight it's bound to cause.

Unfortunately, that hope is quickly dashed when he finds me studying in the Stratos Building tonight.

"You're sure up late, Spy," Xander says with a smile as he sits down across from me. "What're you studying for?"

I keep my eyes focused on the notes spread out before me. I can't look at him. If I do, then I'll want to talk to him and any control I've had since coming back to Arken will instantly disappear.

"I have a test in Poisonous Plants tomorrow" is my clipped response.

"Ah. How's that class going? You learn how to kill someone yet?"

The deep timbre of his voice calms me in a way I hadn't realized I missed. It has my gaze drifting to him in a moment of weakness. He looks happy to be talking to me—which only makes me feel guilty—but he's also drenched in sweat.

I ignore his questions and instead ask my own, "What're *you* doing here at this hour?"

"Tony and I were helping Steven perfect a move he's been struggling with in Weapons Training. They teleported back once we were done, but I wanted to walk since it's a nice night."

A small smile is the only response I give. I'm afraid if I say more to him, I won't be able to stop. I force my attention back to my notes, hoping that's the end of our conversation.

"Did I do something to upset you, Spy?"

The worry in his voice makes the guilt I'm already feeling so much worse. It has me giving him an apologetic look. "No. You haven't done anything to upset me, Xan."

"Then why does it feel like you've been avoiding me?"

Oh gods. It looks like we *are* having this conversation after all.

"I told you. I've been busy with homework and studying," I stammer.

He shakes his head. "No. I don't believe that. When you're stressed, your hair ends up all frizzy because you've been running your fingers through it constantly. And you bite your fingernails until there's nothing left of them." He gestures to my smooth hair and long nails to prove his point. "There's obviously something else going on. What is it?"

I sigh and put my head in my hands. "Alright. *Fine.* Yes, I've been avoiding you, Xan. I'm just trying to focus on my relationship with Graham right now. We were fighting about you all the time by the end of last semester, and it was exhausting. I don't want that to happen again."

His eyebrows shoot to his hairline. "So, you're giving in to your boyfriend's tantrums? What does that mean for us? Are we no longer friends?"

"I didn't say anything about our friendship being over."

"Didn't you?" Frustration creeps into his voice. "You said you don't want to fight with Graham about me anymore. Do you think the fights will ever stop as long as we're friends?"

"I just don't know what else to do." The words come out in a whisper and my response has nothing to do with my relationship with Graham.

I can't fall in love. I just can't.

Xander leans back in his chair and crosses his arms. It makes me feel like I have to explain myself. "He's my boyfriend, Xan. I have to do *something* to stop all the fighting."

"Have you considered breaking up with him?" His anger is now front and center. "He's not good enough for you, Ana. He wouldn't be making you feel this way if he was. I can't believe you're letting him manipulate you like this."

A raindrop hits my hand, startling me. I quickly put away my notes as more start to fall around us. I can't believe how upset Xander is getting over this. I knew he'd be angry, but I thought that'd be it. The hurt in his eyes is a terrible surprise.

It's at that moment I remember what Dr. Farrogow said when Xander and I had dinner at his house. *He needs someone he can count on. I'm hoping that'll be you.*

I told Dr. Farrogow I'd do anything to help Xander, yet here I am abandoning him. I feel awful for going back on my word, but it doesn't change the fact that I need to do it.

I felt something shift between me and Xander when he visited over break, and I can't give it a chance to blossom. Love will only end in heartache. And heartache beats you down until you no longer recognize the person staring back at you. I've seen the effects it has on someone firsthand, and I won't subject myself to it. I can't.

All the emotions I'm feeling have me responding angrily. "Well, it's not like you know what it takes to be in a relationship with someone. Sometimes it requires sacrifice. You wouldn't understand that."

His shoulders tense and I immediately wish I could take back what I said. He knows sacrifice better than anybody.

"Oh, I think I understand it perfectly," he bites back as he stands. His rain falls in thick sheets around us, creating puddles on the tile. "Good luck with that."

When he storms off, it feels like he takes my heart with him.

CHAPTER FORTY-FIVE

XANDER

It's been two weeks since Ana decided she didn't want to be my friend anymore. And it's been over a month since I last heard her laugh or saw her smile. I didn't realize how much of my happiness was dependent upon her until she was suddenly gone. Now, it feels like I'm drifting through life. I don't see the point in anything anymore. The classes. The parties. None of it. Most days, it's a fifty-fifty chance on whether I'll even bother getting out of bed.

Why does it hurt so much? Ana was just my friend. I've lost friends before and it never hurt like this. What makes this time so different?

Tony and Steven have noticed the change in me, and I can tell they're worried. Steven hasn't pried at least. He knows I get like this sometimes and that I need space when I do. Tony, on the other hand, has turned into a mother hen. He's constantly texting, calling, and checking in on me. The unfortunate part of his gift is that I can't ignore him for too long or he'll pop into my room to make sure I'm okay.

I finally yelled at him a few days ago and told him to leave me alone. I couldn't take another minute of his hovering. Thankfully, he hasn't bothered me since, but I know it's only a temporary reprieve.

I don't understand how my life came to this—a constant cycle of waking up and going to sleep with little else in between. I don't know why I survived all I did when I was younger just to end up here in this endless void of darkness. Ana was the light guiding me out of it. Now that she's gone, I'm pulled back in and it's suffocating me.

After my thoughts turned particularly dark last night, I decided I should go to class today. I hoped a few of them would take my mind off my deteriorating mental health.

As I lean against the wall in the training arena, I can't help but feel like fighting my inner demons is better than sitting through this pointless class. Professor Voyd is doing her best while teaching Mastering Your Gift, but her efforts are fruitless. She expects us to follow a long list of safety rules while pushing for us to learn the full potential of our gifts. The two don't meld and somehow, she doesn't see that.

While I watch two of my classmates fail epically at having a productive sparring match, I decide I'm not going to my next class. I've had enough human interaction for the day.

When it looks like the match finally ends—it's hard to tell since they barely did anything—I blow out a relieved breath. I should only have to sit through one more before class is over and I get to go back to my room.

Professor Voyd examines the clipboard in her hand, then shouts, "Thyellas! Pyrrhus! You're up."

I close my eyes and silently groan. *Great.* This is the last thing I need today and of course it's against Kasper. Professor Voyd couldn't have picked a worse sparring partner for me. Kasper Pyrrhus is an antagonistic jerk when he *doesn't* have dirt on you—I've seen it firsthand in this class. I'm not keen to find out how he's going to use Ana against me.

This definitely isn't going to end well.

I push off the wall and slowly approach the center of the training arena, my feet dragging as I do. Kasper's already standing in his designated spot with a smirk dancing on his lips. Yep. He's definitely going to try to get under my skin.

As I plant my feet on my starting point, I take a deep breath and urge myself to remain calm. I don't want to know what I'll do if I let him get to me.

"You may begin," Professor Voyd announces once she sees we're in position.

Kasper immediately throws a fireball at me that I easily dodge. He shoots three more in rapid succession, and I quickly step out of their way.

"What's wrong, Thyellas? You afraid to face me?" he asks as I throw up a wall of lightning to block his next burst of fire. He draws closer while throwing out a few more fireballs that miss me. He then says quietly so only I can hear, "Or are you having performance issues? After what happened between you and Ana, I wouldn't be surprised if you are."

He gives me a wicked grin when he sees my eyes narrow. He knows he's found the only button he'll need to push to rile me up.

His voice takes on a mocking tone after that. "You know, we all told Ana you were bad news and should be avoided. I'm glad she's finally come to her senses." When he smirks again, I know I'm going to hate whatever he's about to say. "Her and Graham are inseparable now and seem unable to keep their hands off each other. I don't think she's missed you at all."

His eyes widen when he's hit with a burst of wind that sends him flying across the room. My classmates' gasps echo throughout the space when he crashes to the floor with a groan.

Kasper slowly stands while my anger boils to the surface. His comments confirm what I always believed. Ana's friends somehow got it into their heads that I was a bad guy, and they didn't want her being my friend because of it. Well, it looks like they're finally getting their wish. If they want me to be the bad guy, then I'll be the fucking bad guy.

I let my wind build in strength around me, no longer caring about hiding the full extent of my gift. Once it's strong enough, I flick my wrists in a circular motion and trap the two of us in the center of a raging tornado.

Kasper's hair whips around his face as he gives me a satisfied smile. "I knew there was more to your gift than you were letting on. My father was never convinced Grand Leader Thyellas was as powerful as he tried to make others believe. It all makes sense now. It was *you*."

I ignore him as lightning gathers along my arms.

"You gotta try harder than that, Thyellas, if you want to hit me," he mocks after he dives out of the way of the two bolts I throw at him.

"Dodge this, *asshole*," I snarl as I place my hands on the ground and electrify the floor beneath us. He tries jumping to avoid it, but he can only stay in the air for so long. When he comes back down, his body twitches violently from the shock and he collapses.

He doesn't pass out, though, which surprises me. Instead, he slowly stands back up and asks through clenched teeth, "How about we make this interesting?" Fire gathers in his hands, and he shoots it at the vortex surrounding us. It combines with my wind, creating a raging inferno. The heat of it singes the hair on the back of my neck.

I can barely hear Professor Voyd shouting for us to stop. I ignore her. Just like I ignore the thought that Ana will hate me for hurting her friend. That doesn't matter anymore.

I call for my rain and feel it gathering within me as thunder rumbles through the room. I dodge another fireball from Kasper, then send a tidal wave of water raging toward him. I note the fear in his eyes as he braces for impact. He ignites himself entirely before he's hit by it. Surprisingly, he remains standing once it does.

"I'll be forced to use my gift if you boys don't stop," Professor Voyd shouts. I'm surprised I can still hear her over the sound of rushing water. Our professor can drain the power from others, often leaving them without a gift for several days. It's useful when teaching a class like this, but she's never tried to drain someone as powerful as me. I'd like to see her try.

The fire surrounding us slowly dissipates, signaling that Professor Voyd is using her gift on Kasper. He falls once it's gone and vanishes underneath the water I continue to throw at him.

I can feel her gift now tapping me, trying to drain me, but it has no effect. Instead, my power continues to rage within the room as my tornado expands. The lights flicker as my gift surges in strength.

"I can't stop Thyellas!" she shouts and I can hear the fear in her words. "Somebody do something! We have to stop him!"

I ignore her cries for help as I continue to send tidal wave after tidal wave toward Kasper. I haven't seen him for almost a minute, but I know he's under there.

I don't feel remorse for what's happening. I don't feel joy either. I'm just numb.

Let them all hate me for this. Let *her* hate me.

Suddenly, I'm yanked out of the tornado by a green vine that wraps around my torso—*Millie*—and the world goes black.

CHAPTER FORTY-SIX
TONY

Steven's phone rings seconds after Professor Hawke dismisses our class for the day. Our professor glares at him, but the man appears to rethink chastising my friend because he shakes his head and mumbles something to himself before walking away. Steven's oblivious to his reaction, but that's nothing new.

My roommate checks his phone to see who's calling and a large grin spreads across his face. He smirks, waving his phone at me. "I told you I'd win her over eventually."

I don't get a chance to ask who he's talking about because he answers the call and says, "Hey, Millie! This is a pleasant surprise. What's up?" His eyes instantly lose their cockiness and dart to me. "Okay. We'll be right there."

When he hangs up, I ask, "What was that about?"

"Apparently, Xander tried killing Kasper Pyrrhus during their Mastering Your Gift class."

"*What?*" Dread settles in my stomach like a weight. Something bad must've happened for Xander to snap like that. He doesn't try to kill people. That's not him.

"Millie said she had to poison him to get him to stop. She thought we'd want to know so we can help him."

I sigh. I'm sure I'll be helping Xander a lot over the next few days. Maybe even weeks. A student almost killing another on campus is not something the school will just brush off. We'll probably have to fight just to keep him enrolled.

I nod my head in the direction of Xander's class. "Come on. He's this way."

A few minutes later, Steven and I approach training arena six. Four members of campus security stand in front of it, blocking our path when we try to enter.

"This training arena is temporarily closed. If you typically have your class here, you'll be in training arena five today," says the security guard who has clearly fashioned himself as the group's leader. His deep voice and stiff posture would certainly back that, but the way he's stuffed his hands into his pockets to hide their shaking suggests it's all an act. The dude has no idea what he's doing. I give him a devilish grin before I ignore his posturing and teleport Steven and I into the training arena.

The scene we're now in is unsettling, to say the least. Chunks of paneling have been ripped from the walls and scattered around the room. There's also an inch of water covering the space. Steven and I slosh through it as we make our way toward Xander's unconscious body. President Forester is already here with a handful of Arken's administrators. They're talking quietly to Professor Voyd, who's visibly shaken. That doesn't bode well for Xander.

The anger I'm trying to keep contained flares when I see Kasper sitting across the room. He's drenched and Millie's crouched next to him, talking to him quietly. It takes every bit of strength I have not to get in his face. I'd love to finish what Xander started. Unfortunately, I can't. Not with all these people here. Instead, I kneel next to my best friend and check his pulse. When I find that it's strong, I examine his arms and face for injuries. Thankfully, I don't find any.

Steven crouches next to me. "Why do you think he did this?"

"Knowing Kasper Pyrrhus, I'm sure he provoked Xander." Kasper seems to get off on provoking people. At least, that's the case in the class I have with him.

"But how?"

I give him a look that says, *How do you think?*

His eyes widen. "*No.* He couldn't be that big of a jerk. You really think he brought Ana into this?"

"I think neither one of us knows Kasper well enough to say how low he'd stoop to get a rise out of someone."

We straighten when Millie's voice sounds behind us. "The poison I used to knock him unconscious should wear off in a few hours without any side effects, but I'll still give you the antidote just to be safe." She hands Steven a small vial filled with an orange liquid. She then looks between us and says, "I'm sorry. I didn't know what else to do. Professor Voyd's gift wasn't working on him, and he was going to kill Kas."

Steven waves off her apology. "Don't be. Xander would've hated himself if he killed Kasper. You did him a favor."

The tension in her shoulders eases. It's her relief that has me asking, "What happened here, Millie? Why did Xander want to kill Kasper?"

"I don't know," she answers with genuine remorse. "Kas and Xander were chosen for our final sparring match of the day. Xander seemed against it and wouldn't engage with Kas, no matter how much Kas taunted him. It wasn't until Kas whispered something to him a few minutes in that Xander finally snapped. He was out for blood after that."

I don't hear the rest of what Millie has to say. Not when I turn to glare at Kasper and see him slowly standing. Whatever leash I had on my anger snaps and every bit of it is directed at the fire bender. He doesn't get to provoke Xander, then walk away while my best friend has to deal with the fallout from all this.

I'm in Kasper's face seconds later. "If you *ever* mess with Xander again, then what he did to you today will be child's play compared to what *I* will do to you." He narrows his eyes as I snarl, "The Pyrrhus name might keep you from facing the consequences of your actions in Fotia, but it doesn't mean anything here."

He smirks and his voice is hoarse when he responds. "I don't know. The long list of people who've willingly fallen into bed with me would suggest my name means something here. Unless you think there's some other reason."

I roll my eyes. It's the only response I have for his stupid retort. "Your pretty face won't matter if I kill you." I poke him hard in the center of his chest to emphasize my point. "Stay the *hell* away from Xander."

"I'm sorry. What did you say? I stopped listening after you called me pretty." His tone is taunting, and it grates on the remaining shreds of my patience.

I snap my wrist, and the dagger strapped to my forearm slides into my hand. I make sure the fire-bending prick sees it before I ask, "You listening now?"

"Careful, Telos," he responds with a wicked grin. "The school's administrators suddenly seem very interested in our conversation. You wouldn't want to risk your *friend* getting in more trouble, would you?"

My grip tightens on my dagger while my nostrils flare. Gods, I'd love to fight him right now—I really, really would—but he's right. If I hurt him in any way, the school will just take it out on Xander, and I can't let that happen.

I use my middle finger to push my dagger back into its concealed position and say, "This isn't over, Pyrrhus. You'll stay away from Xander if you know what's good for you."

I force my hands to my sides and make myself walk away as he purrs, "And miss the opportunity for another exciting conversation like this one? Where's the fun in that?"

I ignore his comment. I have to. If I don't, I'll end up fighting him and I need to be strong for Xander. I can't gut the spoiled nephew of Grand Leader Pyrrhus, no matter how badly I want to. Not when the consequences would be dire for my best friend.

Steven and Millie have finished talking by the time I return to them, so I gesture for him to help me lift Xander. "Let's get Xander to his room, then I'll come back and try to sort all this out."

"I think I overheard one of the administrators say that they contacted Xander's uncle," Millie says, trying to be helpful. "It sounded like he's on his way."

Great. If Sebastian Aeras is now involved, then this whole thing just got infinitely more annoying.

CHAPTER FORTY-SEVEN
XANDER

I wake up in my room, dazed and confused. I'm not sure how late it is but it's dark outside. The only source of light comes from the lamp on my desk.

I sit up in my bed and rub my temples. My head's killing me.

Steven, who'd been sitting at my desk, jumps up when he notices I'm awake. He approaches me slowly while his eyes search my face. "Dude, how are you feeling? Are you okay?"

"I guess. What happened? How did I get back here?" The last thing I remember is being in my Mastering Your Gift class. My eyes widen as the memories of what I did come rushing forward.

Steven must notice the distress lining my face because he grimaces and says, "Millie poisoned you. That was the only way she could get you to stop. She called me once she had you under control and said Tony and I had to come right away. You should've seen Tony when we showed up, dude," he says with a huge grin. "After he knew you were okay, he told Kasper off. I thought for sure he was going to fight him."

My mouth drops open. Tony must've been furious if he did something like that. He's usually the levelheaded one out of the three of us.

"Kasper didn't know how to feel about it," he continues. "From where I stood, it was hard to tell if he was angry or turned on that Tony threatened him. Probably both, honestly."

"Was he okay? Kasper, I mean." The reality of what I almost did to him hits me and I feel nauseous. I hate to think what would've happened if Millie hadn't stopped me.

He brushes off my concern. "Oh, yeah. He's fine." I blow out a breath as a sense of relief washes over me. "He was a little water-logged, but it's nothing he didn't deserve. It was obvious he provoked you. Tony said as much."

"And where's Tony now?" I ask, having just realized how weird his absence is at a time like this.

"He and your uncle are meeting with President Forester now. I guess they're discussing what to do about you," he responds grimly. "Professor Voyd is pushing for you to be expelled. She believes you're a danger and shouldn't be allowed around others."

I sigh, swinging my legs over the side of my bed. "*Great.*"

Steven joins me on my bed, then gives me a concerned look. "What's been going on with you, man? I know you deal with depression sometimes, but this seems so much worse than I remember." His seriousness unnerves me. It's so unlike his usually obnoxious self.

I lean my head against the wall and close my eyes. I contemplate opening up to him, but what would I even say? I'm sad because my friend told me she doesn't want to hang out anymore? That makes me sound pathetic.

"Is this about Ana?" My eyes snap open. How did he know? He must see the question in my eyes because he says, "Tony and I ran into her a few days ago and she acted cagey the whole time, especially when we brought you up. We figured something must've happened between you two."

My voice is a whisper as I say, "She wants to work on her relationship with her boyfriend. Apparently, that means we can't be friends anymore since I was the reason they were having issues in the first place."

"Damn, dude. I'm sorry."

I shrug. "It's whatever."

"You know you don't have to hide how you're feeling from me, right? I'm your friend, Xander. You don't have to be tough for me. Hell, I'm sure you remember how bad I was when Lucy broke my heart. It took a long time for me to recover from it. Heartbreak's no joke."

Heartbreak? That's not what this is. Ana and I were just friends.

"I've always found that the best way to get over one girl is to get yourself under another," he says, cutting through my thoughts. "I say we go out tonight and find you a lady. Maybe two if you think it's necessary."

"Is that even wise? I'm sure the entire campus has heard about what I did by now."

"*Please*," he replies, brushing off my concern. "That's even more reason to go. Guys will avoid you because they're scared of you and girls will flock to you because power turns them on. It's a win-win."

"Let's see what Tony thinks," I state, not committing to the idea. "He seems to be the only one thinking clearly out of the three of us today."

"Who're you kidding, Xander? I'm the only one that thinks clearly out of the three of us *every* day," Tony responds, appearing out of thin air.

His grim face has dread pooling in my gut. "What did President Forester say?"

"She made it clear that the only reason you're not being expelled is because you're the future Grand Leader," he responds with a sigh. "She said if it was anybody else, there wouldn't have even been a discussion." He runs his hands over his face. "With that said, she made it clear that there *will* be consequences for what you did. Starting with academic probation. She said if you step out of line at any point before the end of the school year—no matter how small—then she won't hesitate to expel you."

I blow out a relieved breath. "That's rather generous of her."

"Yeah. I was surprised. But her generosity won't matter if you don't pull yourself together, Xander."

My eyebrows raise in surprise at Tony's frankness. Steven sucks in a breath next to me and asks, "Are we sure that's the right approach here, man?"

"I don't know if we have any other choice," Tony replies, his hazel eyes settling on me. "I've tried to be supportive while you're struggling, dude. I even gave you the space you asked for, but you're clearly not helping yourself. The way you snapped today proves that. Steven and I have both been heartbroken before, so we know what you're going through, man. You can't let it break you like this."

There's that word again: heartbreak. Is that really what this is? I guess it would explain why losing Ana has been so hard on me. But when did it happen?

My chest tightens as I remember all the times we laughed together and the way she'd look at me while teasing me. I don't think it was a singular moment that made me fall in love with her. Instead, I think it was a culmination of all our shared moments: the good and the bad. My heart shatters at the realization.

Oh my gods.

I'm in love with her.

Tony must see the devastation on my face because he pops onto my bed and pulls me in for a hug. Steven leans over on my other side and joins us.

"I didn't know." My voice wavers with emotion as I whisper the words. "I didn't know I love her and now she's gone."

Tony rests his head on my shoulder. "I'm sorry you're going through this, man."

I nod. It's the only response I can give.

"My suggestion still stands," Steven cuts in as he lets go of me. "There are plenty of ladies out there who would love to be a distraction for *the* Xander Thyellas."

Tony lets go of me too and leans back on my pillows with his arms crossed. He glances between Steven and I, but he doesn't give his opinion on what we should do. He won't. He's leaving whatever we do tonight entirely up to me.

"I think a change of scenery would do me good," I admit. "I'd prefer we go somewhere new, though. The last thing I want is to see Ana tonight."

CHAPTER FORTY-EIGHT

XANDER

We find ourselves at a random house party on Barrow Road tonight. It's a few streets over from our usual destination on Wyndell Way. Thankfully, the party consists of people I've never seen before so the possibility of running into Ana seems unlikely.

I thought Tony and Steven would jump at the chance to flirt with some new prospects, but they haven't left my side once. Not even when a few party goers were obviously interested in them. Their care for me warms my heart in a way I desperately need right now.

The three of us have been entertaining ourselves with various drinking games since we got here, and several other guests have joined in. The games have given me a nice buzz that I'm hopelessly clinging to. This is the first time in weeks I haven't felt weighed down by all life's disappointments. It's like I can actually breathe tonight.

All that air is knocked out of my lungs when I see Ana and her friends—except Kasper, who's spending the night in the infirmary—walk through the front door. Whatever progress I thought I was making immediately disappears.

Ana glances in my direction and her eyes widen when she sees me. It looks like she was hoping to avoid me, too. Gods, I hate how much we think alike.

I get up to grab another beer. I'm going to need a lot more alcohol in me if I'm being forced to watch Ana and her boyfriend all night. Tony comes up to me as I down one. "Do you want to leave?"

I shake my head as I grab another, draining that one as well. Ana's already taken enough from me. I'm not going to give her the satisfaction of running away, too. We were here first.

I return to my spot on the couch between Tony and Steven and find that one of the girls playing with us changed the game to Truth or Dare while I was gone. I usually hate the game, but tonight I welcome the distraction it'll provide.

Once I'm seated, the blonde that changed the game meets my gaze and smiles. "Truth or dare, Xander?"

"Dare," I say without hesitation. I've revealed enough truths tonight.

Her smile turns flirty as she says, "I dare you to kiss me."

I'm taken aback by her boldness, but a dare's a dare.

Steven cheers me on as I cross the little circle we've formed and quickly kiss her. It doesn't last long, maybe a few seconds, but the girl is breathless by the time I pull away from her and return to my seat.

When I see her smirk at her friend afterwards, I remember why I hate Truth or Dare so much. The game always turns into a challenge between whatever girls are playing. They always want to see who can go the farthest with me.

Over the next hour, we play several more rounds, but there aren't any more dares of a sexual nature directed toward me thanks to Tony. He steers the blonde and her friends away from the idea every time they call on me. I give him a grateful smile after his third or fourth assist. He just winks at me while stating that Steven must give the blonde a lap dance for his next dare.

As Steven makes his way over to her, I catch sight of Graham glaring at me out of the corner of my eye. I so badly want to ask him what his problem is. He got the girl. Why isn't that enough for him?

When Ana smiles and pulls him in close, I quickly stand and make my way to the cooler. I'm not drunk enough for this.

While I chug another beer, I try to tell myself that I need to accept Ana's happy with her boyfriend. I don't understand it, but she is. And the tension that used to linger between them is nowhere to be found tonight. I guess that means her life really is better without me in it.

I grab what I think is my seventh or eighth beer and chug it too. I'm begging for the alcohol to make me forget her already.

Once I'm finished, I stumble back to the couch. I end up running into some guy I don't recognize as I do, and his drink spills on his shirt. Tony jumps up when the guy starts cursing at me and immediately gets in between us.

"You're *fine*, dude. It's not like that shirt had much going for it anyways. A shirt covered in birds? *Really?* If anything, the spill is a marked improvement to it."

The guy's nostrils flare and he moves closer to Tony in silent challenge. Tony smirks and I see a flash of steel as his hidden dagger slips into his hand. The prick doesn't notice, but he's lucky he backs down when Steven sidles up next to Tony. The guy thinks he's in trouble now because he's outnumbered. He has no idea that Steven's appearance probably saved him from a hospital visit tonight.

"Screw you, guys," he snarls before storming away.

Tony shakes his head once he's gone, then turns to me. "We should probably get you home, dude."

Seeing my best friends standing in front of me with concerned looks makes my heart swell. I'm so grateful for them. They've always made the worst moments of my life not seem so bad.

My words are slurred when I say, "I love you guys. You're my best friends."

The two of them exchange a look. Steven then puts his hand on my shoulder and smiles. "Yep. We're definitely taking you home, buddy."

I try to follow them, but almost fall when I do, so they grab my arms and wrap them around their shoulders. I'm grateful for their assistance. My vision's blurry now and my head feels like a ton of bricks. I have no clue what's going on anymore.

I hear a female voice ask, "What's wrong with Xander? Is he okay?" The voice sounds a lot like Ana's, but I know my mind's just playing tricks on me. She doesn't care. She made her choice, and it wasn't me.

Tony's voice cuts through the fog next. "We're handling it, but you need to get away from him. *Now*. You're only going to make it worse."

I black out before the girl responds.

CHAPTER FORTY-NINE
XANDER

I woke up this morning feeling awful. I've never had a hangover before and after today, I don't plan on having another. It fricking sucks.

Thankfully, Tony and Steven stopped by around noon with a weird smelling juice they said was the best cure for a hangover. To my surprise, it actually worked. My headache practically disappeared once I finished the green concoction. I don't think I've ever thanked someone as profusely as I did them in that moment.

After I felt better, we hung out and talked for a few hours, my heart warming as we did. I don't think they realize their friendship is slowly healing me.

When they finally left just before dinner, I decided I couldn't sit around moping anymore. It wasn't helping anyone. That led to me coming up with a plan to break into the Capitol Building tonight. Just because Ana and I aren't friends anymore doesn't mean I shouldn't find out what really happened the day my father was killed. It's only right to learn the truth so everyone involved can find closure.

It was a few minutes after 11:00 when I made my way to the

Capitol Building. My familiarity with its every nook and cranny made breaking in way too easy. I was in the building and heading toward my uncle's office within five minutes.

My goal tonight is to search through his secretary's things. I'm hoping she's not as thorough as my uncle. I know the documentation I found in his office after he interrogated Metallo is probably long gone, but maybe his secretary kept a document or two without realizing their significance.

I easily find the secretary's desk and begin rifling through her drawers. I'm looking for anything dated around the time of my father's murder, hoping to find something that sheds light on my uncle's connection to all this. It can't be a coincidence that he started following Metallo just a few weeks before he killed my father.

I don't get very far in my search before I find an interoffice memorandum from earlier this week. The bolded red "urgent" at the top of the document grabs my attention immediately. I quickly read it and my stomach sinks.

Apparently, my uncle plans to go to war against Fotia as early as this August, even though I told him not to. That realization has anger erupting inside of me, making me see red. Unfortunately, that's nothing compared to the anger I feel when I read his reasoning for the war. He specifically states in the memorandum that 'they killed our Grand Leader and that will not go without repayment.'

My uncle is planning to go to war against Fotia for a crime he knows they didn't commit. Why? What does he hope to gain from all this?

I have to figure out what he's up to so I can put a stop to it. We both know what really happened that day. If he still plans to go to war against Fotia despite that, then his intentions are darker than I'd hoped.

By the time I return to campus, it's just after 2:00 in the morning and my mind is still reeling from what I found.

As I make my way around the front of the Stratos Building, I run into someone coming out of it. I was so distracted I hadn't been paying attention. I start to apologize but freeze when I realize who's standing in front of me.

Ana's eyes widen when she sees me. I note the athletic wear she has on and the sweat gathered around her brow. She must've been training. But why is she doing it so late? I try to brush away my concern while I note how close she is. This is the closest I've been to her in weeks. All I'd have to do is reach out my arms and I could pull her in for a hug. That realization is torture.

I see a flash of hurt in her eyes as I slowly back away from her. "Xan, can we please talk?"

I shake my head. I can't listen to her tell me that she doesn't want to be my friend again. I'm not strong enough for that. Instead, I turn to walk away but she shouts after me.

"Xander! *Please* talk to me."

I whip around and glare at her while anger suddenly takes over. Her pleading makes it sound like our severed friendship was my decision. "Why?" I snarl. "So, you can blame me for another fight between you and Graham? Not gonna happen."

I'm taken aback when she says, "I deserve that. Trust me, I know I do." She blows out a shaky breath before continuing. "I'm just worried about. I've never seen you black out like you did last night. You also haven't attended Weapons Training in over a week, so I have no idea how you're doing."

"There's no reason for you to know how I'm doing. You ended our friendship, remember?"

"That doesn't mean I don't care, Xan. I want to know you're okay."

I'm pissed now. It doesn't work like that. She doesn't get to cut me out of her life, but still know everything going on with me. I spread my arms wide and say bitterly, "Well, as you can see, I'm fine. So, you can go back to focusing on your relationship with *Graham.*"

Ana flinches and I ignore the urge to hug her when hurt flashes across her face again.

"I messed up, okay? Do you want me to admit that? I messed up." I can hear the desperation in her tone. "These past two weeks without you have been awful. You were right, Xan. I shouldn't have sacrificed our friendship just to keep Graham happy. I was an idiot."

Tears well in her eyes as she once again tries to reach for me, but I step out of her grasp. "I'm so sorry for pushing you away, Xan. I don't think I'll ever be able to apologize enough for how I've hurt you, but I miss you. I miss my best friend, okay? I've realized my relationship with Graham isn't worth losing you over. Nothing is."

She wraps her arms around herself as I struggle to come up with what to say. I feel that familiar stabbing pain in my chest when I realize if I walk away now, then our friendship will be over for good. She won't ever push me again.

A cold rain starts to fall around us.

I don't want to lose her.

When our eyes meet, I see a hurt in hers that mirrors my own. I try to imagine what our friendship might look like now that I know I love her. I'm sure it'll be incredibly hard—our stolen moments will only leave me wishing for more—but I can't imagine a life without her smile or laugh in it. Or that wicked grin she gets on her face right before teasing me.

Screw it. I need her.

I quickly close the space between us and pull her in for a hug.

She starts crying as soon as her arms snake their way around my middle. "I'm so sorry, Xan. You didn't deserve any of this. I was so stupid."

While I hug her, I realize how much I truly missed her. Not just as the girl I love, but as my friend, too. Tony and Steven are great, but the connection I have with them is different from the one I have with her. She truly is my best friend.

My voice is gruff when I say, "I forgive you, Spy." I pull away from her and meet her gaze. "Hell, I might even be happy this happened. Our friendship was starting to have a major power imbalance. You know, with you being the smart one all the time. It's nice to be on even footing again."

She shoves my shoulder when she realizes I'm joking. But then she smiles, and it feels like I'm simultaneously undone and made whole. That feeling confirms how hard being her friend is going to be, but I don't care. I can handle it as long as she's by my side.

CHAPTER FIFTY
ANASTASIA

It's been a little over a week since Xander and I reconnected and I'm so grateful we did. The two weeks I spent without him were hell.

I knew ending our friendship was going to hurt, but I had no idea just how bad. Each step he took away from me the night of our fight felt like a knife stabbing me in my chest. And each day that I didn't hear his laugh or see his cocky grin was a twist of those knives to draw out my pain. I tried everything I could think of to distract myself from it, but nothing worked. Not spending time with Graham, not training, and definitely not homework.

By the second week, it took everything in me not to find him and beg him to forgive me. Honestly, thinking he'd tell me to go to hell was the only thing stopping me. It would've devastated me.

But my fear of rejection no longer mattered when I heard about his fight with Kas and saw him black out at that random house party. Both were so unlike him. I knew then that something was wrong, and I didn't care what he said to me anymore. I wanted to help him.

I didn't see anger in his eyes as I begged for him to talk to me, though. Instead, I only saw how deeply I hurt him. Somehow, that was so much worse. I realized then just how badly I messed up.

I know I had my reasons for distancing myself from him and my justifications seemed sound at the time. But when my plan was put into action, I quickly realized I was a fool. The whole point of staying away from him was to keep myself from falling in love. The pain I felt in his absence told me it was already too late.

I love him.

I thought I felt the beginnings of it during his visit over Christmas break, but I think I fell for him long before that. It's hard to know for sure, though. There was no big aha moment when it came to falling in love with Xander and I'm still struggling to wrap my head around that.

I'd spent the last year pushing away the idea of love. I'd convinced myself it was a death sentence. I even continued to date a man I knew I could never fall for. All to protect myself. Then Xander walked into my life and the barricades I erected around my heart crafted a door just for him. There were no warning bells or sirens as he entered. Instead, my heart greeted him and welcomed him home. I see now that pushing him away was delaying the inevitable. I was always going to love him.

We've been inseparable since that night in front of the Stratos Building, like we're both trying to make up for lost time. I can't say for certain how many nights I've stayed with him, but it's more than I've spent in my own room—much to Millie's dismay.

I think after she watched Xander nearly kill Kas, it changed her opinion of him. I worry she's starting to feel the same way about him as the guys. She hasn't said as much, but she does tell me to be careful whenever I leave to hang out with him now. She never used to do that. I try not to let it bother me, but it's hard not to when it feels like I'm losing the one friend I could always count on to have my back.

Thankfully, my reunion with Xander has softened the blow. I now have a greater appreciation for him. He hasn't once made me feel guilty for what happened between us, even though I know it really hurt him. It makes me think about how Graham would react if I put him through a similar situation. He'd make sure I knew just how badly I hurt him.

The contrast between the two men in my life is unbelievable.

I've found myself doing that a lot lately—comparing the two of them. I guess that's bound to happen when the man you love and the man you're with aren't the same person.

I keep telling myself I need to break up with Graham. It's cruel that I'm even still with him, but I just can't seem to pull the trigger. I think it's because I'm afraid of what will happen once I do. I know our breakup will affect the relationships I have with my friends—especially the one with Kas—and I'm not ready for that yet. Luckily, I have something pretty big to distract me from my worries about them.

A few days after we made up, Xander told me about his uncle's plans to go to war against Fotia. I even read them myself when we snuck into the Capitol Building last weekend and I was in complete shock. Honestly, it feels like me and Xander are having the same awful fever dream. At least, I wish we were, because the reality of the situation is terrifying. In a handful of months, life in Kalyteros could be drastically different. Who knows how a war would play out or how widespread it'd be.

On the way back from the Capitol Building on Saturday, Xander and I both agreed that we need to put a stop to this baseless war. But how?

"My uncle is having his big Formation Day party at his house next weekend. Do you want to go with me?" Xander asked once we got back to his room. "He has his own private office. Maybe we'll find documentation there that proves Fotia wasn't involved with my father's murder."

Excitement bubbled inside of me at the thought. Formation Day is a holiday created by The Sisters to celebrate the day Kalyteros was formed. The ungifted didn't really acknowledge it but I'd always hear how the gifted celebrated it in over the top, lavish ways. Growing up, I wished I could go to one of their parties just to see what it was like.

I accepted Xander's invitation that night, but now that we're on our way to his house, I'm worried I made a mistake. This is the first time I've ever been to an event like this and the last thing I want to do is embarrass Xander or his family.

Xander lightly bumps me with his elbow from the driver's seat. "There's no need to be nervous, Spy. My mom's going to love you."

I give him a grateful smile as we pull through the iron gate that marks the entrance to the Thyellas Estate. My eyes widen as I take in the sprawling brick mansion in front of me. Its white columns and colonial style gives it a stately facade that's every bit the home you'd expect for the province's leader. The large fountain in the center of the drive and the perfectly manicured grounds surrounding the house are the final pieces needed to confirm the Thyellas family's immense wealth.

I can't believe it. You'd never know how rich Xander is by looking at him. He certainly doesn't dress or act like he is.

I stop my gawking long enough to climb out of the car once we're parked. Xander guides me toward the house's entrance and once we enter the foyer, I hear a woman shout, "Xander? Is that you?"

Xander rolls his eyes. "*Yes*, Mom. Just like it is every Saturday at this time."

A beautiful blonde walks into the room with a large grin on her face. She's tall and thin and walks with an air of grace. She's stunning. She's the type of beautiful that'd make a man fall all over himself to impress her. No wonder the Grand Leader wanted to marry her.

She stops when she notices me. "Now who's this beautiful young woman you've brought with you, Son?"

Xander gestures toward me casually. "This is Anastasia Galanis. She's a friend of mine from school. I invited her to Uncle Sebastian's party tonight."

His mom approaches me and pulls me in for a hug as she says, "Well, isn't this a pleasant surprise. Xander's never brought a girl home before." She squeezes me and whispers into my ear, "That must mean you're special."

Xander roll his eyes again, having heard what his mom said

despite her whispering. "I told Ana you'd have a dress she could borrow for the party tonight. She didn't have one of her own."

Embarrassment coils in my gut, but it disappears just as quickly when she grins, clearly excited about the prospect. "Absolutely. I have plenty of old dresses that should fit you." She gestures behind her. "But it'll have to wait until after lunch. I'm in the middle of making shepherd's pie." She gives Xander an admonishing glance. "I hope you like that sort of thing, Ana. I would've made something I knew you'd like if my ingrate son had let me know you were coming."

"Shepherd's pie sounds lovely, Mrs. Thyellas. Thank you."

"Ana, *please*, call me Kate." She loops her arm through mine and guides me into the living room. Xander follows a few steps behind us.

When we enter the large space, I notice a cute little blonde girl playing with some blocks in the middle of the room. She has the characteristic chubby cheeks of a toddler, and her hair falls to her shoulders in little ringlets. She squeals when she catches sight of Xander. My heart swells when I see the huge grin on his face as he squats down to pick her up.

"What have you been up to, my little rugrat?" he asks as he swings her around. Her responding giggles are like music to my ears.

"Can we play horsies?" the little girl asks excitedly.

"Of course, but first I want to introduce you to someone." He carries his sister over to me and gestures in my direction. "Lydia, this is my friend Ana."

Lydia smiles and says, "Hi."

Xander points at Lydia. "And Ana, this is my little sister, Lydia. She's two and a half."

I playfully shake her hand and say, "It's nice to finally meet you, Lydia." She giggles in response, and I'm filled with joy. I desperately want his mom and Lydia to like me. They're the two most important people in his life.

"Why don't we let the two of them play while we chat," Kate says, steering me toward the kitchen. "I want to hear all about you."

CHAPTER FIFTY-ONE
ANASTASIA

Kate finishes lunch while I sit at the island and watch Xander play with Lydia on the floor in the living room. Apparently, playing horsies literally means playing with Lydia's toy horses.

Based on the drama that's unfolding between the horses, I'm beginning to wonder if Xander's seen some of the reality shows Millie and I have. I'm having a hard time smothering my laughter as the scene Xander sets becomes more and more dramatic.

"Patricia! I told you it was my turn on the swing," Xander says in his best little girl voice. "Don't make me tell Sir Neighsalot that you were the one who stole his juice box at lunch."

Lydia's giggles echo through the space as I turn back to Kate. I find her giving me a knowing smile that I do my best to ignore. She's already asked a couple times about the nature of my relationship with Xander. I told her how Xander and I met and that we're just friends, but she didn't seem to buy it.

"So, you've told me about your friendship with Xander," she says while throwing lunch in the oven for its last bit of cooking. "Now I'd love to hear more about you. What part of Zoin did you grow up in?"

I blow out a breath and pray she isn't classist as I say, "I grew up in a small town an hour south from here called Wellington, actually. You've probably never heard of it. It's an ungifted town."

Her eyes widen. "Does that mean you're ungifted?"

I nod.

"Oh wow! You must be pretty remarkable if you were accepted into Arken."

I give her a sheepish grin while Xander chimes in from the floor, "Oh yeah. Ana's practically an expert in all manners of weapons and fighting. Didn't she tell you that's how we became friends? She threatened to kick my butt if I didn't hang out with her."

"Yep. Guilty," I state matter-of-factly. "That's how I make all my friends."

Kate ignores our easy banter. "Well, that's awesome, Ana. Good for you. Kalyteros needs more badass women."

I describe my hometown and what it was like growing up ungifted until the oven timer goes off, signaling it's time for lunch. Xander picks up Lydia and puts her in her booster seat while I help Kate gather what we need for the meal.

Once we're all seated around the table, we dig in and I find myself moaning as the savory dish hits my taste buds. I was starving and the shepherd's pie Kate made is probably the best I've ever had. I make sure to tell her as much and she politely thanks me.

Our conversation then picks up where we left off. I tell Kate about my mom and siblings and Xander catches her up on his classes. He conveniently doesn't mention the part where he didn't attend most of them for two weeks. I assume that means his mom doesn't know what happened between us or the depression he'd fallen into. That's probably for the best. I'm sure she'd hate me if she did.

I hadn't known how bad things got for Xander while we weren't talking, either, until I ran into Tony, and he brought me up to speed.

Xander's best friend was confused when I stopped to say hi to him a few days after Xander and I reconnected. I understood his confusion since I acted all weird the last time he and Steven tried to talk to me. When I told him I was on my way to hang out with

Xander, I thought he'd be happy. I didn't expect his shoulders to tense. Xander told me Tony's always been protective of him, and I saw it firsthand during our brief conversation that day.

"And this will be a permanent thing?" Tony asks with narrowed eyes.

"Of course," I respond, unable to hide how his question offends me. "We just had a fight, but we're good now."

He pinches the bridge of his nose and blows out a breath. It makes me feel like an idiot, but I don't know why.

"You didn't see him those couple weeks, Ana. He was not okay. Xander has dealt with bouts of depression for as long as I've known him, but this was the worst I've ever seen. It was like he no longer had a reason to fight it." There's pain in his eyes when he looks at me. "I was really scared there for a minute. Every time he ignored my calls, I was worried he might've given in to it."

Tears well in my eyes and it's a concerted effort to keep breathing. "I didn't know."

"I didn't expect you to. Xander does a good job of hiding his pain under a mask of anger. It's only because I've known him so long that I can see through it." He puts a gentle hand on my arm. "I like you, Ana. I do. I think your friendship has done a lot of good for Xander over these past few months. But he struggles when people leave him so if you don't think you can be his friend for the long haul, then I ask that you rip off the band aid now. Don't string him along for another few months if there's a chance you'll grow bored of him and leave again. I don't know if he could handle that."

Our conversation ended with me telling Tony that I have no intention of leaving Xander ever again. And I've done everything I can since then to show Xander how much he means to me. I can tell it makes him uncomfortable—we've never talked openly about what we mean to each other—but I don't care. I'll do anything to help him get better. Because he isn't yet, no matter how much he tries to act like he is. I can see it clearly in the quiet moments. That's when his eyes take on a haunted look and exhaustion lines his face.

My thoughts are brought back to the present and the people I share a table with when Xander grabs my hand under the table and gives it a squeeze. There's concern in his eyes when I look at him, so I give him a small smile. He doesn't need to know I was thinking about how worried I am about him.

"What are Formation Day parties like?" I ask, redirecting Xander's attention.

"Obnoxious," he grumbles.

"*So* much fun," Kate responds with a grin. "There's dancing and idle gossip—that part can be fun if you enjoy drama. There's always loads of it. My favorite parts are the delicious food and abundance of mixed drinks. I usually have a little too much fun with the second one." She laughs when she sees Xander nod with an exasperated look on his face. "Though I think you'll love the ending the best, Ana. My brother always puts on a huge fireworks show. It's over the top and spectacular."

My mouth drops open. "Seriously? I've always wanted to see fireworks!"

Kate's excitement is palpable as she nods. "I'll make sure you have a great view of them since it'll be your first time. Xander was obsessed with fireworks when he was Lydia's age, so I know all the best spots to watch them."

Once we were finished with lunch, Xander offered to clean up so that his mom and I could have a head start on getting ready for the party. We thanked him and hurried upstairs, knowing we'd need as much time as possible.

It took a little over an hour of trying on dresses, but we did eventually find one for me. It's a beautiful, black gown with lace detailing throughout. I couldn't believe how well it fit me when I tried it on. It was almost like it was made for me.

I admire myself in the mirror for the hundredth time and struggle to suppress my grin. I think my favorite part of the dress is its cap sleeves. They give it a romantic vibe that makes me feel like a princess.

When I glance at Kate through the mirror, I see her watching me with tears in her eyes. I'm surprised to see her getting emotional, but I know it has nothing to do with me. Not really.

After what Dr. Farrogow told me about her, I have a feeling her tears are actually for her. How many parties with friends did she miss out on because she was forced to marry Alexander Thyellas? And how many school dances of Xander's did she miss because Alexander wouldn't let her see him? I can't begin to imagine her pain.

"You look beautiful, Ana," she gushes when she comes to stand next to me. There's no hint of the sadness I saw moments ago. "This one's definitely the winner."

She guides me to the vanity table next to her closet. Seconds after I sit down, she starts playing with my hair. "I think a half-do would pair perfectly with this dress. What do you think?"

I nod, though I have no idea whether it would or not. I'll trust Kate's judgment on that one.

Another hour is spent on my hair and makeup. By the time Kate finishes, I truly look and feel like a princess. She styled my hair into loose waves and pinned half of it up. She also gave me a smokey eye that perfectly accents my dress.

I thank her when I see how it all comes together, and she squeezes my shoulders from behind. "No. Thank *you*. You've made my son happier than he's been in years. I can't ever thank you enough for that." She lets go of me and smirks. "Even if you swear there's nothing going on between the two of you."

I ignore her teasing as I sit on the edge of her bed. She told me earlier that I couldn't go back downstairs until we're ready to leave, otherwise my grand entrance would be ruined. So, instead, I sit and watch her get ready.

By the time she's finished, she looks even more stunning than usual. She's wearing a form fitting, off the shoulder, navy blue cocktail dress that accentuates her body perfectly. She also left her blonde hair down and went with a natural makeup look. I can already see all the guys that'll be hitting on her tonight.

She checks herself in the mirror one last time, then announces it's time to go. She tells me to head downstairs and says, "I'll be right there."

When I make it to the landing at the top of the stairs, my breath catches in my throat. Xander's standing at the bottom of them, waiting for us, wearing an all-black tuxedo that fits him perfectly.

He must sense I'm standing there because he looks up at me. My heart constricts at the way he smiles once he sees me. He might be the most handsome man I've ever met.

I slowly descend the stairs while I urge my racing heart to calm down. The last thing I want is for it to betray how I'm feeling. Xander extends his hand to me and helps me down the last few.

"You look beautiful, Spy," he says once I've safely made it off the stairs.

I suddenly feel shy. "Thank you, Xan. You don't look too bad yourself."

He hands me a gray coat that was slung over the banister. "I found this coat for you. I figured you'd need one." I thank him as I slip it on, watching him put on his own coat while his mom comes down the stairs.

Once Kate finalizes details with the nanny watching Lydia, she turns to me and Xander. "Shall we?"

CHAPTER FIFTY-TWO

ANASTASIA

The party is in full swing by the time we arrive, and I can't believe the number of cars lining the driveway when we pull into it. The entire capital must be here tonight. How is that even possible?

When the Aeras Estate finally comes into view, I realize how. Its hulking size could hold not only the entire capital's population, but probably a few other cities too. It looks more like a row of homes smashed together rather than a singular mansion for one man to live in. It's beautiful despite its intimidating size. You can tell Sebastian Aeras loves Mediterranean architecture because it influences every aspect of his home.

"My uncle likes to show off" is Xander's whispered response to my amazement.

Kate thanks our driver once he pulls up next to the estate's entrance. I thank him too as I follow Xander out of the car.

My eyes are immediately drawn to the party happening just beyond the open front door. I can see dozens of guests in there, already dancing or talking closely to one another. My hands clench as a feeling of nervousness bubbles inside me. What do I even say to these people?

My gaze snaps to Xander when he grabs my hand. "I'll be right beside you the entire time, Spy. You have nothing to worry about. Just try to enjoy yourself, okay?"

My heart flutters. What would I do without him?

I heed Xander's advice and take a deep breath before we enter the house. I then follow him as he pulls me along through the crowd. We're heading toward the front of the ballroom where Sebastian should be.

We find the host exactly where we expected him, talking animatedly with one of his guests. He has an easy smile and he's giving them his full attention. While we wait for him to finish, I note his white-blonde hair and cobalt blue eyes are identical to his sister's and niece's. I also notice that he and Xander have the same sharp jaw and soft lips. I definitely see how one could find him handsome.

When he's finally done talking to his guest, he turns to us and grins. "Kate! Xander! I'm so glad you guys could make it."

"We wouldn't miss it for the world, Seb," Kate replies as she pulls him in for a quick hug. "Now, if you could just point me to the nearest bar… I'm ready to get this party started."

Sebastian laughs as he directs her to the one just outside the ballroom. Apparently, he has four different bars setup throughout the main level for the party tonight.

"Have fun, Sis. Be safe," he shouts after Kate as she waves goodbye over her shoulder. He then extends a hand toward me. "And who might you be?"

I shake his hand while saying, "Anastasia Galanis. I'm a friend of Xander's."

Surprise flickers in the acting Grand Leader's eyes before it quickly disappears. He gives no further indication that he knows me as he states, "Well, any friend of Xander's is always welcome. You two have fun tonight."

We thank him, then make our way to the outskirts of the ballroom.

"Did you see my uncle's face when you told him your name?" Xander asks once we settle into a corner of the room.

"Yep. He definitely recognized my name. Do you think he'll guess what we're up to tonight?"

"Not a chance," he responds with a shake of his head. "He doesn't know I searched his office after my father was murdered, so he has no idea I know about our fathers' connection. He's probably just surprised to see you here with me."

"Yeah. You're probably right."

Our conversation is interrupted by several guests approaching Xander.

A round man with a rosy face shakes his hand. "Grand Leader Thyellas! It's wonderful to see you here tonight. We don't usually see you at these types of events."

"Yeah... I'm not usually one for social gatherings," Xander replies. "Though, I'm not technically the Grand Leader yet."

A thin woman with sharp features cuts in, "A pointless technicality, Grand Leader." She waves her hand as if to brush it away. "We'd love to hear your thoughts on the housing bill parliament just passed."

The next twenty minutes are spent discussing various political matters happening in Zoin right now. Xander acknowledges all the guests' questions and answers them the best he can. His responses are mature and handled with the sort of grace one needs when dealing with differing political views. He was born to be a Grand Leader, even if he told me it's not something he ever really wanted.

When there's finally a lull in the conversation, Xander thanks each guest for their time and wishes them well. He then steers me toward the bar and whispers, "Sorry about that. I definitely need a drink now."

I brush off his concern. "Don't worry about it, Xan. I actually enjoyed watching you in action. I don't ever get to see that side of you."

He opens his mouth to respond but someone behind us exclaims, "Xander Thyellas? Is that you?" He closes his eyes and sighs before turning to face the source of the voice. "Oh my gods! It is you."

"Hello, Suzie," he replies without an ounce of enthusiasm.

My eyes widen at the mention of his ex-girlfriend's name. I take in the tanned blonde now standing mere inches from him and feel jealousy coil in my gut. She's gorgeous.

This is his ex-girlfriend?

The red dress she's wearing hugs her voluptuous body, highlighting her full chest and round ass. If that's the type of woman Xander's into, I don't stand a chance. My athletic frame leaves little to desire in comparison.

It takes every bit strength I have not to push her away when she strokes his arm. "I'd love to catch up," she says in a flirty voice, but her eyes make it clear she hopes to do more than that. "Maybe we could grab a drink? Find somewhere quiet to talk?"

I feel like I might be sick until I notice the tension in Xander's shoulders. The look on his face makes it clear he has no interest in reconnecting with her. He's just being polite.

I can suddenly breathe again.

When a new song starts in the ballroom, an idea pops into my head. I lean toward him and bat my eyes. "Oh Xan, baby, this is my favorite song. Can we go dance? *Please?*" I whine. "You promised me one dance." I push out my bottom lip to sell it.

Suzie rolls her eyes in my periphery.

Xander smirks, then gives me a flirty smile that has butterflies swarming in my stomach. "Well, a promise is a promise, Spy," he says as he grabs my hand and pulls me onto the dance floor without another glance in his ex's direction.

I can't help the smug satisfaction I feel when I look back at Suzie and see her huff in frustration.

While he wraps his arms around my waist, he whispers into my ear, "If that was you flirting, I suddenly feel bad for Graham, and I didn't think that was possible."

"You're welcome, dick," I say sarcastically, swatting his arm.

He grins and starts spinning me around the dance floor. "Thank you, Spy. *Really.*"

My curiosity gets the better of me when I remember Dr. Farrogow said Suzie broke Xander's heart. "What happened between you two anyways?"

Xander pulls me in close and leans his head against mine as he sighs. "Suzie and I dated for a few months at the beginning of my junior year. We had a few classes together and she was always super flirty. I was already infatuated with her by the time I learned she was also dating Nikolai Ischyros."

I give him a shocked look. "You and Nik were both dating Suzie?" That'd certainly explain why Nik doesn't like Xander.

He nods. "Unfortunately, it took him confronting me for me to realize. We ended up getting into a fight over it. He was smart and broke up with her afterwards. I should've too, but I was stupid. She was the first girl I'd ever been with, so it clouded my judgment."

He blows out a breath as he continues to spin me around the room. "Eventually, Suzie grew bored of me. She'd chosen me and Nikolai because of who our fathers were—what their status was in Zoin. She thought dating us would benefit her somehow. When she realized it didn't, she ditched me. I guess she decided I wasn't worth waiting around for since it was going to be years before I became Grand Leader."

I tighten the hold I have on him and say, "I'm so sorry, Xan. That's awful."

He shrugs. "Unfortunately, that's just part of being a Thyellas. I've had many girls try to date me and plenty of guys try to be my friend solely because I'm the future Grand Leader. Suzie's the only one who fooled me. I've made sure not to let that happen again."

"Yet she had the audacity to flirt with you tonight after what she pulled."

"Yeah, well, that's Suzie. She's trying to weasel her way back in now that I'll be Grand Leader in a few years."

"*Screw* her."

"I appreciate your support, Spy," he responds with a chuckle.

When the song changes, Xander whispers into my ear, "My uncle just went into a room with General Ischyros and a few of his ranked officers. I think this is the only chance we'll get to sneak into his office undetected."

The sudden reminder of why we came to the party has me saying, "Let's go then."

We find a secluded staircase off the kitchen, taking the steps two at a time as we rush up them. I then follow after Xander as he creeps along the hallway toward his uncle's office.

Once we reach the end of the hall, Xander stops in front of an inconspicuous door and ushers me inside while he checks to make sure no one's seen us. Once he's done, he follows after me and shuts the door.

Sebastian's office must double as his library because the entire room is lined with bookshelves displaying a wide range of books. If we had the time, I could easily spend hours looking through his collection. I bet I'd find dozens of books I'd want to read. But we don't have the time, so I peel my eyes away and turn my attention back to the task at hand.

Xander's already rifling through his uncle's desk, so I move to join him. I take the right side while he searches the drawers on the left. As I open the first drawer, I scan for any documents dated around the time of Grand Leader Thyellas's murder.

"Ana, look at this," he says as he hands me a piece of paper. I grab it from him and quickly look it over.

It appears to be a copy of an email from Sebastian's secretary. It looks like it was sent a few weeks ago. In the email, she's questioning his plans for war. She even goes as far as mentioning a memorandum she received around the time of the Grand Leader's murder. My eyes widen when I read it.

'I'm not sure why we're planning on going to war against Fotia when memorandum 6746B stated the Grand Leader was killed by his bodyguard.'

I look at Xander and his shock mirrors my own. "We have to find that memorandum." He nods as he hands me another sheet of paper, a termination letter for Sebastian's secretary dated a few days after her email was received.

"The fact that he fired her after she sent that email confirms my uncle is trying to cover up who really killed my father," he says, pointing at the letter. "He definitely has ulterior motives for going to war against Fotia."

"Definitely. I can't believe our theories were right."

He voices his agreement as we continue our search with renewed enthusiasm. Memorandum 6746B must be here somewhere.

When I pull open the second drawer, Xander's head snaps up out of my periphery. When his eyes then shoot to the door, I instantly recognize the reaction. He must feel someone coming—he told me about his wind and how it works. I quickly shut the drawer I just opened and search the room for a place to hide. When I come up with nothing, worry floods my veins.

I'm caught off guard when Xander rushes to me and spins me around so I'm leaning against the desk. I start to ask what he's doing but he cuts me off. "Do you trust me?"

"Yes." My answer comes easily. I'd trust him with my life.

My heart starts beating rapidly when he pulls me close, and I realize what he's planning. *He's going to kiss me.*

His eyes meet mine again and I sense his hesitation. But then his gaze snaps back to the door and he must realize he has no other option because he pulls my mouth to his. I'm immediately taken aback by the feel of his lips against mine. I've thought about kissing him more than I care to admit, but none of my imaginings did the real thing justice. His lips fit perfectly against mine and they're softer than I thought they'd be. I don't know if the sparks I feel are from the kiss or from his gift, but it's taking everything in me not to give in to it.

I know this kiss is a charade. It'll be our excuse for why we're hiding in Sebastian's office. But knowing it's fake doesn't stop me from hesitating. His lips feel very real against mine. I worry if I give in to it, then whatever barriers remain in place to protect me will instantly disappear.

My resolve doesn't last, though. Not when his hand cups my cheek and he tilts his head the tiniest bit to deepen the kiss. I slip my tongue into his awaiting mouth after that, and he smiles before his starts dancing with mine.

It feels like time stops as I get lost in the moment. Lost in Xander.

While we continue to kiss, he loosens his tie with his left hand while his right pushes down the sleeve of my dress. His hands then tangle in my hair and I have to fight back a moan. *This isn't real*, I remind myself but my hands move to his face, my body betraying me.

As time passes and my desire builds, I start to wonder if Xander actually heard someone coming. When he pushes down the other sleeve of my dress, I realize I don't care. My mind and body are now in agreement, and they don't want him to stop.

In the haze of my desire, I must've missed the door to the office opening. I jump when I hear a booming voice say, "Xander! What the hell are you doing in my office?"

Xander pulls away from me and smirks at his uncle. "Oh, hey, Uncle Sebastian! I'm sorry. I didn't realize this was your office. It was just the first room we found."

In that moment, Xander looks like every other cocky guy we go to school with. I turn and find Sebastian glaring at us while General Ischyros chuckles next to him.

Xander adjusts his tie as he smiles at me. I find myself wishing I could kiss that smug grin off his face, even if it is part of the act. My lips are already begging to feel his again.

Get it together, I scold myself. *You have a boyfriend, remember? The kiss was just to cover up our snooping. That's all.*

I hear Sebastian apologizing to General Ischyros as Xander fixes my dress straps and rights my hair. When he's sure I look okay, he grabs my hand and pulls me away from the desk.

General Ischyros smiles at us and brushes off the acting Grand Leader's apology by saying, "It's okay. I have a kid his age, I get it."

Xander guides me toward the exit as I struggle to compose myself. I keep repeating the same four words, hoping my body will listen.

The kiss wasn't real. The kiss wasn't real. *The kiss wasn't real.*

CHAPTER FIFTY-THREE
XANDER

When the door to my uncle's office slams shut behind us, I finally let go of the incredulous laugh that's been trying to escape since we were caught. We actually got away with it!

I have no doubt, though, that once his meeting with General Ischyros is over, my uncle will go racing to my mom to tell her all about it. He'll demand that she rein me in, and she'll tell him it's not a big deal. That I'm just acting my age. I wish I could say that would be the end of it, but I know my mom. She'll want me to tell her every sordid detail once we're back at the house.

I'm not sure how I'll convince her that Ana and I aren't together now, but that's a problem for me to figure out later. Right now, I just want to celebrate the fact that we found critical information that should help stop the war against Fotia. I feel the lining of my tuxedo jacket and smile at the documents tucked safely there.

I think a dance is in order. I know how much Ana loves to dance so I can't imagine a better way to celebrate a successful investigation.

After everything that happened with Ethan Caravo, I was worried Ana may never want to dance again, but she told me recently that she's fine dancing with others. It's only when she's dancing alone that her anxiety gets the better of her. And since I have no intention of leaving her side tonight, I plan to dance with her for as long as she'll let me.

Eager to have her close again, I pull Ana along as I make my way toward the stairs. I sneak a peek at her while I do, and I'm shocked to see that her cheeks are flushed. I can only think of one reason why they would be: our kiss affected her. A surge of happiness spreads through me that I quickly try to suppress. I know I shouldn't dwell on it. It'll kill me if I do. Ana has a boyfriend. She was just playing her part in our charade. Her flushed cheeks don't mean anything. They can't.

Just like I couldn't let myself get lost in the kiss. I made sure to spend the entirety of it focusing on how to make it look like we were hooking up. I did that because if I'd spent even a second thinking about the kiss and who I shared it with, I wouldn't have been able to stop. Kissing Ana has been something I've wanted to do since the first time I dreamed of her. And that desire has only worsened since I realized I love her.

I glance at her again and my heart rate spikes. She's a vision tonight. When I saw her coming down the stairs at my house earlier, I was speechless. I knew immediately she was going to be the prettiest girl at this party, and I wasn't wrong. No one else compares to her.

You're just friends, I remind myself. *You can't let yourself forget that.*

I ignore the sadness that threatens me. Instead, I bump Ana with my elbow once we reach the top of the stairs. I want to get her out of her head so she can enjoy the rest of the evening. I'm sure she's feeling guilty about what happened, but she has no reason to be. We had to kiss to get her out of my uncle's office safely.

"What do you think about a dance to celebrate a successful investigation, Spy?" I ask. "I'd suggest a dance off since you love competing against me, but I'm not sure the people of the capital could handle that."

She throws her head back and laughs. The sound of it warms my heart. "Could you imagine that? I don't even want to know what types of moves you'd break out."

"Yeah… Now that you mention it, it's probably for the best that we don't," I say as seriously as I can. "I don't want to give any of the older ladies a heart attack."

She laughs again and I'm an addict already wondering when I'll get my next fix.

Since our reunion, I've come to depend on that laugh. It's been the tether that holds me in place, keeping me from getting lost in the darkness of my mind. My depression still consumes most of my thoughts, but little by little each day I feel myself coming out of it. And I owe a large part of my healing to my friends. Their unwavering support is the reason I continue to push forward. It reminds me that I'm worth something. That I matter.

My grip tightens on Ana's hand as I return my attention to the woman next to me—to the light in my darkness. I guide her down the stairs and back to the dance floor, following her lead as she begins dancing to the upbeat song blasting through the speakers. I quickly get lost in the moment. In her. She's so beautiful tonight.

I don't know how much time passes but eventually I see groups of people moving outside, signaling that my uncle's fireworks show will begin soon. I grab Ana's hand to still her and she notices the thinning crowd. A huge grin spreads across her face in response.

"Are the fireworks starting?"

I nod, pulling her along behind me. "Follow me, Spy. I know the best spot for them."

We don't get far before my entire body freezes. Ana runs into my back, but I barely register it. I can only hear the roaring in my ears, feel the weight of the room pushing down on me.

She comes around to look at me. "Xan, what's wrong? Why did we stop?"

Her voice releases whatever hold my fear has on me. *I need to get her out of here.*

"We need to go."

Her brows scrunch together. "*What?* Why? The fireworks are about to start."

"*We need to go,*" I say again, my tone coming out harsher than I intended. We don't have time for her to argue. I need to get her away from this place as quickly as possible. Thankfully, she concedes without further argument.

I drag her toward the front of the house and away from the green-haired torturer I saw lingering outside the ballroom. *Dr. Diavolos.* I don't know what he's doing here but his presence can't mean anything good.

I need to get us out of here before he notices me. Before he notices Ana. The last thing I want is for him to see us together. She doesn't need to be a target in his twisted obsession with me.

Once Ana and I are outside, I signal for an awaiting limo while Ana wraps her arms around herself as the crisp winter air settles over us. I'd rushed us out so quickly I forgot to grab our coats. I give her my suit jacket to warm her as the limo pulls up, then shove her inside it and follow after her.

I don't let myself relax until the limo is on the road, heading toward my house. That's when I finally lean back against the seat and blow out a breath.

Ana gives me a confused look when I do. "What's going on, Xan? Why did we run away from the party?"

I get a sudden, intense urge to tell her everything about my past. About what that evil man did to me. I want her to know every part of me. If there's any hope for her to love me back someday, then she needs to know. I close the partition so the driver can't hear what I'm about to share and throw out my wind as an extra layer of protection.

Her eyes drift to mine after that and it's the warmth I see in them that has the words spilling out of me. How I was punished by my father for years for 'embarrassing him.' How he hired a man to punish me when he became too busy to do it himself. How that evil man would chain me in a storage closet and beat me for as long as my father would allow. How I had to use my own wind to cover my screams, otherwise I'd be punished worse, because gods forbid someone find out what was happening to me.

I tell her how Dr. Diavolos delighted in my pain and actively sought out ways to hurt me worse. How most nights I'd be left hanging there, blood dripping from me, begging for The Sisters to end my suffering. How my father would chastise me for not being stronger when he'd finally come to release me. How the sight of Dr. Diavolos tonight brought back the fear, shame, and desperation I grew up feeling. The very feelings I've been trying to forget for years.

She doesn't say a word while I share what I went through. An occasional sniffle is the only sound that comes from her.

When I finish retelling the horrors I endured and work up the courage to look at her, I don't see judgement in her eyes. I didn't expect there to be, but relief washes over me anyways. I give her a small smile to try to lighten the mood, but it only causes tears to well in her eyes. She wraps her arms around me after that and pulls me in for a hug.

"Oh, Xan, I'm so sorry that happened to you. You didn't deserve any of that."

I melt into her touch. It feels so good to finally reveal that part of my past to her.

She continues to hold me until we arrive at my house. She then thanks the limo driver for both of us as we crawl out of it.

She grabs my hand once the driver pulls away and I suddenly dread the thought of her leaving. "Do you want to stay tonight?" My voice has an edge of desperation to it that I don't like.

Her eyes soften when she looks at me. She knows I need her tonight. "Yeah. Sure. I'm not ready to go back to Arken anyway." I know she's lying for my sake, but I accept it.

We end up spending the rest of the night talking in my room. She doesn't bring up what I shared with her, even though I know she has questions. Instead, she keeps the conversation light. I appreciate it more than she'll ever know.

I lose track of time as we talk. The only indicator that hours have passed is the fire in the hearth slowly decreasing in size, dimming the space more and more.

As the room grows darker, I find my thoughts drifting to the kiss Ana and I shared and how I'd love to do it again. Her wearing my clothes isn't helping that.

She hadn't planned on staying tonight so she didn't pack an

overnight bag. She couldn't exactly sleep in the gown she wore to the party, so I let her borrow a pair of sweatpants and a T-shirt of mine to sleep in. The sight of her in them only makes me want to tear them off her. I resist the urge but it's growing increasingly difficult to. Especially when she glances at my lips a couple times while we're talking. It tells me she's thinking about kissing me too.

Gods, what I'd give to be able to lay her back against my bed and spend the rest of the night making her moan my name. I'd worship every inch of her and show her how she deserves to be loved.

I dig my nails into my palms to prevent my hands from doing something I'll regret. *Get it together, Thyellas.*

By the grace of the gods, I maintain my composure long enough for her to announce that she should get to bed. I show her to the guest room after that and bid her goodnight with the remaining shreds of my control.

When I finally make it back to my room, I throw my head against my pillow and run my hands over my face. I don't know how long I'm going to be able to stop myself from acting on my desires. Especially when Ana looks at me like she did tonight. I know I need to be strong, but her mere presence makes me weak in the knees.

I fall asleep thinking about the feel of her lips against mine.

Ana and I have breakfast with my mom and Lydia before we head back to campus.

I thought my mom would bring up what happened in my uncle's office as soon as we sat down to eat, but she didn't. Instead, she discussed whatever drama unfolded last night between a couple party guests whose names I don't recognize.

But I do know my uncle told her about what happened. The pointed look she gives me when she says she's disappointed Ana and I missed the fireworks last night tells me as much.

I ignore *all* my mom's pointed looks as I eat. This isn't the time to discuss what happened between me and Ana.

Luckily, Ana distracts my mom with questions about the single guys at the party last night. It would seem Ana's intrigued by my mom's romantic prospects. She doesn't know yet that my mom has no interest in dating after my father. His cruelty destroyed any dreams she had of falling in love and growing old with someone. She admitted to me recently that she views marriage as a cage. One she has no intention of ever entering again.

Before long, breakfast comes to an end and we're saying goodbye to my mom and Lydia. I scoop up Lyddy and give her a big squeeze as I tell her I'll see her in a few days. Her tiny arms wrap around my neck as she says, "I wuv you."

I put her down and crouch so that I'm eye level with her. "I love you, too, Lyddy. Be good for Mom, okay?" She nods and gives me a toothy grin.

I hug my mom next and tell her I'll see her at our usual time on Saturday.

She squeezes me and whispers, "Don't think you're getting out of telling me what happened in your uncle's office last night. I expect to hear all about it the next time you come over."

I blow out a breath as I pull away from her, then give her a devious grin. "I have no idea what you're talking about."

"Uh-huh. I'm sure," she responds with an eye roll, then strokes my cheek. "I'll see you Saturday, honey."

"See you then, Mom."

Ana smiles as I approach her, ready to leave. I smile back, unable to help myself.

Our return to campus is a quiet one. We're both exhausted from how little sleep we got. I know Ana needs to study so I didn't want to keep her at my place for too long. Unfortunately, that means we got maybe four hours of sleep last night.

I can see the bags under her eyes when I finally drop her off at her dorm. Her exhaustion won't sway her, though. She'll study for as long as she needs, and she'll somehow retain all of it. Her brilliance never ceases to amaze me.

"Thanks for inviting me last night, Xan," she says with a smile. "I had a lot of fun."

"Of course, Spy. It wouldn't have been a proper investigation without you." I clench my hands, forcing them to remain at my side. "Have fun studying today."

She waves goodbye, then makes her way inside her dorm. My eyes follow her until she disappears. I ignore the longing I feel once she does and return to my own dorm.

CHAPTER FIFTY-FOUR
ANASTASIA

It's been nearly a week since Sebastian Aeras's Formation Day party, but I find myself thinking about that night constantly. A lot of things happened then. Major things.

I'm still shocked Xander told me about the torture he endured growing up. It was so much worse than Dr. Farrogow described. He was not only forced to cover his own screams, but he'd be left to hang there until his father bothered to release him. I can't believe it. Xander was just a kid. He didn't deserve that.

For the first time, I find myself grateful my dad killed that awful man. Alexander Thyellas deserved to die for how he treated his son.

But Xander opening up to me in the back of that limo isn't the part of the night my mind drifts to the most. Not even close. It's the kiss we shared that haunts me and I imagine I'll be chasing its ghost for quite some time.

Unfortunately, I haven't really seen Xander since he dropped me off at my dorm on Sunday morning. Classes have been crazy this week. I had tests in two of them, got assigned a project that's due next week in a third, and had to finish a paper for a fourth. I didn't have any time to spare to see him. Or anyone else for that matter. I pretty much lived in the library all week.

That's why I'm happy the guys wanted to go out tonight. I'm looking forward to blowing off some steam. Though, now that we're out, I'm not sure how much dancing I'll actually get to do. I can usually get Millie to dance with me, but she's visiting her abuelita this weekend. That means I'm at the mercy of whatever the guys want to do and right now they want to play beer pong.

I glance around the room when Kas makes the winning shot. The party's already packed, but it doesn't look like Xander's here yet. I try to ignore the disappointment I feel because of it.

When they swap partners and prepare for a second game, I tell them I'll be right back. I need another drink if I have to watch more of that stupid game.

As I grab a beer out of the cooler, a deep voice says behind me, "I'm surprised you're not on the dance floor. I thought for sure you'd want to show off the moves I taught you last weekend."

A huge grin spreads across my face when I turn and find Xander standing behind me, wearing his usual black T-shirt and baggy jeans, with a smirk dancing on his lips.

"I guess the better question is why *you're* not out there," I quip. "You proved you're quite the dancer at your uncle's party."

He gives me a mischievous look. "My moves are strictly saved for when I'm stuffed into a suit and in the perfect spot for all the wealthy widows to watch. I gotta find my sugar mama somehow. I can't be giving away my moves for free at college parties."

I playfully shove him while fighting back a laugh. "You're absurd."

"Absurd or a genius?"

"*Absurd.*"

He grins and gestures toward the dance floor. "Did none of your friends want to dance with you?"

I shake my head. "But that's okay. It's good to mix it up sometimes."

"*Please.* You love dancing. Especially when you've been stressed, and you just had a very stressful week." He puts his hand out for me to grab. "Come on. I'll dance with you, Spy."

My stomach flutters at his suggestion, but I find myself glancing in Graham's direction. He's still playing beer pong and laughing with Kas. It doesn't look like he's even noticed I'm gone. That fact has me turning back to Xander and asking, "What about your sugar mamas?"

"I'll find a way to make it up to them," he responds with a smile.

I smile back at him and let him lead me to the dance floor. One dance won't hurt. Graham will still be playing this round of beer pong by the time we're done so he won't even notice. Besides, Xander's right, I could really use a dance.

He spins me onto the dance floor when the next song starts, and we sway together in time to the upbeat tempo of the music.

We're about halfway through the song when a familiar voice shouts to our right, "Wait just one minute. Is that Xander Thyellas *dancing*? Somebody, get me a doctor. I must be hallucinating."

Xander gives an exasperated shake of his head, but he smiles when Tony and Steven join us. The first thing Steven does is touch Xander's face. "Oh my gods! It *is* real. Xander's dancing at a party."

Xander shoves his shoulder and says, "Yeah. I am. Let's see if you can keep up, Gi."

Within seconds, the four of us are dancing obnoxiously together and I nearly fall over from laughing too hard when Steven dips Tony with a dramatic flourish. It feels like my heart might explode with happiness. This is exactly why I love parties.

The first song finishes *way* too quickly so I decide to stick around for another. I'm having too much fun. I'm not ready for it to end.

Before I know it, three more songs have come and gone so I tell them I need to check in with my friends. After they wave me off, I hurry to where I last saw Graham. I'm worried he might've seen me dancing with Xander and I know he'll be mad if he did.

I'm already thinking of ways to diffuse the situation when I turn the corner, but I find Graham right where I left him. He smiles when he notices me. "There you are! We were wondering where you went."

I smile back at him, but guilt gnaws at me as I do. I knew dancing with Xander would bother him, but I did it anyway. I really need to break up with him if I'm going to continue to act so self-ishly. The last thing I want to do is hurt him more than I already have.

That guilt keeps me by Graham's side for the rest of the night.

It's now a few minutes past one and the party doesn't seem to be slowing down anytime soon.

While Nik shuffles the deck for our next round of Kings, I head to the cooler to grab a beer. Xander comes up behind me as I do and whispers in my ear, "I'll be taking off in a few minutes, Spy, but if there's any trouble, just let me know. I can come right back. Tony and Steven are staying so they can help too."

I graze the top of his arm without thinking. "Thanks, Xan. I appreciate it." I can't help the smile that spreads across my face as my eyes meet his. I love how he goes out of his way to make sure I feel safe. He doesn't want me to ever feel like I did the night Ethan Caravo assaulted me.

He places his hand on mine and squeezes it. "Have a good rest of your night, Spy."

"Bye, Xan. I'll talk to you later."

I blow out a breath once he leaves and try to ignore how much I already miss him. I then turn to head back to my friends and stop when I find Graham standing in the doorway.

Did he see me with Xander?

I smile at my boyfriend and gesture toward the cooler. "Do you need a beer?"

He nods but the movement seems stiff. *Oh gods, I think he did.* A pit forms in my stomach. When he accepts the drink I offer him with a smile and wraps his arm around me, I feel like I have whiplash. *Did he see me with Xander or not?*

He kisses me on the top of my head once I return to my spot on the couch next to Nik, then says, "I'll be right back. I gotta use the restroom."

CHAPTER FIFTY-FIVE

XANDER

I hate to leave Ana at the party, but I had a long, exhausting week myself and my bed is calling my name.

Thankfully, Tony and Steven are staying behind. That makes me feel better about leaving her. I know they'll take care of her and make sure she's okay if something happens—unlike her useless boyfriend.

I've only made it a few steps down the sidewalk when I hear someone shouting after me, sounding angry. *Great.* Who did I upset now?

I'm surprised when I turn around and see Ana's boyfriend approaching me. He looks furious. "You have some nerve, you know that?" he shouts once he's standing in front of me. "I know you're used to getting whatever you want, but Ana's *my* girlfriend. Not yours. You have no right to be whispering in her ear or holding her hand. Especially when I'm in the other room."

I put my hands up in a placating manner, hoping to diffuse the situation. I'm not trying to fight Ana's boyfriend tonight. "Ana and I are just friends, dude. Nothing else. You have nothing to worry about."

"Did you and Ana rehearse that?" he asks as his eyes flare with anger. "Because she says the same shit to me whenever I bring you up."

"There's nothing to rehearse when it's true," I say, my annoyance with the situation seeping into my tone.

"*Bullshit.* I see the way you look at her. You're just waiting for an opportunity to swoop in and steal her from me. As if you don't already have your pick of women to sleep with." He points at me and snarls, "Stay the *hell* away from Ana."

My eyes narrow at the prick and my voice is icy calm as I say, "You do realize Ana isn't a prize to be won, right? She can decide who is and isn't in her life. Including me."

He gets in my face after that, but I just stare at him, unfazed by his posturing. "What? You don't want to fight me?" he taunts.

"Dude, you're ungifted. I could kill you with a snap of my fingers. I'm not going to fight you."

Suddenly, a fireball hits my left shoulder. I hiss at the burning sensation when a deep voice declares, "Looks like you better take me on then."

Graham steps back so he and Kasper are standing next to each other. I look between the two of them and my expression turns to one of annoyance.

"I'm not going to be fighting either of you so you might as well get that idea out of your head."

"Why?" Kasper asks, feigning ignorance. "You worried you might lose without Professor Voyd here to break it up? And here I thought you were tough, Sparky."

Sparky. A chill runs down my spine. I haven't heard that name in years. The use of it causes something inside of me to snap.

I shoot a bolt of lightning at Kasper and snarl, "If I recall correctly, it was *you* who needed saving the last time we faced each other."

Kasper pushes Graham behind him to shield him, then gives me a wicked grin. "Trust me. I don't plan on letting that happen again."

CHAPTER FIFTY-SIX

ANASTASIA

Kas left a few minutes after Graham did. He didn't say where he was going, but how quickly he moved seemed to indicate it was urgent. Neither one of them has come back yet and it's been nearly ten minutes.

When I start to wonder where they could be, I hear Steven shout from the other side of the room, "Oh my gods!" Tony grabs onto him and they teleport away a second later.

"What do you think that was about?" I ask Nik and Harvey.

Nik shrugs, unfazed.

Harvey glances out the front window, then curses and hurries outside. I look at Nik and he appears just as confused as I feel. We follow after our ice-bending friend while dead settles in my gut.

Something's wrong.

When I step onto the front stoop, shock freezes me in place. Xander and Kas are fighting, and they don't seem to be holding back. I watch Xander use his wind to fling] Kas into a tree behind him. It cracks from the impact and falls to the side, right where Graham is standing. Harvey throws out a wall of ice to shield Graham from it.

The sight of Graham almost dying has fear tearing through me. *No.*

The ground shakes underneath us as Steven asks, "How can I help, Xander?"

Nik snarls from his spot next to Kas, "Don't even think about it, Gi, or you'll be answering to me." Fear flickers across Steven's face in response.

Xander's attention snaps to Nik, preparing to intervene, but Tony steps in front of Steven first and glares at Nik. He pulls out a dagger and twirls it between his fingers. "I'd love to see how tough you are against an opponent you can't touch, Nikolai."

Nik's nostrils flare at the threat but it's Kas who answers. "No one's afraid of you, Telos. You're just Xander's bitch."

Tony teleports so he's mere inches from Kas's face. Kas startles at his sudden appearance in front of him and Tony smirks. "Where was this fire the last time I confronted you, Pyrrhus?" Tony glances at Harvey and Nik before his gaze returns to Kas. "Are you suddenly feeling bold now that your friends are here to help you?"

Kas's eyes narrow to slits as he snarls, "I don't need anyone's help to kick your ass."

My entire body tenses when Tony teleports behind Kas and puts his dagger to Kas's throat. *No.* Kas stiffens underneath it while Tony says, "It's bold of you to assume you could touch me, let alone kick my ass." He leans in and whispers into Kas's ear loud enough for me to hear. "I told you what would happen if you messed with Xander again, Pyrrhus. Did you not care or does that hothead of yours struggle with critical thinking?"

Kas's stare turns deadly, and he throws an elbow back to jab Tony. Tony's gone before it makes contact.

When my two sets of friends gather on either side of the sidewalk, glaring at each other, I finally move. I have to put a stop to this before someone gets hurt.

"What the hell are you guys doing?" I glare at Kas and Xander. "Why are you two fighting?"

Kas crosses his arms. I know he's not going to admit to anything, so I turn to Xander instead. He doesn't say anything either, but his eyes dart to Graham for the briefest of seconds. That's when every-thing clicks into place.

I whip my head toward Graham. "Did you try to start a fight with Xander tonight? Is that what you were doing when you told me you were going to the bathroom?"

Graham gives Xander an annoyed look, as if Xander sold him out, before his gaze returns to mine. "Xander and I had some things we needed to discuss."

"Oh, let me guess," I say in a condescending tone. "I bet it had something to do with the fact that I'm yours and Xander should stay away from me." Graham's eyes narrow, confirming I'm right, and I shake my head. "You're unbelievable."

Kas and Nik position themselves in front of Graham as if they're shielding him from me and I throw my hands in the air out of frustration. "I can't deal with this anymore. I'm going home." I storm across the yard, heading in the direction of my dorm.

I hear footsteps follow after me. "Ana…"

Anger pours off me when I whip around. "Don't follow me, Xander! I'm mad at you, too." I look at the rest of my friends. "None of you better follow me!"

I leave them all behind as I make my way back to campus, my anger guiding me. Something has to change. This can't keep happening.

CHAPTER FIFTY-SEVEN
GRAHAM

The muscle in my jaw ticks as I watch Ana's retreating back. I thought I was angry before, but it's nothing compared to how I feel now.

Who the hell does she think she is? How is she going to scream at me and act like I'm the bad guy here when she was the one openly flirting with Xander a few feet from me?

I'm *done*. I can't keep doing this. For months now, Ana's been playing me for a fool. She made *me* feel crazy for even suggesting something was going on between them. Well, I saw the way they looked at each other tonight and how their hands lingered. If they're just friends, then I'm the fricking Grand Leader of Zoin.

And Xander had the nerve to act like I was being a possessive jerk when I confronted him. As if he has any idea what it feels like to watch the woman you love slip away, knowing there's nothing you can do about it. Of course it's making me crazy. I don't like how I'm acting. Who would? But I don't know what else to do.

How else am I supposed to act? She's breaking my heart, yet she doesn't care.

Xander's obnoxious friend breaks the silence that'd settled over us once Ana left. "Should one of us go after her to make sure she gets home okay?"

Xander shakes his head. "No. She'll be fine. It's best to give her space right now."

His comment has me seeing red. I'm so sick of him acting like he knows her better than the rest of us. Better than me. I take a step toward him and growl, "That's not your call to make."

Kas throws his hand in front of me to make sure I stay behind him as he glares at Tony Telos. The teleporter's now staring at me while he fiddles with his dagger. I get the sudden feeling he could kill me with a single flick of his wrist.

My attention returns to Xander when he sighs and crosses his arms. "I'm not trying to make any sort of call, Graham. I'm just respecting Ana's wishes. She said she wanted to be left alone."

Before I'm able to respond, Harvey cuts in, "I think it's time we all went home before another fight breaks out. You know, to respect Ana's wishes."

Tony looks at Xander to see what he wants to do. When he nods, the teleporter grabs onto him and their earth-bending friend, then disappears.

Once they're gone, Kas blows out a breath and visibly relaxes. He puts a hand on my shoulder after that and I give him a small smile. I might be losing Ana, but at least I'll always have him.

"*Damn*, dude," Harvey grumbles. "Why didn't we recruit the teleporter to our side? I could already be in my room."

Nik pats Harvey on the back and smiles at him. "But then you wouldn't get to see our pretty faces."

"I see your face plenty," Harvey responds with feigned disgust before turning to me with a concerned expression. "You good, Graham?"

I shrug. "I don't know. I'm just so angry right now. I can't really focus on anything else."

Nik and Harvey give me their best sympathetic looks while Nik says, "I'm sorry you're dealing with this, dude."

Kas wraps his arm around my shoulders and steers me toward 306. "I think you could use another drink."

I nod, agreeing with him. I just want to forget about all this and getting black out drunk suddenly sounds very appealing.

"I think Harv and I are going to head back. You guys try not to get into any trouble, okay?" Nik gives Kas a pointed look that has Kas winking at him.

Once we're back inside, Kas immediately drags me to one of the many tables covered with liquor bottles and pours me a glass of whiskey. I shoot it, not caring that it burns my throat as it goes down and gesture for him to give me another.

While I'm downing my second glass, he asks, "So, what did Xander do to piss you off this time? It must've been bad if you confronted him about it."

"*Wait.* You didn't know why I was arguing with Xander? Why'd you fight him then?"

"*Please,*" he responds with a smirk. "I don't need a reason to fight him. Besides, if he did something to piss you off, I'm more than happy to kick his ass." He claps me on the back and smiles. "I'll always have your back, dude."

The sentiment warms my heart, but I don't know if it makes my friend brave or stupid. Xander almost killed him a couple weeks ago, yet he seems unfazed by that fact. I feel like it should've scared him at least.

After a couple more glasses of whiskey, I find myself teetering between being buzzed and outright drunk. I like the feeling. There's a weightlessness to it that makes me forget about all the crap I'm dealing with.

I thought Kas was going to join me in my binge, but he hasn't had a single drink since we returned to 306. It looks like he's being the responsible one tonight. Probably to make sure no one messes with me.

I appreciate his friendship more than I can ever convey. He's listened to me complain about Ana for months now and has never once made me feel stupid for staying with her. And he hasn't judged me when I've acted like everything's okay when I see her. He literally supports me no matter what.

Even now, he's listening to me bitch about Ana and Xander without a single eye roll or hint of annoyance. The realization has me saying, "You're a really good friend, Kas."

He looks embarrassed by my declaration. "I'm not doing anything Nik or Harvey wouldn't."

I dramatically scan the room. "Yet neither one of them are here right now. Only you." I gently shove his shoulder. "Don't sell yourself short, man. I'm lucky to have you."

"The feeling's mutual, dude," he says with a smile while his eyes are locked on his feet.

We sit in comfortable silence for only a few moments before I smirk at him and say, "So… that's the Tony that's been driving you crazy since the beginning of the school year."

He narrows his eyes. "Yeah. What about him?"

"It seems like there's a lot of tension between the two of you." I'm convinced I could've reached out and grabbed it. It was that palpable. "I'm wondering if you plan on doing anything about it. He's your type after all."

"He's *not* my type."

"Oh, he's definitely your type," I respond with a chuckle. "I've seen the kind of guys you've gone home with and he's your type with a capital T." I playfully nudge my roommate. "Didn't you say you were tired of hooking up with people who just fall at your feet because you're Grand Leader Pyrrhus's nephew? That you wanted a challenge for once? Well, I think you've found your challenge."

"No. Definitely *not*," he grumbles, shaking his head. "Tony's a pain in my ass. That is, when he isn't up Xander's."

I don't think Kas realizes he sounded bitter at the end there. It'd seem I'm not the only one Xander's screwing over romantically.

We only stay at the party for another twenty minutes before we decide to head back to our dorm. On the way, I finally ask Kas the question I've been dreading. "If Ana and I break up, will you still be her friend?"

He glances at me out of the corner of his eye and tucks his hands into his pockets. "Ana's like a sister to me, but obviously you're more important. If you don't want me to be friends with her, I won't. She's screwed you over enough that you'd be justified in that. Just tell me what you want, and I'll do it."

What *do* I want? Do I really want to tell my friend I don't want him to hang out with Ana anymore? That seems so childish. And unfair to him. Especially when I know how much he cares for her— she reminds him so much of his younger sister, Tally.

I sigh and run my hands over my face. "I want you to be friends with whoever you want, Kas. It wouldn't be fair of me to expect anything else. Besides, I know Ana cares about all of you. I don't want to hurt her even if she doesn't care about hurting me."

In my drunken state, the truth hits me like a freight train. No matter how angry I get at Ana, a part of me will always love her and hope she chooses me. After tonight, I know that's impossible, but I can't help how I feel.

I know once I sober up, I'll go back to being mad, but right now, I'm just devastated. She was the first girl I ever loved, and I thought she loved me too. She told me as much. I'm starting to think she lied to me because you don't treat those you love like this. You just don't.

Kas bumps me with his elbow. "You'll get through this, man."

"I know."

I just wish I didn't have to.

CHAPTER FIFTY-EIGHT
XANDER

I wake up wanting to talk to Ana. Desperate to talk to her. I want to apologize and let her know how badly I feel that I caused her more stress. I know I should've been stronger last night. For her sake. I shouldn't have let Kasper get under my skin. I messed up.

But despite how badly I want to talk to her, I don't go to her. She was really angry last night. I know she needs time to work through whatever she's feeling. She'll come to me when she's ready to hear my apology.

In the meantime, I need to keep myself occupied. I decide that going to the gym is the best way to do that. I spend the next hour there, blowing off steam, and I'm exhausted by the time I'm done.

Imagine my surprise when I return to my room and find Ana sitting on my bed. "It's about time you came back," she says with a smirk. "I was about to send out a search party for you."

I look between her and my open door. "Did you break into my room?"

She uses her gift to shut it behind me. "I wouldn't call it breaking in. Forced entry, maybe, but not breaking in."

"I'm pretty sure they mean the same thing," I say, unable to stop the smile spreading across my face. She doesn't seem angry anymore and it's a huge relief.

She waves her hand in the air, brushing off what I said, and pats the spot on my bed next to her.

When I settle in beside her, she laces her fingers through mine and leans her head on my shoulder. My whole body relaxes at her touch. I'm glad she's no longer mad at me, but I don't understand why she's gotten over it so quickly. I expected her to shout at me for a little bit at least. Either way, she still deserves an apology for how I acted last night. I shouldn't have fought with her friends.

"Ana…" I start.

She straightens and looks me in the eyes. The anger she felt last night is back, but it doesn't feel directed at me. "Xan, you don't need to apologize. Kas found me this morning and told me what happened. He said he saw Graham arguing with you and wanted to help. That he pushed you to fight him again."

My brows furrow. "He admitted that?"

"He felt guilty about upsetting me," she responds with a nod. "He may be hotheaded, but he does care. I think he knows Graham and I won't be together much longer."

I run my fingers through my hair as I take in what Ana just told me. But there's one question that gnaws at me. A selfish one triggered by something she said.

"You're breaking up with Graham?"

She nods again. "I've needed to break up with him for months now. I've been putting it off because I didn't want to lose my friends. After what happened last night, I know I can't wait any longer. I texted him this morning and told him I need to talk to him. He hasn't responded yet."

I ignore the way my heart leaps with excitement. Instead, I squeeze her hand and say in a consoling tone, "I'm sorry, Ana. I know that can't be easy."

She gives me a sad smile. "It's funny. I know I don't love him, and I know I've wanted to break up with him for months, but now that I'm actually going to do it, I feel a bit sad. I had such high hopes for our relationship in the beginning. He was so kind, and we had a lot in common. I guess I'm disappointed it turned out like this and that he'll probably hate me for it."

I wrap my arms around her and pull her in close when I see the sadness in her eyes. I rub her arm as she leans her head against my chest. We sit like that, in comfortable silence, for a long time.

As I hold her, I find myself wondering what her break up could mean for us. Is there even a possibility she could grow to care for me as more than a friend? I know I'll accept whatever she's willing to give me, but the thought of her loving me back makes my heart pound.

Eventually, Ana pulls away from me and asks if I want to go to the Capitol Building tonight. "We do still need to find memorandum 6746B."

"Yeah. We can do that," I respond. "It'd be nice to get off campus. Do you want to go check out the new Hieran weapons exhibit at the museum beforehand? Maybe grab some dinner?"

She nods excitedly and I feel like I can't breathe. Seeing her happy will always be one of my favorite things.

Ana and I had a lot of fun last night, even if we didn't find any new information during our search of the Capitol Building. She loved the Hieran weapons exhibit, and we learned a lot while we walked through the museum. It was nice to get away from the stress of campus. I know Ana was happy for the distraction from the drama with Graham.

I dropped her off at her dorm last night with a promise that I'd see her soon. My heart has been aching for her ever since. I'm supposed to see my mom and Lydia today and I'm thankful they'll give me something else to focus on for a few hours.

I called my mom yesterday morning and asked if I could switch our visit to today. I lied and told her I was exhausted from a stressful week of classes and needed a day to relax. She didn't need to know that I was moping around because Ana was mad at me.

As I'm on my way to visit them, my uncle's name pops up on my car's dash. I answer his call, asking, "What's up?" He never calls me unless he needs something.

"Hello, Xander." My uncle's commanding voice booms through my car's speakers. "I was just calling to check in on you. Make sure everything's okay."

My eyebrows scrunch together in confusion. "I'm fine. I'm on my way to see Mom and Lydia right now."

"Oh, good." My uncle clears his throat, his voice taking on a serious tone as he says, "I need to know you're making smart choices, Xander. You don't want to do anything that could come back to hurt you. Make enemies of anyone you shouldn't."

What the hell? What is he getting at? My uncle has always loved talking in riddles. I'd ask him to clarify what he means if I cared, but I don't. I don't have the energy to deal with him today.

"Well, thank you for that sound advice, Uncle Sebastian," I say dismissively, trying to get him off the phone. "I'll be sure to take it to heart."

"Good. Just know you can call me if you ever need anything. I'm always here."

"Yeah. I know. Thank you."

We share a few more awkward exchanges before I'm finally able to get him off the phone, but the conversation leaves me feeling uneasy afterwards. It felt like he was trying to warn me about something. I'm not sure what. I highly doubt it has anything to do with Ana, though. We've been very careful during our investigations.

I decide to chalk it up to the ramblings of a paranoid man. There's no other explanation for it.

CHAPTER FIFTY-NINE

ANASTASIA

Graham's been avoiding me.

He won't answer any of my calls or texts and he's gone whenever I stop by his room. I'm not happy about it. He's making this so much harder than it needs to be.

I know I shouldn't break up with him over text—it'd be an awful thing to do—but he's giving me no other option. I've told myself if I don't hear from him by the end of the day, then I'll do it. He's had a week to get back to me. I think that's more than enough time.

Now knowing when I'll officially break up with Graham, I decide I need to distract myself until it happens. Severed relationships are always hard, but this one will be particularly so.

I know once Graham and I break up, it'll mean the end of my friendships with Nik and Kas too. They're both incredibly loyal guys and they'll want to be supportive of Graham through the breakup. That means I not only lose my boyfriend, but I also lose the two guys I look up to as brothers. Two guys who days ago would've laid their lives on the line for me just because I was their friend.

I wonder if they'll even look at me now when we pass each other in the hall. The thought that they won't breaks my heart.

I mourn my friendship with Harvey as well. Harvey isn't one for drama, so I know he'll still talk to me, but it won't be nearly as much as I've grown used to. I'll miss his stupid overly sexual jokes and the way he can ease the tension in our group with a witty remark. I know I won't get to see either in quick conversations with him between classes.

I choose not to think about what I'll mourn when it comes to Graham. He and I have had good and bad times throughout the entirety of our relationship. I've been focusing on the bad a lot lately, but I know as soon as we break up the good will race to the forefront of my mind. It'll be those memories that devastate me.

I decide the best distraction for my spiraling emotions—and my inevitable heartache—is to work on my knife skills in the Stratos Building. I can easily get tied up there for hours working on one technique. There's a particularly tricky move I just read about that I hope will keep me busy for the rest of the day.

I throw on a pair of yoga pants and a loose T-shirt and make my way out of my dorm. I can hear what sounds like a large group of students talking outside the building as I near the exit. The noise reminds me that some stupid 'Welcome to Spring' event is being held in the quad today for all the first-year students.

Imagine my shock when I step outside and see Graham standing in front of my building, mingling with a handful of our classmates. It turns out he can care enough about something to show up for it. Must just be me he doesn't then.

My anger boils to the surface, guiding me to his side. "Hi, Graham," I say in an annoyed tone as I grab his arm. "It's your girl-friend, Ana. Remember me?"

His eyes narrow as he rips his arm from my grasp. "What do you want, Ana?"

"I want to talk to you. I've been trying to for a week now." My tone is sweet, but the words are laced with venom.

"Well, I don't want to talk to you," he responds. I hear contempt in his voice, and it makes me pause. He's never sounded like that. Even at his angriest with me.

"Graham, we *need* to talk." My voice comes out softer than I mean it to.

"*No.* I don't want to talk anymore," he snarls. "Go be with Xander. He's obviously who you want. I'm done with this. All of it."

My eyes widen when his words come out louder than he obviously intended based on the look of surprise that crosses his face. Our classmates are now staring at us—staring at *me*—and my stomach sinks. Graham might not have meant to, but he just humiliated me in front of all these people.

I shake my head at him. "I can't believe you." There's a flash of regret on his face, but it quickly returns to anger.

Before he can say anything else, I turn and make a beeline for my dorm. I need to get away from these people.

Tears are streaming down my face before I even make it inside of the building. When I finally make it to my room, I fling myself onto my bed and let my emotions flow freely as I cry for all I've lost.

CHAPTER SIXTY

XANDER

The campus is buzzing with activity when I return from my visit with Mom and Lydia.

Students are milling about in front of the first-year dorms, and someone is talking through a megaphone. I can't make out what they're saying but cheers erupt in response. It's all very loud so I hurry toward my dorm's side entrance, hoping to avoid the craziness.

I just reach the door when I hear someone shout my name from behind me. I turn toward the voice and my head snaps to the side when I'm punched in the face.

I curse while grabbing my now throbbing cheek. I look up and find Graham standing in front of me, hands clenched into fists and a wild look in his eyes.

"Dude! What the hell?" I snarl at him.

"Looks like you got what you wanted, dick," he says, clearly seething. "I broke up with Ana. I just hope for your sake she doesn't get bored of you too and move onto someone else. I suggest you keep her away from your uncle. She seems to like guys with power."

His remark about Ana makes me see red. I lunge at him and grab him by the front of his shirt. I want to throttle him, but I'll settle for threatening him instead. "If you like breathing without the assistance of a machine, I suggest you watch what you say about her."

He doesn't respond. That's when I see the sadness lingering behind all the anger he's projecting. It's clear he's lashing out like this because he's hurting. That makes me even angrier. I don't care how upset he is. That doesn't give him a pass to talk bad about Ana.

I turn and pin him against the building. "If you weren't such a jealous, selfish prick, you would've seen how much Ana was dealing with this year," I growl. "But no, all you cared about was whether she was spending time with me or not. You *never* deserved her."

His expression turns to one of fear as lightning gathers in my eyes. *Good.* "You better keep her name out of your mouth, otherwise, the next conversation we have won't be as gentle."

I throw him on the ground after that and hurry to Ana's dorm. I need to make sure she's okay.

When I enter her room a few minutes later, I find her curled up in a ball on her bed. She sits up when she sees me and her face crumples. I rush to her and wrap my arms around her while she cries into my chest.

"I'm here, Ana. It's okay. It'll all be okay."

"Graham broke up with me," she says between sobs. "He did it in front of all our classmates. It was humiliating."

I rub her back and continue whispering that everything will be okay. I hate that she's hurting like this.

"I feel like an idiot," she whispers. "I was going to break up with him today. I was ready to. Why am I crying because he broke up with me instead?"

I continue rubbing her back. "The end of any relationship will always be hard. You're not an idiot for being sad about it, especially since you guys dated for a while."

She pulls away from me and wipes at her nose. "I guess you're right." She finally gets a good look at me and her eyes narrow. "Xan, what happened to your face? Did somebody hit you?"

"Don't worry about it, Spy," I say dismissively, hoping she'll drop it.

"*Xander*, did somebody hit you?"

I sigh. *This woman.* "What do you think?"

Her eyes flare in anger. "Oh my gods. *Graham* hit you?" She balls her hands into fists. "I'm going to kill him. I'm going to *fricking* kill him."

She hops off her bed, but I stop her before she gets too far. "I already took care of him, Ana. Don't worry about it."

She gives me a surprised look, but her eyes soften after a moment. She then runs her hands over her face and blows out a shaky breath. I hate how defeated she seems.

"Do you wanna get out of here?" I ask, hoping getting away from here will help her feel better.

She nods, eyes shining.

CHAPTER SIXTY-ONE

ANASTASIA

My coursework has been light lately, but I'm not complaining about it. Not when it means I don't have to spend hours each night studying or working on homework. I don't have the mental capacity for that right now.

It's been a little over two weeks since Graham and I broke up and it hasn't gotten any easier.

Xander has done his best to distract me—going so far as inviting me to stay with him and his family at the Thyellas Estate last weekend—but it's only ever a temporary reprieve.

The minute I'm around my friends again and feel the awkwardness that has become a cornerstone of every interaction I have with them, my sadness always returns in full force. I guess I should be happy that Nik and Kas are still talking to me, even if it's different. It doesn't seem like they know how to act around me anymore. I don't think any of them do.

I glance across the room to where Millie's lying on her bed and a feeling of betrayal gnaws at me. She's tried her best to be there for me whenever I need her, but her relationship with Nik has her spending a lot of time with Graham too. I know it's unfair for me to feel like she shouldn't see him anymore. It doesn't stop me, though.

I just wish things would go back to normal between us.

That thought has me pausing the movie we're watching in its final minutes. "Hey Mills, do you want to grab something to eat once the movie's over? I heard there's a new sushi place downtown." When she grimaces, I ask, "What?"

"I'm sorry, Ana, but I have dinner plans with the guys tonight. I'm supposed to meet them once we're done watching the movie."

My mouth drops open. "You're going to dinner with them *again*? That's the third night in a row."

She gives me an apologetic look. "I know. I'm sorry. They keep making these plans without consulting with me first. I promise I don't let Graham say anything bad about you. For what it's worth, Kas doesn't either."

That should make me feel better. I know it should, but instead I only feel bitter.

"Yeah. I'm sure. It's probably because you guys are too busy talking bad about Xander."

"What? Why would you think that?" she asks, clearly confused.

"I've seen the way you act around him now. You also love telling me to be careful whenever I say I'm going to hang out with him. It's clear you think he's a bad person. Just like the guys."

She shakes her head. "I don't think he's a bad guy, Ana. I..." She runs her hands over her face and sighs. "It's just... I watched him almost kill our friend. He would've if I hadn't stopped him. That's not something I can just forget. Especially when you spend so much time with him alone. I'm always worried he'll snap again and hurt you."

I roll my eyes. Clearly, she *has* been listening to the crap Graham spews about him. If I end up losing her because of it, I'll hate him. She was supposed to be *my* friend. Mine.

"Xander's not like that."

"How am I supposed to know that Ana when you don't tell me anything?" Tears prick the corners of her eyes and it settles my growing anger temporarily. "I always told you I didn't care if something was going on between you two. I only cared about you being happy. I hate feeling like you're keeping things from me. Is it because of Xander? Is he making you?"

Her words hit me as if she'd thrown them and I feel like I could scream. No one ever listens to me. All my friends want to paint Xander as some bad guy who's forcing me to do things. As if I'm not strong enough to make my own decisions. I don't deserve this and neither does Xander. All he's done is be there for me while I've dealt with their crap.

I put my hands up in mock surrender. "You know what? I'm done trying. It's not worth it," I say calmly, my anger simmering just below the surface. "Have fun at dinner with the guys."

I hear Millie shouting after me as I storm out of our room. Her words are cut off once our door slams shut.

I make a beeline for the guys' dorm, following the same path I've taken dozens of times, my destination clear. I reach Xander's room within a few minutes and knock, my anger causing me to pound on the door harder than I intended.

I can feel my gift swirling out of control as Xander opens his door. His eyes widen when he sees the anger and hurt probably still lining my face. He opens the door wider, inviting me in. When I pass him, electricity flares from him in a way I've never seen before.

He shuts the door once I'm inside and turns to me. "Ana, what's going on? What's wrong?"

I move to hug him, but he puts his hands up to stop me. "Look, I know you're not supposed to tell a lady to calm down when they're upset, but you're going to have to calm down before I can hug you." The lights in his room flicker as his electricity flares again. "I think you're bending the electromagnetic field around us and that's what my electricity is responding to. I'm going to end up hurting you if you don't calm down."

Oh crap. I start taking controlled breaths like Xander taught me while I try to clear my mind. The last thing I want is to hurt him because of my spiraling emotions.

Once my gift settles, Xander envelops me in his arms. "What happened, Spy? Why're you so upset?"

"Millie and I just got into a huge fight," I say weakly. "I asked her if she wanted to grab dinner together, but she said she already had plans with the guys. Plans I wasn't invited to because Graham would be there." He strokes my hair while I start to cry. "She said she's worried you're going to hurt me after she watched you almost kill Kas. She also thinks you're the reason I don't tell her anything. I was so upset after she said that. I stormed out of our room and came right here."

I wipe at my tears as I pull away from him. His face is full of concern as he scans mine. "I'm just so frustrated. I feel like I'm losing all my friends, and I don't know how to stop it. It's not like I can tell them what we're doing. Not yet."

He hugs me again as fresh tears streak down my face. "I'm sorry, Ana. I know how much they mean to you. I wish there was something I could do to help."

"Thanks," I say with a sniff. "It's nice to know I have someone in my life who doesn't think I'm a monster."

His right hand continues to stroke my hair as he says, "I'm down to get something to eat if you still want to. Anywhere you'd like."

I lean back so I can smile at him. Despite everything I just shared, he remembered that the whole argument with Millie stemmed from me wanting to grab dinner with her. I don't know what I did to deserve Xander, but I'll forever be grateful for it.

"Honestly, I think I'd rather go search your uncle's office tonight. That's the last place we have to look, and we've been putting it off because of my breakup. It'd be nice to feel like we're accomplishing something. I just need to get my mind off all this."

Xander hesitates. "Are you sure? If you lose control again, my electricity will likely expose us. I don't know if we should risk it."

"Yeah, I'm sure." I put my hand on his arm to reassure him. "I'll be fine. It's nothing we haven't already done several times."

He blows out a breath. "Okay. Whatever you want to do, Spy, we'll do."

It's just before 1:00 in the morning by the time we reach the Capitol Building. As we approach it, I admire the way the dome on top glows in the moonlight.

Xander convinced me I should eat before our investigation, so we went to a local burger spot. It was nice to get away from campus and laugh with my best friend. I was already feeling much better by the time we began our trek through the woods.

We sidle up to the right side of the Capitol Building and crouch down next to the steel door there. As Xander reaches out with his electricity to shut off all the security cameras, I do a few breathing exercises to make sure I'm ready emotionally for what we're about to do.

"We should be good to go now," he whispers a minute later.

I nod and push my gift toward the door to unlock it. Once it is, he opens it wide enough for me to crawl through. As soon as I'm inside, he follows after me and gently closes the door behind us.

It takes a minute for our eyes to adjust to the darkness. We stand once they do, and I trail behind Xander as he moves quietly toward our intended destination.

Sebastian Aeras's office is located in the east wing of the building, adjacent to the Grand Leader's office which takes up the entire end of the hall. Xander's theorized his uncle won't move into the Grand Leader's office until he puts into motion whatever he's planning.

The door to Sebastian's office is unlocked so we quickly sneak inside and turn on the flashlights we brought. I use mine to assess the space. The room feels sparse compared to what I expected. There's a large wooden desk in the middle of it with only a computer resting on top—no family photos or memorabilia in sight. Two large bookcases frame each side of the back wall while filing cabinets fill the space between them. Sebastian's official Vice Grand Leader portrait hangs above the cabinets, looking down on us with silent judgment.

Xander starts searching through his uncle's desk, so I rifle through the first filing cabinet on the left. I don't find anything of note in its top three drawers. As I'm looking through the bottom one, though, a document catches my attention. I pull it out and do a cursory scan of it. It has "CONFIDENTIAL" in red letters at the top and it's dated for the day after Grand Leader Thyellas's murder. It looks like it was only sent to one person: Sebastian's former secretary. I gasp when I read it what it says.

"What is it? Did you find something?" Xander asks from his spot by his uncle's desk.

"Read this," I say, handing him the piece of paper when he sidles up next to me. "I think I found memorandum 6746B."

He reads the document and his eyes widen. "You're right," he says, unable to hide the surprise in his voice. "If we share this with General Ischyros, it should put a stop to my uncle's plans." An excited smile spreads across his face. "I think we got him."

"We should probably make a copy of it, so your uncle doesn't notice it's missing. Do you know where…" Suddenly, I feel like I can't breathe. I try to take a breath, but I can't. Instead, a gurgling noise sounds deep in my throat as water sputters out of my mouth.

"Ana! What's wrong? What's going on?" Xander asks as he grabs my arms to try to steady me so he can get a better look.

We both turn when the lights in the room flick on and a male voice says, "Did you two really think you could sneak into my office and I wouldn't know?"

Xander looks at me while realization dawns in his eyes. He lets go of my arms and electricity flares from his hands. The lights above us flicker as he turns to his uncle and snarls, "Let her go!"

"I recommend you put away your sparks, Xander. If one so much as lands on my carpet, I'll drown her on the spot."

Xander's lightning instantly disappears and the lights stop flickering. I cough as a sudden influx of air rushes into my lungs. Xander checks on me through the corner of his eye, but he doesn't turn his attention away from his uncle.

"We know everything you're planning, Uncle Sebastian," he says. "You're not going to get away with it."

"Oh, on the contrary," Sebastian says with a smirk. "I already have."

I watch in horror as a man with a green mohawk materializes

behind Xander and hits him on the head with a large weapon. Xander crumples on the spot. Three uniformed men then walk into the room. Two pick up Xander and drag him away, while the third grabs onto me and holds me in place.

"No! Xander! Xander!" I shout as I lose sight of him.

Sebastian turns to me and gives me an evil grin. "Don't worry. We didn't forget about you."

A cloth is placed over my mouth and the world goes black.

CHAPTER SIXTY-TWO
XANDER

I come to in an empty room made of concrete with the back of my head throbbing. I have no idea how I got here, but I'm certain my uncle had something to do with it.

I can't say I'm surprised. Clearly my uncle will do whatever he feels is necessary to ensure his plans come to pass. I guess that includes kidnapping his nephew.

My thoughts immediately jump to Ana and dread coils in my gut. Picturing her chained and unconscious in a room like this makes me sick. I'll kill my uncle if he's hurt her in any way.

I pull on the chains binding my hands and legs, but they don't budge. There's an unnatural heaviness to them that tells me they're laced with suppressants. Unfortunately, that means I won't be blasting my way out of here.

I'm scanning the room, looking for a means to escape, when the lone door in front of me opens and a familiar face walks through it. My blood runs cold at the sight of him.

"Look who finally decided to wake up," Dr. Diavolos exclaims with a malicious grin. "Did you miss me, Sparky?"

I know better than to answer him, so I just glare at the monster from my past.

"Really? You have nothing to say to me after all these years?" He puts his hand to his chest as if I hurt his feelings, then slaps me across the face and gives me an evil grin. "That's fine. I always did prefer your screams."

My cheek's still throbbing when he turns and waves his hand toward the front corner of the room. A table materializes there and my stomach drops when I see the weapons lined on top of it. He walks over to it and begins examining them. I assume he's deciding which one to use on me first.

When he picks up the mallet, a nostalgic smile spreads on his face before he turns to me and sighs wistfully. "Do you remember how you used to scream and scream when I would smash your fingers with this?" He sighs again. "I miss that."

"Well, I was eleven, so…"

His eyes widen with excitement. "He speaks!" He fans himself dramatically before turning back to the table to pick up another weapon. "I always did love that deep voice of yours," he muses while turning over the knife in his hand. When he puts it down and picks up a different one, a sudden realization hits me. If he's in here with me, then he isn't hurting Ana.

I resign myself to what I must do.

"You're pathetic," I snarl, pouring every ounce of hatred I have for the man into the statement.

The green-haired torturer whips around and glares at me. "*I'm* pathetic?" He tightens his grip on the knife he holds and walks toward me. "You're the one squandering a chance at unbelievable power. All you'd have to do is agree to the war against Fotia, but you refuse. For what? That hot piece of ass in the other room? She'll just use you, then dump you like that little blonde did a few years ago."

Him mentioning Ana has me seeing red so I do the only thing I can. I spit in his face. He slowly wipes away my saliva with an amused grin, then lifts the knife in his hand and slices me across the left eye with it. I fight back a groan as a searing pain emanates from the wound. I don't want to give him the satisfaction of seeing me hurt.

He smiles at the gash now marring my face. "That's even better than I imagined," he says excitedly. "I can just see your mom's face now. She'll be weeping over you at your funeral and all she'll be able to focus on is this one flaw on your otherwise perfect face." He sighs. "Why didn't I do this years ago?"

"Go to hell," I growl.

The torturer's eyes darken. He walks back to the table and picks up a whip this time. With two sharp flicks of his wrist, the whip cuts open my shirt and slices lines across my chest that form an X. I hiss in a breath, unprepared for the pain.

"You think you're so tough now, huh? You obviously forget how easy it is for me to break you. I'll have you begging for me to kill you before you know it."

My eyes widen when the torturer picks up the mallet again. I try to fight back as he grabs my right hand, but the chains make it impossible. I'm at his mercy.

While he forces my hand to lay flat, he looks at the tattoos on my arm and tsks. "I can't believe you covered up all your scars." He looks me in the eyes with a face of pure evil and says, "I guess I'll have to give you more."

I bite down on my bottom lip, holding in a scream, as the mallet smashes my index finger. His face is one of pure joy as he examines it afterwards. Once he's satisfied with what he sees, he moves on to my next finger and then the next. He takes his time with each of them, savoring the pain etched across my face as they shatter. When he finally finishes minutes later, I feel faint. Blood trails down my arm and drips onto the ground beneath me.

After that, he puts on an apron and picks out another weapon. He returns to my spot on the wall and takes in my pale face. He smirks as he leans in and whispers, "Don't give up on me now, Sparky. We're just getting started."

The next several hours pass by in a blur of pain. To get through it, I keep repeating to myself, 'He's not hurting Ana. He's not hurting Ana. He's not hurting Ana.' I can take whatever he dishes out as long as I know she's okay.

When I just start to feel like I can't take anymore, Dr. Diavolos punches me and steps away from my damaged body. I work my jaw, trying to ease the pain as I spit out blood and a few teeth. They land at my feet, adding to the pool of blood already there.

"It feels so good to be reunited, don't you think?" he asks with a satisfied smile. I don't think there's a single part of me that remains untouched by his evil hands. I can barely stand as the pain he's inflicted wracks every inch of my body.

"Unfortunately, I have to end our time here," he says with another sigh. "I've already spent more time than I should've with you. Your uncle said I could play with you first, but now I need to go interrogate the girl."

He must see the anger gathering in my eyes because he pats me on the shoulder as if to comfort me. "Don't worry. I'll be back. I just need to pay a visit to your girlfriend first." He acts like he's going to walk away, but then pauses, seeming to contemplate something. "I wonder how easy it'll be to make her scream. Got any advice?"

I lunge at him and try to grab him while electricity sparks around my eyes. It quickly dies out due to the suppressants lining the chains that bind me, but not before a look of fear crosses the torturer's face. It disappears within seconds and is replaced with a smirk.

"I'll make sure to give her your regards."

As the door shuts behind him, I try the chains again, ripping and pulling at them in desperation. They still don't budge.

CHAPTER SIXTY-THREE
ANASTASIA

I woke up hours ago in an unknown location and my thoughts have been spiraling since.

The room I found myself in was cold and unfeeling and made completely out of concrete. The drain in the center of it gave me a good idea of its purpose.

Torture.

I stared at that drain as the minutes ticked by, wondering how I ended up here. And where the hell was Xander.

When I pictured my own blood pouring into the drain, I told myself I had to get out of here. I began fighting against the chains that bound me with all the strength my tired body could muster.

After an hour of trying, and failing, I concluded there was no escaping my current predicament. The chains weren't budging and the suppressants in them were preventing me from using my gift. I was well and truly trapped.

I spent very little time worrying about myself, though. All I could think about was how the man that knocked out Xander matched the description of the monster that tortured him for years. Was he with Xander now? My heart dropped at the thought.

It didn't take long for guilt to mix with my worry.

The only reason we're even in this mess is because of me. I'm the one who pushed Xander to search the Capitol Building tonight. He didn't think it was a good idea, but I didn't care, and he was going to do whatever made me happy. I couldn't deal with the drama with my friends and made a stupid decision because of it.

This is all my fault.

I have to find a way out of these chains. I don't care what it takes, I *need* to get out of here. I'll never forgive myself if something bad happens to Xander because of me.

I perform the breathing exercises Xander taught me and keep repeating them until a sense of calm finally settles over me. Once it does, I reach out to the chains and will them to open. I outright beg for them to open.

Please. I need to save my friend.

I can feel a whisper of my gift swirling underneath my skin and though it's nothing compared to what I usually feel, I pray it's enough. I reach out and caress the chains with that little bit of power.

Please open.

The next few moments are excruciating. Despite my power swirling around them, the chains remain in place, and it has my anxiety ratcheting up to an unhealthy level. My pleading doesn't seem to be working. Nothing seems to be working. What am I going to do?

Please. Please let me save my friend. I can't lose him. I just can't.

Suddenly, the chains binding my wrists loosen and a jolt of excitement passes through me at the realization. Unfortunately, that's when the door in front of me opens. My eyes snap to it and my stomach's instantly in knots when I see two men walk into the room and close the door behind them. The first man, Xander's uncle, has an expression of annoyance on his face, but I don't pay much attention to it. Not when the sight of the second one makes my heart stop. The green-haired monster's wearing an apron soaked in blood.

On my gods. Is that Xander's blood?

The man notices my gaze and smirks. "Xander sends his regards."

It feels like all the air rushes out of my lungs. *No.* No, no, no. What have I done?

Sebastian Aeras clears his throat, dragging my attention to him. "We have some questions for you, Ms. Galanis."

"Yeah? Like what?" I quickly shift my demeanor into one of arrogance. I don't want either man to know how badly the sight of Xander's blood affects me. I don't want to give them any reason to hurt him further.

The Vice Grand Leader smiles as if he can see through my charade, then asks, "What were you doing in my office last night?" He pulls a document from his back pocket and waves it in front of my face. "You seemed rather excited to find this. What did you hope to accomplish with it?"

When I just stare at him, not saying anything, he sighs. He nods toward the green-haired man and the monster grins, sending a chill down my spine.

He approaches me slowly after that and says sweetly, "Hello, beautiful." My skin crawls as he trails a finger along my cheek. "I've been told I can hurt you whenever you refuse to answer a question. I'd keep that in mind. You wouldn't want me to scar this pretty face, would you?" When the torturer's gaze darkens, nausea roils in my stomach. The man truly is evil. It's clear he gets off on the pain of others.

I don't have time to change my mind about answering Sebastian's question because the monster punches my left eye so hard I see stars. My head hits the wall behind me while I gasp. The pain radiating from my eye now is excruciating, but I breathe through it and somehow maintain my composure.

My eye's watering when I finally look at them, but anger laces my words as I declare, "I'll only answer your questions if you answer mine."

The Vice Grand Leader looks annoyed again but says, "Fine. I'll play your little game, girl." I notice a gleam in his deep blue eyes, almost like he's impressed with me. "Ask away."

I think about all the information Xander and I've gathered over the last few months and my first question is obvious. "How'd you know I was gifted?"

He smirks. "Why, your father told me. Or, rather, he showed me. He was getting more and more agitated with the breakdown in our relationship with Fotia. I wanted to know why, so I followed him for a few weeks. Imagine my surprise when I saw him purchasing the materials needed to make a suppressant from a random apothecary in Fotia." He shakes his head and smiles. In that moment, I want nothing more than to punch him in his handsome face. "After that, I had to know who Nicholas Metallo was hiding. When I watched him train you one evening, I knew I found who I was looking for."

"But why'd you care? I was a nobody."

"Eh, eh, eh," he says while wagging a finger. "I answered your question, so now you have to answer mine. Those are our terms."

I roll my eyes. "Fine. Ask your damn question."

"I'm going to circle back to my original question." He waves the document in front of my face again. "What did you plan to use this for?"

I contemplate how best to answer it. We planned on giving the document to Nik's dad, the General of Zoin, in the hopes he'd put a stop to the brewing war. I don't think it'd be wise to tell Sebastian that, though. The Vice Grand Leader might think Nik's father is working with us and I don't want to put the General in any sort of danger.

After several seconds, I decide to answer with a partial truth instead.

"We were going to present it to parliament. We hoped if they saw the truth, they wouldn't approve of your plans to go to war against Fotia."

He narrows his eyes, seeming to assess the validity of my answer, so I quickly ask my next question, "Why did my dad kill Grand Leader Thyellas?"

A grin spreads across his face and it's one of pure evil. "Because I told Alexander about your gift. I knew he'd try to exploit you because of it. I also knew your father would rather kill the man he was hired to protect than let that happen. I figured with the two of them out of the way, I could swoop in and take over as Grand Leader. Then I could finally start the war I'd been pushing Alexander to wage for years."

My eyes widen. My dad killed the Grand Leader to protect me. Oh my gods.

That means Sebastian Aeras is the one who put all this into motion.

And then he killed my dad and covered up his death with a mine explosion.

It'd been Sebastian Aeras all along.

"But you murdered all those innocent men. Why?"

He smirks again and decides to answer my question without him needing to ask one first. "It's not like their deaths meant anything. They were just some ungifted men from a town nobody cares about. The last thing *I* needed was people looking into your father's death, so it was the perfect cover up."

He's a monster. I'm looking at a real-life monster right now. That's the only explanation for the lack of guilt I see on his face. How could he do that to all those poor men? Their families?

"Do you think my nephew will ever support my plans to go to war against Fotia?" he asks, dragging my spiraling thoughts back to him

I hesitate before answering. I know I'm now crossing into dangerous territory. "I think your nephew will be a great Grand Leader who'll be able to weigh the risks and benefits of any plans brought to him. If you give him a convincing enough argument, he might."

Sebastian nods at the torturer and my body immediately tenses. The monster approaches me with a wide grin on his face, then punches me so hard in the stomach that it knocks the wind out of me.

As I'm gasping for breath, the Vice Grand Leader says, "Dancing around my question doesn't count as answering it, Ms. Galanis." His tone is no longer professional. It's angry. "Do you think my nephew will support my plans to go to war against Fotia or not?"

The torturer stays near me, prepared to strike again if needed.

Before I answer, a thought comes to mind that has my blood running cold. If the Vice Grand Leader brought on the assassination of Grand Leader Thyellas—his own brother-in-law—for this plan, then he's just as likely to kill his nephew. What better way to convince the people of Zoin to go to war against Fotia than to tell them that Fotian assassins killed the last two storm benders in existence?

Xander isn't going to make it out of here alive if Sebastian Aeras has anything to say about it.

I do my best to steady my breathing. If I can convince this awful man that Xander would support his plans, maybe he'll spare him. "I don't think it'd take much to convince him. He already can't stand Grand Leader Pyrrhus's nephew."

Sebastian grins. "I know you're lying, but at least that means you're not stupid. You know the truth would be a death sentence for Xander." He approaches me slowly and stops mere inches from my face. "I have news for you, Ms. Galanis. My nephew isn't making it out of this alive, no matter what you say." Any plans I had to ask him why he wants this war to happen so badly immediately disappear. It feels like he stabbed me in the chest and twisted the knife. The pain is so loud I can barely hear him say, "But that doesn't have to be your fate."

His voice takes on a charming tone as I try to keep myself from spiraling further. "I'm very impressed with your gift, Anastasia. I saw the way you were able to bend metal even while taking suppressants. You never noticed, but I did. You're more powerful than you realize and I'm in need of an assassin. We could really benefit each other."

He takes a step back, giving me space to think about what he just offered me. My eyebrows shoot to my hairline when I realize he's serious. "So, I'll live if I agree to be your assassin?"

"Precisely," Xander's uncle responds with a beautiful smile. "What do you say?"

What do I say? *What do I say?* Is he serious?

Every ounce of hatred I feel for the man pours into my response. "*No.* I'd *never* work for you. You killed my dad and now you plan on killing my best friend too. I'd rather die than help you."

He sighs. "Very well." He turns to the monster beside him and signals that it's time to leave. They both exit the room, but Sebastian pauses with his hand on the door. "There's no hope for my nephew, Ms. Galanis. Dr. Diavolos will be killing him within the hour. Don't waste your potential on a lost cause. The war against Fotia is happening." He sighs again when he sees the stubborn look on my face. "I'll give you time to think over my offer. I hope you make the right choice." The door clicks as he closes it behind him.

Once the two men are gone, every emotion I'd been suppressing is finally released. Tears stream down my face as I think about my best friend and what they plan to do to him. Xander's going to die and it's all my fault. Why couldn't I just stay on campus like he suggested?

I have to do something. I can't let him die. Not when there's still so much life for him to live. A life I hoped to spend together.

I glance at the chains again and feel my gift building within me.

I can do this. I can get us out of here.

I have to.

Minutes pass while I weep and urge the chains to let me go. As I do, flashes of Xander and I laughing together hit me. So does his smile. And the way he'd protect me while also making sure I never forgot how strong I am. Life won't mean anything without him in it.

That realization has my emotions tangling with my gift, strengthening it. While my desperation increases, so does my gift. When I think I might burst because of everything I'm feeling, the chains snap off my wrists and fall to the floor. My heart leaps in triumph. I look at my legs next and repeat the process for the chains binding them. They fall off instantly.

I waste no time with my newfound freedom. I quickly shake out my hands and legs, getting blood flowing to them again, then rush to the door and throw it open.

I find a dimly lit hallway on the other side and step into it. As I do, my gift spreads out, searching for the chains that bind Xander.

I'll tear this place apart if I have to. I'm not leaving without the man I love.

CHAPTER SIXTY-FOUR
XANDER

I'm struggling to remain conscious when Dr. Diavolos enters the room. I breathe a sigh of relief when I don't see any fresh blood on him. *Ana's okay.*

I groan when he walks up to me and grabs my face, moving it back and forth to examine his handiwork. When he finally releases me, he sighs and says, "Unfortunately, Sparky, it looks like our time together is coming to an end. Your uncle says it's time for me to kill you."

I don't have it in me to react. I'm too exhausted to. I just hang my head, accepting my fate.

My voice is hoarse when I ask, "What about Ana?"

"Your girlfriend seems to have impressed the Vice Grand Leader. He offered her a job as his assassin. She turned it down, but he's giving her time to think about it. He's hoping she'll change her mind once you're out of the picture."

My eyes snap to the torturer's. "Tell her to take the job."

He laughs, clearly surprised by my demand. "What?"

"I know how much you love when I beg. Well, here I am. I'm begging. Please tell her to take the job. She doesn't need to lose her life over this."

The monster smirks. "And what do I get if I do?"

"Anything you want. Just please tell her."

He grins and it's nothing short of evil. "*Anything?*" He smacks me after that and I suck in a sharp breath while he shrugs. "I'll think about it."

I hang my head again. I knew it was a long shot.

He pulls a knife out of his back pocket and begins playing with the tip of it. "Any last words, Sparky?"

"Yeah," I manage to growl. "I'll see you in the Underworld."

The torturer smiles and that smile's all I see before he stabs me in the stomach. I groan as a burning pain radiates from the spot, unable to muster the energy for any other reaction. He twists the knife before he removes it and I groan again. He then tosses it onto the table and makes his way toward the door.

His fingers have just wrapped around the handle when gunshots ring out. My head snaps up in alarm.

"Huh," he muses. "Your little girlfriend must've escaped. The Vice Grand Leader thought that might happen." He smirks. "Looks like I'll get to play with her after all. Guess I won't be upholding the little bargain we made."

Something inside of me snaps at the thought of him going near Ana. At her being shot at. I channel all the energy I have left into my gift, urging it to work. A few seconds pass, but a small wind starts to blow around the room. Dr. Diavolos stops, doorknob in hand, when he feels it and turns to give me a surprised look.

I continue to channel my energy into my gift, praying it'll get stronger. Within the span of a breath, my wind is blowing the weapons off the table and electricity is sparking from the ceiling. The torturer's eyes widen when he realizes what's happening.

Four bolts of lightning strike my chains, breaking them into several pieces. Once I'm free, I step from the wall and crack my neck, a feeling of calm settling over me as I do.

The monster turns invisible when he sees I'm unchained. I smirk at that. *Oh, how the tables have turned.* My wind now blows around the tiny room at dangerous speeds. I stand in the center of it, waiting for Dr. Diavolos to show himself. He'll have to at some point.

"You may be invisible, but you can't hide from my wind, asshole."

After several seconds, I notice the weapons bouncing off an invisible spot a few inches from the wall by the door. *Gotcha.*

With adrenaline coursing through me, I approach that spot with an evil grin. He materializes in front of me a second later, knowing he's been caught. I can't help the joy that fills me when I see the fear in his eyes.

Electricity gathers along my arms as I grab the front of his shirt and snarl, "You'll never hurt another person again." A bolt of lightning strikes his heart, killing him instantly. I let him go and his body drops to the floor as more shots ring out. I summon as much of my gift as I can and head for the door.

I'm coming, Ana.

CHAPTER SIXTY-FIVE

ANASTASIA

The hallway opens into a large warehouse full of shipping containers.

I look around the space, trying to figure out the building's layout in the hopes it'll help me find Xander faster. It's impossible, though. The large containers take up too much space. I can't see anything but them.

Where are you, Xander?

My gift is useless in this situation. Xander's chains must also be laced with suppressants because my power doesn't feel them anywhere. That means I'm stuck wandering through the building to find my best friend.

I turn to the right and follow along the wall. Eventually it should lead me where I need to go. At least, I hope so.

I've only made it a few feet when gunshots ring out, echoing throughout the space. I dive behind the shipping container closest to me, hoping to get out of the line of fire, but a stinging sensation on my left ear tells me I've been hit. I curse under my breath. *I don't have time for this. I need to find Xander.*

Vice Grand Leader Aeras's voice booms from somewhere above me. "I thought you might escape. I had my guys posted up here for that very reason." I hear his sigh of frustration. "You're not going to be able to save him, Anastasia."

I peek around the container and follow the sound of Sebastian's voice. I find him standing on a platform on the other side of the room. I also find eight uniformed men with assault rifles flanking him.

"Come on, Ms. Galanis. Join my team. You're incredibly talented. Don't you want to show the world how gifted you are? Don't you want to prove those who thought of you as nothing more than ungifted trash wrong? I'm offering you that opportunity."

While Xander's uncle tries to persuade me to be his assassin, I send out my gift, feeling for the bullets that were shot at me. I gather any that I find, then stand up and face the awful man. Our eyes meet at the same time I shoot the bullets back at him and his men. Two of them fall when they're hit and don't get back up.

Sebastian's able to stop one of the bullets from striking him with a wall of water he throws up at the last second. When it dissipates, he looks at me with pure outrage. "Very well. Goodbye, Anastasia."

He signals for his men to kill me, then makes his way toward the back door and disappears through it.

I duck behind the shipping container again as more shots ring out. With a quick glance, I see that two of the uniformed men remain on the platform while the other four descend the stairs, coming to find me.

When a uniformed man comes into view, I gather more bullets to me and slip around the side of the container. I quickly shoot one at him and grin when I hear him hiss in pain. I'm about to shoot another when someone grabs me by the hair from behind and yanks me toward them. A gust of wind blows past me as I try to twist out of the soldier's grasp.

The soldier presses me against him and sneers, "I'm sure going to enjoy killing you. It's rare we get a target quite so pretty." He puts a knife to my throat as he breathes in my scent.

I'm preparing to bend the knife to my will when I hear a deep voice behind me say, "Let her go. *Now*."

I suddenly feel like I can't breathe when I recognize the voice.

Tears sting the corners of my eyes when the soldier turns us, and we come face to face with a walking tornado. Wind spirals around Xander at dangerous speeds and lightning cracks throughout the vortex. A chill runs down my spine as I look into his eyes and only see white orbs staring back at me.

The remaining soldiers join us, staying as far back from him as they can. The jerk holding me seems unfazed, though. He just smirks and pulls me closer to him, taunting Xander.

Xander's white eyes scan the room, assessing the situation. I gasp when two lightning bolts streak across the ceiling and strike the gunmen that stayed on the platform. They collapse to the floor, along with the guns that were about to fire at us.

Xander's voice has an otherworldly quality to it as he asks, "Does anyone want to join their friends?"

The soldiers exchange nervous glances, and I see fear etched across their faces. The one holding me decides to finally release me and throws me at Xander.

Xander drops his wind and catches me. He then does a quick once over to ensure I'm okay. When he doesn't find anything of concern, his attention returns to the soldiers in front of us. They all have their hands raised in surrender.

"*Go,*" says that otherworldly voice.

The soldiers waste no time. Within seconds, they're gone, and the warehouse is empty. Relief floods me and I'm seconds away from crying happy tears. *We're alive.*

I turn to hug Xander, unable to contain my excitement, but he slouches against me. "Xan, are you okay?" I ask as I crane my head to get a better look at him. What I see makes my blood run cold.

I grab him and try to get a better hold on him. He's now unconscious and so pale. There are so many cuts and bruises covering the parts of his body I can see. I feel sick when I notice the fingers on his right hand are bent at unnatural angles. But none of that compares to the stab wound in his abdomen and the large bruise forming around it.

I choke back a sob. "Oh Xan, what did they do to you?" I ask through my tears. I take a deep breath and try to gain some semblance of control over my emotions. Xander needs me. "Don't worry. I'll get you help."

I throw his left arm around my shoulders and proceed to drag him toward the exit. Once we're outside, a quick look around tells me the building we left is part of an abandoned Fotian shipping facility. It's near a large body of water so I deduce we're in the Fotian city of Pyr. It's about an hour away from Arken.

I send out my gift, searching for anything that can get us away from here quickly. It detects a small car a street over. "You're going to be okay, Xan," I whisper while I drag him in that direction.

I give a relieved sigh when I round the building across the street and see an old, maroon Sedan sitting a few feet in front of me. I use my gift to unlock its doors as I approach it, then lay Xander down gently in the backseat.

When I sit down in the driver's seat, I tell myself I need to remain calm. *He needs you. You're the only one he has right now. It's up to you to save him.* I grab his left hand while my gift turns the car's engine over. "Stay with me, Xan," I plead, pouring all the love I have for him into that statement. "Just stay with me."

I put the car in drive and head toward the only place I can think of to go.

It's nearly midnight when Dr. Farrogow opens his front door. His eyes widen when he sees me holding an unconscious and bloody Xander. He checks to make sure no one's seen us, then ushers me inside.

Once we're standing in his foyer, he picks Xander up with ease and makes his way toward the back of the house. "Come on."

We pass through his living room and enter the small guest room off it. He lays Xander down on the bed, then asks me to fetch his medical bag from the front closet. By the time I return with it, he's removed Xander's shirt and jeans so he can better assess his injuries.

"Who did this?" he asks, voice grave.

"Vice Grand Leader Aeras gave the order to kill Xander, but the damage was done by the man that used to torture him."

Dr. Farrogow shakes his head. "I don't know why that shocks me. I've seen what those in power are willing to do to keep it." He looks at Xander with tears brimming his eyes. "I'm so sorry this happened to you, Xander."

"You'll be able to help him, right?" I ask, struggling to keep my voice from wavering.

"I hope so. I'll certainly do everything I can." He meets my gaze, then grabs my hand. "But I have to be honest, Anastasia. I have no idea how he's even alive right now. Some of his injuries are pretty bad." He sighs and returns his focus to Xander. "We have a long night ahead of us."

I sit on the bed next to Xander and say, "Tell me what I can do to help."

Hours later, I'm shaken awake by Dr. Farrogow. I jolt upright and reach for Xander, worry instantly sinking into my gut. I must've dozed off.

"It's okay, Anastasia. You only slept for an hour. Everything's okay." His words calm me, but the look of concern in his eyes threatens it. "Why don't you go lay in my bed and get some sleep? It's just down the hall. There should be some pajamas laid out you can use."

Before I can protest, he says, "Xander's stable now. I'll be monitoring him the rest of the night to make sure he stays that way." He puts a gentle hand on my shoulder. "He's going to wake up needing a friend. A *rested* friend."

I nod, giving in to my exhaustion. "Come get me if anything changes," I state, my tone leaving no room for argument.

I cast one final glance at my friend before I leave and note how much better he already looks. The hope it provides helps me fall asleep quickly.

CHAPTER SIXTY-SIX
XANDER

I jolt awake and wince at the pain that shoots through my entire body. While I slowly sit, I look around the unfamiliar room and try to figure out where I am. The room is simple but outdated. I'm tucked into a full-sized bed that takes up most of it. A simple nightstand, a full dresser, and a rocking chair round out the space.

As I lean against the bed's headboard, I notice I have on a clean pair of shorts and a loose T-shirt. *Did somebody change me?*

"Oh good. You're awake," Dr. Farrogow says from the doorway. He sips from a mug in his hand and the morning paper is tucked under his arm.

"Dr. Farrogow?" I'm unable to hide my surprise. I look around the room and notice the old quilts and knickknacks that decorate it. I should've known I was at his place. "How did I end up here?"

"Ms. Galanis brought you. She showed up late last night and begged for me to help you. I obviously couldn't say no." His eyes give me a once over. "How are you feeling?"

"Sore," I admit. "Confused. I thought I was going to die."

"I did too," he responds with a sigh. "I don't know how you survived long enough to get here. You were knocking on death's door by the time I started treating you. I honestly didn't think you were going to make it through the night."

"How bad was it?"

"*Bad*." He counts my injuries on his fingers. "You had three broken ribs, a punctured lung, a stab wound in your gut that was bleeding internally, a mangled hand, and a shattered tibia. That was on top of all the cuts and bruises that were causing their own problems. It was the worst I've ever seen you. My biggest worry, though, was how much blood you'd lost." He rakes his fingers through his hair. "It took hours of healing for you to stabilize. Even then, your blood pressure continued to drop to dangerous levels. Anastasia ended up having to give you some blood. Thankfully, hers was compatible with yours."

"Where is she now?" I don't like that she isn't here. Did she need to be treated too?

"I finally sent her to bed a few hours ago. She was determined to stay by your side throughout the entire process, but I could see how exhausted she was."

"Is she okay?" My worry instantly switches to fear. If she's hurt in any way…

"Yes. I checked her out despite her protests. All I found was a bruised eye, some bruising on her abdomen, and a scrape on her left ear from a gunshot. She wouldn't let me treat any of them, though. She said you were the priority."

I sigh. *Sounds like Ana.*

He clears his throat, changing the subject. "I was going to make some breakfast before I leave for my first class. Would you like anything? I have eggs, bacon, and some toast."

"Toast is fine. Thanks."

"Coming right up," he says with a smile.

Before he leaves, I state, "I'm sure Ana would love some eggs and bacon."

He nods, a small smile forming on his lips. "Got it."

Once he's gone, I blow out a relieved breath. *I'm alive.* Thanks to Ana.

When the smell of breakfast cooking floats into the guest room, I finally climb out of bed and limp to the kitchen. Dr. Farrogow smiles wide when he notices me, then gestures for me to sit at the table. Seconds later, he places a plate me with two pieces of toast on it in front of me.

"There's bread in the pantry and butter in the fridge if you decide you want more," he says while grabbing his satchel from a hook on the wall. "I put Ana's eggs and bacon in the microwave. I have to leave for class now, but I'll check in as soon as I'm able. You two take it easy today and lay low. You never know who Vice Grand Leader Aeras has roaming the campus."

I nod. "Thank you, Dr. Farrogow. For everything."

"Of course." He hesitates. "Xander?"

"Yeah?"

"Feel free to stay here as long as you need. You won't be a bother."

I give him a sad smile. "I'll probably have to take you up on that."

He gives me a smile that mirrors my own, then leaves.

CHAPTER SIXTY-SEVEN
ANASTASIA

When I wake up, it takes me a minute to adjust to my surroundings and remember where I am. The first thing I do is check the clock on Dr. Farrogow's nightstand. It says it's past nine, so he probably already left for class. That means I should get moving. I'll need to keep an eye on Xander in his absence.

I sit up and stretch, trying to convince my body to wake up, and wince at the twinge of pain that shoots through my abdomen. While I was changing last night, I noticed a black bruise forming where the green-haired torturer punched me in the stomach. The sight of it instantly angered me, but I know I should consider myself lucky. It could've been much worse—if Xander's injuries are any indication.

My stomach tightens with worry as my thoughts drift to my best friend. I really hope he's okay. I know Dr. Farrogow wouldn't have left if he wasn't, but I don't think I'll be able to relax until I hear his voice or see his smile.

Unfortunately, his injuries aren't the only thing we have to worry about now. His uncle tried to kill him. He probably won't stop until he does. That means Xander can't go back to class or live in his dorm anymore. At least not until we stop Sebastian Aeras.

What a mess I've made of things.

Will I have to go into hiding, too? I guess that's something I need to discuss with Xander once he's feeling better.

I wonder if anyone's even noticed I'm gone. Today will be my second day of missing class and I never missed a class before. Are my friends worried? Do they even care? I bet Millie thinks I'm just staying with Xander after our fight.

I could've died and no one would've known what happened to me. Or why. The thought makes me sick. Maybe I should tell my friends what's been going on. It'd probably be good for someone else to know the truth in case Sebastian does end up killing me and Xander.

Before I can talk myself out of it, I dial Millie's number using the landline in Dr. Farrogow's room. I'd use my cell phone, but I left it in Xander's room the night we were captured.

Millie answers on the second ring. "Hello?"

"Millie, it's Ana."

"Ana? Oh my gods! Where've you been? I've been worried sick. The guys told me you weren't in class yesterday. I tried calling you, but you wouldn't answer your phone." Her voice is full of regret as she asks, "Is this because of our fight? I didn't mean for it to get so bad. I'm sorry."

"No, Millie. This has nothing to do with our fight. I promise." I suck in a breath and blow it out slowly. "Listen, something's happened. I want to tell you about it, but it'd be best to discuss it in person. If I give you an address, could you meet me there?"

"Of course. Whatever you want. I can come during my lunch break as long as it's not too far." Millie's eagerness to make up with me after our fight warms my heart. Maybe our friendship is stronger than I thought. "Is it okay if the guys come? They'll want to know you're okay."

At this point, it feels like my heart might burst from all the happiness flowing through it. My friends were worried about me. They noticed I was gone. They still care.

"Yeah. Bring them along. It's something they should know, too."

I give her the address to Dr. Farrogow's house, and we hang up with promises of seeing each other soon.

Once my conversation with her is over, I decide to check on Xander to see if he's awake yet. A quick glance at the oversized T-shirt and plaid pajama pants I borrowed from Dr. Farrogow has me sighing. It's not the most flattering of outfits I've worn, but it's clean and unbloodied so it'll do.

As I make my way toward the guest room, I catch sight of something in the kitchen that has me stopping in my tracks. I'm overcome with emotion when I see that it's my best friend sitting at the table.

He notices me in the doorway and slowly stands as I rush toward him. I fling my arms around his middle—making sure to be gentle—as his find their way across my back. I lean into his chest and sob, the events of the last few days finally taking their toll on me.

He strokes my hair and repeats, "It's okay. I'm here, Spy. I'm alive."

The sound of his voice breaks something inside of me. I'd come so close to losing him. What would I have done without him? My tears flow freely as the ache in my chest sharpens. Xander tightens his hold on me and leans his head against mine, seeming to understand my spiraling thoughts.

When my tears finally slow a few minutes later, I lean back and look up at him, needing to know it's really him. He cups my cheek as he looks me in the eyes and says, "It's me, Spy. I'm here." It's then I see the cut on his left eye that's healed into a white scar.

Fresh tears well in my eyes as I lean my forehead against his chest. "I'm so sorry, Xan. I'm so, so sorry. You didn't deserve any of this. It's all my fault."

"No, it isn't, Ana," he whispers. "I don't want you to think like that, okay? The only person at fault is my uncle and I'm going to make him pay for what he's done."

He pulls away and gestures for me to sit at the table. As I do, he limps over to the microwave and grabs a plate out of it. My stomach growls when he places it in front of me and I see it's full of eggs and bacon. I give him a gracious smile as he sits down next to me.

While I eat, I catch him examining my black eye. "How bad did Dr. Diavolos hurt you?" he asks, clearly concerned.

So, that's the name of the torturer.

"He barely touched me," I say, pointing at my black eye. "He gave me this when I refused to answer one of your uncle's questions. He then punched me in the stomach when I didn't answer another question the way they wanted. They don't really bother me other than a slight twinge here and there."

His entire body sags with relief. "Good. I don't know what I would've done if they'd hurt you worse than that."

My heart warms at his worrying over me, but the guilt I feel about him being hurt as badly as he was overrides it. I grab his left hand and graze my thumb over his bruised knuckles. "Xan, can you tell me what happened?"

"I don't know if there's anything to tell," he responds, raking his now healed fingers through his hair. "Dr. Diavolos tortured me using his usual methods, except this time he wasn't limited on his time with me. He took advantage of that."

He stares at the table in front of us, refusing to meet my eyes as he continues. "I was told my uncle ordered him to kill me—and I thought he had—until I heard shots ring out and Dr. Diavolos said they were being fired at you. Suddenly, it was like the suppressants no longer worked on me. I was able to escape my chains using my lightning and once I was free, I killed him and went looking for you."

"You killed him?" I ask, unable to keep the surprise out of my voice.

He nods, his face solemn.

My mouth drops open at that. I don't know if I'm more surprised Xander killed that evil man or happy he can never be hurt by him again. Either way, it's a good thing that monster's gone.

A thought pops into my head, stemming from the way Xander explained what happened last night. "You say you went looking for me, but do you remember finding me?"

He shakes his head.

I think about those white eyes and the otherworldly voice that came from Xander's body and a chill travels down my spine. Who was that? It's probably best I don't dwell on it. We both made it out alive and that's all that matters.

I squeeze his hand, deciding to drop the topic entirely once I see how tired he looks. We can discuss this further after he's had more time to rest.

Once I'm finished eating, I grab our plates off the table and head to the sink to wash them. Xander joins me, leaning against the counter.

We enjoy the comfortable silence and the fact that we're together.

As we stand there, mere inches from each other, I realize it's going to be a while before I feel comfortable leaving him. One look at Xander and the way his body's leaning toward me tells me he feels the same.

I almost lost him…

My thoughts drift over the last six months and everything we've been through during that time. None of it was easy but he was with me through it all. He supported me and was there for me when no one else was. He quickly became my best friend because of how easy it was to talk to him and how freely I laughed when we were together. I never once felt like I had to hide any part of me. He fully accepted me as I am.

I glance at him through the corner of my eye and feel my heart constrict. I really am in love with my best friend. He's everything good in my life right now and he's the type of person I could only dream of having. Is there even a remote chance he feels the same? What will happen to me if, gods forbid, his uncle kills him? Will I become a shell of myself like Mom did after Dad died? I know I love Xander with every fiber of my being, but it doesn't change the fact that love terrifies me.

When I'm finally done washing the dishes, I face Xander and find him already watching me. "What are you thinking?" he asks. I must not be doing a good job of hiding what I'm feeling.

It's the concern in his eyes that has me thinking, *screw the risks.* Xander's worth every heartbreak I might go through.

I blow out a long breath and say, "I'm thinking I almost lost you before I had a chance to tell you how I feel." Confusion flickers across his face. "I'm also thinking I'm not going to make that mistake again."

"I don't understand."

I reach for his hands as my eyes lock on his. "I love you, Xander. I think there's a part of me that always has. I told myself I'd never fall in love—that it only leads to pain—but I finally see that my mom was right. Love *is* worth the risk. And I do love you. So very much.

"You've seen every side of me, and I've never once felt judged by you. Instead, you accepted each part with open arms." I brush away the tear rolling down my cheek. "It's been an incredibly tough year for me but somehow you made it not feel so bad. You've always been there to wipe away my tears, and you've been by my side cheering me on as I learn the truth about who I am.

"But it's not just about how you make me feel, Xan. I want to be that person for you, too. I want to be by your side as you fight whatever battles come your way. I never want you to feel alone again. I don't know what life holds for us now, but I know it'll be okay as long as we're together." I squeeze his hands. "You're the person I want to be with, Xan. I've been fighting that feeling for too long, but I don't want to anymore."

CHAPTER SIXTY-EIGHT

XANDER

I focus on the feel of Ana's hands holding mine to keep my legs from giving out. My entire world just shifted off its axis and I'm stunned into silence.

I can't believe what she's saying. It's everything I've dreamed of but never thought would be possible.

She loves me.

My beautiful, unbelievably strong friend somehow fell in love with me.

What did I do to deserve it?

I feel like the luckiest guy in the world.

I must be quiet for too long because a look of concern crosses Ana's face. "It's okay if you don't feel the same way, Xan. I won't hold it against you. We can pretend I never said anything if you want."

I quickly close the space between us and grab her face gently so as not to hurt her black eye. "Oh, Ana. You have no idea how happy you just made me." She gives me a shy smile and my heart feels like it's floating. My thumbs graze her cheeks as I smirk at her. "When I first met you, I wondered which god I pissed off to get you thrown into my life. Since then, you've challenged everything I've said and flicked me off more times than I count. You should drive me crazy. Instead, I've completely fallen for you."

Her breath catches as I lean my forehead against hers and close my eyes. Here, in this moment, I'm exactly where I need to be. I've spent so much of my life feeling lost and untethered. There was nowhere I could truly call home until I met Ana. *She's* my home. When I'm with her, all the thoughts in my head quiet and I'm finally able to relax. Her presence is a comfort I've been searching for since I was a kid.

I'm now addicted to the drug that is her and I don't ever want to be clean.

"You've healed parts of me I didn't think ever would, Spy. And you've made my life better in every way possible. I honestly don't know what I'd do without you." I open my eyes and stare into the silver pools of hers. "I love you, Anastasia Galanis. I love you for all that you are and all that you've made me. I think I started falling for you when I confronted you in the woods that night. The passion you poured into everything reminded me what it's like to care about something and you very quickly became that for me." My thumb grazes the outline of her mouth. "You're *everything* to me."

Before she can say anything, I pull her mouth to mine and kiss her desperately. My lips have been begging to kiss her again and I'm grateful I can finally give them what they want.

I nearly lose my balance from the feel of her soft lips against mine. Kissing Ana—I mean, really, truly kissing her—is better than I ever imagined. My dreams did *not* do it justice and I'm reeling from the way my heart and body responds to her. I already know she's ruining me for anyone else, yet she has no idea.

While my fingers tangle in her hair, she parts her mouth, inviting me in. A purring noise comes from the back of her throat as my tongue begins teasing hers. The sound of it has one of my hands drifting to her lower back so I can pull her closer. The feel of her body now rubbing against mine has my own groan falling from my mouth.

When her hands grip the front of my shirt, begging for more, I give in to her silent demand. My right hand releases her hair and finds its way under her shirt.

She groans as I gently graze the bottom of her breasts. With a sharp intake of breath, she pulls away from me and asks, "Are you sure this is okay? I don't want to hurt you."

I smile against her mouth. I'm touched that she's worried about me, but there's no way I'm stopping this now. Not when this is what I've wanted for months. "Don't worry about me, Spy. I can handle a little pain." I pull her mouth back to mine while my fingers find her left nipple.

She groans again and presses her chest into my hand, clearly loving what I'm doing and wanting more of it. With that, I slip my other hand under shirt. I massage and tease both nipples until she's whimpering for relief.

I break our kiss and quickly pull her shirt off before I pick her up. Her legs wrap around my waist as I walk us to the table and it's a miracle my brain doesn't turn to mush. I kiss along her collarbone and neck as I lay her on top of it, making a slow trek to her breasts. When my lips finally find her left nipple, her fingers tangle in my hair while her hips grind against me.

"Hold still for me, baby," I whisper against her nipple. "Otherwise, I'm not going to be able to focus on you for as long as I'd like. I'm already dying to be inside of you. You rubbing against me like that is not helping."

"You mean like this?" she asks innocently while her hips move against me in a torturously slow rhythm.

I fight back a groan, then shift so my mouth is inches from hers. "I'd be careful if I were you, Spy. I'm the one in control here. That means I determine how quickly you orgasm, and I can drag this out all day."

"Oh, really?" Her tone is taunting, and I instantly realize my mistake. My dick is now lined up perfectly with her groin. She angles her hips in such a way that she's able to grind along the length of it. I curse and drop my forehead to hers. That felt so good.

Any control I thought I had over the situation immediately disappears. I'm now putty in her hands, waiting to be molded.

"I want you inside me, Xan," she whispers into my ear, causing every muscle in my body to tighten. "I've wanted you for so long and I'm tired of waiting. I don't need you to draw out my pleasure. I just want you inside me."

My eyes find hers and I'm mesmerized by the mixture of love and desire I see there. My dreams did not do this justice, did not do *her* justice, but how could they? I'd never seen something so beautiful before this moment. Not even my wildest imaginings would've been able to capture how perfect she looks pinned beneath me.

She's *so* beautiful.

A groan slips from my mouth when Ana takes my right hand and places it over the seam of her pajama pants. Her obvious need has me pulling them off her with a speed that shouldn't be possible. My eyes then skim greedily over her naked body.

My gods.

She's perfect.

All the training she's done throughout her life has given her a toned physique that somehow highlights every beautiful curve she has. I could easily spend hours worshipping every inch. And I will. Later. Right now, I'm going to give her what she wants.

I pull my shirt over my head and slip off my shorts too. Ana's eyes roam over my body and there's a hunger in her gaze that has my dick aching, begging to feel her heat wrapped around it.

I lean over her, and she adjusts her legs so I'm lying in between them. The nervous smile she gives me only lasts for a second. It's quickly replaced by moans as I slowly ease into her.

"*Fuck*, Xan."

I take my time, making sure she can handle my size, but any hesitancy I have disappears the moment I'm fully inside of her. That's when she swirls her hips, begging for more.

"Again, baby," she pleads in a whisper.

Damn. I love that she's not afraid to tell me what she wants.

I pull out of her slowly until only the tip remains, then thrust back into her with a speed that has her nails digging into my back. I can't tell if she's praising the gods or cursing them as my dick slides into her again.

After that, I'm unleashed and moving inside of her at a pace that has both of us cursing and moaning each other's names. I'm nearly dizzy from the pleasure.

Sex has never been like *this* before. Her body is my source of life and I'm its humbled servant. I need her in the same way I need air to breathe. I can never go back to just being her friend. Not after this. I'm hers. Mind, body, and soul.

When her nails dig into my back, urging me to go faster, I know she's almost there. I do as she asks, but I also wrap my lips around her left nipple and tease it with my tongue.

"Oh my gods. *Xander*," she groans while her nails carve fresh lines into my back. The pain only spurs me on, so I pinch and tug on her right nipple with my free hand. All the stimulation has her orgasm hitting quickly and with an intensity that has her shouting my name.

The feel of her tightening around my dick has my own orgasm crashing over me. I moan her name and have to remind myself to breathe. I'm so lost in the moment that I forget where my body ends and hers begins. Honestly, I just want to stay like this forever.

After our orgasms pass, we lay there, intertwined on the table for several minutes, neither one of us wanting to break the spell.

My heart beats rapidly while I replay what just happened in my head.

Holy shit.

So that's how good sex can be when you're in love with the person.

Wow. I'm well and truly done for.

Unfortunately, we can't lay here forever. We have no idea when Dr. Farrogow will be getting home and the last thing we want is for him to find us in this state. Especially on his dining table of all places.

I slowly stand and reach for my shorts. I groan when the motion causes a shooting pain up my side. I definitely overdid it after almost dying, but I don't regret it one bit.

Ana's gaze snaps to me with concern lining her face. I try to ease her worries with a joke, "Are you trying to kill me, woman? I could barely walk as it was. Now I think I'm going to be bedridden."

She playfully shoves me, and it takes every bit of strength I have not to lay her back down on that table and find more ways to make her moan. Instead, I force myself to focus on putting my clothes back on.

Once we're finished getting dressed, I hear a knock at the door that has my eyes widening. Who could that be?

She gives me a horrified look. "Oh my gods! I totally forgot my friends were coming over during lunch. They were worried about me, so I told them I'd explain everything in person. That was before this happened," she says, gesturing between us. "Do you think they'll know I had sex?"

I give her a quick once over and state matter-of-factly, "Oh yeah. You're screwed." When she shoves me again, I laugh and answer honestly. "No. You're fine, Spy. They won't be able to tell."

When her nervousness persists, I rub the tops of her arms and say, "Everything will be fine. They're your friends and they're here because they're worried about you."

She visibly relaxes. "You're right. Thanks, Xan. I needed that reminder." She grabs my hands and squeezes them. "I think I should talk to them alone at first. I'm not sure where their heads are at and the last thing I want is one of them coming after you. Especially while you're still recovering."

I hate the thought of her having to relay everything that's happened alone, but I can't argue with her logic. Her friends and I don't exactly get along and I don't want my presence to take away from what needs to be said.

"I'll do whatever you think is best, Spy," I say while sitting back down at the table. She gives me an appreciative smile, then hurries out of the room.

CHAPTER SIXTY-NINE
NIKOLAI

I wouldn't say I'm an angry person—my temper doesn't boil just below the surface like Kas's—but there are certain things that set me off easier than others. Xander Thyellas and his annoying friends have always been one of them.

Growing up, there was so much pressure on me as the General's heir. I couldn't express interest in anything other than my training without being criticized by my father's colleagues. They expected me to be an example of Zoin's strength, discipline, and determination even from a young age.

I think that's why I hated Xander and his friends so much in high school. Despite them being heirs for equally important roles, it didn't seem like they were held to the same standards I was. Why did *they* get to be normal when I could be nothing more than a soldier for the province?

I know now that it was immature of me, but I was hell bent on making the three of them feel as bad as I did. I felt it was only right.

I did and said a lot of things to them—especially Steven—I'm not proud of.

It took me meeting Millie and falling in love with her for me to realize why I hated them so much. I guess I wished I had the sort of joy that seemed to come so easy to them. Thankfully, Millie gave that to me.

Now, with her in my life, I'm trying to be better.

When I realized Xander, Tony, and Steven were also going to Arken, I made a point to keep my distance from them. I didn't want to fall back into my old ways.

I think I did a pretty good job of it, too. That is, until Ana's friendship with Xander started causing my friends to get hurt. Xander doesn't know how lucky he is that I didn't find him and beat him to a pulp after he nearly killed Kas. And all three of those idiots don't realize how close I was to kicking their asses when they were threatening me and my friends outside of 306. The only reason I didn't was because I kept imagining how upset Millie would be if I did. She's everything good in my life and I don't want to do anything that could risk our relationship.

Though I doubt I'll be able to exercise the same restraint if I see Xander now.

Ana was missing for almost two days. No one could find or get ahold of her during that time, and it terrified us. I was so worried that something bad might've happened to her and that it was all Xander's fault. I never cared that she was friends with him, but now I think that was a mistake.

Millie said Ana was vague when she finally heard from her this morning. We're on our way to meet her now at some random house on the outskirts of campus and a feeling of unease has settled in my gut. Something's not right.

If I find out that my friend's been hurt in any way and that Xander had something to do with it, I don't know if I'll be able to stop myself from hurting him too. I just hope Millie will understand.

"I think this is the place," Millie says as she looks at the piece of paper in her hand and compares the address on it to the one in front of us.

My brows furrow as I look at the homes surrounding us that belong to Arken faculty. They all have the same one-story brick facade. Why the hell does Ana want us to meet her here of all places? Kas and I exchange a concerned look. Something definitely isn't right.

"I guess I should knock, right?" Millie looks to me for answers.

Before I can respond, Kas's deep voice says behind me, "I'll do it." He makes his way to the front door and gives a forceful knock. It's one that echoes around us, causing my unease to grow.

Please let Ana be okay.

A few minutes pass without answer so Kas goes to knock again. The door opens before his knuckles make contact and we find Ana suddenly standing before us with a nervous smile.

Kas instantly goes still in that eerie way I know means he's angry, but I don't have time to worry about him. Not when Ana has a black eye and looks like she's been through hell.

I move past Kas and grab Ana while I get a closer look at her eye. "Who did this to you, Ana? Was it Xander?" The tone of my voice does little to hide the anger I'm feeling.

I look past her into the house to see if Xander's inside. If he is, then I'm going to show him exactly what I do to those who hurt my friends. I won't let him get away with it this time.

She steps in front of me, blocking my view. "Xander didn't do this to me." She looks past me and says to Kas, "I promise he didn't. If you guys could come inside and sit down, I'll explain everything."

CHAPTER SEVENTY

ANASTASIA

My friends slowly file into the house as Nik follows after them, grumbling to himself.

Kas and Harvey sit down on the loveseat with a seriousness to them that tells me they're prepared for a fight. Millie and Graham sit on the adjoining couch and I note the worry dancing in Millie's eyes. Nik refuses to sit down, choosing to stand next to Millie instead.

I position myself so I can stop anyone from approaching the kitchen, then blow out a breath, preparing myself for what I must say.

"Where are we?" Nik asks, eyes narrowing on me.

"This is Dr. Farrogow's house," I explain with a wave of my hand. "He told me I could come here whenever I needed to. Well, I needed to." My friends exchange confused glances, so I say, "I'll try my best to explain everything and hopefully it'll all make sense by the time I'm done."

My friends settle in, clearly ready to hear my explanation, though their shocked expressions makes it clear they didn't expect what I'm telling them. I don't blame them. I'd be shocked too if I hadn't lived through it.

When I'm finally done, they sit in silence for several seconds until Millie asks, "So, you're really a metal bender?"

I nod. "I'm really a metal bender."

Graham's eyes look like they're about to pop out of his head. I don't think I've ever seen him look so shocked. "Why didn't you tell us any of this, Ana? Or about your dad passing?" He finally meets my gaze and the hurt lining his face has guilt twisting in my gut.

"My dad's death wasn't something I was ready to talk about when school started. When I finally was months later, it felt weird to just drop it on you guys, so I didn't." I run my fingers through my hair. "Regarding the investigation, the things Xander and I were looking into were actively being covered up by Zoin officials. We were worried the information could start the very war we're trying to prevent." I give them all an apologetic look, then shift my focus to Nik, Harvey, and Kas. "You guys are the heirs of the three Generals of the kingdom. It wouldn't have been fair for me to tell you to hide all of this from your fathers. Especially you, Kas."

Thankfully, my fire-bending friend nods his understanding.

"Up until two days ago, the only thing we thought we had to worry about was the war. We had no idea how bad things truly were."

"What happened two days ago?" asks Nik.

I cross my arms in preparation for what I'm about to share. "After Millie and I argued, I wanted to get off campus and clear my head. I thought going to the Capitol Building was the best way for me to do that. We searched Sebastian Aeras's office that night, looking for a memorandum that'd prove he was lying about who killed Xander's father."

The guilt I've been feeling about what happened hits me again with a force that nearly knocks me over. "We did find what we were looking for, but we were caught by his uncle in the process." I hear Millie gasp, but I refuse to look at her. I need to get through my explanation without breaking down. "Sebastian Aeras took Xander and I to an old, abandoned warehouse in Pyr. That's where he interrogated us and tortured Xander to find out what we knew."

Nausea coils in my stomach as I recall just how bad Xander had been tortured. He really is lucky to be alive.

"Sebastian confirmed everything we found and said he was going to kill us. Honestly, we're lucky we escaped alive. We..."

Nik puts up his hand, signaling for me to stop. "I'm sorry, Ana, but I'm having a hard time believing what you're saying. Why would the Vice Grand Leader hurt his own nephew?" He looks around the room to see if anyone else agrees with him. When they avert their eyes, he sighs. "I guess I find it a little too convenient that Xander isn't here to confirm your story. I mean, you say you're lucky to be alive, but it looks like you only have a black eye."

I look down at my feet, not wanting Nik to see how bad his words hurt. I don't know what to say to make him believe me. I hate that I even have to.

My head snaps up when Xander's voice cuts through the silence like a knife. "Is this enough proof for you, asshole?" I turn and find Xander shirtless with his arms spread wide. His injuries are on full display, and they somehow look even worse in the warm lighting.

Nik shuts up instantly and crosses his arms. The muscle in his jaw is working, though, so I know we haven't heard the last from him.

Xander puts his shirt back on while he moves to stand next to me, limping as he does. His presence helps me finish what I need to say. "I asked Xander to wait in the kitchen because I wasn't sure how you guys would react if you saw him before I explained everything." I force myself to remain calm as I look at Nik. "I understand your thinking Nik, but I was in the room when Sebastian Aeras gave the order for Xander to be killed. If you can look at him now and still question the validity of what I'm saying, then I don't think there is anything I can say that'll change your mind."

Nik huffs. "My father would never let this sort of thing happen. He would've put a stop to it immediately."

"That's kind of the whole point of a cover up, don't you think?" Xander bites back. "Your father is only told what my uncle wants him to know."

In an instant, Nik's in Xander's face, pulsing with rage. "I could snap you like a toothpick before you even know what's happened, prick."

Electricity flares in Xander's eyes while he says with scary calm, "Try me."

I'm between them within seconds, pushing them gently away from each other. "No one's accusing your father of letting this war happen, Nik. Obviously, the Vice Grand Leader is only sharing what will ensure the war happens. Besides, I doubt anyone would see through his lies without doing the sort of digging Xander and I did."

Nik runs his hands over his face before his eyes settle on me and Xander. "I'm sorry. Clearly, I'm a little on edge. I just hate to think my father hasn't bothered to question the validity of the Vice Grand Leader's claims."

"Sometimes, it's easier to accept that evil's an outside force you can fight against," Xander explains. "It's a lot harder to come to terms with the fact that the villain's someone you've known and respected for years. I don't blame your father. I don't blame anyone who's fallen for my uncle's lies."

My friends fall quiet, so I ask, "Are we good now? Is there anything else you guys would like to air out?"

Graham clears his throat, and Xander tenses next to me. He must have the same reservations I do. What could Graham possibly have to say after all he's done?

"Why didn't you tell *me* about all this, Ana? I get not wanting to tell Nik, Harvey, and Kas. I can even understand not telling Millie since she's dating Nik. But why not me?" The sadness in his voice has all sorts of conflicting feelings washing over me. He casts his eyes downward as he says, "It would've helped me understand. Maybe I wouldn't have acted like such an idiot."

"Honestly, Graham, I didn't tell you because I was doing these investigations with Xander. And I couldn't mention Xander without it turning into a fight."

He nods, knowing I'm right, then whispers, "I'm sorry."

I leave it at that. There's nothing for me to say. I'm certainly not going to tell him that it's okay. Because it isn't. He argued with me for months because he couldn't get over his own insecurities. That wasn't fair to me.

Nik breaks the silence that had fallen over us once again by asking, "So, you guys figured out what Sebastian Aeras is planning. What now?"

Xander and I look at each other and shrug.

"I have no idea," Xander responds. "What I do know is my uncle needs to believe I died last night, or he'll continue to hunt me down until he actually kills me. Maybe if he thinks I'm dead, it'll give me time to figure out how to stop this war."

"How can we help?" Nik asks.

"I think you and I should gather whatever documentation we can to prove my uncle's true intentions for the war. Once we have it all together, you can give it to your father. He'll never approve of the war once he knows the truth."

"And what are the rest of us supposed to do?" Millie chimes in.

"Go about your lives as if everything's normal. The last thing we need is for Uncle Sebastian to realize you guys know what he's planning too. Who knows what he'd do. Nik and I will loop you in if we need you."

"What about Tony and Steven?" I ask, suddenly realizing they should've been included in this.

The guilt lining Xander's face while he shakes his head makes me realize just how much he's sacrificing to stop this war. "No. Only those in this room can know I'm alive. If my mom and my best friends don't act devastated by my death, my uncle will never believe I'm gone."

Oh gods. I didn't even think about his mom. That's going to be awful.

Once our discussion is over, my friends realize how much time has passed and announce they need to get back to campus. They all leave except for Graham. He hangs back, wanting to talk to me. Xander whispers that he'll be in the guest room if I need him, then leaves me alone to talk with Graham.

I cross my arms as I face my ex-boyfriend. So many conflicting emotions battle in my head while I look at him. Honestly, I don't know if I want to fight to be his friend or settle for whatever *this* is.

"I'm sorry you didn't feel like you could tell me what was going on," Graham starts. "I know my jealousy didn't make it any easier for you. I don't think I can apologize enough for that. I felt you pulling away from me and I was so desperate to keep you that I turned into someone I never wanted to be. You deserved better than that. I'm sorry."

Friend. I want to be his friend.

Despite everything we went through, I still care about him and want him in my life.

"Don't beat yourself up, Graham. I could've been more honest with you from the beginning. I should've been." My shoulders sag and I feel months of tension suddenly disappear. "I have no hard feelings regarding the way everything played out between us. I still care for you, and I hope we can remain friends despite everything."

"I'd like that," he says with a sad smile. "You mean so much to me and I'd hate for you not to be in my life anymore." He pauses, eyes darting toward Dr. Farrogow's guest room. "Even if it means I have to watch you with someone else."

We hug each other goodbye after that and make promises to talk soon.

"I'll see you later, Graham."

"See you later, Ana."

Once the front door closes behind him and I lock it, I'm overcome with joy. The conversation with my friends might've started out rocky, but it ended better than I ever could've imagined. I'm so grateful everything is out in the open and I don't have to lie anymore.

A grin spreads across my face as I turn toward the back of the house and think about who's waiting for me there. While I make my way to him, I come up with a plan that involves the two of us staying in that bedroom for the rest of the afternoon.

CHAPTER SEVENTY-ONE

ANASTASIA

Xander and I spent the few days I stayed at Dr. Farrogow's getting to know each other in ways that were previously unexplored. I thought we had a great connection before, but it was nothing compared to what we have now. My love for him only deepened during our time together and I wish we could've stayed in the little bubble we created there forever.

Unfortunately, Dr. Farrogow could only provide an excuse for my absence for so long before I had to return to campus.

Returning to Arken without Xander was like going home and finding all your furniture rearranged. It didn't feel right, and I found myself wishing constantly that I could go back to the way things used to be.

The hardest part about coming back, though, was lying to Tony and Steven, telling them I had no idea where Xander was whenever they asked. Watching their worry grow as days turned into weeks broke my heart.

Thankfully, my evenings are spent with my friends again. They're able to provide a distraction from the guilt warring inside of me.

Since we only have a couple weeks left of class, my friends and I are taking advantage of the lighter course load by having movie nights as often as we can. Xander told us to act like everything's normal so that's what we're trying to do.

Tonight, we're holed up in Nik and Harvey's room and it's Harvey's turn to choose what movie we're going to watch. He ends up picking some spy movie and we're just settling in to watch it when the TV beeps loudly, announcing that there's an urgent message from the capital. I have a feeling I know what it's about, but I still feel anxious when Sebastian Aeras's face appears on the screen.

"Oh gods. What does this clown want now?" Kas grumbles from his spot on the floor next to me.

"It shouldn't be about the war," Nik answers while readjusting Millie on his lap so he can get a better view of the TV. "When I talked to my father today, he said things were at a standstill on that front."

"So, what could he possibly have to tell us?" Millie asks, looking to me for answers.

I turn my attention back to the screen and say matter-of-factly, "He's going to announce Xander's death." My friends' eyes widen, and it feels like we're all holding our breath until the Vice Grand Leader speaks.

"Citizens of Zoin, it's with a heavy heart that I come to you today." Sebastian pauses, then scans the crowd gathered before him. I have to give it to him, he looks genuinely sad as he takes a deep breath and says, "Our greatest fear was realized a few weeks ago... My nephew, Xander Thyellas, was murdered in his sleep." A gasp can be heard from the crowd and he nods, lip wobbling as he does. "My team analyzed the scene as thoroughly as they could and are confident Xander was killed by the same individuals that murdered his father."

Kas snarls, "Oh, screw you, dude."

I can't believe it. Sebastian's doing the exact same thing he did last time—putting the blame on Fotian assassins. I figured he would, yet I still find myself shocked that he is. The man must have no shame. That's the only explanation for it. He'll do whatever he must to get what he wants. Unfortunately, I don't think there'll be anything left standing in his way after tonight.

I'm shaking my head out of frustration when my phone rings. Xander's voice sounds from the other end once I answer it, asking, "Are you hearing this?"

"Yep. We're in Nik and Harvey's room watching it. I can't believe your uncle's actually doing this."

"I know. Me either. It's insane."

We all fall silent when the Sebastian Aeras starts up again. "Xander was a good kid and would've made a wonderful Grand Leader someday. I hate that we won't get to see all he would've accomplished." He feigns wiping a tear from his eye and I resist screaming at him through the TV. "I know things might seem crazy right now, but I promise we'll get through it together. Zoin is comprised of some of the strongest people I ever met and it's your continued strength that'll help me do what is needed." He takes a deep breath and scans the crowd again before continuing, "Without a straight line of succession, I fear I'm the only one who can fill the role of Grand Leader until we're able to find someone more suitable. I feel that's what's best for our province right now. The people of Zoin shouldn't have to worry about who will lead them. They just need to focus on their grief over the loss of our young leader.

"For those of you who'd like to say goodbye to Xander, we'll be holding a funeral for him at Zaxton's Funeral Home on the last Saturday of the month. You're all welcome to attend. I know it'd help his mother greatly to see how loved her son was."

Xander sucks in a breath when the camera pans to his mom and you can clearly see that her eyes are red-rimmed. She looks devastated.

Poor Kate. I wish I could be there for her through this. I hate that she even has to deal with it after everything she's been through. She doesn't deserve it.

When Sebastian starts to discuss the logistics surrounding his appointment as Grand Leader, Nik turns off the TV and I put Xander on speaker so he can be involved in our conversation.

Graham asks me from Harvey's bed, "Are you gonna go to the funeral?"

I'm taken aback by his question. I hadn't considered it, but now that Graham mentions it, I probably should. At least for Kate, Tony, and Steven's sake. Besides, it'd probably be a good idea to play up my grief to convince Sebastian that Xander really is dead.

I sigh and fist my hands at my side. "Yeah. I probably should."

Harvey gives a low whistle. "Man, that's going to suck."

"Do you want us to go with you?" Kas asks, gently bumping my arm with his.

"No. This is something I need to do alone."

CHAPTER SEVENTY-TWO
ANASTASIA

I was six years old when I attended my first funeral. It was for a great aunt on my mom's side I never met. I didn't understand what was going on. I only knew that everyone around me was crying, and it felt weird that I wasn't.

I went to a couple funerals after that, and they were all the same. People were upset, yet I didn't feel a single thing.

It wasn't until my dad's funeral that I understood how upsetting they could be. I knew he was dead for days before it but being surrounded by people who were all grieving him made it real in a way it hadn't been before that moment. It was devastating and I hoped his funeral would be my last for a long, long time.

I certainly didn't think I'd be attending my boyfriend's funeral nearly a year and a half later. Even if I know it's not real, it feels real. Everyone's talking about how Xander was too young to die or how much potential he had and it's taking every bit of strength I have not to break down.

I spot Kate across the room and know I can't put off talking to her any longer. I force my legs in her direction, even though it feels like my shoes are made of bricks.

When I'm only a few feet away, Kate catches sight of me and a fresh wave of pain mars her beautiful face. She opens her arms and beckons for me to hug her. My face crumples as I close the distance between us and allow myself to get wrapped up in her warmth.

"Thank you for coming, sweetie," she says through tears as she rubs my back.

"I'm so sorry for your loss." My own tears fall and I'm unable to stop them.

She leans back and rubs the tops of my arms. "I'm sorry for yours, too, honey. I know how close you were to Xander."

My lip wobbles. "I loved your son so much."

She hugs me again and we sit there holding each other for a few minutes, clinging to this brief moment of comfort. We finally break apart when the sound of a throat clearing comes from behind us.

Some man I don't recognize is the one who interrupted us, clearly too impatient to be polite, but it's not him my eyes are drawn to. It's the sight of Tony and Steven lingering near the outskirts of the room that catches my attention. I gently squeeze Kate's arm in farewell, then make my way toward them.

Once I reach them, I pull them both into a hug and offer them my condolences. They lean their heads on my shoulders and squeeze me tightly.

When they let me go, my heart breaks for the hundredth time today. The pain they're feeling is clear in the way they're holding themselves. Even in the way they ask how I'm doing.

"I'm okay. What about you guys?"

Tony shrugs and the concerned look Steven gives him tells me Tony is not handling Xander's 'death' well. Steven shrugs too and gives me a half smile. "We're managing."

I grab Tony's hand and squeeze it. When his eyes meet mine, guilt is interlaced with his pain, so I hug him again. "There's nothing you could've done, Tony. There's nothing any of us could've done."

"I was supposed to be his protector" is his whispered response. "I've always been his protector. I should've known something was wrong and been there to help him that night."

I hug him tighter while Steven puts a comforting hand on his back. I hate that he feels that way and I really wish things could be different. If anyone deserves to know that Xander's alive, it's Tony and Steven. They've been loyal friends to him for years and they've loved him like a brother. I hate that they have to go through this.

I pull away from Tony and cup both his and Steven's cheeks. "Xander really loves you guys. I hope you know that. You're his best friends." I can't say he *loved* them. I just can't. Not when they look as sad as they do. I want them to read into what I'm saying, and I want it to give them hope. Please let them believe this isn't the end.

"I hope we still get to see you, Ana," Steven says with a sad smile. "We don't want to lose you, too." My tears are flowing again after that and Steven curses. "Oh my gods. I'm so sorry, Ana. I didn't mean to make you cry."

I wipe my eyes and say, "It's okay, Steven. I'm okay. My heart just breaks for you guys."

"We'll be okay," Tony says, staring at the ground. "It'll just take some time."

A man who looks a lot like Tony approaches us and I leave so they can talk to him alone. After that, I head for the exit, eager to get away from this place. If I see another person I care for heartbroken over Xander's 'death,' I don't know if I'll be able to keep the truth in any longer.

I've only made it a few feet out of the building when I hear someone say my name from behind me. I turn and my whole body goes rigid when Sebastian Aeras approaches me, clearly angry.

"I don't know what game you think you're playing, girl, but it's a dangerous one," he snarls. "I know my nephew is still alive out there somewhere and I *will* find him. I won't let the two of you stop my plans."

I feign offense. "You have some nerve, you know that? Confronting me at Xander's funeral of all places? I had to bury him because of what *you* did to him." Sebastian's eyes narrow as I raise my chin in defiance. "You better hope your sister never finds out what you did, or you'll have bigger things to worry about than me stopping your war."

Several people exit the building behind us, abruptly ending my conversation with the awful man. I turn and leave without another word, and I can feel Sebastian's eyes following me all the way to the car Harvey let me borrow.

Once I return to campus, I rush to Dr. Farrogow's place in a haste that's probably stupid considering Sebastian could have people following me. But I don't care. I need to see Xander. I need to be reminded that he's alive and well and that we're doing all of this for a reason.

Xander opens the front door after my third knock, and I collapse into his arms. He carries me inside, whispering that everything's okay, while I sob.

"That funeral could've been real. It *was* real for so many people today. You should've seen your mom, Xan. She was so sad. I hate not telling her the truth."

"I know, Spy. I do, too," he says while putting me down. "But we have to. At least for now. It's the only way we'll be able to stop my uncle."

"I just hate this so much."

"Me too," Xander responds while stroking my hair. I feel him tense before he asks, "Did you see Tony and Steven? How were they?"

I pull him toward the couch and force him to sit while I relay everything his best friends said. He puts his head in his hands and shakes it while mumbling, "This sucks."

"There's more..." Xander slowly lifts his head, and I can see the worry in his eyes, so I quickly say, "Your uncle confronted me."

His expression instantly turns to one of rage. "Did he hurt you?"

"No. Nothing like that. He just told me that he knew you were still alive, and he was going to prove it. He also said we weren't going to stop him."

Xander stands and a look of determination comes over his face. "Oh, we're going to stop him alright. My uncle has no idea what's coming for him."

CHAPTER SEVENTY-THREE
ANASTASIA

I've been home for summer break for a little over a month now. It's been a nice reprieve from the craziness that had become the norm at Arken.

Thankfully, I finished my classes and passed all my finals without any further run-ins with Xander's uncle. It was a small blessing, though I'm sure it's one that'll be short lived.

Once my last final was taken and my room was packed, I found each one of my friends and hugged them goodbye. It was a lot harder parting ways with them than I anticipated. I couldn't imagine not seeing them every day after all we'd been through together. And knowing how drastically things could change if we're unable to stop the war had me holding onto them a little tighter.

I was terrified of what might happen if Sebastian gets what he wants. There's always risks involved with war and I worried my friends would be thrust into the middle of it. My fear has only grown as more time has passed without us finding a way to stop it. Nik has been searching for the proof Xander and I found, but every bit of it has disappeared.

Xander's efforts to stop his uncle has only incensed the interim Grand Leader and he seems more determined than ever to find

Xander. And because I'm Xander's girlfriend, he's been paying extra close attention to me. I constantly feel metal in the woods that surround my house, telling me there are soldiers out there watching me and my family.

The constant presence of Sebastian Aeras's men means I haven't been able to see Xander since I left Arken. I wasn't sure I was even going to get to say goodbye to him until he suddenly appeared outside of my room as I was grabbing my last bag. He smirked when he noticed my surprise and I couldn't help myself after that. I leapt into his arms and hugged him so tight that he grunted.

"You really thought I wouldn't say goodbye before you left? Come on, Spy, you know me better than that," he teased.

I didn't care about the risks as I pulled him into my room and shut the door behind us. I wasn't going to go a whole summer without a proper goodbye. Unfortunately, we could only be together for a few minutes before he had to leave.

I've missed him terribly since.

To distract myself from everything else going on, I've been spending time with my family and helping out around the house. It hasn't helped as much as I'd like, but it does provide some reprieve.

Tonight, my family decided to have a relaxed evening at home. Even Daphne skipped a party at her friend Samantha's house to spend time with us. We cooked dinner over the fire my mom started, then spent the evening reminiscing and playing games. Surprisingly, no fights broke out this time.

We were having so much fun that it's well after midnight before we drag our butts inside and go to bed.

I'm not asleep for long when the sound of rain hitting our tin roof startles me awake. I sit up and look outside my bedroom window and find that it's pouring—which is weird because I didn't think it was supposed to rain for another week.

When I glance at the clock on my dresser and see that it reads 2:10, I lay back on my pillow with a groan and close my eyes in an attempt to go back to bed.

Any thoughts of sleep escape me when I hear a familiar rumble of thunder. It has me bolting upright with a feeling that something's wrong settling in my gut.

I scramble out of bed and look out my window again. This time, I see Xander walking up my driveway, completely drenched from the rain. I quickly throw on sweatpants and rush outside.

Within seconds, I'm in my front yard, approaching Xander while goosebumps crawl up my arm due to the cold. I stop a few feet from him and my toes squelch in the mud.

My heart stops when I finally get a good look at him. His shirt is torn, and I see the shadow of a bruise forming on his left cheek.

Something's definitely wrong.

"Xan, what happened? What're you doing here?" It's an effort to keep the worry out of my voice.

His eyes flare in anger as he states, "Nik and Millie betrayed us. My uncle knows I'm alive, so we have to get out of here. It's no longer safe."

ACKNOWLEDGEMENTS

I would like to thank my husband, Sterling, for not only supporting me when I told him I wanted to write this series, but for listening to me talk about it constantly since. I appreciate your willingness to listen to all my favorite quotes/plotlines, whatever crazy ideas I've come up with, and for offering your own suggestions when I'm stuck. I couldn't have done this without you, my love.

I would also like to thank my sweet daughter, Elodie. Thank you for all the hugs, cuddles, and laughs throughout this journey. You're the reason for everything I do.

A huge thank you goes out to all my amazing friends, family, and beta reading team. Thank you for not only being willing to read my story, but for caring about it as well. Your comments, notes, and feedback have helped me so much during this process. I cannot thank any of you enough. I appreciate anyone who reads my book or is willing to talk with me about it—at this point, I think it's become my love language.

I would specifically like to thank my friend, Grace Marino. I love that we're on this writing journey together. I've loved being able to bounce ideas off you and whine about the struggles of writing/publishing. You've made this entire process so much easier.

Thank you to my awesome editor, Mallory Day. You sure had your work cut out for you with this one, but you helped shape it into something I'm so incredibly proud of. I appreciate you so much. I'll work on my overuse of then and ellipses before the next one.

Thank you to my incredible cover designer, digitaldreams_designs. You have taken every idea I've given you and turned them into incredible covers I'm obsessed with. I'm looking forward to continuing to work with you.

Thank you to my formatter, InksparkDigital. I appreciate you formatting my book so that it's perfect for release. It was a pleasure working with you.

Lastly, thank you to my readers. You're the ones who give my work purpose. I hope in some way, no matter how small, my stories make you feel seen.

About the Author

A.M. Wentworth has dreamed of being an author since she was a little girl. She spent much of her childhood with her nose in a book and stories bouncing around in her head. In August 2024, she decided to finally make those dreams a reality. Since then, she's poured her heart and soul into a story, cast of characters, and universe she hopes readers will love just as much as she does.

When she isn't writing, she enjoys listening to screamy music, reading, and spending time with friends and family.

Website: amwentworthauthor.com

instagram.com/amwentworth94
facebook.com/A.M.Wentworth-Author
tiktok.com/@amwentworth94